THE STORM WITHIN

A Dark Fantasy Adventure

THE SPLINTERED LAND
BOOK II

RICHARD PARRY

Contents

REQUIEM'S JUSTICE

The Storm Within

Assassins strike. Rebellion rises. And a dragon stirs in the north.

Geneve and the sorcerer Meriwether are ambushed while burying their dead. **Their attackers can wear any face—even the one she loves.** Their goal is simple: erode the Queen's power and **tear the crown from her trembling fingers.**

To stop them, Geneve and Meriwether must race to the north and **cut the head from the serpent.** But the fires of rebellion are already blazing. The Feybrind and Vhemin march to war. The gods turn their faces away. **And in a madman's grip, a dragon wakes—ancient, unstoppable, and bent on destruction.**

Geneve has faced horrors before, but even the ancients feared the beast that now threatens to burn the world.

Her blade is ready. She only hopes she is strong enough to wield it.

You're Awesome

You could have picked any book, but you chose this one. That means a lot.

Your support keeps independent authors like me forging ahead, writing the stories we love (and hopefully, the ones you love too). Whether you're here for the characters, the worldbuilding, or just a little escapism, thank you for being part of this journey.

You. Kick. Ass.

Roll for Narrative

WHERE WORLDBUILDING AND OVERTHINKING COLLIDE

Love stories that linger in your brain long after The End? Ever wonder why some books hit like a natural 20 and others critically fail their way into the 1-star abyss?

Join *Roll for Narrative*, my hub for sci-fi and fantasy lovers. I explore storytelling like a rogue casing a dungeon, review movies, books, and games, and dish out writing tips like a chaotic-good bard with a grudge against bad prose. No spam, just good stuff.

Join the quest:
https://rollfornarrative.parrydox.com

For my Rae, always.

Dramatis Personae

KNIGHT CHEVALIER GENEVE

Geneve serves the Three: Cophine, Ikmae, and Khiton. She is a Knight Chevalier, master of the Storm.

She knows the heft of Requiem better than the lines on her palm, but the demands of the Tresward now seem foreign. Her order commands death to sorcerers, but her dearest friend is one of their kind.

Geneve will use her blade, and the Storm inside her, to protect the innocent, and hold the guilty to account. She only need work out which is which.

MERIWETHER DU REEVES

Meri has found a friend in the unlike-liest of people: a Tresward Knight.

His modest skills with illusion have stood them in good stead, but his journey isn't over. He will go with Geneve on her quest to uncover the rot within her order.

If the world gets saved on the way? So be it. But that's not why he's here. Red hair and a pure heart call to him. He used to be smarter than this.

It's time to stop doing the smart thing, and do the right thing instead.

SIGHT OF DAY

One of the secretive Feybrind, Sight of Day leaves his forest home on a mission to the human kingdom of Or'sen.

Skilled with a blade, bow, and wit, he is friend to all except the hated Vhemin. Sight of Day is a craftsman of great skill, whether making weapons or pancakes.

He has lived many years longer than even the oldest mayfly humans and Vhemin. The Feybrind can't talk, so he communicates with the People's beautiful handspeak.

ARMITAGE

Vhemin. Hunted. Hunter. That's Armitage.

Some jobs take longer than others. This one might take him the rest of his life. And that's fine, because his tribe's gone. Too brittle to find another, he'll stick around with the Knight, runt, and cat until the end comes.

He's got nothing better to do.

VERTILINE

Knight Chevalier Vertiline commands the Storm in one hand, the bitter whip of sarcasm in the other.

She's in the Tresward for the wrong reasons, but she's still the second best swordswoman the world has ever seen. If she can hold on to her courage, Vertiline might just stop stupid people from doing stupider things.

If not, well. She wasn't a proper Knight anyway.

Facing the Night

They came for Geneve while she buried her dead.

The air of Ravenswall smelled of smoke and rot. A sky forged of lead and sorrow hung overhead, threatening rain. It was cold, as cold as the south was, but with a malice that got into the bones. Geneve stood within the city's Tresward keep. Its walls held supplicant hands to the clouds, but the Three didn't answer. The gods had been silent for so long, she wondered if they were real.

The city mourned. Thousands died, and her losses were tiny compared to that. *Just one man, and perhaps not a very good one. Why am I here?*

The keep's courtyard was empty of anyone except her closest. Armitage glared snake eyes at the pyre, the torch in his hand a licking, hissing statement of anger. Sight of Day clasped hands before him, head bowed. Geneve didn't know if he prayed, or who to. The Three had forsaken his kind long ago. Vertiline leaned on a cane with her remaining hand, a bloody bandage covering the stump of her other. It was stained, but couldn't come close to the redness of her eyes. Tilly hadn't cried in front of Geneve, but the evidence of her grief was written on her face.

Meri stood out of sight behind her, but she could *feel* his presence.

Still reed-thin, shivering in borrowed, tattered clothes. But here all the same, because he had her back when sense suggested he should run. Or hide, to get away from her, and those like her.

The pyre waited. It held two bodies. Nicolette, Knight Champion, and Israel, Knight Valiant. Both were Tresward, but so much more. Nicolette died a long time ago and walked as risen.

Israel was her father.

Both seemed peaceful. Sight of Day, Armitage, and Meri dressed them in Smithsteel, because she couldn't bear to, and Tilly couldn't anymore. The burnished sun on their breastplates stared at the heavens as if demanding an accounting from Cophine, Ikmae, and Khiton. The gods didn't seem to care. Not about their shield for the world, or perhaps the world itself.

A scuff of shoe on stone, and then a touch at her elbow. "Would you like to say anything?" Meri's voice was calm, even, and stronger than she felt.

"I have nothing to say. Burn them." Geneve nodded to Armitage.

The monster's snake eyes looked past her to Meriwether. The young man's hand left her elbow. "I have a few words. If nobody minds."

Geneve swung to him, voice dry as old leaves. "They're not your dead."

He nodded, not arguing, but not stepping back. "I don't know who Nicolette was. A Champion for Light? We've seen it. But corrupted by the dark, dragged low. Forsaken. She doesn't deserve our anger, but instead, our pity. Our memory of the good she did." He sighed, a bellows running low on wind. "I know who Israel was, though. Dedicated. Honorable."

"He tried to kill you a handful of times," Armitage grunted. "This torch isn't getting any lighter."

"Who's to say I didn't deserve the killing?" Meriwether shrugged. "I'm no god. But I think Israel wasn't guided by the Three."

{The Justiciars,} Sight of Day suggested, his golden eyes soft. {They are just people.}

"Maybe. But I'm not talking about him hunting me. I'm an accident of thought here. A red herring to cloud the mind." Meri stepped away from Geneve, holding his hand out as if to display her as an exhibit. "His most important thing in all the world wasn't his honor, or his dedication. It was something more ... precious." Meri's hand fell. "I would have liked to know him better. I feel the lack is mine." Geneve felt something in her chest give, just a little. "He gave up love," Meri's eyes found Vertiline's, "and duty," he turned to the keep, before finally looking at Geneve, "to pursue something more."

"Treachery?" Geneve felt the anguish in her voice.

"No, Red." Meri's eyes turned sad, but she saw the understanding there. "Hope."

"A time when he could leave the Tresward?" Tilly's coldness rivaled the cloud's. "He was their man. He was—"

"*Here,*" Meri insisted. "*Right* here. Always." He tried for a lighter tone. "Trust me. As a man with an absentee father..." The joke died on his lips. "But this isn't about me." He raised his eyes to the keep's walls. "This is ... hang about. Who's that?"

Geneve followed his gaze. Standing atop the keep's walls, frozen against the skyline, stood a hooded figure. They held a bow. In a single smooth motion, they raised it. "'Ware!" she screamed. "We're under attack!"

Vertiline spun, the motion no longer smooth enough. The loss of her hand unbalanced her. She swept her glass blade from its scabbard. The figure loosed, Vertiline sidestepping, slicing the arrow from the air. But she wasn't perfect. Not anymore, and the Storm didn't answer her call. The arrow and blade both shattered, the clatter of the shaft against stone accompanied by the tinkling bells of glass rain.

More assailants boiled from the shadows. Geneve counted five, Requiem finding her hand like a lover in the dark. An arrow spat toward Meri, and she swung the steel in a beautiful, wondrous arc. A flight of vermillion sparrows fluttered skyward in the blade's wake, the arrow shattered to fragments.

Sight of Day turned, tail swishing. He met an attacker head-on. His assailant leveled a pike, but the Feybrind slipped around the thrust like his body were air. The cat disarmed his opponent, spun, and beheaded his foe, golden eyes seeking others.

Two rushed Armitage. The monster laughed, using the torch like a cudgel. Flame and justice hammered the face of one using a short blade. The second used a rapier, darting in, hoping speed would be better against bulk. *He's not seen the monsters fight.* The Vhemin jinked left, then clotheslined his enemy. He followed the man to the ground with brutal punches.

Two came for Vertiline. Geneve called, "Tilly!" then tossed Requiem. The skymetal hungered across the distance, turning in a vicious spin. It collected one of Vertiline's attackers, knocking the woman from her feet. Tilly followed the sword's path without looking, putting her hand on hilt as the blade thrummed in the corpse. She drew Requiem from the body, swinging low, then high. Her strikes no longer held perfection, but that didn't stop her attacker losing his left leg followed by his head.

Geneve looked up. The bowman still stood on the walls. Tribunal's range would be insufficient. She ran forward, eyes resting on Armitage's dropped torch. Geneve grabbed it, felt its weight, and eyed the distance. One of Khiton's seven hundred patterns came to mind. *Return What is Owed.* Her stance was faultless as she wound up, throwing the burning brand.

It spun, arcing across the distance. She heard the song of the Storm, the scream of vengeance, the cry of justice. The torch burned brighter, exploding as it hit the archer. His body erupted into burning fragments, charred gristle and ash hurrying away on the cold wind.

"Fuck me," Armitage said.

Sight of Day walked past her, eyes on the battlements. *{I always said there was a storm inside you, Daughter of the Three.}*

"I'm not their fucking daughter," Geneve spat. She whirled, red locks angry. Vertiline met her glare first and tipped her head, half tiny bow, half acknowledgment.

Armitage's eyes were wide, slitted snake pupils still on the burning ruin above. He held an assassin in one hand, but almost like he'd forgotten about the man. "Lemme get another torch."

Behind them all, Meri. The still calm in the eye of the storm. The young sorcerer walked past Vertiline, and sidestepped Armitage to stand before Geneve. "You're not their daughter, no. You're his." A slight nod to the pyre, and Israel.

He held his arms out as if he knew what was coming next. *Israel doesn't deserve my tears. He lied to me my entire life. He turned his face from my mother. He and Vertiline slaughtered a village. They conspired with a Justiciar to keep everything from me.* But those were just words, and words were nothing against what she tried to keep inside. *Tresward don't crack. We don't break. We are the world's shield.*

Meriwether didn't move. His eyes were kind, and sad, and asked nothing of her. His arms were still waiting for ... for what? For her to bend? To fall apart, for a man who didn't deserve it, in a city that didn't care?

Her heart didn't care what she thought. Geneve felt the crack in her chest break open, and she huddled into Meri as the tears came. He put his hand on her head, stroking her red hair. "It's okay," he said. "It's okay."

But it wasn't. Geneve sobbed by the pyre of a man she'd never really known. She'd thought him a friend, a mentor. A guide through life. But she'd not known him as her father, and she never would.

It wouldn't be okay ever again.

TIME PASSED. THE MINUTES SEEMED INFINITE, YET INSUFFICIENT.

Geneve walked the halls of Ravenswall's Tresward bastion. Things felt familiar enough, yet she was a foreigner here. She didn't know why. It wasn't the emptiness. Geneve remembered the smell of oil and sweat. Could almost hear steel on glass, the huff of breath, the cry of the Storm unleashed. The training halls here were smaller, designed for Knights to practice rather than train Novices, but they had the same equipment. Heavy things to lift. Solid wood and stone to hit. Ropes, and unsteady bridges. Blindfolds and shields, spears and Smithsteel. Glass if she wanted it.

Her fingers trailed over a wooden mannequin. The face was pitted and scarred, rough under her fingers. It felt like bark, not the polished training dummy that'd been delivered here, shiny and new.

Geneve left the training area. She found the barracks. All cots were empty. Possessions, gone. Drawers held no keepsakes. *Have they aban-*

doned me? The city? Or the world? Whatever called the Tresward away at Ravenswall's hour of need, they'd left no trace. She found no books in the Cleric's library, the shelves empty. The kitchen ovens were cold, and bathing water was freezing.

Her armored boots clacked against the stone floors. Geneve's echoes kept her company. She'd left the burning pyre behind. The regard of her friends felt too heavy to carry, so she'd walked inside. *I look for solace where I don't belong.*

Am I still Tresward? I command the Storm. But my brothers and sisters left me.

Her feet knew where to go. They led her down steps worn with use. The Smithy was empty. Gloom lay like a gray blanket, broken by shafts of dusty light from small windows set high in the walls. It smelled of a man she didn't know. Not Kytto and the warmth beneath his anger, but someone like him. It was as familiar as dirt. The armory held no glass or steel, but the air remembered the scent of hard work. Her fingers ran across the empty racks.

They didn't even leave dust.

Geneve's fingers ran along her sash. The black strip, and its single bar of gold. *Knight Adept Geneve.* Her lips twisted into a sneer, fist clenching around the sash.

"Don't do that."

Geneve whirled at Meri's voice. He stood in the Smithy's gloom, face shadowed, but she heard the care, layered brick by brick, in his voice. Cautious, because this was her place. *Maybe he fears his voice isn't welcome here.* "Do what?"

"Your sash." He moved through the shadows, rags whispering as he came. He touched her armored hand above the fabric. She couldn't feel his fingers but wanted to.

"I'm no Tresward."

"You are all the *way* Tresward."

"We hunt sinners." Geneve jerked her hand away. "You've no idea what that means."

He sighed, lowering his fingers. "Maybe I don't. I thought it meant someone who was strong but kind. Brave when it made no sense. A person who put shoulder to the heaviest weights, giving all, letting nothing go."

Geneve fingered the sash, then slipped it over her head. She let the black puddle to the floor. "I didn't earn that, you know."

"Hah. Oh, you're serious." He paced. "Tell me, then."

"I drugged my opponents before my Trial. I couldn't use the Storm. They'd have swept me aside like pieces from a board." Geneve hung her head.

"So?"

"So, I cheated!"

Meri laughed for real this time. "Everyone cheats. *Everyone.* You just feel bad about it. Tell me, oh doubtful Knight, what's so wrong about using your mind?"

Geneve sighed. "It wasn't ... honorable."

"But you passed the Trial?"

"The Clerics thought it an amusing trick. They let me carry my single gold bar." She nudged the sash with her boot. "But Vertiline and Israel had to carry the rest of me. Until—"

"Until you saved a city. Yeah, I was there." He scuffed a hand through unruly hair. It'd grown longer on the road. It had a curl to it Geneve liked. "Why are you here?"

"I miss him." Geneve unbuckled her gauntlet. "I can't stand it, this, this..." Her words ran out as she tore the metal glove free. It hit the ground with a clatter. Her fingers found the clasps on her other gauntlet. "This *cage!*"

Meriwether was by her side. Hands over hers. "What are you doing?"

"Will you help me?" Eyes on his. Heart hammering. Chest pounding.

"Always."

"Get it *off* me." Piece by piece, he helped her take off her Tresward armor. The golden sun clattered to the ground, face down. Pauldrons, greaves, and gauntlets. Steel, chain, and leather, all in a heap. She stood in the cellar, wearing only padding. Feeling her heart grow lighter with each piece removed.

Kytto wouldn't be pleased at the mess. Geneve picked up the armor, returning it to the racks. Last of all was the sash. She felt the fabric in her hands. It was almost new, holding the black like a moonless night. Vertiline's was a little frayed, and Israel's had been gray.

"You should keep that, at least." Meri tried for a grin, but it was sickly, born feeble. "You never know. You might need something to guide you home."

She fetched holster and scabbard, then turned to the stairs. "Come, Meri."

"In a minute." The young wizard lingered, eyes roaming the room. "I'll be right behind you. I just want to ... understand."

Geneve nodded, leaving him to his peace. But she took his advice, clutching the black sash in her fist. Its single gold bar felt almost as heavy as the steel she'd shed.

Chapter One

It took a while for Meriwether to find everything he needed. The Tresward did an excellent job of stripping the place of anything that wasn't nailed down, but it wasn't the first time he'd robbed someone. A cabinet in the scullery, forgotten by even the spiders who'd woven ancient silk above the lock, yielded a suitable sack. It'd held desiccated remains of what might once have been onions, but there was no one to ask, and Meriwether wasn't an archeologist.

Geneve was long gone once he'd collected the things he thought they'd need. Armitage and a glowing pile of coals waited in the courtyard. The Vhemin grunted when Meriwether emerged, hauling his sack. "You need a hand with that?"

"I got it." Meriwether joined the monster by the pyre's remains.

"Good. I wasn't going to help anyway." The creature reached a scaled hand into the coals, rooting about. He pulled free a burnished gauntlet. No soot clung to it. It wasn't the blackened Smithsteel of a fallen Champion, which meant it was Israel's. "That Tresward armor's really something, isn't it?"

"It's the people within it that are the real marvel."

"Don't be a dick." Armitage tossed the gauntlet back into the glowing heap, then brushed soot from his hands. "That's not what I meant, and you know it." He eyed Meriwether's sack. "What's in the bag?"

"Something I think we'll need."

"Weapons?"

"Of a sort."

"I heard it's legal to kill a man for being an asshole," the Vhemin warned. "The guard don't come looking or nothing."

Meriwether laughed. "This isn't for you. Not for me either, really."

Armitage sniffed. "Smells like bullshit."

"Could be." Meriwether headed toward the gates, avoiding the fallen bodies of their attackers. "I feel we should be worried about these guys."

"Worrying won't help," the monster warned. "They know where we are."

"Who?"

"Whoever's behind all," Armitage waved his arm at the sky, "this shit. We got undead fuckers. We've got turned Knights and fallen heroes. Some asshole's even worked out to get my kind," he slapped his chest, "working together. And then we kicked 'em in the balls. That's a thing a man doesn't soon forget."

Meriwether paused half-way to the gates. "We did, didn't we? Kick 'em in the balls, I mean. Geneve killed their Champion."

The monster squinted. "You got a point, or are you just seeing if your teeth still meet in the middle?"

"Why would you send six normal people against the Savior of Ravenswall?" Meriwether eyed the battlements where smoke still curled from the remains of an assassin. "It doesn't make sense. Not unless..."

They both stood like posts for a handful of heartbeats. Armitage scratched his armpit. "Oh, fuck."

"That's what I was thinking." Meriwether turned for the gate, putting a little curry in his stride. "Why didn't I bring a horse?"

THE JOURNEY TO THE QUEENSFANE WAS A HURRIED AFFAIR. Meriwether's burden was too heavy to run with, and he wouldn't surrender it to Armitage. The monster jogged at his side, glaring snake eyes at any humans who got too close.

Vhemin weren't welcome in Ravenswall, and it was a wonder he hadn't been murdered. *Still, plenty of time for that. It's only mid-week.* Meriwether didn't know why Armitage was still with them. Or Sight of Day, for that matter. The cat had promised to bring Meriwether to the queen, and he'd delivered. The Vhemin's deal was up, too. They'd opened the temple, and he'd taken them across the desert.

We're worlds apart, the four of us. A sinner, Knight, monster, and house cat. But Meriwether admitted he was glad of the Vhemin's company. Armitage might've been a murderer, but he was *their* murderer. And being a wizard in a city brought low by vile magic wasn't the safest place to be.

The streets wound toward the Queensfane. The pair ducked through the Artists Borough, ignoring the misery they found. No actors practiced for play. No artists painted. The city mourned, and none felt it so plain as those tuned to the heart.

The castle was quiet enough, no alarms crying a warning. That didn't mean they weren't too late. Meriwether puffed. "We need to hurry."

"Gimme the sack, then."

"Get your own." Meriwether flashed the Vhemin a quick grin. The monster answered with his horror-show teeth. "The only reason to attack us was a diversion. There's only one target more important than the Savior of Ravenswall."

"The queen," the monster agreed. "Don't know why you runts bother. The woman can't lift a sword. She'd die in three days on the plague lands. Maybe it's a mercy to rid you of weakness at the top."

"Sometimes it's not about our outer strength." Meriwether ducked around a cart. "It's what's inside."

"Blood? No?" Armitage shook his head. "I've no idea what you mean, then."

"I think you do, monster."

"I think you need to run faster, runt."

The sack didn't get lighter, or the breathing easier. But that wasn't the worst thing that would happen today. So, they ran.

THEY CAUGHT UP WITH GENEVE AND SIGHT OF DAY OUTSIDE THE castle. Vertiline was nowhere to be seen, her pale skin and almost white hair absent. Geneve marched with purpose toward the castle gates. The Knight's hair was teased into red strands by the wind. The cat appeared unruffled by the wind and current events both. "Geneve!"

She turned, a smile touching her lips as she saw him. "Meri." Her eyes found the sack. "What's that?"

"Why's everyone worried about my luggage?" Meriwether paused, sucking air. He waved at Armitage to continue, as the monster didn't seem winded at all.

"The runt ... your pardon." Armitage wiped his mouth, starting again at Geneve's glare. "I mean no disrespect, and you know it. It's just, we've got a thing going on. He calls me monster, I call him runt, and neither of us knifes the other in their sleep."

"Wait, there are knives involved?" Meriwether adjusted his load, expression astonished.

{We're going to die, and we won't even know why.} Sight of Day rolled his eyes.

"Shut it, cat." Armitage scratched his gut. "Here's the thing. You don't attack the Savior of Ravenswall—"

"The who?" Geneve glare turned to an overcast scowl.

{He means you.}

"I'm not—"

"This will go faster if you shut up," Armitage suggested. "You don't attack the slayer of a Champion with six grunts. Doesn't matter if you've got the element of surprise or not. The only way you kill a Knight, and take this from someone who knows for sure, is from a distance, with an arbalest."

"The queen," Geneve hissed, whirling to the keep. Her fingers clutched her empty scabbard. "Vertiline has my sword."

{She'll probably need it more than you. They will send many, and in great

numbers, against a Chevalier.} Sight of Day's tail swished. *{I hope her shopping expedition is important.}*

Shopping? Meriwether frowned. "She's going to get drunk?"

{That's what I said.}

"She's not a Chevalier. None of us are what we were a week ago." Geneve looked to the castle. "Let's get inside."

☂

THEY BURST INTO THE QUEEN'S THRONE ROOM. QUEEN MORGAN WAS in deep conversation with one of her Coterie when they slammed the doors open. The queen's house guard arrayed before her throne came to attention, blades already out of scabbards before recognizing Meriwether and Geneve.

Maybe we should've knocked first.

Morgan's eyes widened, lips pressed into a line. "Knight Adept Geneve. Lord du Reeves." Morgan looked across the monster and cat. "And ... friends. I trust this intrusion has purpose?" If she was surprised at Geneve's appearance, all white cotton and no armor, she didn't let it show.

"Assassins," Geneve said. "They came at us at the Tresward bastion."

The man the queen was talking to straightened. Meriwether didn't recognize him, but there was a lot of that going round. His robe said *I'm a wizard, stand back* better than the small silver broach the queen gave to her favored. The broach was fine and all: the Coterie's symbol was a stylized lightning bolt, which Meriwether felt overemphasized the benefits of evokers, but everyone needed a mascot. "And yet ... we are perfectly safe."

Meriwether glanced at the ceiling. *That's where they came from last time.* The rafters were free of clinging assassins. "This is ... unexpected."

"Not at all, Lord du Reeves," the man oozed. "While you've been playing at wizardry and grandstanding, a few of us are trying to save the kingdom. I thought you might try a little more showmanship. It's what your kind is," he sneered, "good for."

Geneve bridled, but Meriwether touched her arm. *I've got this.* Gentle fingers, a passing touch, but she stilled. "And how many Champions have you killed, hmm?"

The man cleared his throat. "That's hardly—"

"Or risen dead?" Meriwether leaned forward, ear cocked. "Is it more or less than one?"

"Lord du Reeves." Queen Morgan stood.

Meriwether winced. "Please don't call me that."

"My throne room, my rules." A smile, a hint of the young woman behind it. "Please, let me introduce Vikander. He is the new head of the Coterie. He holds sway over the elements."

Meriwether felt his gut churn. *This asshole?* "I'm sure he'll be fine. Back to the assassins—"

"That means you report to me," Vikander said.

Meriwether frowned. "What a curious notion. What gives you that idea?"

"I, uh, am in charge of the—"

"The Coterie, I know." Meriwether waved his hand. "You're under some kind of fantastic illusion I'm a member of your special club." Geneve snorted. "I've got friends aplenty."

The queen patted the air with her hands. *{Calm down.}* "I meant to make this offer more formally, but since you're here..." The queen's eyes slid off Meriwether, finding Geneve at his side. "I've need of people with specialist skills. Those who can hunt threats against the kingdom."

"The kingdom, or the throne?" Geneve's voice was clear, betraying none of the morning's emotion. If she felt self-conscious without her armor, white cotton hanging in soft lines down her frame, she gave no hint.

"They are the same thing." The queen's voice held a little ice mixed with steel.

"They are fucking not," Armitage said. "One's a person, who might be an asshole. The other's a group of people, which I'll admit, might mean a group of assholes."

Morgan spared the monster a withering glare. "Both, then."

"I'm not working for him." Meriwether eyed Vikander. "I don't think anyone else will, either."

Vikander's eyes held amber fire, the faintest hint of power deep within. "You'll come to heel, you little—"

Geneve took one perfect, flawless step forward. When her foot landed, a distant peal of thunder touched the air. Her eyes were locked on Vikander.

"Hi," Meriwether said brightly. "Look, before this gets out of hand, I think it's worth finishing the introductions. I'm Meriwether, this is Sight of Day," he pointed to the cat, "the warlord Armitage," the Vhemin cocked an eyebrow but said nothing, "and the Savior of Ravenswall, Knight Adept Geneve."

Vikander's throat worked like he was swallowing a live cockroach. "That's the—"

"Knight Adept, yes. Keep up, man." Meriwether beamed, then faced the queen. "You want to offer us a job?"

She nodded. "I need people..." Morgan quieted, raven locks framing her face, then eyed Armitage. "I need humans I can trust."

Geneve shook her head. "If one of us works for you, all of us do."

The queen's smile faded. "Perhaps I could ask the Feybrind Kingdom, but the Vhemin—"

"All or none, your majesty." Geneve glanced to Meriwether. "I've friends aplenty, too."

"Also, we need to think about it," Armitage said. "The cat thinks so too." Sight of Day nodded. "Mostly, we need to get drunk."

Before the queen could answer, a bell pealed, high and clear. It wasn't the regular cadence of a clocktower, but the panicked frenzy of an alarm. More of Morgan's house guard streamed into the throne room, readying to whisk her to safety.

Armitage sighed. "I guess that's a no to the drink."

"I need steel." Geneve faced Meriwether. "Go with the queen. Stay out of sight."

"I can—"

"I need you *safe*," she hissed. "I've lost so much already." Red hair lashing, she stormed from the room, Armitage and Sight of Day on her heels.

Meriwether watched them go. "But I need you safe, too."

Chapter Two

Geneve knew the castle wasn't under attack. The alarms came from outside, the high peal carrying across the sea air near the keep. She ran through the keep, seeking anyone with a sword who didn't look like they needed it.

A mace would do.

She didn't find any conveniently laying about. The three made the keep's main portcullis. It rumbled closed behind them as they squinted in the overcast glare. Geneve visored her eyes with a hand, trying to work out where the crisis was. The bell tolled from the Artist's Borough, but she couldn't see the cause. "Where do we go?"

{Over there.} Sight of Day arrived at her shoulder, pointing. *{See the flame?}*

The cat's golden eyes were sharp. She'd missed it at first: a tiny plume of smoke was chased heavenward by licks of fire. A fire could be disastrous, but didn't explain the alarm. The sound demanded *attack!* not, *get a bucket!* "Let's find out what's going on."

They ran from the keep. Soldiers and the queen's house guard readied defenses in the grounds. People hurried, but none seemed to have clear purpose. Panic was everyone's constant companion after the living dead walked these streets.

The roads outside the keep were more choked than usual as some ran toward the alarm, others away. Armitage bellowed, bulling his way through the crowd. Sight of Day slid between people like water around rocks, and found an underused alley. *{This way.}* He waved them over. *{As happy as Armitage looks bashing skulls, it'll be faster if we avoid people.}*

Geneve and the monster joined Sight of Day. She clutched useless fingers over her empty scabbard. "I need a blade."

Armitage snorted. "You also need armor, but you had to go all melodramatic."

{The creature speaks truth. There's a first time for everything.} Golden eyes found hers. *{We could leave this to those with arms and armor.}*

"Tilly's out here somewhere. Knowing our luck, she'll be at the heart of the ruckus. Come on." Geneve headed down the alley at a run, eyes up to the roofs for danger from above.

The Feybrind paced past her, making her speed look like the slow amble of a racing snail. He leaped up a wall, bounced to the other, then hauled himself onto a balcony. Another jump, a ricochet from the opposite wall, and he was on the roof. He peered over, then pointed north. *{That way. I'll guide you from up here.}*

"Fucking cat." Armitage glared. "Always running away."

Geneve headed north. She felt light without her armor. Faster, more fluid. *The feeling is dangerous. I've nothing between my heart and harm but a thin cotton shift.* Their path crossed a busy street. Armitage stampeded through, parting people like a ram through a rotted gate. Geneve followed on his heels, ignoring scared eyes and more immediate cries of alarm. *Vhemin!* and *monster!* filled her ears, and then they were past.

Sight of Day waved from a rooftop, directing them to the west. Geneve rounded a corner, finding a short alley and a closed door. She slowed, but Armitage didn't. The Vhemin sped up, shoulder down, barreling through the closed door as if it were parchment. Geneve jumped debris. Her eyes said *you're in a kitchen* and her mind screamed *no time! Run!*

Another door, and into a small shop front. The smell of pastry and panic. More cries, and a blade bared, steel hungering for the light. Armitage slugged the man who'd drawn. Geneve grabbed the dropped shortsword—*at last!*—in passing. Her hand measured its weight and said *this is a flimsy weapon*, but there were no others.

With the Storm backing her swing, she didn't need strong steel. Geneve could fight with brittle glass and carve apart the Three's enemies.

Except I don't know if these are enemies of the Three. I've no idea what's ahead.

She brushed rebellious hair from her eyes. Geneve's heart said something terrible was coming, and her heart hadn't lied. The same heart told her Meri was a good and true friend, the Vhemin wouldn't turn on her, and that Sight of Day would stand with her.

The street outside clotted with people. Two broken carts lay tangled ahead. One was lashed to a horse, which lay on the ground on account of being dead. The other was headed by a donkey, braying in pain, while people milled about in confusion. Armitage slowed, charting a course for the trapped animal.

"Armitage! No time!"

"We make time," the monster roared, not slowing. He slammed into a man in argument with another by the tangled donkey, knocking him into the broken cart. A scaled fist dropped the other, and the Vhemin grabbed the fallen man's belt knife. A few slashes, and the donkey was free of bonds, but still trapped by the wreckage.

Armitage got beneath the cart's seat, shouldering the weight. He heaved, feet skidding against the cobbled ground. *We don't have time for this!* But Geneve saw the monster's eyes as he looked on the donkey. Something like remembered pain, or borrowed sympathy.

She vaulted the wreckage, getting to the other side. Geneve got her hands under the cart, heaving. Wood splinters fought against callused palms, but she ignored them. She strained, and the cart rose. The donkey brayed, back legs spasming, then it was free.

Armitage dropped his side, Geneve following suit. He reached for the donkey, but it kicked, hitting him in the chest. He staggered, and the beast used the time to make a quick getaway. Armitage righted himself, horror teeth split in a grin. "Got a good kick, that one."

"Didn't it hurt?"

"Hurt plenty. Not the worst thing that'll happen to me, though." Snake eyes found her own. "Why are we standing around?"

She bared her teeth, half snarl, half grin, then looked for Sight of Day. The Feybrind waved them on from the rooftop corner of a building by an alley. Geneve ran, passing a gentlemen's clothier, a barber, and an empty store before hitting the relative quiet of the alley.

The Vhemin will kill people without pause, but stops to help an animal. Her mind wouldn't leave it alone. The monster chugged along beside her, snake eyes front, paying her no mind. *He is like that with his bear, Beck.*

Her thoughts were waylaid as they burst into a small courtyard. It was the type used by carts to deliver raw materials and pick up finished goods. Back to a wall, pale face a contrast to the bloody bandage at her severed wrist, leaned Vertiline. The Chevalier held Requiem steady enough, but Geneve had seen enough people lose blood to know Tilly was standing on grit alone. Requiem's fang tasted the enemy, the blade a ruddy, wet red.

Arrayed before her like the scattered leaves of a deadly flower were black-clad bodies. None moved, because Tresward didn't strike to injure. Vertiline might not hold the Storm on a tight leash anymore, but she knew the blade, the body, and how the former was the key to the latter's lock. Release, and you free the soul within.

An open door to Geneve's left disgorged thick, black smoke. The building's windows vomited flame. *This is where the fire is. But also, enemies intent on Tilly's murder.*

The dead were many, but still outnumbered by the living. Geneve's quick count said *ten still breathe.* Armitage, never one for complex math, charged into the fray. He grabbed a man by his belt, then swung him like a club into another.

Tribunal was in Geneve's hand, the scattergun roaring like a lion, calling all eyes to her. *That's right, ignore my friend. Pale Vertiline trembles like a leaf in a storm.* The gun's first bite chewed a woman's arm and shoulder to the bone, the second tearing the jaw from another.

She threw her shortsword, the blade whistling through the air to lodge in the skull of a man preparing to throw a spear at Vertiline. The hilt snapped off as the blade hit, confirming her belief it was a shoddy weapon. Geneve followed the weapon's path, halting her charge in the middle of the courtyard. Weaponless, and with five opponents still standing.

They spread around her, ignoring—*blessed Three*—Vertiline. Two went for Armitage, three still on Geneve. A *snick-thud* announced the arrival of Sight of Day's attention, an arrow shaft sprouting from the skull of a man with hard, gray eyes. The Feybrind was invisible in the pall of smoke above, but his arrows still found their mark.

A woman to Geneve's left threw a javelin. Geneve caught it, letting the momentum take her arm back, then tossed the shaft on the same path back to its owner. The Storm trembled along the javelin. It hit, shearing the woman in half like the hand of Khiton himself knocked her apart.

Three left. A crunch and a scream behind her suggested Armitage had dropped that number to two. Geneve faced her remaining opponent, nothing between her heart and his stiletto but thin cotton, stained with sweat and blood. His eyes roamed her, then he turned on his heel to flee.

Another arrow *snick-thudded* from Sight of Day's vantage above, hitting behind her. Armitage's last opponent gone, with but one remaining. A whirl of bloody skymetal, the unmistakable flash of Requiem as it spun past Geneve, hitting the man in the chest. He gurgled, fingers clutching steel as he fell.

Geneve turned, seeing Vertiline so very pale, her stump dripping blood through its bandage. The Chevalier gave a crooked smile. "You throw your sword so often, I wanted to see what it was like."

The burning building's heat was like a forge. Geneve shielded her eyes with her hand, coughing at smoke that hadn't found the heavens. Armitage kicked a woman at his feet. She had an arrow through her neck. The monster squinted at Sight of Day, who gave a cheery wave. "That one was *mine*, cat! You don't steal another man's kill."

The Feybrind landed cat-perfect on the ground beside Geneve, bow in hand. *{You looked like you could use the help.}*

"It's just not done!" The monster kicked the corpse again.

Geneve made it to Vertiline's side before she could slide to the ground. She held her friend up, one hand on her shoulder, the other resting light fingers above her stump. Vertiline's breath hissed through clenched teeth. "It stings."

"You shouldn't have exerted yourself. It's not healed, Tilly."

"Tell them. I just..." She trailed off, eyes unfocused for a moment. "I came here to get—"

"Drunk," Armitage snarled. "While the rest of us were working for a living."

"Armor." The pale woman sighed. "I need to sit."

"Hold her. Don't let her sleep." Geneve waited for Armitage to step in. The monster's snake eyes met hers. His look said, *She's probably going to die.*

Geneve turned aside. She didn't want to hear it. A quick rummage among the dead yielded a strong leather belt. She bound it around Vertiline's wrist, closing off the blood flow. *I used the Sway on her to stop the bleeding before. Can I do it again?* She leaned close to Vertiline's ear. The Chevalier smelled of smoke, sweat, and a sickly kind of fear, but mostly of regret. Geneve tried to ignore Tilly's feelings, reaching inside herself.

It was difficult to remember what happened when—

Don't think about it.

—the Valiant fell. Geneve felt into the core of her, the place where she kept her feelings locked away. Her mind's fingers found one that felt like terror, then discarded it for one that tasted of love. She whispered, "Vertiline, your body doesn't bleed. You know this to be true." Geneve drew back, then kissed Tilly on the forehead. *//BE WELL.//*

Vertiline's eyes were closed, her breathing shallow. She'd passed out. But Geneve liked to think her skin looked a little less pale, her skin less pinched in pain.

"Well, hell, I'm glad you did that. We should wheel you out to kiss everyone better on the battlefield." Armitage hefted Vertiline, but gently, so carefully, like she was made of the glass she used to wield.

"Don't get any ideas." Geneve retrieved Requiem, then slipped shells into Tribunal. She scanned the courtyard. "Why was Tilly here?"

{Why did someone set fire to this perfectly fine building?} Sight of Day's tail swish, swished. His golden eyes squinted against the blaze's heat. *{Perhaps we should get clear. Fire is bad.}*

Geneve made a quick search of the dead. As expected, they had no papers, no convenient scrolls showing their mission, and no helpful tattoos or clan markings. Clean skins, near as her hurried search could tell. Professionals, sent for one purpose. She eyed Vertiline, who looked like a child in Armitage's massive arms.

They were sent to kill a Knight, and they almost succeeded.

Geneve almost gave up, then saw a too-familiar wave of hair defying the constraints of a hood. She knelt, pushing the hood aside, then stumbled back, hand to her mouth. Geneve wouldn't mistake that face, not in a thousand lifetimes. The hair her fingers wanted to feel, the beard that never seemed short or long enough.

It was Meri, sightless eyes staring skyward.

Chapter Three

The book Meriwether found was useful in two specific ways. Most important, it was old, but not in a fancy, you-shouldn't-read-this way. No runes embossed the leather cover. The parchment was ancient, sure, but not vellum made from the skin of virgins. It didn't smoke or emit eldritch light. The interior was free of pictures that would make it more accessible to younger readers. He'd found it in the queen's library, specifically inside a locked cabinet that no one seemed to have a key for. He'd tickled the lock open with ease. A quick word, a gentle touch, and the rusted clasp popped aside like a pimp once he'd got the feel for your regals. No one missed the book, and when they saw Meriwether with it, they didn't want it.

The second reason he liked the book was he couldn't understand it. Not a word. The language was ancient, or at least from a part of the world Meriwether had never been to. While not experienced in all customs and peoples, he'd been across the continent often enough to meet traders from all lands, and steal from them. Meriwether spoke a handful of languages, and learned to read more through stolen manifests and shipping labels. He could order ale in most places without drawing the eye, or ear, and he fancied himself accomplished with the gentle arts of communication. The book remained steadfastly resistant to telling him what it contained.

The cover held no words, but the inside facing page showed just three: *ET MAGIA HIGH*.

'High' seemed one he could work with. 'Magia' was another he felt comfortable taking a guess at. Lined up, he thought the book was perhaps *A High Magic*, or *The Magician Supreme*.

Of course, it could be a cookbook. He sat on an overstuffed chair big enough for two, but had no companions. The chair was in a small chamber deep within the keep, alongside various other couches, divans, and tables. The tables held refreshments, of which he'd eaten enough for two, despite Geneve being Three knows where. *I hope she's safe.*

'Small' was relative; it was still large enough to hold twenty souls. A collection of guards, all piercing eyes and ready steel. The queen, of course, and her parasite Vikander. A collection of her Coterie, some less starved-looking than others. Fatter ones he imagined had been here longer. News of the queen's safe haven for mages traveled slow by design. She didn't have an army capable of defending against the Tresward if they decided to snare a whole net of sinners in one go.

This is where I sit: the queen and her pet mages, a viper, and a handful of men and women who will murder us if they think we mean her majesty harm. The hardest part of all this was he hadn't accepted Morgan's offer. He didn't know if they should work *for* her, or even *with*. Meriwether's past lent him a dislike of royalty. He didn't know if it was the sloping foreheads or sunken chins, but they didn't think like regular folk. They had the most, but wanted more, and trod all over everyone to climb higher.

Fairness, Meriwether. The queen's already at the top. It made her motivations slightly less suspect, but only marginally. For all he knew, she wanted a group of wizards to incinerate the Tresward, and then all threats to her crown. In her shoes he'd probably do the same, because Meriwether knew his father, and his father was exactly the sort to want a pretty hat and a kingdom to go with it.

He paged through the book, trying to fathom what it said. The cookbook idea wasn't without merit. It held neat, ordered rows of things that could be ingredients or methods. Steps to do *something*, and the devil was working out exactly what. Meriwether loved a mystery, and the book gave him his heart's desire. It's a shame it didn't have red hair and piercing eyes...

Meriwether jerked upright, the book snapping closed. All eyes turned to him for a moment, then with varied amounts of eye-rolling looked away.

"Something you want to say?" Vikander looked down his nose at Meriwether. His hands were tucked into his sleeves, his almost-a-smile-in-the-right-light condescending, his tone worse.

Meriwether ran his fingers across the smooth, aged cover of *Et Magia High*. The book felt like a hundred others might have done that, or perhaps one or two people who did it a lot. "Where do you come from, Vikander?"

"The western reaches." The Coterie's leader beamed. "It's a wealthy land. People know their place."

"Probably why they threw you out, no?" Meriwether stood, ignoring Vikander's outrage. He walked to the refreshments table. An unused goblet beckoned, so he filled it with a wine so red it could put hairs on his descendant's chests. "Hard to be hated by those with everything and nothing alike."

Vikander turned to Morgan. "My queen, this is exactly why we need to have a single leader. A unified force. If you would let me lead all your specialists, I'd be able to coordinate a response at all levels."

The queen raised an eyebrow. "My lord Vikander, if you think one man holds control of all my forces, you haven't been paying attention."

"I'm sorry?" His eyebrow rose.

"It means she doesn't trust you either." Meriwether walked to a bookshelf. He'd have preferred a window, but it was a tall order from a basement. The books were tales of bravery for the challenge-starved, and romance for the heart-weary. "I haven't read this one."

"Expanding your knowledge with tawdry tales?" Vikander's sneer was evident without looking at him.

"Always." Meriwether tapped a book's spine. *The Missing Maiden*. "There's more to the world than earth and sea, Vikander. We can learn things from the imaginings of a madman, or the shy heart of a poet.

Only those dead inside would spurn stories of feeling in favor of just the knowing." He left the book alone, facing the room. Most looked at him, or Vikander, the exception being the guard, who watched everyone, always. "I'd have thought someone who aspired to lend agency to the queen would look for all sources of truth."

The evoker's hands came free from his robe. "Perhaps we should talk privately, Meriwether."

"If you think it'd help, sure." Meriwether tossed him a wink. "But I suspect a good round of hide-the-bishop's more what you need. Sadly, I don't see anyone stepping up as your partner. You can," he tapped the side of his nose, "always play solo."

"You little—"

The door opened, revealing two guards working to restrain Geneve. Armitage followed behind, three other humans grappling with the monster. House guards within the room surged to assist. Sight of Day slipped in behind the ruckus, ducked a woman's outreached arms, sidestepped a man with hands like hams, and arrived at Meriwether's side. *{You seem suspiciously alive.}*

Meriwether blinked. "What?"

"Meri!" Geneve dropped a guard with a punch, took one in return, and felled her opponent with a knee to the groin. She still wore nothing but plain cotton, but had her sword back.

Meriwether looked behind her but caught no sight of Vertiline. He felt his stomach roil, a sickly queasiness he wasn't used to. It said *you owed that one* and *she better not be dead.*

Morgan rose, red gown a squall of fabric. "Hold!" Everyone ignored her, guards trying to fell Geneve with some enthusiasm, and trying to fell Armitage with more.

Vikander threw his arms wide. A trail of lightning crawled between his fingers. *That won't do.* Meriwether eyed his cup, took three paces to Vikander, and smashed it on the back of the man's skull. The evoker dropped to the floor, a snaking trail of electricity fleeing his body. It galloped up the bookshelf, cindering three books, one of which was the excellent *Trials of Marcellus.*

"*ENOUGH!*" Queen Morgan's voice cracked like mace to the jaw. She leveled her finger at a house guard with captain's stripes. "Regan,

RICHARD PARRY

contain your men. They live because the Tresward lets them. And you,"
she swung her gaze to Geneve, "*learn to fucking knock!*"

A stillness settled on the combatants. Armitage shook a woman
free, then casually elbowed a man in the jaw, dropping him like a sack.
"I told you we should have—"

"The mistake was mine, your grace." Geneve bowed her head, but
didn't bend the knee. *Knights kneel only to the Three.* "I saw," her eyes
found Meriwether's, "something that I couldn't bear, and I had to be
certain." She took a deep breath, putting the palms of her hands on the
guard to her left. The man had a split lip and an eye already swelling
closed. Geneve appeared unharmed. "I beg forgiveness."

"Uh," the man said. "Sure." He gave a nervous laugh, as if realizing
he'd been wrestling with a Tresward before his brain got involved in
the conversation.

Queen Morgan eyed the Knight for a handful of heartbeats. Meriwether winced, fearful of what would come next. Most historical
monarchs would put imbeciles to the sword, starting with the most
dangerous fools and working down the ladder. While separating
Geneve's head from her shoulders would take some effort, and no
small number of soldiers, a dedicated leader could see it done. The
queen's eyes found the Vhemin, then swung to Sight of Day. She
continued her circle, a slight raise of the eyebrow showing her surprise
at Meriwether above the prone Vikander. "Leave us."

"Right away," Meriwether agreed.

"Not you, fool. And by 'fool,' I of course mean, Lord du Reeves."
The queen pointed at Sight of Day. "You, take the monster out of my
sight. Captain Regan, clear your team out."

"Your majesty—"

"*Did I stutter?*" Morgan's face was paler than Vertiline's. "And take
this," she nudged Vikander with her toe, "with you. Knight Adept
Geneve and Lord du Reeves, you will stay."

Geneve looked to Captain Regan, and perhaps sensing his discomfort, unbelted her scabbard. She handed the weapon to him. "Will you
keep this safe for me?"

"Thank you." The captain glanced to the queen. "I appreciate your
understanding." Meriwether thought Geneve could commit regicide

28

using a handful of grapes from the table, and he suspected Captain Regan knew this too. But it was a small courtesy, extended from one professional to another. *And if the good captain knows how much she loves that sword, he'll keep it close.*

People trickled from the room like rats leaving a sinking ship. Vikander was hauled out, perhaps less gently than his condition required, and the door closed with a click.

Morgan sat, eying the spilled wine. Her gaze moved to the burnt bookshelf, where a brave curl of smoke still rose. She took a deep breath, then held her hand out to a divan across from her. "Please, sit."

Geneve clenched her hands. "Your majesty—"

"You will sit, Knight Adept Geneve, because no one stands higher than the queen except the Three themselves." Morgan showed no fear of the Tresward.

Meriwether slunk to the divan, Geneve joining him. "I must say—"

"I feel standards haven't been set, what with the attack on Ravenswall." Morgan leaned forward in a rustle of silk. "It's customary to allow your monarch to speak before you put your foot further in your mouth than it already is. Do you understand, Lord du Reeves?"

He nodded. "I, uh. Sure. Absolutely."

"Here's the simple truth." The queen looked to Geneve. "My kingdom is under siege. It's burning right to the waterline. I need people who can help put out the fires. Are you one of those?"

Geneve glanced at Meriwether. "Your grace—"

"Before you tell me no, consider." Morgan smoothed her gown. "The best allies are those who need each other the most. Your Tresward have abandoned you. I see you've left their colors in your past. You..." She winced, pressing a hand to her temple. "This blasted headache."

Meriwether perked up. "Headache, your grace?"

"It's nothing. As I was saying—"

"It's possibly something." Meriwether shifted the *Et Magia High* on his lap. He wasn't sure how he'd retained the tome in the ruckus. "There are magics—"

"I'm savior to mages." The queen's lips pressed in a line. "They wouldn't attack me."

Meriwether and Geneve exchanged a glance. Meriwether chalked that one down to look into later. "Of course, your grace."

"I've made it clear what the kingdom needs, but you hesitate." Morgan leaned back, headache clearly not the mild sort. "Knight Adept Geneve, tell me what caused the alarm in my city."

"Assassins." Geneve glanced at Meriwether. "And, I think, sorcerers."

"I told you, the mages wouldn't attack me—"

"Your majesty," Geneve stormed on like someone with little experience in the wrath of tyrants, "I don't mean to anger, or to jest. By battle's end, I counted twenty-five dead in an attempt to assassinate Knight Chevalier Vertiline. The enemy seek to end your most powerful allies." Geneve's hands curled on her lap, fingers clenched so tight they were bloodless. "They had mages among them. Or at least one mage."

Meriwether swiveled to face her. "What?"

She focused on the queen. "It was in the Artist's Borough. We need the whole of the tale from Tilly, but it seems she found them at an armorer's. There was a fire." Red locks lashed. "That's not important. Among the dead was a man wearing Meri's face."

Meriwether tried to get a foot in the conversational door again. "I said, what?"

The queen eyed them both beneath hooded lids. "He is not an uncommon-looking man. Nor unseemly, yet—"

"I would know his face anywhere, your grace." Geneve shook her head. "It was him. Not someone who looked *like* him, but *him*. The body wore his hair. His chin, and his beard. Beneath the smoke, he smelled like Meri."

Meriwether wished Sight of Day were handy for a quip, or Armitage to interrupt with something disastrous. *No? It's just you then.* He cleared his throat. "A thaumaturgist and an illusionist working together could do this."

Geneve nodded. "The seeming to the eyes is one part, but the essence needs transference."

"You're telling me there are at least two wizards allied against the throne?" Morgan glared, face bleak.

Meriwether spread his hands. "Not necessarily. We can guess two wizards are working together against the Tresward. Or the Champion of Ravenswall." He looked away, aware of how little a part he played in saving the city. "They need not be concerned with the throne."

Morgan gave a slow nod. "That is true, but I don't believe in coincidences. Tell me of them. What did they look like? Clothing? Symbols?"

"Nothing." Geneve gritted her teeth. "No symbols. No scrolls, potions, or other elements of magika. Plain steel weapons made well enough, but not *too* well. Javelins and spears, wood strong enough for the work. Unremarkable armor."

"Did they wear black?" The queen dropped the question in an offhand manner, but Meriwether heard the subtle tension behind it. The faintest tremor as if she knew the answer and didn't want to ask.

"They did. It is the costume of villains everywhere. They were attired similarly to those who attacked your grace before the Knight Champion breached the city gates." Geneve brushed red hair aside. "You know these people?"

"Hold up." Meriwether leaned forward. "All black. I'll admit, it's not a remarkable element by itself, but ... Red, do you remember Calterburry?"

"Aye." She gave a smile, half hidden by her hair. "You were focused on freedom."

"For those of us not familiar with the events in Lord Symonet's citadel, what happened in Calterburry?" Morgan had the look of someone reaching her patience threshold with fools.

And she's aware of which city is run by which lord. Keeps the information in her head, not trusting it to advisors or books. Worth bearing in mind: this queen puts in the work. "Back when we didn't ... understand each other so well," Meriwether squeezed Geneve's hand, "the lordling Symonet had me captured from under the Tresward's noses. He wanted to Harvest my skills. The people who extracted me were similarly attired in black."

"Good enough with steel, too." Geneve nodded. "But they broke against Tilly and..." She wound down, a catch in her voice.

The queen rose, walking to the bookshelf. She ran her fingers along the tomes, selecting one. Returning to her seat, she handed the volume to Meriwether, the book open to a page already. "Read it."

He flipped the book over to check the title. *An Honest Account of the Denizens of Crime*, by *Mercer*. "I've not heard of Mercer."

"That's because anyone writing about the criminal underworld needs to keep their name to themselves." Geneve reached over and turned the book back to the open page, a half-smile trying its best to hide on her face. "Read it, Meri."

He cleared his throat. "The page is titled 'The Vide.'" He frowned. "'Black of attire, the now infamous assassins of Tebrani extend their network of murder-for-hire to the Kingdom of Or'sen. Known for high fees yet excellent service, they guarantee death to anyone, regardless of rank or station. Having accepted a contract six years prior, the Vide assassin Jasmijn was said to have murdered the monarch Kacper while awaiting beheading in his usurper's lock-up.'" Meriwether raised an eyebrow. "That shows a work ethic. 'The Vide are known for no uniform other than black attire. They carry no markings, tattoos, or special effects. The only way you know their work is by the guarantee of death. It is said they are the living Will of the Precept, eternal emperor of all Tebrani.'"

"They sound a cheery bunch." Geneve frowned. "We don't know the Vide within the Tresward."

"Too busy with sinners, I expect." Morgan smiled to take the sting out of it. "Mercer is a ... person I hired to write what they knew of the criminal world. I asked them to record their knowledge after my father's murder. I felt I needed to know a little more about what went on in the dirty grouting of my kingdom." Her eyes grew distant with memory.

"Do the Vide have a line on mages?" Meriwether closed *An Honest Account*. "And who'd have a contract out on Geneve?"

Morgan counted on her fingers. "Tebrani is a different land. Their rules aren't ours. The Tresward hold no influence there. They are a legend only. And the contract was put out on you first, Lord du Reeves."

Meriwether winced. "I wish you wouldn't call me that. At least until the dear old man's dead."

The queen considered him for a moment, and Meriwether had never felt more measured. "Leander du Reeves is said to be in excellent health. Do you mean to kill him?"

"No!" Meriwether tightened the ratchet on his smile. "I just mean ... I haven't earned it, your grace. Titles and such are best saved for those who've done the work."

Morgan muttered something that sounded like *that's a shame*. "I think I understand more about you every day, Meriwether."

Geneve's hand tightened in Meriwether's. "What are you going to do about the Vide?"

"Me? Nothing." The queen rose, smoothing her gown. "You, on the other hand, are free to defend yourselves as you see fit."

Chapter Four

Night came soon enough, and with it, her weary body demanded rest. She found their quarters and threw herself onto her cot.

Geneve swam the murky shoals between sleep and waking. She was pulled by currents she couldn't control. The waters about her held her friends. Meri, of course, but also the golden-eyed Sight of Day, and the monster Armitage. Her friends cried out for help, the water closing above them, heads vanishing from view. Geneve tried to save them. She was a Knight Adept of the Tresward. They'd trained her since she was five to be strong. But when she grabbed Armitage, the Vhemin slipped from her hands. Sight of Day's panic was swallowed by the waves just as easily.

Meri tried to swim to her. She held his hand just once before he vanished, the dark water swallowing him without a sound. She screamed his name, but no one answered. The water around her was cold, dark, and bottomless. Geneve couldn't save them. She couldn't save anyone.

Above, hidden by clouds almost as dark as the waves, a vast form flew. Geneve heard the flap of wings so large they sounded like ship canvas. She couldn't see anything, but she felt fear. Fear not for herself, but for the world. Fear for what she'd made.

When the thing above her spoke, it had the voice of gods, of angels, and of demons. The water about her shook with the weight of it. She turned her face away, terror tearing at her, regret dragging her deep.

//YOU HAVE BROKEN THE WORLD AGAIN. ALL WILL PAY THE PRICE FOR YOUR FAILURE.//

GENEVE WOKE WITH A CRY HALF-LOST TO SLEEP. SOMEONE HELD HER arms, golden eyes staring from the gloom. She wanted to scream, to punch out. Geneve swung, her arm half-fouled by the blankets.

Sight of Day swatted her strike aside as if she were a bumbling Novice fresh to the Tresward. His soft hand touched her face. When she stilled, he let her go. *{You make more noise than a pig at slaughter.}*

Geneve gave a shuddering half-sob, half-laugh. "I'm sorry."

Her room was dark. The hearth had long burned low. The coals gave almost no light back, a ruddy pool lapping beneath her bed. The Feybrind sat by her side. He wore pants and a shirt, but no shoes. *So, the hour's early. I woke him.*

They shared joined rooms. The four didn't want to be separated after their time on the road. Geneve's room was the smallest. A simple bed, coarse woolen blankets, and a pillow. She tossed the blankets aside, shivering in the cool air. Geneve navigated to the window by memory, throwing the shutters wide. Sea air and moonlight greeted her. She eyed the three moons, judging the hour a whisker before fourth bell. Habit made her glance to the corner. Requiem's hilt gleamed above its scabbard, touched by the moonlight. Tribunal hung from a hook, ready and waiting. "I'm sorry I woke you."

Sight of Day shrugged. *{I'm a light sleeper. Especially light when my neighbor flounders like a landed whale.}*

"You could always swap with Meri." Her room was the most easterly, followed by Sight of Day, Vertiline, Meri, and Armitage.

{I don't think that's a good idea. Also, the monster snores.} Sight of Day

stood, padding on noiseless feet to her side. His gentle hands found her bare arms, rubbing them for a moment. Golden eyes looked into hers. She saw nothing but care and worry there. *{There is a storm inside you, Daughter of the Three.}*

"I know. It came out when ... with Nicolette." She scrubbed fingers through red hair. "And I don't think I'm their daughter. Not anymore. Not after ... everything."

He nodded, not disagreeing. *{That's not the storm I mean.}* He slipped to the door, tail cutting the night, but cast a backward glance. *{You're not alone in sleeplessness. Be careful with your heart, Daughter of the Three. It's the only one you've got.}*

She watched the empty door for a moment. Cold air breathed against her neck. Geneve retrieved her blanket, draping it about her shoulders, then went in pursuit of tea. She wouldn't sleep again, not if her dreams were filled with warnings of world destruction.

Geneve walked the short corridor connecting their rooms, blanket following like a train. Sight of Day's door was open, the cat sitting cross-legged on a rug, golden eyes closed. Tilly's door was closed. Geneve leaned her head against the stout wood. *My friend. They tried to kill you.* Always, Vertiline had been her teacher. Not as skilled as Israel with the Storm or Sway, she was somehow more ... approachable. Yesterday was hard for both of them. The Chevalier's command of the storm slipped away, as gone as her missing hand. Better with a blade than any normal human, she was still ... *ordinary*. Geneve tried to consider pale Vertiline in any light other than *magnificent* and found it a struggle.

Behind the wood, she heard a sleepy moan. Vertiline had been dosed with medicines. Without Tresward Clerics, she was reliant on earthly cures for healing. The pain of her arm bothered her terribly, but she faced it as she had all dangers: shoulders square, chin out.

She isn't ordinary, and you know it. Vertiline has more splendor in her broken body than you've seen another match. Geneve touched fingers to wood, whispering, "Sleep well."

Meri's door was open, his bed a circus of disarray. His blanket was tossed to the floor, shutters thrown wide. A book lay open on a small desk beside his bed. The sack he'd taken from the Tresward garrison lay to one side. *Best leave that. He's earned a few secrets.* Ignoring the rampant snores from the room holding Armitage, Geneve padded into Meri's room. She held the book up to the dim light. The language was foreign to her. She supposed it was something he was working on while she...

While I left him like the ordinary man I thought him as. Geneve sucked air, then bit her lip. *I pushed his aid away, leaving him here like a castoff toy.* She knew the truth of the words, felt the sting of them without another speaking. Geneve put the book back. "I must treat my precious things with more care." Her eyes found Cophine's pale face through the window. Behind the goddess, Ikmae's gray, and the shroud of Khiton's dark regard. She felt them *watching* her, merciless, eternal. An echo from her dream surfaced.

All will pay the price for your failure.

"What do you want from me?" She didn't know who she asked, but it didn't matter. No one answered.

Hugging the blankets about her, Geneve set out again. She left Meri's room and her regret behind, focused on finding that cup of tea. The queen's castle was a multi-level monstrosity. The advantages were that she could pretend to be an unknown among the thousands here. Her status as the Savior of Ravenswall didn't matter. Also, there were kitchens *everywhere*. She trailed wool behind her as she followed her nose. It told her bread baked ahead. Bakers kept uncivilized hours so the rest of humanity could get crusty, warm treats with their breakfast.

In the distance, she heard fourth bell. It tolled its chimes against the night, as if mournful.

You have broken the world again.

The warm light of hearth called her forward. Geneve dodged the bustle of people full of their self-importance as she ducked into the kitchen. Warmth rolled over her, the smell of food, and the soft hum of conversation. She sheltered by the door, taking it in. A man and woman worked by a stove. Another man chopped by a bowl, his knife a blur. Above them, pots and pans hung on hooks.

A stove smoldered by the wall. A teapot was already set atop. The cook doing impressive bladework caught her eye, then used the knife's tip to sling a mug in her direction. "For the Savior of Ravenswall."

Geneve caught the cup with a wince. *So much for it not mattering here.* She pointed to the pot. "May I?"

"Not my pot, Knight. It's his." The cook jabbed his blade past Geneve, then went back to his cutting.

She turned. In a corner with shadows moody enough for a storm of crows sat Meri. He lounged on a hard wooden chair, a cup resting beside a pot of honey on the table before him. His hair was a tousled mess, but his eyes were bright, a smile bringing them alight. "It's your favorite."

Geneve wrapped her hand in a blanket, snaring the pot and pouring a cup. "My favorite?"

"Angels kiss."

She laughed, then sniffed the brew. She caught the aroma of cloves and cinnamon. "It smells like the tears of heaven." Geneve walked to his table. "May I sit?"

He seemed surprised. "You don't need to ask."

She settled across from him, sharing the smell of cinnamon and their own pool of quiet for a time. "I do, though."

"You what now?" He blinked, the early hour clearly making his mind crawl at a pace closer to her own.

"Ask, I mean. I ... should always do that." She sipped tea, then spooned honey into it. It might smell like heaven, but it tasted like unsweetened trash without it. "Yesterday, I left you here."

"There were people to fight." He looked away, trying to save her from the sting of what she'd done. "Not my thing."

"It is. You've traveled across the plague lands with me. Us, I mean. We faced a dragon, Meri. A dragon! And a temple of the ancients. You and I faced the Vhemin. We fought a Champion."

"You did the fighting, as I remember—"

"*We* fought a Champion. There was no one else who stood by me."

"To be fair, they were all dead or dying."

She laughed. "You held a blade against Nicolette. For me."

"That seemed dumb." He rubbed his face with a hand. "I wasn't really thinking about it."

Geneve watched him over her cup, steam wisping about her face. She ignored the lie for the comfort it gave him. "I pushed you away, instead of remembering how strong you are. How wise, and smart. I wonder ... I wonder if you may have seen something I didn't when we faced the Vide."

Meri pushed his cup about, chasing a trail of water back and forth. "Thank you for saying that. It warms my heart you can lie as well as me." He offered her a tired smile, about fit for the hour. "So. You're up early."

"Bad dreams."

He nodded. "There's little to be festive about, it's true. I like kitchens. Did you know that?" He looked past her, perhaps at the cooks, or something in his past. "They were a place I could be safe. Always have been. Good things come from them. I think cooks love the world and show it through what they make for us."

Geneve blinked. "Meri, if you want to—"

"Thing is, there's scarce been a time I've had a moment to rest in one. Always running, always hiding. Stealing." He glanced at her from under a rake of hair that fell over one eye. "Thank you for lifting me up from the muck, Red."

"I captured you. I dragged you into danger!"

"Same thing." He shrugged. "Journey's not done though, is it?"

She nodded. "I dreamed of... I'm scared."

The statement lay between them, as real as the honey or the tea. He sighed. "Me too. And not a regular kind of scared. I'm ... terrified. Do you play chess?"

"I ... what?"

"Chess. It's a board game. You—"

"I know what chess is."

"Why didn't you say?" He brushed his hair back. "In chess, you never lead with your queen. Always, the game starts with a pawn. I'm scared because we fought a Champion who almost bested a whole city with her army of dead, and I'm pretty sure she was just a pawn."

Geneve drew her blanket closer. "What's the book on your desk?"

He gave her a blank look. "The book? Oh. *Et Magia High*. It's a cookbook." He pointed with his cup behind her where the chefs were hard at work. "Remember how cooks make everything with love? The ancients knew the rule too."

"It's a what?"

"A cookbook. But, instead of making eggs, or a souffle, you can remake the world." He rubbed his nose. "I think, anyway."

"You *think?*" She leaned forward. "I know it's early, but you need to start making sense."

"I thought it was just a fun puzzle. Old book, unknown language, something to pass the hours while you were off doing," he waved his hand, "hero stuff."

"Meri—"

"But the thing is, I've worked pieces of it out. I had to use another book to do it. Some of the words were similar enough. Behold! I know what the title is." He waited her out.

"Well ... what is it?" She gritted her teeth. "You're the most frustrating—"

"The High Magic." He leaned forward, face close, eyes brighter than she remembered seeing. "The book is a cookbook of High Magic, Gen."

"What's ... High Magic?" She huddled close with him, their heads almost touching, voices dropping to a whisper unconsciously. "The Tresward talk of lots of magics. Evocation. Enchantment, and illusion. Thaumaturgy, necromancy, and summoning. And—"

"I know all those." He leaned back. "The really neat part is, I have no idea." He laughed. "None! I've got a book about the High Magic and I can read about one word in fifty. It's—"

"I will never understand you." She relaxed into her chair. "I need your help."

"Oh? Pray tell, what can the high magician help you with?"

Geneve snorted. "The bad guys. Will you come with me into certain danger?"

Meri watched Geneve across the table. Balancing and measuring her? Surprised at her request? She didn't know. He tapped his cup with a fingernail. "I thought you'd never ask."

Chapter Five

Meriwether watched Geneve head off, red hair jouncing. She would never be a slender, elfin waif, and he liked that. Geneve walked with *power*, like her steps held a meaning of their own.

She catches the eye, and no mistake.

She was heading for arms and amour, and that was a task he couldn't help with. His knowledge of swords was the obvious. *They are excellent at cutting people, and make lousy plowshares, despite what romantics would have a man believe.* Geneve left the kitchen, leaving him to his thoughts. The first to gain entrance to his sleep-starved consciousness was:

There could only be so many attacking Vertiline if she happened upon their hideout.

Despite his breezy attitude, he wasn't fond of following Geneve into death and destruction, but something about the Vide's presence in Ravenswall ... *itched*. They were here to kill Knights, but that was something you could do anywhere. Assume they were well-informed, and they could easily waylay the party on the road. Which meant Vertiline stumbling across twenty-five while shopping wasn't a carefully laid plot to assassinate them. She'd put her foot in a hornet's nest by accident. Meriwether would stake a fistful of silver regals on it.

Squaring that idea away into an uncomfortable corner of his mind left room for another:

Tilly will die.

So, he needed to fix that. He owed the pale Knight for many things. He slurped the last of his tea, then bussed his cup and Geneve's to the scullery. Meriwether made short work of the dishes. He wasn't the kind to be waited on; it was just that kind of presumption that gave asshats like his father the reputation they deserved.

The queen's keep was coming alive as the sun rose. *Not much time— get about your business.* His room was as he'd left it. He sidestepped to Sight of Day's quarters. Meriwether rapped on the closed door, then made the short voyage to Armitage's door. This one he hammered, because the monster wasn't a light sleeper.

Snoring was replaced by cursing. Meriwether thought he heard *best way to die is to disturb a man's sleep*, and *maybe I'll kill someone before breakfast this week*, before the door yanked open. Armitage's snake eyes blinked, clear as the dawn itself. The Vhemin looked like he'd been up for hours, no hint of post-dream fatigue about him. The only giveaway was his lack of clothes; Armitage wore a towel about his middle. The monster was muscled like he'd stocked up at a sale. His scaled skin rippled with it. *Curious: he has no scars.* "What is it, runt?"

"I hoped we could share a passing tale of delight over breakfast."

Armitage squinted. "You trying to be funny?"

"I *am* being funny."

"Let's put it to the vote. Cat?"

Meriwether looked to his left where Sight of Day had materialized. The Feybrind was fully dressed, leaning against the keep's stone wall, eying his nails. *{I think the human can sometimes be funny, but those occasions are when he's fallen over.}* Golden eyes winked. *{There was one time when he—}*

"The thing is, we've got a bit of a problem." Meriwether cocked an eyebrow. "If I'm right, we're all in terrible danger."

Armitage sniffed, hawked, and spat. *Someone's going to have to clean that up.* "What else is new?"

"Vertiline lost her hand." Meriwether spread his hands. "She's not at her best. I've no doubt she's better with steel than anyone in this corridor, but her injury isn't the kind you walk off. Tilly will ... get hurt. But, she's also proud. It's like they give Knights a blade of glass and an extra helping of pride before sending them off into the world."

"She ain't better than me," Armitage said. "Course, I'm not in the corridor, so I'll let it slide." He eyed the Feybrind. "You want breakfast?"

Sight of Day nodded. *{I've been up for some time. Everyone has very loud dreams.}*

"Good. Let's go kill it, then." Armitage barged past Meriwether, holding up at Vertiline's door. He hammered it so hard it shook in the jamb. "Girl! Get out here."

Meriwether winced. *Girl?* Sight of Day shook his head, also wincing. After a five-count, the door flew open. Vertiline stormed into the corridor, getting right up into the Vhemin's face. "Do you want to *die*, monster? The best way to achieve that is to disturb a woman's sleep."

Armitage grinned his shark teeth. "I thought the same thing myself. We're," he jerked a thumb at Sight of Day, "going to murder breakfast. You know, outside the walls. There's some disagreement on who's the best at killing, so you need to come along."

Tilly's long hair wasn't bound in its usual braid, but that didn't make it unkempt. It flowed like a white wave as she nodded. Her hand found her stump as if by accident. Meriwether saw her fingers trembled, but her voice was hard as she said, "I've a need to stretch my legs. Castle life's not for me." She went back into her room.

Armitage made to follow, stopping short as the door slammed in his face. His grin didn't vanish. "I don't like many humans, but this one's a keeper. Come on, cat. Let's get ready." He walked off, clothed in nothing but a towel and a *I-don't-care* attitude.

Sight of Day raised an eyebrow. *{It's a wonder any Vhemin survive. I best make sure he doesn't surprise someone.}*

Meriwether stopped the Feybrind with a touch on his arm. *{Thank you.}*

He got a half-smile in return. *{We will keep this one from harm. You've* *only got to worry about yourself.}* Sight of Day frowned. *{Oh dear. Are you sure you don't want to come as well?}*

"Try not to trip and die," Meriwether suggested. "It'd be a shame if you had a tragic hunting accident."

{You say such hurtful things.} The half-smile fell away. *{You are very precious to us, child of man. Please don't have a hunting accident of your own.}* The cat sauntered off, slender sword at his waist, bow across his shoulders.

A moment later, Vertiline appeared in the corridor. Her hair wasn't braided, rather lashed into a long tail. The Knight wore no steel, favoring supple leather for the day, but she'd magicked up a sword from somewhere, the thin blade hanging from her belt. Vertiline almost made the exit before slowing, steps uncertain, then looking at Meriwether. "The Storm no longer answers my call."

"Aye."

"It's been at my shoulder for so long. I've ... faltered." She put her hand on the old stone of the keep. "The Three turned their faces from me, but it wasn't when we fought Nicolette. They stopped watching over me a long, long time ago."

Meriwether wasn't sure what to say. *Make something up. It's what you're good at.* He made the short journey to Tilly's side. "So?"

She whirled. Her eyes were hard and cold as southern ice. "Don't—"

"Peace!" Meriwether took a step back, hands up. "I meant no offense, Knight. I mean that you've all you need right here. A Feybrind and a Vhemin to hunt with. And a fellow Knight has your back."

"I'm no Knight. Not anymore." Those hard, cold eyes thawed a little. "Was this your idea?"

"That depends. Are you going to hit me?"

She looked away. "No, sorcerer. Not you or your kind, ever again."

"Then it was all my idea." He smiled. "I'll happily accept the credit."

Vertiline nodded. "Sounds like the Meriwether I know." Her hand found his arm, holding him tight. "Keep her safe, you hear me? Israel and I were her guardians. He's," her voice cracked, "gone now, and I'm worthless. That leaves you."

Meriwether wanted to say, *By the Three, how am I supposed to keep her safe? She's a Knight, and I'm a fallen sinner!* But Tilly's eyes left no room for sidestepping. This close he could see the tiny details. The red-rims, evidence of a lost battle within. A slight pinch by the corners, as if she was in pain. "You're not worthless. No, listen! The Storm doesn't make us worthy. Geneve walked the world for years before it became her ally. Was she ever less than wonderful?"

A grudging nod. "No. But the matter remains. Swear you'll keep her safe."

"Don't worry, Knight." Meriwether covered her hand with his own. "I'm pretty sure the Three put me here to be a thorn in her side. She won't get into terror without me, I'm certain of it."

"Good enough." Vertiline freed her hand. "Perhaps spare a thought for yourself, while you're dodging danger. There are precious few made of such bright cloth." Then she was gone, leaving a faint scent of oiled leather and steel.

He tugged his borrowed clothes tighter. *Bright cloth? Steel would be best, but at least* someone *admires my fashion sense.*

MERIWETHER MADE HIS WAY TO THE STABLES. HE CARRIED THE knife Geneve gave him, and slung a cloak over his borrowed clothes. People of the keep paid him little mind. Meriwether hadn't summoned lightning from the skies, or wielded Divine Storm against the vile fallen Champion who assailed Ravenswall. He'd run panicked through the streets while everyone else did the hard work, and that made him better than invisible: it made him *irrelevant.*

Best place to be.

The stables were of a size fitting royalty. Meriwether saw tens of horses waiting on the queen's favor. He found Tristan's pen. The blue roan shifted in his stall, chewing something that seemed surprisingly tasty for vegetation. *I need to get more greens in my diet, obviously.* Meriwether let himself in, running a hand down the horse's flank. Tristan tossed his head, then nosed Meriwether's face. "Hey! It's okay. I know, you've been stuck in here for days. No one loves you, and the food's terrible."

The horse *wuffed* in response. Meriwether found his saddle, tossing it over Tristan's back. "Let's see if we can get you saddled before your boss arrives." He worked fast and smooth. The horse sucked in air as he went to tighten the girth, so Meriwether jabbed him. Tristan tried for a nip, but Meriwether was wise. He ducked low, then hauled the cinch tight.

"Like a true master."

Meriwether whirled at Geneve's voice. She leaned against the opposite bank of stalls. Her red hair was unbound, falling in curls about her face. She wore black amour, plain guardsman's steel, but the familiar hilt of Requiem peered from around her hip. Meriwether saw she also wore her Tresward sash, the single gold bar looking brilliant against the night of her attire. Tribunal's worn grip watched him from her shoulder. "I, uh." He blinked. "Uh."

She detached herself from the stalls. "He *always* tries to bite whoever's about to tighten the girth strap." Geneve reached for Tristan's nose. The horse bowed his head, clearly loving her touch. "He's a brat."

Meriwether smiled. *She has that effect on me.* "I didn't mean offense. Just trying to get him ready. I'll find another horse."

Geneve shook her head. "We'll ride together. You're barely competent on a steed."

Meriwether laughed. "I resemble that remark. Try not to terrify me too much this time." This close, he caught her scent. Metal and leather, and beneath that, something softer, warmer. "Are we ready?"

She raised her eyebrow. "*I'm* ready. I can't speak for you."

"Then we're good to go. To certain terror and doom!" He let himself from the stall.

Geneve took Tristan's halter, leading him from the stables. The sky held the colors of orange, burnished gold, and behind it, the sandstorm yellow of the plague lands. She paused outside the stables, eyes on the heavens. "I hope I haven't killed us all. This is too wonderful to replace."

Meriwether did a double-take. "You what?"

"Nothing." She gave him a small smile, the kind reserved for honesty between friends. "Just a dream I had. Let's go, high sorcerer."

THE RIDE TO THE ARTIST'S BOROUGH WAS TERRIFYING. HE RODE behind Geneve, arms about her armored waist. She leaned forward, urging Tristan to new feats of speed and daring-do. The horse's hooves sparked on the cobbles. His mane flew, fingers of wind stroking it to wild, long lengths.

He's having such a good time, yet I fear immediate death. A mad grin broke out on Meriwether's face. Geneve's flowing hair caught in his teeth, and he laughed. *Death can be fun! Keep telling yourself that.*

They rattled through the streets. People gave way, because that was the kind of thing that kept your soul in your body. Ahead, a cart had broken down, its load scattered across the street. "Geneve?" She glanced at him, something joyful in her face. Meriwether saw her teeth bared in challenge and delight. "Geneve, no!"

She paid him no mind, putting her heels to Tristan's flanks. The horse, confined to the stables for the better part of a week, leaned into his gallop. The fallen crates blocking the road approached faster than a dead man's fate. Meriwether wanted to scream, but all his energy was focused on holding Geneve.

Tristan reached the barrier, feet leaving the ground. They soared over, and Meriwether felt his stomach was left behind them. The horse crashed to the ground, but Tristan's footing was sure. He clattered on, the cursing of merchants and wagoneers falling away behind them. It was replaced with something far more heartwarming: Geneve's laughter. She cackled like a crazy woman, hands intertwined with the reigns.

She's earned it. A little joy, salted in the middle of all this misery.

Meriwether realized he was grinning like a Three-touched fool. The streets flashed by, the horse and his rider in perfect harmony. *The Tresward don't just teach them bladework. She's a rider the likes of which I've never seen.*

The short minutes to their destination felt like seconds, and in the impossible manner of time, also like hours. Meriwether wished it could continue, but their duty waited. Geneve reigned Tristan in, the horse puffing like a forge's bellows. They headed between two buildings and down an alley designed for carts. At the end, a ruin of soot and smoke marked where a building burned right to the waterline. There were no bodies.

Either the queen's guard collected them, or the Vide swept up their leavings.

Meriwether slipped from the horse, Geneve clattering beside him in her borrowed armor. The smile left her face as she looked at the scene of Vertiline's attempted murder. She strode to a wall, different to the others only in that it held a smear of blood. "Here's where Tilly stood."

"Stay there, then." Meriwether turned a slow circle. "What did she see that marked her for death?"

"I see nothing."

"Hmm. I wonder." He peered at the buildings surrounding them. "I've never seen riding as fine as that."

She looked at her feet, color coming to her face. "If you'd seen Israel—"

"Hah! Israel was the size of six other men. No chance he'd ride so well." Meriwether crouched, eyeballing things from a different altitude. "Tilly came here shopping?"

"So she said."

"What for?"

"I don't know." Geneve shrugged, then tugged at her collar. "This armor's nowhere near as well-fitting as good Tresward Smithsteel."

What's for sale here? Three buildings remained. One looked to be a cloth distribution warehouse. Another held the organic smell of produce. When Meriwether pried the back door of the third open, he saw hanging sides of beef and pork. It didn't feel like Tilly came here for bacon, cauliflower, or a length of canvas, so her destination must have been in the burned-out building. "In there."

Geneve put her hand on Requiem's hilt. The motion looked unconscious, like stuffing hands in pockets. "It's charcoal."

"But it's our kind of charcoal." Meriwether stood, then headed for the ruin. There wasn't much of a doorway, but he tried to honor the intent. He stepped inside, trying to make out what this place might have been. A crumbled collection of metal and brick looked like it could have been a massive hearth. And those big hunks of metal held a familiar shape. He headed toward them, rubbing soot away with his cloak. "This was a forge."

"An armory?" Geneve drifted in behind him, eyes roaming the wreckage. "Tilly wanted weapons?"

Meriwether wiped his fingers on his cloak, trying to get the soot off. *I barely touched anything and I look like a chimney sweep.* "Or armor. Perhaps she's not the only one who wants to leave the burnished sun behind her."

Geneve looked away. "She has nothing to hide from the Three."

"Some might say you don't either." Meriwether kicked a pile of charcoal, unearthing carbon dust. "She can't call the Storm."

"It's because she's imperfect." Geneve held her hands out like two scales. "The Storm needs perfection to work."

"Perfection is unattainable." Meriwether found a pile of wreckage that looked promising. "Help me with this."

"You want me to help you get dirty?" Geneve didn't move. "Perfection is how we call the Storm."

"I want you to help me get in here." Meriwether tried to put a little honest pleading in his tone. "There's the forge. Anvils by the wall. Squint right, and you might see racks of weapons and armor lined up over there." He directed her attention to blackened sticks. "So, you might wonder why there's a stone structure under a bunch of wood. Rewind the imagination a little, and this could've been a closet, with a hidden door."

"You see all that?" Geneve glanced around.

"I'd see more if we could move all this rubble." Meriwether kicked at the collection of coal-black wreckage. *One day, I'll be big and strong, just like dear old Dad. Until then... I'll use my wits.* "I'll be right back."

He left Geneve staring in surprise and headed across to the butchery. Inside, he ignored shouts of alarm as he helped himself to a mattock. Closing the door behind him, he hot-footed it back to the ruin. He even managed to make the inside when a couple of louts from the butchery caught up with him. The largest one—*why is it always the brutes who go for me?*—grabbed Meriwether's shoulder. "That's enough of that, lad. Hand it over."

"I'm on," Meriwether searched for a credible excuse, and risked the truth, "the queen's business."

"The queen wants a cheap mattock?" The brute looked like he tasted the truth for the vile flavor of almost lie it was. "Try again."

"Hold, sir." Geneve strode toward them. "He speaks the truth. Of a fashion, anyway."

The brute and his companion goggled. The companion, a smaller man who looked like he needed to eat a decent pie, said, "You're the Savior of Ravenswall."

"I'm just a soldier," Geneve said.

"Who saved Ravenswall," Meriwether agreed. "And we're here on the queen's business."

"The queen doesn't need your mattock." Geneve put her hands on her hips, armor clinking. "Meri needs it, to uncover an evil plot against the throne. We think."

"Think?" The brute chewed it over. "How sure are you?"

"About fifty-fifty sure. At the glass half-full, half-empty stage." Meriwether detached himself from the thug. "I need to get in there," he pointed with the mattock's business end, "because I think it's a trapdoor to the underworld."

"Sounds bad," the thug said. "Lemme see that." He took the mattock from Meriwether, then went to work with an enthusiasm Meriwether couldn't have matched. Broken, burnt timber was cleared in less time than it took to scream *larceny and lies*. He surveyed his handiwork. Sure enough, a metal-bound ruin masquerading as a trap-door was set into the floor. The brute set the mattock into the seam between trapdoor and floor, heaving.

A creak, a pop, and a crunch later, the trapdoor groaned free. The thug handed the mattock to his companion, grinning gap teeth at Geneve. "Just wait until the missus hears we met the Savior of Ravenswall."

"By your leave, miss." The thinner one doffed an imaginary cap. Then the pair left.

Meriwether goggled at their backs. "Usually I avoid the truth. It never helps ... and yet here we are."

Geneve peered into the gloom uncovered by the trapdoor's removal. "You were right, there's a passage to the underworld here."

Meriwether drew his cloak closer. The air didn't feel as warm as it could, and he imagined the darkness below wouldn't greet them with cheer. "Do you feel it?"

She glanced at him. "Feel what?"

"The Storm." Meriwether pursed his lips. "When I work illusion, it doesn't feel like much at all. A tingle, perhaps. Sometimes my nose itches. But I *know* it's done, nonetheless. If others work more powerful magic nearby, I can feel that too. Like hearing someone shouting in the next room." He let his cloak drop. "I imagine the Storm must feel ... magnificent. I've seen butterflies take flight, and heard sparrows sing. The powers of creation answer when you call. We saw," he struggled for the right words, "lightning smash the world, cast down by the Three as Israel fought ancient guardians. So ... what does it feel like?"

"Like nothing at all. Like everything at once." She shook her head, eyes down. "Well, that's not quite right. You know when you do something so well, so perfectly, your body feels *right?* Everything in a line. Like you could push through rock with a finger, or balance the world on the palm of your hand."

"I've no idea what that feels like." Meriwether joined her at the tunnel's lip. "I'm just a sinner, and a long way from home."

"Here." She drew Requiem, handing the sword to him. "Balance that."

"You must be joking." He took the blade, turning it about. Even to his inexperienced hand, it felt a marvel. "This is the work of a true master."

"It's the work of a true friend. His name is Kytto, and he loves Tilly so much it hurts to see." She shook her head. "Balance it."

Meriwether put Requiem's tip against the ground. He tried to feel where the metal would fall, then let go, stepping back. The sword held for a moment, then began the inevitable topple to the sooty ground.

Geneve snatched it up without breaking her gaze from him. "The Tresward teach us everything about weapons. What they look like, and what they feel like. I know where this blade is without looking. I saw as you balanced it—"

"Tried to."

"I saw where it would fall. Now, see. This is the perfection we strive for." She put the tip of Requiem against the ground, finger on the pommel. Geneve closed her eyes, a smile touching her lips, then stepped back.

The sword stood straight and true, standing tall like a reed. She opened her eyes. "That is perfection."

Meriwether didn't want to move. "How did you do that?"

"Practice." She eyed the blade. "It's not quite right. It will fall soon."

"How do you know?"

"Because I'm not a god, Meri. Any of the Three could place that blade there, and untouched, it would remain there for eternity." Requiem wavered, then began the certain journey to the ground. Geneve grabbed the hilt, sheathing it. "All things we do will fail, given time."

"Tilly could balance a sword like you, no?" Meriwether crouched, running his finger through the spot where the sword's tip rested. He could detect no trickery. "So why has the Storm left her?"

"A sword is only as good as the body behind it. When my memories were ... stolen, I was unbalanced. Imperfect. Her body is like a door-frame out of true. It works, but still the door squeaks in the rain." Geneve ran armored fingers through red hair. "In time, she might learn to balance. Become perfect again."

"That makes no sense." Meriwether stood, crossing his arms.

"She must be straight—"

"Not that." Meriwether gritted his teeth. "I'm sorry. I didn't mean to interrupt. I ... misspoke because I don't understand. I meant, this ... Storm? It shakes the world. When I saw you fight Nicolette, I swore the Three were there, with you." He tasted the truth on his tongue. "I was afraid, because I've done precious few things right, and so many wrong. I thought they might see me. The heart of me."

"Oh, Meri." She took his hands. He felt the steel around her fingers, but the gentleness within. "The Storm is their gift to us. Their blessing, so we remember their footsteps upon the world." She let him go. "If they didn't see the light in you, they wouldn't be the gods they are."

"You believe so much?"

"Time is wasting." She investigated the pit. "I *remember* believing. I live with doubts as my armor. My shield of faith cracked when Israel fell."

"Seems shitty armor."

Geneve laughed. "Israel would admit his failings. It's one of the things I loved about him." She stepped onto dark stairs. "We could really use a fairy about now."

The thud of footsteps announced someone's approach. Geneve turned, blade in hand, but it was only the reedier of the two from the butchery. He held a lantern. "I saw you had none, and thought this might be of use."

Meriwether took it from him. "Friend, what's your name?"

"Cable, m'lord."

"I'm no lord." Meriwether opened the lantern's hood.

"You walk like a lord. Talk like one. Stand like the ground's your own." Cable smiled. "No disrespect, but if you ain't a lord, they best watch out." He doffed his imaginary cap, leaving them alone.

"How curious," Meriwether managed.

"Come, Lord du Reeves." Geneve smirked. "Certain death awaits, your lordship."

Chapter Six

L ight lapped around Geneve's feet. Meriwether walked behind her, and it warmed her heart to have someone at her back again she could trust. She'd never felt so *right* since part-nering with Iz and Tilly.

I need to speak with Vertiline about the lies we share.

Yes, she did—but later. Now, there were those with blades hungering for their hearts. Meri unearthed their lair, right in the middle of the Artisan's Borough. All knew Queen Morgan favored artists and creatives, and her enemy took advantage of that, building their nest right in the heart of the good she tried to do.

The stairs led down. Geneve felt they'd made it at least ten meters down before the floor leveled out. There was no evidence of soot and ash here. The fire hadn't made it through the trapdoor. *Either a stroke of amazing luck, or they warded their entrance. More evidence of sinners.*

She bit her lip. *They aren't sinners. Meri's not a sinner. I've done more wrong than he.*

The corridor led forward a short distance. A handful of doors held secrets and mysteries aplenty. Geneve tried one, finding a bare room. Another held a treasure of dust and not much else. "There's nothing here."

Meri coughed. "There. A spider."

She laughed. "The fearsome Vide. Spiders."

"Don't mock. Spiders are plenty bad. The Llyrrad Spinners of the Naraku forest contain a toxin so deadly, it was harvested by tribes of the region for warfare." He held the lantern up, emphasizing the emptiness of the room. "Sadly, we don't know who won the war, because they're all dead."

"You made that up."

"I made *parts* of it up." He tried another door. "Behold, a stray square of vellum." He retrieved it from the floor. "False alarm. It's blank."

"Which parts did you make up?" Geneve's shoulders tensed. She wanted Meri to keep talking, because his words carried her on a long lake of calm.

"Most of it. There is a Llyrrad Spinner, though. It's about the size of a parakeet." He frowned. "At least, that's what the book said. The poison causes paralysis and agony. I'm pretty sure the size part is accidental. Otherwise those spiders are showing off."

She led them down the corridor. It opened into a larger room, marked by passages at the major compass points. The room held nothing. Geneve growled her frustration. "The Vide are clearly excellent at cleaning house. They should hire out for that as well as assassination."

"Perhaps they do. Cashflow is king." Meriwether walked to the middle of the room and crouched. He touched the ground.

"Find something?"

"Yes. Or the absence of something. Here." He pointed. "And there. Marks cleaner than the rest. I think a table sat here. Heavy, perhaps six meters a side."

"That's not a table." Geneve walked the imaginary border of the 'table.' "That's a fighting ring. They trained here. Sparred in the middle while people watched. All under the streets. Safe and quiet. No noise would travel above."

"Devious and clever. Just the wrong kind of enemy to have." He pointed to the eastern passage. "This way?"

"May as well." She took the lead again. Four steps down the passage Geneve heard a *click*. A tiny slice of motion alerted her. Requiem flashed, the blade finding her hand as if by magic. She sliced an arc before Meri, cutting a dart in two.

The pieces clattered to the floor. Meri's eyes were wide. "What just happened?"

"A trap. Stay behind me."

"Wait a second." Meri wiggled an eyebrow. "I'm good for something. Just watch." He headed off.

"Meri!" Worry gnawed at her. How could she protect him if he triggered another trap? *But you can't lock him away in the keep. There are dangers everywhere.*

"It's okay, Red." He crouched, fingers sweeping a flagstone. "This one's different."

She approached, footsteps careful on the pavers. "I see nothing."

"Hah! A flaw in the mighty Tresward's otherwise excellent schooling." He closed his eyes for a moment. A softer *click* sounded from beneath the paver. "There we go."

"What did you do?"

"I can tickle locks. Talk the right way to them, and they'll go out to dinner with you. A few whispered words, and afterward they open up like—"

"Aye, aye, I'm sure they become less than modest company. What about the traps?" She crossed her arms.

"Oh. Right. Well, a mechanism is a mechanism. These are the same. I asked *her*," he stroked the paving, "for her hand in marriage. She said yes!"

"You're impossible."

"I'm magnificent. I understand how the two are easily confused." He pushed forward a few more meters. "What do we have here?"

"I'm getting tired of seeing nothing and having to be inspirationally shown," Geneve warned. "Out with it."

"The last two traps were weighted affairs. Place your foot wrong, and—"

"I understand the core principles," Geneve growled.

"You should get more sleep," Meri winked. "It adds to calm. Anyway, this one is magically bound."

"How do you know?"

"Because there's no physical arming mechanism." He pointed to the ceiling. "All of that comes down if it's triggered."

"How do we avoid it?"

"We don't trip it. I thought that'd be obvious." He gave her an eye-roll fit for the ages. "The good news is, this trap isn't paying any attention to you at all. She's got eyes for me alone." Meri held up his hands in a *please-don't-kill-me* gesture. "By that I mean, she looks for magicians. This ward's designed to murder sorcerers. I'd imagine the Vide don't want the queen's Coterie coming down here."

"But I'll be fine?"

"Probably."

Geneve whirled on him. "How certain are you?"

"Almost all the way." He stood, holding the lantern toward her. "Take this. If you trigger the trap, we both die. I guess you could say I'm interested in the outcome."

"No. We take you out, then I come back."

The smile fell from his face. "Geneve, there are a thousand reasons why that's not a good idea. First is, of course, what happens if the Vide return and I'm up there? But most important is this: what happens if you encounter more magic?"

"The Tresward—"

"The Tresward teach you to work as a team, no?" He offered her the lantern again. "Go. I'm not afraid of the dark. There are worse things."

Geneve felt the truth of his words. The Vide would make short work of Meri if they caught him in the open. Down here, she had a chance at protecting him.

And he, me. 'There are worse things.' Perhaps he feels my fall as much as I, his.

She took the lantern. "I won't be long." Geneve glanced ahead. "I promise."

"I believe you. I don't think there are more traps." He sighed. "I'm almost all the way sure this time."

Geneve tried for a smile, but it felt brittle, so she headed forward. The corridor ended at a stout door. It was unlocked, opening on well-oiled hinges for her. Instead of the emptiness she expected, she found a small room with a single table. The table held an envelope.

It could be poisoned. She bent, examining the letter. The paper was of fine quality, and bore a single name on the front.

Meriwether.

She straightened like someone knifed her in the spine. *There's a letter for Meri* here? *How can this be?*

Geneve touched the letter with gauntleted fingers. It didn't burst into flame. The floor didn't drop her into a pit of spikes. She grabbed it, stalking from the room. The lantern's light groped ahead, looking for her friend.

She found him sitting by the wall. He nodded, a ready smile fading from his face as she approached. "What's wrong?"

"This." She offered him the letter.

He took it, eyes going flat and hard. "Oh."

"Who knows your name in the Vide?" She crouched before him. "Meri, what's going on?"

He turned the letter in his hands, lips pressed into a line. "I don't know, but I know who penned this." His finger ran across his name. "This is Leander du Reeves' handwriting. I'd stake my life on it."

"Your ... *father* wrote this?"

"Aye." He held the letter with trembling hands. "I don't think there's anything he's got to say that I want to hear." He offered it to her. "It's yours, if you want it. But be careful. The man is made of pure spite."

She took the letter, opening it by sliding her thumb under the seal. Wax cracked to the stone floor.

> *Meriwether—*
> *The Vide are gone. If you want answers, come home. You know where to*
> *find me.*
> *—L*

Geneve turned the letter over. There was nothing else. "This is ... bizarre."

He nodded, not looking at the letter. "Let me guess. It's cryptic. It says to go find him."

"How did you know?"

"If I wanted to attack the queen and remove all credible aid, that's the way I'd do it." He rubbed his eyes. She'd never seen him look so tired. *What happened between Meri and his father?*

Let it be. He'll tell me if he wants to. Or when he needs to.

"What if he wants to make amends?"

Meri scoffed. "Leander's not the type who makes mistakes to make amends for." Beneath the anger, buried under a mountain of hate, she heard a young boy's longing in his words. "He *never* makes mistakes."

Geneve stood, crumpling the letter in her hand. She opened the lantern, feeding the parchment to the flames before dropping the burning remains to the floor. Snapping the lantern closed, she held out her hand. "Come."

"Where are we going?" He took her hand, and she helped him up.

"The queen offered us a job. I don't know if I can work for her. I'm not sure of much." Her eyes found her feet. Borrowed boots, because she couldn't bear to wear good Tresward Smithsteel. It encased her in lies. She felt Meri's fingers on her chin. Raising her eyes to his. Always at her side, lending her his shoulder when hers was weak. Geneve wanted to touch his face, to smooth the frown wrinkle on Meri's brow. She wanted to unmake the pain he felt by reaching into his past, but not even the Three could do that. "We're going to teach your father about all the errors he's made."

Chapter Seven

The trek back to the queen's keep proved much slower. Meriwether and Geneve walked either side of Tristan, the Knight leading the horse. Meriwether kept his thoughts close, but they were moving much faster than his feet. A thousand ideas worked through his head, principle among which was:

If she knows about my dirty, filthy family she'll never look at me again.

Aside from that minor concern, because Meriwether had no plans to tell Geneve about Leander, his mind juggled other ideas like a street trickster. Was he right to send Sight of Day, Armitage, and Vertiline away? Was the queen safe? She could be a powerful patron, but there was a greater power out there toppling Champions and Justiciars of the *Tresward*, for fuck's sake, and putting paper soldiers in their place.

Would the queen be next? Would his friends be taken? How could he protect Geneve from a magic he didn't understand himself? This was a battle neither of them had faced before. She met things with blade and teeth bared. He ran away. It seemed like neither approach would work here.

Tristan nudged Meriwether. The horse wasn't his usual shake-rattle-and-roll self. His big brown eyes were soft, as if he smelled something wrong in the air. Meriwether patted his nose, then hugged the beast on a whim. "Sorry. We're not as much fun on the return trip, are we?"

Geneve glanced at him around the blue roan. "We've saved Ravenswall. Some might say we've earned a piece of time to look after things closer to our hearts."

Meriwether nodded, but more out of habit than agreement. "Some might. Others will look at it as a weakness, and try inserting a knife between our ribs."

"A frontal attack would be a courtesy we've not seen from the Vide." Geneve brushed red hair from her face. "Meri! Look at me." He slowed, eying her around the horse. Tristan took a step back, clearly not wanting to be between this, whatever *this* was. "You helped Sight of Day. Armitage and his people, as best you could—"

"But we couldn't save them, could we?"

"And then you walked by *my* side. All while you thought Israel and Vertiline would haul you to Judgment. You've done nothing for yourself—"

"Except survive! I've done plenty of that. It's what I'm good at." He tasted bitterness enough for three in his words.

She sighed in exasperation. "We must see Leander. If he's behind the Vide—"

"It's a big if." Meriwether encouraged his feet back to walking, Geneve following suit. He surveyed the street, avoiding her gaze, but felt her eyes on him nonetheless. Her regard felt like the heat of a forge, the burning of coals, as if she could see all the petty things that made his family terrible. "I learned from the best. He's a liar and a thief, but on an epic scale. If he's asking us to go somewhere, we should look at the spot farthest from that for the real truth."

"There are many kinds of truth." Geneve's voice carried over the street noise, for all the softness of it. "There are the lies we tell ourselves, hoping to make them real. Those can be the worst of all."

"Aye. Aye, Red, you're right." Meriwether bit his lip. "I don't want to make a mistake. There are kingdoms at stake."

"You call yourself a liar and a thief, yet always you look to others. Your gaze rides high, sorcerer. Never in the muck. One day, you'll see yourself with my eyes, and be amazed at what you find." Geneve pointed ahead, her arm directing him to a stall selling spitted meat. "Hungry?"

She drops the truths of the Three in one moment, then thinks with her stomach in the next. By Cophine, Ikmae, and Khiton, she's a marvel only they could make. "I could eat. I don't know how to save a kingdom, but I figure I could work out how to chew."

They shared a grin. There'd be time enough for saving the world after second breakfast.

THE KEEP HUMMED LIKE A HIVE. SINCE THE BREACH OF THE CITY'S wall, the queen worked tirelessly with advisors, artisans, and merchants. Morgan needed supplies brought in by sea: food for her people, alongside stone and wood for rebuilding. The queen had precious little time for worrying about the Savior of Ravenswall and her small troupe, and that suited Meriwether just fine.

He and Geneve went their separate ways. She said she needed to *blow off some steam*, and he winced internally at what would happen to her sparring partners. Meriwether was tempted to trail along and watch, because Geneve in motion was poetry on the eye.

But, no. I've my own jobs to attend.

He found the queen's library suspiciously quiet and unoccupied. Her Coterie were off doing amazing magics, and there wasn't much call for a man skilled with tricks of the eye, no matter how many locks he could tickle. Meriwether felt an itch behind his eyes, a sure sign magic was being worked. It was continuous, and he wondered what the queen had her sorcerers and witches working on that required so much effort.

Whatever it is, I've got the day off! Use it well.

The library held many secrets. He'd never read it all in his lifetime, but musty tomes weren't his ideal way to while away the day anyway. He wanted answers. *Somewhere in here* must *be the secrets of the ancients. Hints at what they made, and why.* Meriwether wanted to know about the temple they found in the plague lands. He hoped to find more about dragons. The temple held so many mysteries. How did the artifacts of the ancients bedevil the Feybrind? Why did they turn Vhemin into monstrous oatmeal? Where did the dragon come from? How had the temple stolen time from him and Geneve, giving nothing in return?

He went through progressively older books, finding nothing but dust and sneezes. Light from the big arched windows fell across the pages for a time. It wasn't until he was squinting, eyes red with exhaustion, that he realized he was working in gloom. No one came to light candles, or stoke a fire in the library's hearths.

Odd. Still, the keep has bigger issues than a lone sinner toiling in a worthless pursuit.

Meriwether stretched, his back popping. He'd been working at a table, and eyed the tomes he'd strewn across it. *Arphanel's Mysteries* was a lie; the man made up huge tracts of fiction, welding them together with an amalgam of truth. Seriously: he swore the ancients could use the sun to power the world, a fantasy of the highest order. *Lady Ellen's Facets of the Fallen* was somewhat more interesting but focused on tales of the heart. The ancients, it seemed, loved and lost like any other. Meriwether suspected Lady Ellen wrote her tales as a vehicle for self-exploration. The devices she described were ... unique.

He was about to call it a day when his eye snared on the corner of a book buried beneath a pile of scrolls. Meriwether dragged it into the fading light. Black cover, tattered with time or use. Binding gnawed by mice. He blew dust from the cover, revealing gold filigree. *IMMENSAE.*

No author. No subtitle. Meriwether waved the dust cloud he'd disturbed aside, but it paid no mind, settling on his person. He coughed, then opened the book at a random page. The volume was filled with intricate, excellent penmanship, of which he could understand not a word. It looked to be the same language as *Et Magia High*. A lost tongue, but by the Three's mercy, this one had pictures.

The pages he'd settled on seemed to be a feature spread. The left page held an illustration, the right a description that defied decipherment. Ignoring the text, he let his eyes wander the picture. It was a person. Armored, certainly, and drawn in an imposing style. The figure's chest was out like a barrel, hands on hips. A sword was belted at hip, but that wasn't the fascinating thing. The figure took up a tiny fraction of the page. Behind them, the mighty form of a dragon.

Meriwether thought back to when he and Geneve found the dragon skeletons. *They rode dragons, Meri!* She'd been so excited by it, and here was something that may support that. While not proof, this book showed a picture of a dragon rider, armed and armored, ready to wage great battles.

The image was faded by time, and the light didn't help. Meriwether bustled to an armoire, rescuing a lantern. Quick work with flint and steel set a delicate flame to bloom within. He shut the lantern, because only an imbecile worked with an open flame around books, then returned to his table.

Under the brighter light of the lantern, further details came to him. The first made him bend almost close enough to touch his nose to the page. Sure enough, the illustration showed the armored figure's breast-plate sigil. Time moved the details somewhat, but he'd stake his life on that being the blazing sun of the Three. "Were these Knights? The dragonriders were Tresward? Or the Tresward came from drag-onriders?"

He studied for more details. His eye snared on the figure's breast-plate. It didn't look much like Tresward armor, so there wasn't a lot of hope there. But the figure wore something else that made him swear. Meriwether slammed the book shut. He grabbed the lantern, blew it out, then sprinted for the door.

There was something he needed to see, and he needed to see it *now*.

MERIWETHER MADE THEIR SHARED CHAMBERS AFTER TAKING THE stairs three at a time. He skidded to a halt outside Geneve's room. *Get yourself together, man.* He scrubbed a hand through his hair, took a couple calming breaths, then rapped his knuckles on her door.

Footsteps. Hand on metal. The rattle of a lock, then the door opened. Geneve was dressed in a white cotton shirt, hair a wet disarray. Her eyes brightened when she saw him. "Meri!" She gave him a once-over, taking in his state. "Is everything okay?"

"No. Yes. I mean, sure, I think so!" He agitated from foot to foot. "Can I come in?"

"Sure." She stepped out of the way, and he breezed past.

Her chambers were spartan. A bed, more of a cot than anything royalty would dare put their heads on. Armor, hung on a rack, but not the kind he needed. Requiem leaning by the bed, Tribunal's holster draped over it. A collection of white cylinders sat on a small table, a few others studded about the scattergun's belt. *Cartridges for the boom stick. She's running low on those.* He did a circle. "Where is it?"

"Where's what, Meri?" She crossed her arms. "What's going on?"

"Dragonriders," he said. "Ancients. Magics and mysteries!"

"More specifically."

"Ah." *Get your head together.* "I read a book in the library."

"Just the one? You should start a club. Get a few more people, and together, you might make a second tome." Her lips hinted a smile.

"Oof. I walked into that one."

"Like a low-hanging beam." She gestured to the cot. "Sit."

"I'd rather stand."

"I'd rather know what's going on."

"Point taken." Meriwether sat on the edge of the cot, clasping his hands to settle them. They felt like wild animals, like as not to tremble in fright. "The book's called the *Immensae*. No, I don't know what that means. Big? Probably something like that. Doesn't matter." He screwed his eyes shut, remembering. "There's a picture in it. A person, beside a dragon."

"A dragonrider?" Her voice held interest.

Meriwether opened his eyes, saw the light in her eyes. "Yes. The book's old. Couple hundred years at least. Maybe more. Same language as the High Magic. This next bit's important." He took a calming breath. "Where's your helmet?"

Her eyes shifted sideways, remembering. "I put it in the Tresward armory."

"Not that one. That's shitty steel, no offense."

"It's Smithsteel!"

"Less shitty steel, then. The helmet from the temple. Tell me you kept it." His hands clutched so tight he thought they might break.

She nodded, but her lips pressed into a line. "I still have it."

"Can I see it?"

"It's from a horrible place. We shouldn't—"

"*Please*, Red." He shifted on the cot. "If you want me to beg, I'm happy to." He dropped to the floor, taking a knee. "Knight Adept Geneve, by the Three, may I see your rusty desert souvenir?"

She laughed. "Get up, idiot." Geneve dropped as he rose, hunching beside the cot. She whisked out a small box. Opening it, Meriwether glimpsed the fragments of a life. A necklace with a broken pendant. Her Tresward sash. *No, that's not hers. It's too gray. That's Israel's—mark the gold bars. Five, to her one.* Beside those humble remnants, the ancient helmet.

Geneve offered it to him. Meriwether took it. It was light, as if it were made of dreams, not metal. A visor of glass covered the faceplate. He turned it over, just to make sure. The picture was crude, but as dissimilar as her Tresward armor was, this was the *same*. "This is the helmet the dragonriders wore."

She took it from him, putting it on. "It's light. I can see through clearer than the day." Geneve took it off, red hair spilling out. "So, what does this mean?"

"It means where there's a helmet, there's a suit of armor to go with it." He stood, moving to the window. "There's a dragon out there looking for its rider."

Geneve joined him. They stood, shoulder to shoulder. He smelled rosewater, and felt the heat of her through thin cotton. "It's alone. It's the only one like it in all of the world."

"Aye." He cocked his eyebrow. "Just like its rider."

She blinked. "I'm not a dragonrider!"

"Spoken like a true dragonrider." He sobered. "We need to leave."

"To find the dragon?"

"To do lots of things." He pointed out the window. "We misplaced a dragon. That's a ruinous thing to leave roaming the land. Worse than standing on a rake in the dark, I'd expect. But I fear betrayal."

"Here?"

"Yes." He left the window, charting the short journey to the door. "They'll come tonight. Be ready for it."

"How do you know?" Geneve stayed by the window, a breeze lifting her hair. Her voice wasn't hard with doubt. Curious, like she needed to understand how he knew when the knife would strike their backs.

"Because it's my father. It's how he came for me, last time." He gave her a sad smile. "Don't sleep too deeply. Not tonight." He shut the door behind him. Meriwether told himself it was to stop questions he didn't want to answer. But really, it was because he couldn't bear the compassion in her eyes. He didn't deserve it.

Chapter Eight

G eneve made sure her things were squared away. She didn't
have strong feelings about the queen's keep. It wasn't
Tresward, which meant she had precious few memories of
being at home in such places. Her earliest memories with her mother
were in a lordling's keep. Nothing this fine, but similar. Built by men,
for a greater man. But not for the gods.

But do I still serve them? Will they accept me?

So, she readied herself. First stop was the castle kitchens. The
Savior of Ravenswall was welcomed by all, in a *please-let-us-get-on-with-
our-jobs* kind of way. She dodged cooks while stealing provisions.
Cheese, hard bread, and smoked sausage jockeyed for position in a bag.
Her mind listed the preparations of the Tresward. *Food for two, for at
least three days. Water, and a little wine. Don't forget the tea. No angel's kiss this
time*. She stilled a smile, remembering, then made the jaunt to the
quartermaster.

He was a dour man who looked like a smile would cost more than a
life's worth. She asked to borrow a few things. His face remained
closed, hard as marble, before splitting into a gap-toothed smile.
Anything for the Savior of Ravenswall. Geneve didn't feel comfortable

with the fame, but it made acquiring flint, pans, and lanterns a lot easier.

Next stop, the stables. She made sure Tristan's saddle was ready in his stall. She filled saddlebags with provisions and equipment, stowing those in a pile of hay at the back. The blue roan watched all this with the uncaring eye of a beast content with his oats and barley. Soft munching kept her company while she worked.

I've done it all. There's nothing left but to wait. Geneve wondered whether Meri had set this up as a prank, but discarded the thought. He claimed to be many things. A liar, and a thief. A cheat, and a meister. A cunning man, a burglar, and a sorcerer on the run.

Geneve wasn't sure about all those things, but one fact she was certain of: he never wasted her time.

She returned to her room. It waited, barren, cold. Lifeless. She eyed the wall. *If they come, we should be together.* Geneve gathered her things, making a pile outside Meri's door. She knocked.

He hauled it open. His eyes were wild, almost feverish. "Hi?" Meri scanned the floor where her belongings were. Armor, sword, scatter-gun, and ancient helmet. The only possessions that mattered. "What's that?"

"If they attack tonight, we should be together."

He nodded, stepping aside. "You can have the bed."

"I'll not take your bed—"

"Take the damn bed. I won't need it." He bustled toward the desk, slinging himself into his chair. She saw *the High Magic* was open. "I've almost cracked it. The first word here? It's 'the,' I'm sure of it."

Geneve laughed. If he worked, she wouldn't sleep either. "I'll get some tea on."

❦

GENEVE LEANED AGAINST MERI'S HEARTH, HOLDING HER NOW COOL cup of was-tea. It was now tea dregs, a far less interesting thing to sip. Meri worked without break, head down in his book. She'd never been much for academia. The Tresward taught them enough to know the shape of the world. Letters and numbers, sure, and who ruled where. How to find Tresward-friendly inns, or how the best weapons could be sourced in remote regions. Functional knowledge for doing the Three's work.

But nothing like learning for the sake of it. She wondered what it would be like to have his kind of burning curiosity. Scattered pieces of parchment marked his attempts to decipher a language lost to humans. The ancients had dragonriders, and the dragons to go with them. Their Artifices still straddled the land, forever frozen and immobile, the magic powering their hearts gone forever. But the metal machines didn't age. No rust touched them.

Geneve wondered about the name of the dragonriders. *Immensae.* Meri thought it meant *big*, but it didn't feel right to her. It felt more like *immeasurable*.

She felt the hair on the nape of her neck rise. Meri felt it too, jerking upright. He winced. "I should move more often."

"What was that?"

"Magic." He stood, rotating his shoulders. His borrowed clothes made him seem so out of place. She wore fine cotton, but he made do with castoffs. "And I'd bet a lot of power, if you noticed."

"I didn't feel the magic." She mentally reached for what set her off. "Hear that?"

"I hear nothing."

"My point." She tossed her dregs into the fire, set the cup down, and flowed to her feet. "The castle noise is gone."

Meri cocked his head. "There are no night birds or insects, either."

"Help me with my armor." He didn't need much guidance, having worked with her armor before. She set Requiem's sheath behind her for a rear-draw style, then settled Tribunal against her back. "What could make the noise go away?"

"My kind of trickery." He held his hands up in mock surrender. "Don't fret. I can't do it. But illusion is the seeming of things, just as it's the un-seeming of others. You say they wore my face before? Well, someone who could do that could make a dog's bark disappear, or fashion a chorus of angels from a drunkard's lament."

"Can they do anything else?"

"I don't know. We don't have a secret club. I've heard whispers. Rumors. Rumblings among the street folk. There was once—"

His door shattered inward in a shower of kindling and fire. Geneve moved before conscious thought entered her head, sweeping Meri into an embrace, sheltering his body with her own. Wood rattled against her armor, and something heavy hit the back of her head. She shook it off, spinning to the door.

Requiem hungered into her hand. The skymetal glinted its anger.

The first through the portal wore Meri's face, just as the one in the burned-out courtyard had. Lightning danced between his hands. She held Requiem in both hands cross guard. Her stance was perfect, and a single blue butterfly came into being on the point of the blade.

Lightning leaped for her, and she caught it on the steel. She felt her skin come alive, her teeth bright, every nerve in her body tingling. Geneve stumbled, smoke coming from her armor. *My guard was perfect!* She wheezed, her body feeling *hot* and *heavy*. The sorcerer with Meri's face and lightning hands leered, stepping forward.

He dropped as Meri shattered his chair across the man's head. The young illusionist grabbed her hand, wincing, but hauled her upright. She smelled burned hair. *Is that me? Or him?* There wasn't time to check. Meri led her into the corridor outside their rooms, then through the door into the castle guest thoroughfare.

Five waited for them. All wore his face. *They dare!*

She pushed Meri to one side, ducking to the other. Fire billowed from the hands of a fake Meri. The orange-red caught in his eyes, making him look a demon. Geneve kept her momentum up, drawing Tribunal. The scattergun roared, and two enemy sorcerers dropped in boneless heaps. She threw the scattergun with the Three's perfection. It sparked as it passed through the air, hitting a third in the chest. His body caved in, the remains slopping against the wall.

Geneve spun Requiem through the air, hitting another man center-mass. The blade tore him from his feet, nailing him to a door. One remained. The sorcerer raised his arms, a mad grin on his face. She imagined him thinking, *You're out of weapons, Tresward.* The stone above groaned as he worked his will against it.

Behind him came a roar. Geneve heard it once before, in her

dreams. The anger of a creature so mighty, the world shook at its weight. The sorcerer's concentration broke, and Geneve took three perfect steps to him. Her arms shivered with Light as she struck three times, breaking his clavicle, ribs, and burying the last punch in his gut. He fell, gurgling.

Geneve whirled to Meri. "Dragon!"

"It's fine! That was me. I wasn't sure I could do it." He gave her a weak grin, his face paler than Tilly's. "First time for everything."

"How do you know about my dreams?"

"Dreams? No clue. I heard that," he pointed at the corridor's end, "while you slept through our daring escape from the temple. Wait. You dream of the dragon?"

"Later." She fielded Tribunal's red, glistening form from the floor, then hauled Requiem from the door. Geneve slicked blood to the floor. "To the stables."

"A moment." He went back to their rooms, returning with loaded arms. He tossed her the dragonrider's helmet, but kept a book and his precious sack. "We'll need these later, I'll wager."

She thought of asking—again—what was in the sack, but it was a question that would keep for another time. The run through the castle was fast. No one was about. The kitchen fires burned, but unattended. They passed guards aplenty asleep at their posts. A few doors were broken in, bloody ruin showing murdered occupants. Meri looked in one such room at a family butchered in their sleep. "They're cleaning house."

"What do you mean?"

"It's the signature of those taking all the power for themselves. Take the throne, then all viable opposition. I've seen it before." He turned away from the misery. "Let's be away, and keep our wits sharp. There's no telling who's in on this."

A scream carried on the night air. Shouts, and the clash of steel, before the sounds vanished, as if muffled by a pillow. Geneve loped ahead, steel ever ready. No one guarded the gates. She led them through the gardens toward the stables. Legs sprawled in a pool of blood marked a fallen guardsman. Someone unlucky enough to be on duty at the wrong time, or an agitator against the throne? In death, it was impossible to know.

Meri's sack *clinked*, and he clutched it close. "Sorry."

"Don't worry. I've not been fond of the stealthy approach." She crouched behind a hedgerow, peering toward the stables. "This isn't good."

He joined her, face by hers. "Ah." By the stables stood a group of Queensguard. She counted fifteen. Black armor, stern eyes, no humor about them. But also, no bodies. No fallen stablehands lay on the ground. There was no dark slick of blood to be seen.

"Let me speak with them." Geneve slid Requiem into its sheath.

"Are you mad?" He made a show of looking her over. "Did that hit in the head addle your wits?"

"I won't leave Tristan here." Geneve jabbed her finger toward the stables. "He's—"

"Aye, aye. A true companion, that one." Meri's voice held no mockery. "I'm fond of how he doesn't try to bite me too often."

"Let's get him out, then." She strode from the hedge's shelter, holding her hand up in greeting. "Ho!"

The guard turned to her in a single, smooth motion. Steel glinted in torchlight. Geneve smelled the familiar scent of horses and hay, mixed with the hardness of oil and leather. A man wearing captain's stripes strode forward, blade out but pointed to the dirt. "Ho, Tresward."

"I need my horse." She held her palm out toward the stables. "He's in there."

"Aye." The captain nodded. "I need your head. Orders, you see." He glared at the night sky, as if counting stars was the most important thing he could be doing. "Doesn't feel right."

"You question your command?" Geneve eyed the guards. They shifted, fanning out to surround her and Meri.

"Never questioned the queen's orders. It's why I wear the stripes, and only a few times felt the lash." He slid his blade into its scabbard, offering her his hand. "They call me Heser the Cheg."

Geneve slid Requiem home. If there was treachery, the blade would be in her hand faster than the eye could follow. She clasped Heser the Cheg's hand. "Geneve."

The captain gave a grim smile. "Not 'Geneve, Savior of Ravenswall?'"

"That title carries to much weight," Geneve admitted. "If you must use something, Knight Adept works. I've earned it."

Meri agitated behind her. "Red? This—"

"It all feels wrong, does it not?" Heser the Cheg ignored Meri as if he wasn't there. *A man of action, used to the blade and its silvered promise.* "As if the world's tipped. We've all gone cock-eyed and can't see the truth of things." He spat. "The orders tonight were to place the head of the Savior of Ravenswall above the portcullis. A warning, if you like. There were two things wrong with the order."

"The first?" Geneve edged in front of Meri, keeping her armored body between him and the captain as best she could.

"Never in all my time serving the Raven Queen have we done such things. Her father was also a man of honor. Dealt with villains, but fairly. If they needed killing, the murder would be done, but the bodies set to rest. Not used as a parody for the eyes of folk to see." Heser the Cheg took his gauntlets off, tossing them to the ground. "The second problem is the order wasn't given by her majesty. A different set of lips gave them."

"Vikander," Meri hissed.

"You know the snake?" The captain nodded. "I've not been well for days. Some say the water's turned, but I fear it's something else. We've not felt the touch of magecraft before, but I think this is what it must be like."

"If you let us go, your life is forfeit." Geneve searched the man's face for signs of deceit, but found none.

"I'll get bawled out. I've been bawled out before. Especially if we never saw you." He glanced at his men and women. Solders with grim faces, but all offering grudging nods. "Might feel the lash for this one. A few more stripes on my skin, to replace those I'll lose from my collar." He nodded to Geneve. "It was good to meet you, Knight Adept Geneve. If you're in these parts again, come say hello."

"Wait!" Geneve looked at the guard arrayed around her. Steel returned to sheaths. Eyes softened, but remained wary. "Thank you, Heser the Cheg. I'll pray for you."

He gave her a lopsided grin. "My thanks, but I'd ask a different favor. The queen needs your regard more than me. She's in danger. Alive, but ... different. We need," he eyed Meri over her shoulder, "cunning men who can work for the throne. Not play act at it."

Meri took a step forward. "Heser, what—"

"It's Heser the Cheg." The captain sniffed.

"Of course." Meri gave a small bow of apology. "I meant no offense. Heser the Cheg, how is the queen different?"

"Absent, even when there. Complains of headaches. Irritable, more than exhaustion warrants." He sighed. "I claim no knowledge of her cares. But I've served her family since I could hold a blade."

Meri nodded. He pressed his palms together, as if in supplication. "If you find her the way she was, even for a moment, would you give her a message?"

Heser the Cheg eyed Meri. "Will it cost me the lash?"

"It might. But it will help her headaches." Meri looked at his feet. "They're caused by a weight on the mind. I'm offering you a few small ways to help shoulder the load."

The captain nodded. "I'll give your message."

"Tell her," Meri glanced at Geneve, "we accept her offer."

⁊

THEY GALLOPED THROUGH THE STREETS OF RAVENSWALL. FEW challenged them, but the night was alive with people. Folk pulled from their homes, buildings burning again, but this time set alight by those who used to be friends or protectors.

Meri held her waist, but each time she checked on him, he wasn't looking away. His eyes saw everything, caught the flames of burning buildings, and held them tight. He wasn't afraid. What she saw in his face seemed foreign there. Geneve knew he carried no skill with a blade. His magics were humble, small, the kind unlikely to change the world. And for all that, she saw him make a promise for each person fallen, each home burned, each family tossed aside.

Meriwether du Reeves was going home.

Chapter Nine

T he city fell behind them like a bad dream. Meriwether sat behind Geneve. He wasn't the most comfortable. It wasn't the speed; that seemed fine. Tristan ran at a steady canter that gathered the klicks like a squirrel harvesting nuts. The horse stored them as a promise for tomorrow.

The discomfort wasn't because of the saddlebags. He'd ridden behind Geneve before. The saddle was for one, so he spent most of those trips in direct contact with the horse. Anyone who told you riding two up was easy street hadn't spent enough time on the business end of a horse.

No, the problem's because you're running away from a problem. Again. The Knight taught you how to face challenges, but this is another you're leaving in your dust.

Was that fair? The thought line was unfamiliar, like cakes with a pickle filling. It could be a new flavor sensation, but it could be gastronomical doom. *And here, I'm thinking about food. I lasted for years without regular meals. These Knights stuffed food into me at every opportunity, and now I want seven squares a day.*

They had spent most of the night awake, with nothing but tea. Tea warmed the heart, but the stomach thought it sucked as a steak substitute.

Geneve broke his wagon train of thought by turning to him. "Where are the others?"

"Ride north." Meriwether tried for a smile, but wasn't sure she'd see it in the dark. "Also, keep your eyes on the road."

He got a tight grin in response. "Scared, wizard?"

"Terrified," he admitted. "But not of your horsewomanship. I'm afraid I've guessed wrong."

Geneve's expression faded to a warm smile. "You've not done it before, except that one time you underestimated the Tresward. And that turned out okay."

"The road!" Meriwether saw a bend in the road approaching at speed.

"The road's not going anywhere." Tristan turned, taking the curve without breaking stride. Geneve laughed at his wide-eyed look of fear. "Enjoy the journey. The start and end contain trouble enough."

"Aye." He clutched her tighter anyway. Geneve turned eyes front. "We should see it soon."

"See what?" Her words came to him on a river of wind.

"That." He pointed to the sky. The Three watched from on high. Before Cophine's luminous face a bright spark of color bloomed, all reds and yellows.

"Fireworks? Someone will see!"

"I'm experimenting with something. I've fashioned a trick of illusion that only we can see. Bound it to a rocket, and gave it to our friends. The explosion's audible if you're close enough—I can't do much about that. But the light shouldn't be visible to any but us."

"You've been busy, sorcerer." Geneve sounded *pleased* or *proud*, rather than suspicious. "Where do you find the time?"

"I don't sleep much." He didn't tell Geneve her nightmares woke him too. Meriwether didn't know what she dreamed, but he felt her terror. It dragged him awake. *No need to burden her with that pestersome detail. She'd worry, and there's nothing to fix.* "When I can't sleep, I read. The queen's library was wonderful." He felt a little wistful at the lost access to all that knowledge. *It'll be there when I get back.*

If I get back.

Another flare scorched the sky. Meriwether felt the tug of his illusion magic, a mask he'd constructed for a heavenly show. Another sorcerer might feel it too and follow the sensation, but he doubted any were close enough. They were all in Ravenswall, murdering innocents.

"Do you think the Coterie is in on the attack?" Geneve's words mirrored Meriwether's thoughts. It was uncanny.

"Some of them." Meriwether tried to settle himself on Tristan's backside, but that annoying jolt of guilt kept him from comfort. "I think it likely the Vide collected their own wizards, infiltrating the queen's advisory. A long game, a backup for Nicolette's failure."

"Should we go in?" Geneve slowed Tristan as they approached another bend in the road. The flare came from straight through the trees to the northwest, but the road jinked back east.

"Aye. They'll be off the road aways."

"Then we walk. Eating bark isn't on the menu tonight." Geneve reined Tristan to a halt.

They slid down. Meriwether frowned. "Or."

"You want to eat bark?"

"Not that." He glanced back toward where Ravenswall lay. The city was far distant, hidden by the curve of the world, the night, small hills, or all three. "It's possible this wasn't a plan for Nicolette's fall, but a parallel plot. That they meant to take the throne by stealth and murder. She followed *us*, remember? Because she couldn't get into the temple anymore."

Geneve nodded. "And I can't imagine a Champion following the beat of another's drum unless it suited her. The Vide have many pies in the oven."

"Don't talk about food." Meri rubbed his stomach. "Breakfast feels a long way off."

She nodded. "I could eat. Oatmeal would be fine, but eggs and sausage would be better."

"What did I say? No food talk." Meri headed for the tree line. Another flare burst in the heavens. It felt closer, almost above them. Geneve followed, leading Tristan. Her black armor was almost invisible in the night. The trees hid the Three's gaze from them. Even Cophine's pale face was a memory.

"A fire." Geneve's voice was a whisper, perhaps as respect to the woods.

He saw it. The crinkle of orange-red through the trees, hinting at warmth and company. A gentle wind touched the boughs around them, urging them on. Meriwether picked up his pace, a few minutes' hurry rewarding him with a break in the trees.

A small clearing held a campfire. At one time it had been massive, but now a small blaze sat in the middle of charcoal. *Armitage was here, heating his rock.* Despite the recent evidence of people, not a soul waited.

The *crack* of a broken branch arrived a moment before the cool kiss of steel on Meriwether's neck. He swallowed. "Hello, Armitage."

The knife vanished, and the monster hauled Meriwether around. He held a vicious-looking curved knife. Armitage sheathed it, then clasped Meriwether's shoulders. "It's good to see you, runt. How'd you know it was me?"

Meriwether looked into snake eyes. "You told me you wouldn't kill me this week. I figured if the Vide were after us, I'd be dead already."

"Huh." Armitage stuck fingers between his lips, blowing a shrill whistle. "It's safe! It's just the runt and Gen."

Sight of Day slipped from the shadows. {*All with ears could hear that for klicks. You are quiet for a Vhemin, but still have their ... enthusiasm.*}

"What are you trying to say?" Armitage squinted at the Feybrind.

"You're very loud." Pale Vertiline stepped from the trees. She wore leather armor, a slender blade belted at her hip. Geneve hurried across the clearing, embracing her friend. Meriwether noticed how Vertiline moved her injured arm with exquisite care, as if it were packed inside jagged glass, the tiniest motion causing pain.

"We just fired rockets into the sky. Doesn't get much louder than that." Armitage sniffed, then spat into the fire. The gobbet sizzled and hissed. "How'd the fuck-up party go?"

"About as expected." Meriwether approached the fire, spreading his hands to warm them. "There were a couple surprises."

{*How marvelously evasive.*} Sight of Day's golden eyes were warm.

Geneve faced the firelight. The rest circled the flames, building a huddle of friendship in the night. "The queen's ... fallen. There are assassins called the Vide. They have plots to control everything."

"My father's an asshole, too, if that helps." Meriwether shrugged. "He left a letter and everything. Apparently we need to see him to find answers."

"Sounds like a trap." Vertiline hugged her injured arm to her chest.

"Sounds like fun." Armitage adjusted his hot stone backpack. "He's rich, right? A lord? Human lords have all the best stuff. Wine and food. Their whores are a little scrawny—"

"We have to go." Geneve looked to each of them in turn. "Meri and I will, anyway. You should go somewhere safe."

"Fuck off." Armitage laughed. "Oh, you're serious? Well, shit. You suck at reading people."

{The monster means there's nowhere safe in the world. We'd rather fall with friends than die alone.} Sight of Day sighed. *{The Feybrind Kingdom needs the world whole as much as any.}*

"I ... can't be much help." Vertiline's eyes seemed locked on the fire, as if the flames held safety. "I'll do what I can."

"Tilly." Geneve turned to the Chevalier. "I—"

"Oh, hell, I almost forgot." Armitage scratched an armpit. "Where'd I put it?"

{Tell me you remembered it. This is not a good time to revert to being like an ordinary Vhemin.} Sight of Day rolled golden eyes.

"We had to tether the horses off a bit. Didn't like the rockets, see?" Armitage rooted in their pile of luggage. "Carrying all this shit here wasn't fun. Where ... ah. Here it is." He surfaced with a shield. It was circular, the surface mirror-bright metal. Studs circled the rim. Armitage spun it like a huge coin, then held it out to Vertiline. "Here."

"I can't use a shield." She held up her stump. Meriwether saw the jut of her jaw, perhaps hiding the hurt within. "You imbecile."

"Oh, good golly, I didn't think of that." The monster's shark-toothed grin didn't hold malice. "Take it."

{What he means is, we made it for you.} Sight of Day took the disc from Armitage, flipping it over. *{Here. The clasps are designed to bind to*

your injured arm. The cup here holds you, rather than you it. With a little practice, you can protect the world again, Daughter of the Three.}

"You ... made this?" Tilly took the shield from Sight of Day. "It's light."

"The cat knows smithing. I'll not deny that." Armitage hunkered by the fire. "Can't swing a hammer for shit, though. Call it a team effort. While you lot were off kissing babies, we tried to be a little more proactive."

"You made this in three days?" Geneve ran her finger along the shield's rim. "It's exquisitely crafted." She looked at Meriwether. "Did you plan this?"

"Me? No. All I did was measure her arm." Meriwether held his apart. "Illusion has its uses. I watched Vertiline, then gave them a simulacrum of her arm to use as a guide. It was their idea."

{It was Armitage's idea.} The cat held his hands out. *{He has an old soul, full of wisdom.}*

"Take that back or I'll punch your teeth in," the Vhemin warned.

{Perhaps not as old as I thought.} The cat's tail swished.

Vertiline squatted, the motion slow, tired, and full of pain. She rested the shield beside her. Her eyes were wet. "I don't know what to say."

"Don't say anything. Just, don't walk off." Meriwether crouched opposite her. Fire licked the air between them. "We need you."

Vertiline nodded, slow and steady, like the idea of being needed was new. Her voice held warning. "I can't call the Storm."

"Neither can I." Meriwether shrugged. "Where we're going, we need trust more than good weather."

Ice-blue eyes met his across the flames. "Where's that?"

"We're going to visit the head of the Vide. Their marshal in the Kingdom of Or'sen, unless I miss my guess." Meriwether stood. "If you three will join Red and I, that is."

"If I get to swing steel, I'm in." Armitage's voice was a growl of intent.

{I've nothing better to do.}

"I'd like to come." Vertiline stood. "I'd like to find a purpose again."

Meriwether smiled. "I haven't told you of the certain death we'll face."

"Same old bullshit," Armitage said. "The smell of it's around you like an outhouse."

{Who is the head of the Vide?} Sight of Day began to pull together cooking accoutrements. A pan for the fire, and eggs alongside sausage. *Geneve will get her dream breakfast.*

"Oh, no one important." Meriwether's grin turned feral. "Just my father."

Chapter Ten

I t was Meri's idea all along to get Tilly free of danger. He can't fight like her, and Vertiline's pride wouldn't let her sit on the sidelines. He is a marvel with people, using his heart like a Smithsteel shield. Geneve munched her breakfast, enjoying the smokey flavor of the sausage and the gentle butteriness of the eggs. Sight of Day scrambled them better than any chef she'd met, and he managed it over a campfire in the woods.

They broke camp with the easy familiarity of people used to working together. Vertiline did as much as she could with her arm as it was. Sight of Day fashioned a sling for her after checking the wound. His eyes were soft as he unwrapped the bandage, but he nodded. {No infection. We might be cursed with your company a few more days.}

The horses were tethered a short jaunt away. Geneve led Tristan, the blue roan surging ahead when he smelled his companions on the wind. Five hundred meters through the woods they arrived at a stream. Beck roamed free, the big bear serving as a cuddly guard. Troubles and Fidget stood together, as if talking about the price of silks.

Chesterfield stood alone. The black charger's head was low. Geneve let Tristan's reins go, the horse prancing to join Troubles and Fidget. She walked to Chesterfield. {I know how you feel.}

The huge black horse nodded, as if he understood what lay in their shared past. A missing piece, made of strength and Light. *Israel. My father. Why didn't you tell me?*

She felt a familiar presence at her shoulder, turning to find Meri there. "Hey."

"Hey, yourself." Geneve pressed her hand to Chesterfield's nose. "He misses Iz."

"I've a feeling that's shared between you. Tilly, too." The young sorcerer eyed the sky as the stream burbled behind him. "There are things too great to lose without the world feeling it."

"He never told me."

Meri didn't ask her *what*. He knew, like he knew water was wet, or that her hair was red. "He couldn't. He made a promise." His hands came up, guarding as her expression went hard. "I'm not saying he made the right call. But some asshole in a fancy hat said, 'Keep this secret, and your daughter will be safe.' So, he kept it secret. Fancy hats are the downfall of the world." He sighed. "I don't mean to tell you what's right to feel, or how to grieve. I'm here for talking, if an easy ear will rest your heart. I'll keep your silence just as well, because sometimes the whispering of things makes them cut too close. I don't know which of those is the right path, but I'm certain of one thing. Israel loved you more than his own life. More than duty, or the Tresward. It must have hurt like a brand to see you and keep his silence." The sorcerer's eyes found Vertiline. "If it's not me you can talk with, perhaps there are others you can share your heart with."

She nodded, eyes down. "I ... thank you, Meri. I will talk when the time is ready. I don't fear your council. I fear how it will make me feel."

"Fair enough." He put his hand against Chesterfield's flank. The big charger stood, steady as a rock. "Will you ride him?"

Geneve shook her head. "I've a horse already. You should take him."

"Me?" Meri laughed. "I don't want to be eaten."

"The rumors of Chesterfield fueling himself on the souls of the damned are exaggerated." She smiled, heart warmed by Meri's presence. Geneve wished she could talk to him, but he had cares enough of his own. Leander, and all that meant. Her grief was a simple thing in comparison. "Chesterfield doesn't need a strong hand. An honest one. Kind, but certain. I can think of no better rider."

She left Meri gawking at her back, striding toward Tilly. "Vertiline."

"Geneve." The pale Knight lifted her chin. "What wind blows?"

"The tired kind. I've not slept. We need to head north, and at speed. We can rest tonight, but I don't think my head's clear. Yours, neither. How do we proceed?"

Vertiline's chin lowered a fraction. "Why ask me?"

"You're the Chevalier." Geneve blinked. "I'm an Adept."

Tilly laughed, a sour, dry sound. "I'm no Chevalier, no more than you're an Adept. You hold the Storm in your fist, and I've heard the Sway on your tongue." She bowed, arms out in a courtly gesture. "Where you lead, we follow."

"But—"

"Ikmae's sometime balls," Armitage rumbled. He approached with his bear in tow. "We've followed you for weeks. It ain't gonna change now."

"But—"

"Get your horse, and start moving." The Vhemin's snake eyes watched her, considering, measuring. "If you like, we can arm wrestle for who's in charge. You'd lose, and then I'd abdicate, and we'd be where we are. Happy to do it if you think the theater will help."

{Who better to lead a handsome cat, a horrible monster, a wounded soldier, and a sinner?} Sight of Day half-smiled. {We're only offering you the job because none of us want it.}

"He's right." Meri stood with arms crossed. "It sounds like real work, and that's for suckers."

THE JOURNEY NORTH FELT LIKE THE END OF SOMETHING PRECIOUS, and the building of something fragile. Not their party—that was sound as bedrock. Geneve felt them *with* her, not just sharing the same road. No, the feeling was because they'd fallen from the Three's eyes. They were trying to save the world with steel and strength, and mortals weren't made for it. It's why the Three put the Tresward here.

Still. If there were five souls up to the task, it's these ones. Geneve looked to the skies. The moons no longer lay above, morning blue as brilliant as your heart's wish, but she prayed anyway. *Please, Cophine. Tell me how to start. Ikmae, I need your counsel. The middle can be the hardest, and I don't know the way. Khiton, always we've ended things as you intended. Help me do it one last time.*

The gods didn't answer. They never did.

They set a steady pace. The day turned warm, then hot. Geneve felt the sweat slick the middle of her back beneath her armor. Pale Vertiline fared better in armor made of leather, not steel. Armitage and Sight of Day paid the day no mind, swapping barbs, half-lies, and truths.

Meri sat astride Chesterfield like he wasn't sure how he'd got there. His eyes kept straying to the horse. She watched him countless times as he leaned forward, touching the black charger's neck, whispering something to the stallion. Each time the horse flicked an ear, nodded, and kept walking, one foot after the other.

They stopped for lunch. Bread, cold sausage, and hard cheese. Sight of Day wrinkled his nose at the bread, but ate the rest. Armitage ate the cat's share of the loaf.

Geneve chewed, thinking. "Meri, where is your father?"

"Casa du Asshole." The sorcerer kicked a clump of grass. "He has estates spanning much of the north."

"But you think you know which one he's at?"

"Pretty sure." Meriwether's face grew dark. "He'll be at Lakewell Stronghold. It's a nice enough place if you ignore the company. Surrounded by farmland as far as the eye can see. Mostly vines. They're old. Good rootstock." A smile touched his lips with the memory. "There's an old mine nearby. It gave up good gold before the earth got tired of it. The wine's still good, though. Also, there's a harbor. It's right there in the name. 'Cept it's not a lake, which I'll admit is confusing."

"Why there?" She kept her voice soft, so only they could hear. "Why is Lakewell important?"

"It's not, really." He turned away, eying his cheese as if it was swarmed with maggots. "It's not important at all. And neither are the people who live there. My father's a sociopath, and my mother's dead."

"Your brother?" Geneve remembered the queen words. *Lord du Reeves lost a boy.*

"I don't have a brother." Meri tossed his cheese into the trees. "I never did. Come on. Let's be about it."

THEY PLANNED THE PACE OF THEIR JOURNEY TO TAKE A FEW DAYS. First stop, Parnear Harbor, two days easy ride north. There, they'd charter a ship for the three-day voyage to Whisperwind Port. Whisperwind was due east of Lakewell Stronghold, and a further two days' ride would see them at the vineyard estate in time for dinner.

That was how Meri described it, anyway. He spoke with confidence, like a man who'd done the journey a hundred times before. *Or just once, but the hard way.* Geneve didn't question his directions, and neither did the rest. Time pressed, and the longer they delayed, the worse things would get for the queen.

Seven days. A week's effort, unmask the villain, and save the kingdom. It seemed easy if you said it fast enough.

That night, they sheltered in the arms of an Artifice. This one was unusual in that it had fallen. Geneve couldn't tell if it fell when the ancients walked the land or later. It was an eight-legged affair, but unless her eyes missed their measure, this would've been squat, perhaps two stories tall when upright. The Artifice's belly gave a shelter at their back. Canvass stretched between two legs afforded a simple roof.

Meri spent the time after setting camp brooding in the dark. Or that's what she thought, until she went to find him. She'd let her armor fall, stacking it in an orderly pile. She and Armitage played Three's Bastard while Sight of Day made a big show of not joining in, instead going to hunt, and Tilly huddled about her arm. Sometime during the exercises Meri walked off.

Hair wet with sweat, Geneve stalked after him. To lend him comfort, as he had her. She haunted the glum dusk about the Artifice, walking around the fallen machine until she reached him. He stood by it, staring long and hard at what would've been the top if it still stood upright.

"Meri?" He turned at her voice. "All's well?"

"Fine," he said, in the universal way people did when it wasn't. "I'm not an Artifice expert."

Geneve frowned, running that through her head a few times. "What?"

"Here." He touched the machine. "I don't think I've seen this before."

She joined him in the fading light. "I'm not sure what I'm looking at."

"Hah! Not an Artifice expert either." He leaned closer, fingers brushing the metal. "There's a seam."

Geneve squinted. He was right. The Artifice had a square panel, recessed from the rest of it. A ridge rimed with moss and lichen showed the joins in the metal. "Is that a door?"

"Crazy, right?" He kicked the metal. "These were their servants, not their vehicles. That's what people say. The Artifices didn't have riders. Not like the dragons."

"Perhaps it's a ... wagon?" She shook her head. "Does it matter? It's a dead relic from a time we should forget. The ancients touched the world and broke it. The Three tried to hold the brittle remains together, and we're all that's left."

His eyes glinted in the dark. "But what a cool remnant we are." He straightened, stretching. "There's something else. Come on."

Meri led her around the fallen Artifice to the front, if there was such a thing. Firelight tried to reach them in fits and starts through the scattered foliage and splayed legs of the Artifice. The machine rose above them. *By the Three, it must have been wide.* "What are we looking at?"

"This is a head, of sorts. See how it joins to the body?" He pointed at a segment of overlapping metal plates. He directed her to above the snout. "There. Tell me what you see."

The face of the Artifice was a featureless gleaming black strip. "I don't—"

"Like your helmet." He hugged his arms to his chest. "The black glass. You can't see through from one side, but it's clear from the other. This was a carriage with a really big window." He held his palm out in a *behold!* gesture. "Notice anything else?"

"This is getting tiresome."

"I'm having fun with it." He took her glare at face value and backed up a step. "The plants, Red. They grow here. Artifices don't have greenery around them. Except this one does."

She looked at the machine again. "What's it mean?"

"No clue." He patted the ancient relic. "But I think there are people inside who might. Or they did. Before they died, I mean. This thing's their tomb."

"We're having dinner beside a mausoleum?"

"That's one way of looking at it." Meri eyed the night sky where the Three eyed him right back. "They've watched this world for hundreds of years. I wish I could ask them what they saw."

"They don't answer." Geneve tasted bitterness on her lips. "They never do."

He cocked an eyebrow. "Maybe you're asking the wrong questions. No, don't hit me. I don't mean our hearts aren't with them, but rather we're looking at the wrong place for answers. What if the Three aren't there?"

Geneve glanced at the sky, then Meri, then the heavens again. "What?"

"We live in a world where a Champion fell and became risen. A Justiciar died, and something wears his skin as a mask. People storm the castle with *my* face, which is flattering, but shows a pattern of deceit." His finger jabbed skyward. "What if they're gone?"

She stood with her mouth hanging open like a broken hinge. "Where would they go?"

"It might be better to ask, who would have the power to take them? How do you bend a god to your will? And *then* we get to worry about where you stash the bodies."

"The Three aren't dead!" Geneve didn't mean to shout, and wanted to take the words back as Meri retreated a step.

"Aye, Red. I think you're right, and I don't know why. It's the reason I'm asking questions, you see. If you ask them hard enough, often enough, you can break through to a new truth." He took a cautious step toward her. "A question for you, then. I see you've struggled with your faith. Worried the gods won't love you, or that you've done wrong, when all can see the right of where you place your feet."

Geneve brushed back her hair. "That's not a question."

"Of course." He touched the fallen Artifice again. "If we find the Three fallen, what will you do?"

"I'll..." She trailed off. Geneve wasn't a god, to be saving other celestial powers. She was a Knight, and not a very good one. "It doesn't matter. The Three are *there*, Meri." Geneve jabbed her arm skyward. "We can see them."

He nodded, not disagreeing. "Or something that once was them."

"Why ask these questions? Do they serve a purpose?"

"Maybe." Meri patted the machine's nose, then let his hand fall. "There's something wrong with the world. Has been, for hundreds of years. The ancients fell. They left little trace. Their cities are ruins within blasted wastelands. Yet we know they flew dragons and harnessed machines like this. You've got to wonder what kind of thing would toss them into the gutter like trash. You've got to think," he tapped his head perhaps with more force than it needed, his voice turning to a hiss, "something that could kick aside a world of wonders might joust with the gods themselves."

Geneve joined him, touching the machine. The Artifice was cold, lifeless, and hard as sin. "Do you know something?"

"Very little. But I *think* I know what *Immensae* is." He sighed like the old wind traveling through the Artifices feet. "It's 'Boundless,' Red." Meri left her by the machine's nose, trudging toward the light and companionship of their camp.

"Meri, wait." He turned to look at her. "What does 'Boundless' mean?"

"Imagine the Storm and the Sway. Magic and machines. All that together, but without rules. A people who could command the wind and seas, and step on a dragon like a tame gelding. *They* were the Boundless, Geneve. As close to gods as people could be. And you know what? They're all gone, too. Everything that shouldered the sky fell."

She felt a shiver touch her spine, deeper than the wind on cold sweat. "Gone?"

"It's okay." She caught his smile in the dark and returned it. "If we fall too, we're going together. Maybe you didn't step from the path. Maybe the path's been gone a long, long time."

He left her in the lee of the Artifice, a lone Tresward under the Three's watchful eyes. *Maybe the path's been gone a long, long time.* She glared at the sky, but no answers came.

Perhaps it was time to find her own path. And with it, the answer to the greatest question of all: what broke the world?

Chapter Eleven

A good night's sleep helped Meriwether's world view a hundredfold. The air smelled cleaner, sharper, and he didn't feel the pervasive need to strangle someone. He woke after a dream of eating pancakes with lemon honey to find Sight of Day making pancakes. Armitage crouched to the Feybrind's right, next to a small cookfire of his own. A pot steamed before him.

Meriwether levered himself off his bedroll, scratched his beard, and inhaled. "Are you making pancakes with lemon honey?"

{I'm making pancakes. The monster's burning lemon honey.}

Armitage growled. "This isn't as easy as it looks. Busting open the hive? No problem. Vhemin skin is stronger than it looks. Making this over a cookfire in the woods? Well, it's a special kind of bullshit."

Meriwether swung his gaze about, looking instinctively for Geneve. Her bedroll was empty, as was Vertiline's. *Probably off scouting the terrain, or just taking a leak.* "Can I help?"

"No. And I don't need advice, either." The monster hunched. "Fuck *all* this."

"Give it here." Meriwether walked to the Vhemin's side. The pot bubbled, a little hot, but not so far gone it couldn't be rescued. "Gently. You're not smelting iron."

"How do you know how to make lemon honey?"

"Doesn't everyone?" Meriwether glanced to Sight of Day. "What I want to know is where you found the lemons."

{Life has supplied them in rich amounts recently.} The Feybrind's golden eyes were mirthful. *{We lack tequila and salt, so this was the best alternative.}* He flipped a pancake. *{We only have a little flour, but it's enough for a meal between friends.}*

The three made breakfast. Beck ambled closer, interested in the largess afforded by breaking into a natural hive, and Armitage shoved the bear away, but only after a rough hug. The morning was aways from warm, but the small comfort of a shared fire made it seem less cold despite the clear air.

Geneve and Vertiline returned before breakfast was ready. Geneve carried Sight of Day's bow, and Vertiline held a brace of rabbits. The Adept looked at the fallen Artifice at their backs, considering. "Now would be a good time to have a travel device of the ancients."

"Last time we found the ancient's stuff still working, we almost died," Armitage reminded her. "Almost dying seems to be the base water level around you, so I don't want to appear fretful. But, pretty please, with lemon honey on top, can we not be dicks about this?"

Vertline laughed. "The monster makes an excellent point. Danger dogs your heels, Adept."

Geneve glared. "*Me?* What about you?"

Tilly spread her arms, smile going wider. "If we're keeping score, you freed the Vhemin. Opened the ancient temple. Bested the Champion. Me, I just look good on a horse." She offered the rabbits to Sight of Day. "You don't eat pancakes, so we picked you up something extra."

It's good to see her humor return. The ghost of Israel walks with us, watching all the time. He haunts these two, but they press on regardless. Is this what Tresward existence is like? Cherishing those you love, but accepting they may fall at any moment? Meriwether watched as Geneve put the Feybrind's bow down. She swept red hair from her eyes. "I didn't know if I could still shoot. Thank you for the loan."

"You can shoot too?" Meriwether looked from the bow to her. "I thought the scattergun was your thing."

"Geneve favors the loud, upfront approach it's true, but Tresward use all weapons." Vertiline sprawled her lean form against a pack. "The Storm is harder to use at range. Almost impossible."

"But I saw her when we set Israel to rest." Meriwether frowned. "She knocked that Vide asshole off a parapet."

"Harder. I didn't say impossible." Vertiline winced, favoring her stump. "The best can do it, and Geneve's form is better than any I've seen."

"Oh, gosh." Armitage batted nonexistent eyelashes. "You've got yourselves a budding circle jerk there."

Meriwether laughed, then handed out plates. Pancakes set by the fire to warm were distributed. Armitage and Geneve ate most, with Vertiline and Meriwether taking merely a double share each. Sight of Day skinned rabbit.

The morning didn't suck. No, not at all.

THE ROAD PASSED SWIFTLY BY. FARMLAND WAS GREENER HERE. Trees stood taller. The warmth of the north didn't press against life as much as the cold in the south. Meriwether wondered if the plague lands kept warmth one side and cold the other, because such a rapid change of season didn't feel right for the distance traveled.

That, or it's spring. Relax. Not everything's an ancient curse.

The party passed through a small town called Garen's Well. Armitage took the long way around, not wanting to terrify villagers, or possibly get shot. He led his bear off amiably enough, promising murder if they stopped for ale without him.

Garen's Well was new since Meriwether passed this way last, wooden buildings structured around a mine burrowed into the earth. For all the grubby dirt on people's faces, there were smiles too. They bought a few more supplies, and put a new shoe on Chesterfield, who'd no doubt buried the lost one in someone's face.

The big charger felt powerful beneath Meriwether. Like he was built to haul mountains, and he didn't even notice the thin man on his back. Meriwether took it as a kindness the beast hadn't tried to kill him. *Friendships are forged by time and pressure.* It didn't hurt that Meriwether kept whispering to the horse. Things like *I understand what loss feels like*, or *I'm not who used to ride you, but I'm doing my best*. The horse might not understand the words, but his ears flicked like the tone of them was pleasing.

Garen's Well dropped behind them. They'd made no friends or enemies. If anyone thought Geneve was the Savior of Ravenswall, they made no comment. She didn't wear the Tresward's burnished sun, nor carry a glass sword. There was no reason for them to be noticed. Meriwether stopped at a ramshackle construction that the smith said was the closest thing to a tavern, picking up a wineskin or three and a small cask of something else. He paid with the queen's gold, not illusory coins, and felt better for it.

Armitage rejoined them at the far side of the village. He wore a sour expression. "I can smell the booze on you from here."

"Peace, Armitage." Meriwether pulled the cask from Chesterfield's saddlebags, tossing it to the Vhemin. "There. Copper wine, they called it."

"Is it made from copper?"

"Might be the color," Vertiline suggested. "Or the smell."

"Smells fine." The monster re-corked the cask. "Thanks for not being a dick, runt. I appreciate it."

Meriwether grinned. The journey north might not be as hard as he feared.

⁙

THEY FOUND A SMALL CAVE OFF THE ROAD. BECK NOSED IT OUT AS dusk gathered shadows. It was dry, a hollow worn into a cliff face that would house them well enough. They could have pushed for the next town, but Vertiline didn't think the best approach to avoiding the Vide was going to a conveniently signposted inn.

Geneve gave grudging assent. Meriwether figured she wanted to test steel against them again, but each fight carried risk. Her eyes met Meriwether's when she agreed to hold her peace. *Risk for all, but less for her. She makes this choice for me, despite what vengeance demands of her.*

Armitage hauled a fallen trunk close, and they built a fire with that sheltering the flames from the road. Meriwether couldn't have said what they talked about, but he remembered the inner pinch for days after. The special feeling that said, *ware! Magic.* He jerked to his feet, plate rattling to the hard stone ground.

Geneve stood, her motion oiled and smooth. "Meri? What is it?"

He peered into the night. "They come."

"Who?"

"All of them, I think." He looked at his dropped plate. "Well, that's unfair. The feeling of foreboding and dread I've got is because one particularly powerful mage is coming from there," he jabbed a finger southeast, "and he's focused on us. Recent history says mages hunt in packs."

She retrieved Requiem, belting the sword to her hip. "Then we teach them to avoid us."

"Aye, that's one approach." Meriwether bit his lip. "But what about a trap? All this time we meet them head on, and they're ready for that."

"A trap?" Vertiline pushed herself upright, pale face drawn with pain. The day's ride hadn't been kind to her, and her bandage was spotted with red. "With what bait?"

"The kind they're already after." He jerked a thumb at his chest. "I think the magician's after me. Kind of like a lodestone." Meriwether shook his head. "Look, that's not a good analogy, but I don't have time for a better one."

Armitage scratched his belly, then stood. "You want to sit in a trap, it's your funeral. People keep saying you're smart, but it seems you're the opposite."

"Hear me out," Meriwether said. "This is what we'll do."

WHEN THEY APPROACHED, MERIWETHER WAS READY. HE SAT ON the log Armitage provided, back to the cave, eyes to the night. Their arrival came with the whisper of wind, a too-urgent shake of trees, and the quieting of night insects.

When terror showed its face, Meriwether wasn't surprised. He smiled, but without much feeling. "Vikander. What a pleasure."

The mage strode forward. The firelight didn't touch him courtesy of the trunk, but Meriwether wouldn't mistake the arrogant set of his shoulders even in the pitch of midnight. "Save your pleasantries. We've not much time." He looked about, face falling. "Where are they?"

"Who?" Meriwether examined his fingernails.

"The Savior of Ravenswall. The Vhemin and the Feybrind. And the pale soldier. *Where are they?*" Vikander took another step forward.

Meriwether could make out the glint in his eyes, like a fever burned the man from within. "Long gone. They've business to attend, and don't need an illusionist's help for that."

Vikander made a small noise, half grunt, half growl. "You're no illusionist. Did your father teach you nothing?"

"My father taught me a few things. How to fear the lash, and what good wine tastes like. We failed to come to terms on much else." Meriwether's mind raced. *Why is Vikander mentioning dear ol' Dad? What's his play?* "Allow me to answer your question with a question. Where are the Vide?"

The mage turned, scanning the night. "Not far away, now. This is why we've not much time. I *must* speak with the Savior of Ravenswall."

"Pretend she's out to lunch. Would you like to leave a message?"

Vikander took a long, steadying breath. He closed his eyes, lips moving like he was counting to ten. *Good work. I'm getting to him.* Meriwether wanted to grin, to cackle, to let the terror of facing an evoker bubble forth, but he kept all that buttoned down. *Dear ol' Dad also taught me to show nothing, despite feeling everything. The lash hits harder each time you cry.*

The mage's eyes popped open. "I've no time for games."

"Excellent. You'd suck at playing them."

Vikander's fists clenched. "You must take me to the Champion slayer. I've a message for her. The queen's under threat."

"Hah! Oh, you're not joking. Of *course* Queen Morgan's under threat. From *you.*" Meriwether crossed his arms. "Slithering into an advisory position. Warping her thoughts against us. I'll admit though, this new dissemblance of yours is a surprise to me."

"No. I mean, not anymore." Vikander ran a hand through close-cropped hair. "Here's the truth."

"At last! Behold, gospel from a liar's tongue."

"I've earned your ire, I agree." Vikander glanced at the trees again, as if fearing night terrors. "Until yesterday, I worked for the Vide. They approached me. They needed mages, you see."

"Uh huh."

"Get close to the queen. Turn her. If not, break her." He shrugged. "Royalty's no friend of mine. Not yours either, I'll wager."

Meriwether raised an eyebrow. "This feels a convenient bond of brotherhood."

"Hold a moment longer. We arranged the coup. I've some small skills with enchantment alongside evocation." Vikander crossed his arms. "Job done, so to speak. Then they came for me. Tidying up loose ends, I expect."

"So you want the Savior of Ravenswall to shield you from their blades?" Meriwether scoffed. "That's a pitiful level of angst, even for a snake like you."

Vikander held his hands up, palms out. "*Hold.* My time's done. I want two things. Vengeance for my death, as they'll have it one way or the other. I pay my tithe with honesty." He drew his robe about him, trying to marshal a little regal bearing from the dregs of his shattered pride.

Meriwether chewed that over. "The second thing?"

"That's for her, and her alone." Vikander shrugged. "Take me to her, or the secret dies with me."

"Then I guess the secret dies with you." Meriwether patted the air. *{Calm down.}* "Not because I'm the asshole here. It's because of them."

Vikander whirled. Five black-clad figures walked from the trees, weapons drawn. They wore hoods, their faces wrapped with cloth so only their eyes showed. The Vide had arrived, and they were here to kill a pair of mages.

Chapter Twelve

T he hardest thing to do was stand still.

Geneve waited, Requiem in hand. She held the north, Armitage to the south, and Tilly a hard edge to the west, near the cave. Sight of Day held position above.

All were invisible. Geneve couldn't see anyone but Meri. The snake Vikander approached him, and holding herself from killing the Coterie's leader was one of the hardest things she'd ever done. The evoker got close to her best friend, and she felt the terrible fear of it. The sickness in her gut, the pressure behind her eyes. Every part of her wanted to take seven perfect steps toward the enemy wizard and cut him down.

This is what we'll do. Meri laid the plan out for them, gram by gram. He smiled as he spoke, a softness in his eyes as Geneve watched him. Something about him said, *I'm terrified, but this one thing I can do.* When he'd said their part was easy, she hadn't believed him.

I've never been good at standing still. But if the monster can do it, so can I.

The Vhemin was hidden beneath the seeming of a bolder. The illusion of a rock sat atop his position. It was old, weathered, with lichen growing at the base. Meri's illusions had every detail perfect. Where time chipped the rock, or the jagged face where it may have broken from the cliff above. Armitage huddled within, waiting for their signal.

Tilly's illusion was a pile of fallen wood. The branches were old, worn, some rotted, others calcified. She crouched, ready to strike. Geneve knew her blade was ready, as she knew her friend was tired, worn thin by the world. This fight could be her last, but like Geneve, Vertiline was a Knight of the Tresward. She faced death like she always had: with calm.

For Geneve, Meri fashioned a tree, straight and true. The bark was gnarled, weathered, and above a bird's nest waited for the return of its ward. She stood within the trunk's seeming, Requiem held vertical, the blade before her face. When the illusion dropped over her, she'd wondered if it worked. She could see her sword. Geneve could see herself, and nothing made the world any different. No gauze of filmy light. No dulled sound. Everything looked normal.

A step to the left, and she was outside a tree. Geneve tried to touch it. The bark gave with a feeling like parting cobwebs. Meri said, *It's because your mind believes. It's not really there.*

So, she returned to the tree, watching. Waiting.

I hate standing still.

Vikander and Meri exchanged barbs. Every time the evoker moved, she itched to slice him. He was *most likely* the queen's downfall; he all but confirmed it to Meri. When he demanded to speak with Geneve, she thought of striding forth.

But Meri had said, *I know you'll want to dive right in. Don't.* She'd thought he was talking to Armitage, but his eyes were on Geneve. *Red? This is serious. Wait. Listen. Watch.*

I really hate standing still. But I hate it most when those I love are in danger.

When the five Vide came from the trees, Genve glanced at Meri, expecting him to give the signal. The illusionist did nothing of the sort, instead braying with laughter. He stood, brushed his pants off, and said, "Is this *it?* You brought five assassins to deal with the Savior of Ravenswall? The one who dropped a Tresward Champion?" He jabbed his hand out at Genve's head height. "About this tall? Red hair? Striking in pose, and beautiful like the dawn?"

Beautiful like the dawn? Geneve's wagon train of thought de-hitched as Vikander stepped forward, arms raised. "Die!"

Lightning arced from his palms, turning the five to pillars of ash. The soft hiss of sand accompanied the human-shaped charcoal forms sliding to piles on the ground, along with the *tink* of metal weapons falling to earth.

Hold still. There's been no signal. Besides, I'm night blind. Geneve blinked, trying to clear her eyes after the storm of power that incinerated the Vide. Her vision cleared, showing Meriwether also blinking. The young illusionist clapped. "Well done! Now we'll never get anything out of them."

"I saved your life!"

"You saved *yours*. I'm fine, thanks." Meriwether sat on his log again. "See, the problem is you're under the impression I need your help. I don't! What I need is answers."

Vikander, realizing his hands were still raised, lowered them. "I've offered to give you—"

"You've offered to give me a *version* of the truth, aye. I'll not deny it, or turn away its usefulness. But what you don't have a firm grip on is how precarious your situation is." Meriwether glanced skyward. "What do you see?"

Vikander's mouth hung open. He checked the sky. "The moons. Any imbecile can. Well, Cophine and Ikmae, of course. Khiton's a bit difficult to make out this time of year—"

"Aye, Khiton's a man of mystery. Shadows and secrecy." Meri mock-shivered. "What you don't see is cloud. Not a one in the sky. And here you are, blasting lightning like only a thunderstorm would. If you were a Vide, what would you think?"

"I..." Vikander whirled in a panic. "You've got to help me!"

"*I've* got to do no such thing." Meri examined his nails. Geneve smirked from her tree illusion. "*You've* got to run, Vick. You've got to run like the hounds of hell dog your heels. You'd better get started before..." He trailed off.

"Before what?"

"Before that." The illusionist cocked an ear. Geneve heard it too— the tremble of horse's hooves, the urgency of their beat unmistakable.

"Sounds like your friends are on the way. Cheer up. There's some good news here."

Vikander faced Meri again. "Good news?" His voice was hollow, like a rotted trunk. "I can't do that many more times."

"Aye, that's a piece of good news, but not the slice I had in mind. The Vide coming *en masse* means you were telling the truth. Or enough of it." He stood, rolling his shoulders. "Best come over this side of the log, Vick. It's not safe where you are."

"Safe?" Vikander's voice was as pale as his skin. "There's nowhere in Or'sen safe for me!"

"Be as may, it's slightly steadier ground over here. Come on." Meri nodded encouragement.

Vikander vaulted the log like a rabbit, scurrying behind the fire. Meri stayed where he was, peering into the night. Vikander looked at the cave wall. "Why are you standing there?"

"Fire makes you night blind." Meri drew his knife. Geneve smiled to see it was the same one she'd ... gifted him. "Won't be long now."

The sound of hooves vanished, replaced by silence that could only be called eerie. The world seemed to still as it had in the queen's keep. *The Vide come, and with them, sorcerers who can steal sound.* It was a good trick, and would stop any here crying for aid.

Meri had anticipated this too. He rummaged in his pack, hauling out a single rocket. *The signal.* He stuck it beside the fire, quickly as you please, then let the long tail of fuse fall into the flame. It started to burn with a sparkle, a tiny fairy in the night. Geneve heard nothing, but there was no mistaking the brightness. Vikander's lips moved, no noise coming out. The man touched his lips, surprised, and shifted from foot, a picture of agitation.

I know how he feels. I HATE being still.

The Vide swarmed from the trees like black-clad nightmares. Their movements were fluid, almost magical. All wore hoods, steel in hand. A few carried bows. Geneve counted their number while she waited. The men and women of the enemy streamed past her, intent on the two sorcerers within the cave.

Meri flung his arms wide and was *transformed*. Instead of the thin man in borrowed, scruffy clothes stood a Knight of the Tresward.

Armor, gleaming and gold. The burnished sun of the Three shone in the night. His hand held a long blade of shimmering glass, not a knife.

Oh. Oh, he's beautiful too.

She caught the gray-black sash across his breastplate. Five gold bars challenged the Vide. Geneve blinked, her heart hammering her chest. *Meri wears Israel's sash. A seeming, but he offers me a memory. What it is to fight with friends, and have the Valiant at your back.*

The Vide didn't slow. The rocket in the flames ignited, spitting at the sky. It shot high and fast, birthing a ruddy star in the heavens. That was what she'd waited for: Meri's signal. Geneve screamed a war cry, jumping from her illusory cover.

The Vide already past her didn't know what was happening. The illusion that stole sound also took the cry from Geneve. They had no warning. The ones still coming saw her step from the bark of a tree, and she marked a not insignificant amount of surprise in their eyes.

Vertiline leaped from her woodpile, stepping into view like a ghost sent from the underworld. Her face was death pale, eyes blue and glass hard. She had her new shield buckled to her stump, slender steel in her other hand. Armitage tore free from within his boulder, snatched a Vide from her feet, raised the body above his head, and dropping her across bent knee. Sound rushed back with a shudder and a thump.

Arrows announced the arrival of Sight of Day's attention. She didn't know where the Feybrind hid, but he needed no illusion. A moment later, he landed cat-perfect beside Armitage, blade in hand, back to back with the monster.

The hammer of steel on steel flowed over her, a music she knew, a dance she loved. Geneve swept Requiem, clearing space. Two perfect steps took her closer to Meri. Each footfall landed with a thunder crack. That alerted the Vide at the fore, who turned. She heard the young illusionist yell, "Do as I do! If you value your life, do it!"

He raised his hands to the sky. Geneve raised her blade, the steel waiting. From the heavens a brilliant blue lance dropped to it. While illusion, a seeming of lightning and nothing more, she felt the tingle on her arm. *I want to believe.* Vikander, clearly a fast learner, raised his arms. Real lightning arced from him to the tip of her blade.

Now, Ikmae's Dance of Storms. Geneve stepped into the motion, letting the Storm free. Lightning snared on her blade, the Storm holding it close. She didn't burn as she had within the keep. The Three prepared them for this, if only the Tresward knew they were supposed to have wizards as their allies.

Geneve swung her blade overhand, blue light crackling along its length. The steel carved through a Vide before her, a massive man with greatsword raised in defense. Requiem chimed its laughter as it shattered her enemy's steel. The Storm followed her perfect strike, the force of the Three coupled with the evoker's borrowed energy.

The man exploded in a burning shower of agony. Pieces scattered like a red fan before her.

Now this *was worth holding still for!*

Geneve stepped through the Dance of Storms. Meri called lightning to her as she'd told him to, Vikander lending substance to the illusion. She spun, taking the head from an enemy, the power of the Light tearing him to ash. The evoker panted exhaustion for a moment, leaving Geneve and the Storm to themselves.

As I've trained, so it will be. Geneve took three faultless steps over uneven ground, embracing Khiton's Rush of Devils as she reversed Requiem in her grip. The blade held backstyle, she swung twelve times as she advanced, eyes closed in an ecstasy of Light. Her sword carved arm from chest, head from neck, and cleaved torsos.

Thunder rolled. Geneve opened her eyes. Requiem glowed with Light, the blade silver-white. She bared her teeth in challenge, ignoring Vertiline's astonished stare. Geneve took a man's blade on her steel, the Storm holding Requiem true. Her enemy's blade sheared through on the force of the block. Thunder shouldered the sky once more.

Armitage dropped a body, sharing astonishment, while Sight of Day's golden eyes were the widest she'd seen, but Geneve paid no mind. *Next, the Harmony of the Wind.* She lopped the arm off an opponent, stealing the fallen shortsword from her. Geneve tossed Requiem to the sky, slicing a man from collarbone to groin with her borrowed blade. She held her hand out, Requiem falling into her palm.

Geneve whirled, slashing the blade overhand. There was no one in front of her, but five Vide stood ten meters off. Requiem fell, and so did the heavens. Lightning hammered the earth. Not the petty magic of an evoker past his prime. Not the seeming of an illusionist, no matter how grand. This was the raw, brutal power of the Three. The ground erupted on impact. Geneve saw the silhouette of the Vide's bodies, hard black within the brilliant white of the gods' fury.

She held her blade high, calling stormlight to her. The heavens granted her wish, lightning coiling in glowing, arcing lengths to her blade. Three Vide remained. The assassins ran, trying to get away. Geneve hurled Requiem. The blade whirled across the clearing, lightning reaching clawed fingers to the ground as it flew. Skymetal hit, electricity discharging through her foe.

Smoke. Whimpers and hard breathing. The delicate tread of passing thunder, distant now. Geneve panted, chest heaving. She stalked to her blade, freeing Requiem from the char that used to be a human. The blade was everbright, clean, like fresh forged steel.

Geneve spun to Meri. He stood, eyes wide. Vikander had backed against the cave wall, mouth slack. Armitage and Sight of Day held their distance, shoulder to shoulder. "Meri! Did you see?"

"Aye, Red. Are you well?"

"I feel *alive*, Meri! I feel so alive!" Her heart pounded, but like it wanted *more*.

"Okay." He scratched his head, then sighed. He came to her, picking his way around the smoking, ruined dead. When he reached her, he took her gauntleted hands in his. "It's just, your eyes are glowing."

"They're what?"

"They're like the lightning." He cocked his head, smile somehow sad. "They're like ... what the dark fears."

Sight of Day looked at his blade, as if wondering why he'd bothered drawing it, then slid it into its sheath. *{There is a Storm inside you, Daughter of the Three.}*

"What the *fuck* was that?" Armitage bellowed.

Vertiline approached on slow, cautious feet. She examined her bloodless blade with a critical eye, then slipped it away with a flourish. Tilly gave a tight bow. "Well met, Chevalier."

"I'm no—"

"When Israel and I fought the sentinels of the ancients, he called the lightning. But he didn't command it. It was an accident, as are many of the gifts of the Storm." She shook her head. "Only Champions bend it to their will. It seems you've at least earned a step up from Adept."

Meri reached out, touching her sash. His fingers tapped twice. He looked to Vertiline. "Is that right?"

"Aye, sinner. It's right." Tilly turned away, and worked her way through the fallen, making sure they were dead.

Geneve looked at her sash. Three bright gold bars ran along its length. "What's this?"

"A promotion." Meri gave her a lopsided grin. "Hail, Chevalier. I guess? Something like that."

Vikander chose that moment to make a break for it. It was inevitable. The man felt he controlled the powers of creation, and he'd seen something he had no answer for. He sprinted north.

"Don't make me run!" yelled Armitage, sprinting after him despite his words. He needn't have bothered.

A fallen Vide raised a crossbow. Geneve screamed, "'Ware!" grabbing Meri and shielding him with her armored body. The crossbow *thwacked*, followed by a grunt as Vertiline finished the Vide.

Vikander stumbled, falling to the earth no more than twenty meters into his escape. Armitage slowed, grabbed the man, and dragged him back. The Vhemin dropped the evoker at Geneve's feet. He was still alive, but bloody froth bubbled through his lips. Geneve crouched. "You've not much time. You wanted to meet the Savior of Ravenswall. Here I am, sorcerer. What's your message?"

Vikander's words were a whisper. She leaned close, to better hear him. "...du Reeves is the most powerful mage the world's ever known. Why the Vide want him." A cough, blood rattling in lungs. "Why his father... needs him. Why they tried to kill me. Not because I ... toppled the queen. But because I *failed*."

"Failed? Failed what?" Geneve hauled Vikander close. She could feel the soul leaving him, yearning for the Three's embrace.

"I couldn't leash du Reeves." And like that, Vikander was gone.

Geneve let the body go. *Leash du Reeves? Were the Vide after Meri's father? Is he under their sway?* More useless questions, and not enough time for answers. Geneve stared at her friends. She sensed a shift in them, a cautiousness that hadn't been there before. In all, that is, except one. Meri stayed by her side, hands clasped. "Are you sure you're okay?"

"I've never felt so good," Geneve said. "I know I should feel something. Fear, or guilt, or ... anything. But all I feel is ... *bright*."

"That's okay." Meri raised an eyebrow. "You look bright too, so it's fitting. I wonder if your eyes will ever stop glowing. It'll be hard to blend in if they don't." He turned to go.

She grabbed his arm. "You're not afraid? The others are—"

"They've seen something shake the world. Give them time," he suggested.

"But not you?"

He considered the question for a moment. "I'm kinda used to it. See, you've shaken my world since the first moment I saw you."

Chapter Thirteen

What the hell kind of cheesy line was that? Meriwether wondered how his mouth and brain were connected at times, as evidence suggested he was both smart and stupid at the same time. They'd left the dead Vide behind, making it to Parnear Harbor without further incident.

The port city was every centimeter the shithole Meriwether remembered. He smelled rotting seaweed well before they got close enough to see the cloud of gulls that circled the city like aggressive, loud locusts. Sight of Day's entire face puckered, but Armitage breathed deep, a contented smile on his face. Geneve's lips were pressed into a line, and Vertiline spent a lot of time breathing through her mouth.

The outskirts of the city weren't patrolled. Parnear ran under the seedy scheming of pirate captains who kept order because it was marginally more profitable than war in the streets. The gates of the city lay wide, an easy feat as one of the massive metal-bound doors was missing. *You'd have to be a desperate warlord to invade. There's little here worth stealing except trade goods, and those are in constant flux.*

The good news as far as Armitage went was Vhemin were tolerated here. Parnear was one of the few locations humans and monsters traded in uneasy peace. Meriwether didn't remember seeing Feybrind here before, the smell and noise far too much for their sensitivities. He shifted on Chesterfield's back to face Sight of Day. "Are you good?"

{I fear I'll never be good again.} Sight of Day gagged. *{How can you stand it?}*

"Smells like home and hearth. Chin up, cat." Armitage urged Beck forward. The bear growled at a merchant who strayed too close. The startled man picked up his feet and ran.

"I've fought Vhemin. Jousted men and women on the field of battle. Felt the Storm along my blade. Held glass and wore steel, doing the Three's will. Never did I think I'd be brought low by stench alone." Vertiline ran her hand through near-white hair.

"We should find a ship, and quickly." Geneve scanned the flock of gulls circling above. "No telling what'll land on us if we linger."

"Well, there's the thing." Meriwether tugged his ear. "Hiring a ship? I don't think that's how it'll work."

"Come again?" Armitage hauled Beck around. "That's why we're *here*, runt. A ship."

"Sure." Meriwether brightened up a smile, testing its gleam under the sun. "But why hire one? Too much risk. Out at sea, someone could toss us over the side, or sell us out to the Vide. We need a better plan."

{Oh, no.}

Meriwether's smile felt about the right level. "Oh, *yes*. We're getting into the shipping business."

THE TRICK WAS FINDING JUST THE RIGHT KIND OF SCUM WITH A perfect ship. Meriwether spent a good hour walking the docks. Ships eased against their moorings, the tide lifting them with a gentle hand. Geneve agitated at his side, hissing things like *Meri, we've got no time*, or, *Why are we here?*

Each time he'd said the same thing: *An hour here saves six hours or an easy death on the waves.*

He paused by a billboard. It offered jobs for hire, bounties on renegades, and want ads for crew. In the middle was something that took his fancy: a parchment almost untouched by the weather. He grabbed it, read it twice, then pocketed it.

It's not the ships, but the crews. Meriwether discarded the *Saratoga* for being the fat sow she was. Her crew wore bright clothes and seemed content with carrying linens north to south. *The Raven* looked a pretty hull, but her crew were hard, bright steel close at hand. Her captain had a shrewd nose, and the likes of him wouldn't make mistakes. A sleek vessel bearing the name *Stargazer* had promise, but was perhaps too small, her wooden skin too thin.

The *Chimera* seemed to fit. Her crew looked down in the mouth, with patched but not threadbare clothes. When Meriwether asked after the captain, there were shifty looks and sour twists of the lip. They'd been on hard times and asked to do harder things. The yoke didn't sit well on their shoulders. *Somme's not here.* Meriwether nodded his thanks, taking Geneve to the captain's last known location: a tavern called *The Bloody Fire*.

The Bloody Fire didn't live up to its name. It was underground, the hardpacked dirt of Parnear's streets giving way to a gloomy burrow only vipers would be comfortable in. The pair stepped over a drunk sailor passed out on the steps, Geneve's face puckering in distaste. "Meri, why are we here?"

"To get a ship. We've talked about this."

"We don't have enough money to buy one."

Meriwether paused before they reached the bottom of the steps. "Who said anything about buying one?" With that, he breezed through a flap of fabric demarcating outside from in, Geneve's protests behind him. *The Bloody Fire* oozed dockside tavern chic. The hapless fellow outside was merely a signpost to others within. The bar was a square affair, around which stood stools of various states of repair and occupancy. A few gentlemen were passed out on the bar top itself, half- or mostly-empty bottles nearby. The bartender was absent. It seemed likely they were on break, or perhaps their field of fucks needed re-sowing.

The walls held small alcoves adzed into the rock. Blankets and pillows tried to provide a tacky sort of comfort to occupants. Meri-

wether pointed to an occupied one at the rear right of *The Bloody Fire*.
"There."

"How do you know that man is the captain of the *Chimera?*"

It was a fair question. Meriwether sighed. "See how his skin is
tanned from the sun? Craggy, like a cliffside. Strong shoulders, and
arms like Armitage's. Used to working the waves, but above a belly
gone to fat, because he relies more on others for that work now."

Geneve nodded. "I see it."

"Good. No matter what happens, don't interfere." He headed over.
The *Chimera's* captain was dressed more opulently than his crew, but
unlike his crew he was passed out, dead drunk. Meriwether slid across
from the captain, kicking the man's boot.

The captain startled awake. "Whaa?"

"Hello, sir!" Meriwether kept his voice over bright, a shade too
loud. "Captain Somme? I understand you have a ship to sell."

Somme bestirred himself, big shoulders rolling as he floundered for
altitude. He glanced at Meriwether, then looked up at Geneve,
standing with her arms crossed, a black-armored bulwark. Eyes back to
Meriwether, he squinted. "No?"

"Yes," Meriwether insisted. "You've debts, my friend. You owe
Pirate Lord Rama twenty-thousand silver regals. Pirate Lord Amsen
insists you owe him a similar sum, but won't accept payment in
anything other than platinum solars due to the debasement of the local
currency. You're racking up more debts here, and I'm guessing you've
not a copper baron to your name."

Somme turned his squint to a glare. "Not for sale."

"A ship's a pricey thing, I'm sure." Meriwether examined his nails.
"Forty-thousand silver regals is more than the *Chimera's* worth, even
with the crew paid up, and they're not. Am I right, or am I right?"

The captain glared harder. "Still not for sale. I've got myself a
proposition that'll allow me to keep my ship, my crew, and assholes like
you far away."

"As I thought." Meriwether nodded his thanks, stood, and walked
away.

Geneve hurried to keep up. "What was that about?" She looked
back at Somme. "What just happened? Why were we here?"

"Gambling," Meriwether said, trying for an air of mystery. "A long bet against short odds. Now, let's find us a pirate lord."

AMSEN AND RAMA WEREN'T ON MERIWETHER'S MUST-SEE LIST. He instead wanted to speak to Pirate Lord Picotee, a woman whose reputation was almost unknown elsewhere. Meriwether heard last time he was in this neck of the woods Picotee had the largest house in Parnear Harbor.

"She rarely takes to the waves these days," Meriwether said, as he and Geneve wound up gently sloping dirt streets toward the large house atop Parnear's house refuse.

"And you know this how?"

"Last time I was here she made a bet with a young illusionist. Lost it, fair and square." He winked. "She and I got to talking while she had me strung up."

"Wait. You won the bet? Why'd she string you up?" Geneve wiped sweat from her brow.

Meriwether sympathized. The heat was ramping up, and she wore black armor. Still, the Knight made no comment of discomfort; her shoulders were square, spine unbowed by the mere throw of mother nature. "Picotee doesn't like to lose. Which is why," he fielded the paper from his pocket, "we're going to her."

"What's that?" Geneve's eyes narrowed in an overly-suspicious manner.

"It's a winning ticket. Trust me." Meriwether dodged around a cart laden with furs. "It's just up ahead."

Picotee's fortress was a vast sprawling estate. The main building was mud brick with vast windows overlooking the harbor. *Once you get used to the smell here, the view is spectacular.* White-capped blue as far as the eye could see. The estate was fenced with iron. Hardpacked dirt streets on the city side gave way to green manicured lawn within the fenced area. Rumor had it that Picotee had an army of slaves carry buckets up each day to water the grass.

That was, of course, ludicrous. She had a private well. Meriwether liked Picotee's style, despite her having him at knife point last time he was here. She could tell a good lie, almost like she believed it herself. Picotee's reputation was half teeth, half bark, and the marvel was not even Meriwether knew which was which.

The gate guard was a massive Vhemin wearing boiled leather. His cold-blooded kind didn't mind the heat at all. He held a pike ending in a blade as long as Meriwether's arm. The creature came to attention, pike lowering as Meriwether and Geneve approached along a narrow path. "Hold, humans! Unless you want to die, that is." He leered, snake eyes hard.

Meriwether held, but Geneve kept walking like the Vhemin and his pike were obstacles for other people. The monster, clearly used to casual slaughter, tried to stick her with the pointy end. She slipped around the thrust, grabbed the haft, and brought the blade of her armored hand against it. Wood snapped. The guard was left holding a stick with no point. Geneve flourished the pike's blade. The guard looked to the blade, then to his much less effective staff. "Do you have an appointment?"

Geneve tossed the blade aside with a clatter. "I do not."

"What she means is," Meriwether stepped between them, "we're here to speak with the Countess du Parnear. It's a matter of some urgency, involving waifs and strays. I'm sure you understand the critical nature of this, along with the sensitive need for secrecy."

Geneve leaned close to Meriwether's ear. "Countess?"

The guard measured Meriwether, gave a nod, and tossed his pike haft aside. "I'll get someone to take you up." He turned to the house, bellowing, "Dammel! Dammel, get your drunk ass out here! Some asshole wants to see the mistress."

Dammel, a *drunk ass* by the list in his bearing, arrived. He was a thin man, wisps of hair combed over an otherwise starkly bald pate. He had the dark skin of the Tebrani, but the clear blue eyes of the south. Alcohol might have tripped his feet, but his words were unslurred, those blue eyes missing nothing. "Ah. Meriwether. I'd hoped you might have had the common decency to die."

"The feeling's mutual. Is the countess in?" Meriwether straightened his shirt. "It's about a tattoo, a girl, and a lot of gold."

"She is. This way." Dammel waved them in.

"Countess?" Geneve asked again.

"Later," Meriwether said. "What happened to doing nothing, no matter what?"

"What happened to telling me what's going on?"

"Fair," Meriwether admitted. "Allow me a few secrets."

"A few?" Geneve's voice went up at least three octaves.

"One does not become a pirate lord of Parnear by accident." Meriwether grinned. "I told you, all royalty are scum."

Dammel led them through a well-tended garden festooned with guards and into the house itself. The entranceway was huge, the kind of thing Queen Morgan might have created if she was in exile. A wide staircase of imported elm wood took center stage. The drunk led them up. "The countess is enjoying the view after her morning constitutional."

"Countess?" Geneve didn't sound like she held much hope of an answer this time.

They made the second level, slipped through a huge room with couches and tables, and onto a balcony overlooking the grounds. Surrounded by seven guards, two of which were Vhemin and one Feybrind, was the Pirate Lord Picotee. The years had been kind enough, Meriwether supposed. She was still waif thin, with beautiful elfin features set in pale skin beneath hair black as raven's wings. A pixie-like smile lit on her lips. "Meriwether, you little cunt. I hoped you'd died."

"My Countess du Parnear." Meriwether bowed. "It's fortunate for you I didn't."

"I very much doubt that." The countess's eyes, green as sun-touched coastal waters, slipped from him to land on Geneve. "Who is your unlucky friend?"

"I'm not unlucky." Geneve looked the guards over, her face showing how lost at sea she was. "I don't think so, anyway."

"Ah. Honest enough. By her bearing, a soldier. By her stance, Tresward. And by her armor, fallen as low as you, you shit." Picotee's eyes landed on Meriwether. "I should have you killed."

"Probably," he agreed. "Before you murder me on a whim, I

thought we might share some wine. Talk over old times. Speak of things—"

"Get to the point."

Meriwether produced the flyer from his pocket with a flourish. "Behold."

Picotee's eyes landed on the parchment, lingering for the barest moment too long. "You bore me."

"If I may." Meriwether cleared his throat and read. "'Whomsoever shall find a maiden with ebony-black...' Hang about. 'Whomsoever?' Who wrote this? It was that ass-hat Dammel, wasn't it?"

Dammel coughed. "I don't know what you mean."

"Where was I? Here we go: 'Ebony-black hair and a trident birth-mark above her left ankle will bring her to Otto the Collector for a reward of ten-thousand platinum solars.'" He whistled. "Ten *thousand*. *Ten* thousand. That's a lot of solars."

Picotee's eyes went hard. "What do you want, Meriwether? I could have you put in a box and returned to your family."

"You could *try*," Geneve said. "Or you could talk to Meri. We're going there anyway."

"I've got this," Meriwether said. "I've really got this. Stop helping."

"You've got nothing," Picotee hissed, leaning forward, "except an active imagination and a death wish." Her movement disturbed the flowing cloth of her skirt, revealing a birthmark above her left ankle. It was a darker pink against her pale skin, and had the seeming of a trident.

"I've got a keen eye and a good memory." Meriwether rolled the parchment, tapping his chin with it. "Last time I was here, we got ... acquainted. During our ... conversation, I couldn't help but notice the birthmark on your leg. How is Ekua, by the by? Your daughter must be near full grown by now."

Picotee's guards burst into motion. A Vhemin hurled a spear at Meriwether, the other tossing a curved axe at Geneve. The Knight snatched the spear from the air and caught the axe in her other hand. Geneve spun, using the spear shaft as a bolas, dropping one of Pico-tee's human guards to the floor with a thump. Without looking, she jabbed the spear butt behind her, collecting Dammel in the solar plexus. The man had drawn a long thin knife, which he dropped along with the rest of his groaning self on the ground.

Geneve tossed the axe in a spin against the wall. It ricocheted off, bouncing into the back of a guard's skull. The woman dropped like a poleaxed steer. She vaulted Picotee, spear held horizontally, slamming into the Vhemin. The creatures were launched backward over the balcony rail, falling to the ground below.

The Knight turned, spear lancing out. The blade held a hair's breadth from Picotee's throat. The remaining four guards froze. Three had made it to Meri, and one stood between them, as if at a loss where to go. "Should I stop helping, Meri?"

"No, that was good." Meriwether untangled himself from his assailants. "Believe it or not, Picotee, we're here to help."

The countess's eyes were wide as she looked at the spear held against her neck. "This doesn't look like help."

"We need a ship." Meriwether tossed the parchment to the table. "You need your kid. We can work something out here."

"Why do you care?" Picotee growled.

"Because I know what it's like to be tossed out like trash too, Lady du Parnear. I've felt the ice wind as family falls far behind. You've made it good, here. A few loyal retainers from your days playing lady at an estate." Meriwether bent, helping Dammel up. "None of us deserve the hearts of people like these. Our blood's too blue and cold, but what can you do?"

"What'll it cost me? Do you want the solars?" She sneered, as if the spear blade at her neck were a feather.

"Do I look like I need the money?"

"Frankly, yes."

"Ah. Truth is a painful thing." Meriwether smoothed his borrowed shirt. "I don't want your coin, Picotee. One day, I want harmony and peace on the world. Before that, I need a ship, and to be on my way. Also, I want your daughter to not be kept hostage, or sold to a worse master."

Picotee nodded, but like her neck was full of rust, the motion painfully slow. "You want to do a good thing, to make up for all the bad." Her eyes turned sad. "I think I understand that."

"Maybe. But I really do need a ship." Meriwether sighed. "Here's how it is. Your daughter's aboard the *Chimera*. She's got a crew of twelve souls, docked here at harbor. Her captain's a drunk and a louse named Somme. He means to use Ekua as leverage, getting you to keep the blades of Amsen and Rama from his neck."

"You've told me everything and kept nothing for yourself." Picotee eyed the spear again. "Do you mean to kill me? You've no leverage, now."

"I don't need leverage."

Picotee laughed, despite the resolute bastion of Geneve beside her. "Of course you do. This is *Parnear* Harbor, du Reeves. It's *my* city. I own it, mud and all. What do you hold in reserve that could possibly get you the ship you want?"

"Oh, that's simple." Meriwether gave her a smile, small and honest. He'd saved it for times just like this. "You want to do something good to make up for all the bad, too."

⚓

THEY WAITED UNTIL NIGHTFALL, BECAUSE ONLY SUCKERS TRIED TO steal an entire ship in broad daylight. Geneve lingered at Meriwether's side. Her black armor seemed inky in the night. The Three watched from above. Cophine's pale face shone on waters gone still. If all went well, she wouldn't need to use her sword. It'd be a bloodless coup, and they'd have a ship.

Armitage had muttered *that's a special kind of wishful thinking we call lunacy out on the sands*, but Sight of Day gave Meriwether a half-smile. He'd said {*My friend, you'd save even the pirates from themselves,*} which felt weird, but there it was. Vertiline offered no opinion on the matter, returning to the sharpening of her blade. The five of them waited behind a low wall by the docks. The ships dotting the harbor were lit by lantern light. It looked like the sea was alive with fireflies.

"I guess it's time to go on stage." Meriwether pulled his cloak tighter.

Geneve held his arm. "Meri, I—"

"It's okay, Red." He looked into her eyes. There he saw focus, sure.

Dedication, honor, and a willingness to do what must be done. But also he saw concern, or a shading of fear. "*I'll* be okay."

"Will you?"

"I've survived eighteen long years without getting my fool self killed."

"That's because you've been around inbreds and amateurs," Armitage rumbled. "If you want to die, come see me. I'll square you away."

"I thought you weren't going to kill me this week."

"Always next week." The monster's snake eyes held no malice. Armitage ruffled Meriwether's hair with a massive hand. Meriwether felt the weight and strength there. *So much power. So misunderstood.* "If you get yourself into strife, call out. We'll just be over here, feeling useless."

"I *hate* standing still," Geneve said.

{I quite like it. Very peaceful.} Sight of Day stretched, then sat with his back against the wall. *{I've always thought if someone volunteers to die in your stead, you take them up on the offer.}*

It's go-time. Meriwether vaulted the wall, almost ending the night in an inglorious heap as his cloak snared on it. The fabric tore, and he managed to land on both feet. While not Feybrind-perfect, it was close enough for dirty work in the dark.

He walked down the docks, offering a nod to a man drinking wine from a throne made of coiled rope. Meriwether sidestepped a pile of fish guts, almost not noticing the smell over the general miasma of Parnear. The docks beneath his feet were weather-stained wood, hardened by salt and time. The gentle roll of the seas lifted the *Chimera*. The ship flew lanterns like her sisters in the bay. The gangplank was down, no guards at the base. *So far, so good.*

Meriwether walked up the boarding ramp, made the top deck, then stopped as the cold touch of steel pricked his throat. "You little fucker," hissed a man by his left ear.

Turning, but very slowly so's not to give the wrong impression, Meriwether took in the well-muscled form of Somme. "Hello, sir! I hear you have a ship to sell. I will give you ten thousand platinum solars for the *Chimera*."

Somme blinked. "You what?"

"Solars for sail. That's the bargain."

"You ... you sold me out to Rama!" The knife pressed against Meriwether's neck.

He backed away a half-step. "No, that's not quite right. I sold you out to Rama *and* Amsen. It's just M'lord Amsen hasn't caught up with you yet." Meriwether gently pushed the knife away from his throat. "Now, where is it? Ah, there it is." He set off.

"Where do you think you're going?" Somme caught up with him about two steps too late. Meriwether had his hand on the ship's storm bell and managed three hard rings before Somme grabbed his shoulder, slugging him across the jaw.

Meriwether landed on the deck, hard. He tasted blood and fear. Somme's knife thirsted, the steel glinting in Cophine's gaze. "I'll gut you!"

A *hiss-chunk* marked the arrival of an arrow, pinning Somme's hand to the bell mast. The knife clattered to the deck, and the captain bellowed in pain. Meriwether stood, retrieved the knife, then gave the bell another five loud rings. He wiped bloody drool from his lip, then yanked the arrow from the bell mast.

Somme screamed.

"This is a present from a friend of mine." Meriwether examined the arrow. "It's quite exquisitely made. Better than human artisans can produce for a quick copper baron. The Feybrind make everything well. Arrows, swords, clothes, and friends." He let the arrow drop to the deck.

A few sailors arrived, alerted by the storm bell's ring. Meriwether waited until the full crew compliment was here. He stood on the deck of a might-be-pirate ship ringed by ten uncertain faces. He saw no calm there. No level heads ruled the opposing forces. That was okay; he didn't need level heads. Anger and fear would work better here.

"I've come to buy this ship, and with it, her crew." Meriwether reached beneath his cloak, slow enough to not generate undue excitement, and pulled free a sovereign. He let the gold drop to the deck by the arrow. All eyes followed it, rather than focusing on Somme's mewling. "I appreciate loyalty can't be bought." Another sovereign, more lost gold at his feet. "But it can be squandered. It's a fickle currency understood by only a few." Meriwether let two more sovereigns drop.

"He's leaking gold," laughed a gap-tooth man with sunburned skin. This got a chortle.

"Aye." Meriwether let more gold tinkle to the deck. "I'll wager it's more than you've seen in a long while, while your captain amasses debts to go with his hangover, no?" That got a few sober nods and thoughtful looks. "You've got to wonder what kind of stash he's got squared away against the debtor's ledger."

"I pay my debts," Somme hissed, hulking over Meriwether.

"Do you want to get shot again?"

"I ... no."

"Then back up. No, keep going. That's right, about there." Meriwether waited until Somme was five meters back. He scanned his audience. *There. That one.* A woman with hair faded to rust by the sun, with dark eyes that'd seen more than they cared to. "Hello, sailor."

"I ain't your—"

"I'm Meriwether." *Don't push. Don't goad.* "There's a pirate lord who owns this town. Aye, aye, I know you may never come back here. A wind at your back's as good an escape as any. I've tried the trick myself, and yet Parnear called me back anyway. There's a curious thing about this city not many know. It's ruled by the pirate lords."

"Rama, Amsen, and Picotee," a nut-brown man said.

"Three for three," Meriwether agreed. "What many don't know is there's a prince among equals there. Or, perhaps, a countess. Picotee comes from a family with blood blue as the seas. Before she staked her claim atop the hill," he cast his arm toward her mansion, "I knew her as a clever girl learning tricks from a mother hard and cruel. Her family and mine go back, and then back some more."

"Bullshit," the nut-brown man said.

"It makes excellent manure." Meriwether scratched his beard. "Picotee is the Countess du Parnear. The curious thing, friends, isn't her name, but a singular trait of the women in her family. When I was five or so—she's older than me, don't let her youthful looks fool you— she showed me her left ankle." Meriwether turned to the rust-haired woman, her eyes growing more haunted with each word. "They carry a birthmark. It's a trident of sorts. Picotee has it, and so does her daughter Ekua."

"Three's mercy," rust-hair whispered.

"Roya? What do you know of this?" The nut-brown man stepped forward. "What's this stranger mean?"

Roya scrubbed rust-red hair from her face. "We're all going to die, Jan."

"Maybe not. Picotee loves me like a brother," he lied smoothly, pointing to Somme. "All she wants is this man, and her daughter Ekua returned."

Nut-brown Jan squinted. "We've no Ekua here."

"That's not true, is it Roya?" Meriwether gave an encouraging nod. "You've seen her."

"Captain's quarters," the woman whispered. "Wasn't supposed to go in, but I needed the key to the supply room, and..."

"There's no fault of yours," Meriwether said. "Not if you hand her over. Picotee might have been a countess once, but she's a pirate lord now, and she'll murder you all without a second thought if her daughter's harmed."

"Lies," Somme hissed.

"There's the matter of a reward," Meriwether added. "Ten thousand platinum solars." He made a show of turning. "Ten crew. A thousand platinum solars apiece. With that, you could go your way. Or stay. I mean to take the ship, but I'm no slaver. I'll only take honest workers, for honest pay. People who want a stake in the cargo, and a say in which winds we take. After one tiny, insignificant job's squared away, that is."

Jan turned to the captain, expression thoughtful, then slugged him in the gut. As Somme bent over, the nut-brown man hammered him across the jaw. Three of his fellows rushed forward, grabbing Somme by arms and legs.

They marched the captain off. He began struggling when he saw the hard face of Picotee at the base of the gangway. Or perhaps it was the ready blades of her men. Meriwether winced when his scream cut short. He faced Roya. "First mate Roya—"

"I'm no first mate."

"Welcome to your first field promotion. I really do need to have Ekua. She probably misses her mother very much." Meriwether held his hand out, palm up. *After you.* "Please take me to her."

The captain's cabin spanned the width of the stern, large windows looking out on the not-quite-majesty of Parnear. Huddled on herself, a raggedy blanket pulled close, sat a young woman. Thirteen, not a day older, with dark eyes, raven's wing hair, and pale skin. Her ankle held the muddy smudge of a trident. Meriwether walked to her, stopped a couple paces away, then crouched. "Hello, Ekua. Do you remember me?"

The girl shook her head. "Are you going to sell me?"

"No. I'm here to take you home." He nodded to the windows. "It's a special fashion of cruelty to see your mother's hearth and be unable to reach it. Come. She's outside." Meriwether held his hand out for Ekua. The girl took it, and he led her past Roya to the deck outside.

Picotee stood with tear-bright eyes, her face so brittle it might shatter at the lightest touch. Meriwether wondered what went on behind her eyes. *Show no weakness. We both learned that. And yet, by the Three, this is her daughter.* Picotee held a longblade, the length of it wet, almost black under the starry sky.

Ekua ran to her mother. Picotee swept her into her arms, hugging her daughter fiercely. Meriwether waited, looking over the sea. Minutes passed before Picotee joined him at the rail. "Du Reeves."

"My Lady du Parnear."

She laughed, the sound as brittle as her face had been. "Not for a long, long time."

"The world's changing, Picotee. Might come a time when we need the du Parnear family back in their residence."

"And what would your father say about that?" She offered no emotion with the words.

"I'm not sure I care." Meriwether sighed. "Perhaps a du Parnear in their home is too much to ask. Just, next time..." He trailed off.

"Ask your boon."

"Maybe don't try to cut out my liver."

A pause, then she laughed. "You've not changed, Meriwether. The world has, but you're the same. All armor of wit around a soft heart that's unready for this time. People like you don't survive." The breath gusted out of her, a shuddering gale of relief. "Thank you for giving me back my daughter. I will never, for all time, forget this."

He nodded. "You'll spare the crew, as we discussed?"

"They've done no wrong. Our bargain holds. The *Chimera* is yours. Ten thousand platinum solars, to be given to the crew. Your life, and your friends, and forever passage to Parnear, for as long as my word holds as law."

That last wasn't part of the bargain, but Meriwether didn't argue. "Thank you."

"Do you love her?"

He turned, startled. "Who?"

Picotee nodded, wistful. "Aye. I see it in you. You fear the color of your blood will drench her in sin." She pushed away from the rail like a ship launching. "Don't worry. Your blood might be blue, but you're nothing like the dirty rest of us."

Meriwether stood gaping at Picotee's back as the pirate lord strode away. The once Lady du Parnear draped her arm about Ekua, walking her daughter from the decks of the *Chimera*.

After Picotee left, Geneve strode up the gangplank, eyes hard until they spotted Meriwether. She hurried to his side. "Are you well? Your lip is bleeding."

"It's nothing." He winced as she grabbed his chin, turning his face to Cophine's light. "I'm fine!"

Geneve growled. "Stop being a baby and let me see." After a few moments, she let her hand fall. "You saved a pirate lordling tonight. Was that wise?"

"I'm not sure." Meriwether considered the question as he watched the crew open a longbox. Within, ten long, shining platinum fingers. They laughed as they distributed their wealth. "But I think so. It's things like this that show the Three what they bought when they saved the world."

Chapter Fourteen

Of course there was a party.

The whole town was invited, or that's what it felt like to Geneve. She'd never seen so many people so drunk before in her life. Parnear Harbor was in the business of trade, including many fine Trebani liquors, and it seemed more than a little of that largess was up for consumption tonight.

I guess it's not every day you get reunited with your family. Admit it, you're just jealous. Geneve turned a half-drunk goblet in her hands, feeling the slight relaxation as the ale took hold of her thoughts. *I wanted to sail on the first tide, but Meri said we should stay.* The illusionist had said *you never know where your next friend's coming from*, and it made a certain sense, but it also cost them time.

Geneve could feel an urgency the ale couldn't take away. The need to escape the Vide, or dispatch their leader. The *wanting* feeling inside attached to her displacement in the world. She was without Tresward, and above all, without Iz.

My father, why didn't you tell me? Geneve huddled in a dark corner designed for brooding. An awning blocked her view of the Three above. The table before her was empty of friends, but had a jug of ale waiting for her to finish what was in her cup. She sat by a large square that might have been for merchants to display wares, but was used for the business of celebrating. Fires burned. Meat sizzled on spits. In the center, Parnear citizens danced in various stages of drunkenness. Geneve spied guards strolling about, all with tankards, cares set aside for the night.

Picotee was seated on a raised platform along with two other pirate lords. Geneve didn't know which was Rama or Amsen and couldn't work up the enthusiasm to care. She spied Ekua near her mother, the girl's cheeks dimpled with laughter. If there were dark thoughts behind her eyes, Geneve couldn't see them.

She envied the girl. *You've still got at least one parent. All mine are dust.*

Through the throng Geneve spied a familiar face. Pale Vertiline navigated the revelers with expertise won through long hours in the training room and battlefield. The Chevalier nodded to some, smiled at others, and glared once or twice at those whose hands got too close to hip or buttock. Hands were retracted, because while Tilly held a mug in her hand, the sheathed blade at her hip reminded any with eyes to see what she was.

Geneve wondered where Vertiline headed. *Does she need quiet?* The Chevalier's course circumnavigated the throng, stopping by a spitted pig. She spoke with the vendor, negotiating for a platter heaped with steaming meat. Mug on that, she balanced the platter on her stump, holding it steady with her hand, then strode straight for Geneve.

Vertiline stepped around empty tables, depositing the platter before Geneve. "Eat."

"I'm not hungry."

"Don't be stupid. You're always hungry." Vertiline speared a piece of smoking pork with her dagger, popping it into her mouth. "This is beyond good."

"Okay, I'm a little hungry." Geneve's stomach growled despite what her heart thought was best. She drew her own knife, helping herself to the meat. It was moist and juicy, the crackling perfect and crispy. "Oh, my. Who knew pirates could cook so well?"

"I imagine it's to do with seaboard rations. Works up an appetite for the finer things once you're ashore." Vertiline munched. "Why the sour face?"

"I'm brooding."

"I can see that. Anything in particular? I've a few things on my mind. I could help you."

"Help me brood?"

"Exactly so." Tilly watched the crowd whirl. The people were all brightly-colored clothes and smiles, laughter and joy. Only a few knew what the fuss was about. Picotee hadn't let it known her daughter was missing, so a party celebrating her return was surprising to many but no one turned down free ale. "You know how Iz and I joined the Tresward?"

"Knights are inducted young, and you—"

Vertiline snorted. "Not at all. We served a lord before the Tresward. Both our blades were steel, our armor ordinary. Young, aye, I'll not deny that. He was a man at arms while I was still in training. You'd never seen such use of steel." Her eyes went distant. "Knights came to town. They were on the trail of a sinner, or other great injustice. Three, as there always are."

"Did you pick a fight?"

"Me? No." Vertiline nibbled more pork. "Neither did Iz. Respectful as he always was. Asked about joining the Tresward. Told them he saw their cause as just and wanted to raise arms to champion the Three." She looked at the table, or perhaps her stump resting on it. "There were a lot of problems. The lord didn't want to let us go. Leastways, not Israel; he was the best of his men. He disarmed all who came against him, not injuring a single one. I think that's what convinced the Knights to take him with them. Me, also."

"But you didn't want to join?" Geneve considered while chewing.

"Oh, I did. But for all the wrong reasons." Tilly's breath shuddered out a sigh. "It's taken me a long time to realize it, you see. I was in love, Gen. I was in love."

"With Iz?" Geneve blinked.

"Aye. Perhaps I worshiped his use of steel, or fancied his manner. But really, it was his looks. Never has a man had a jawline like his." She tried for a smile, but her lips only turned down. "So, we joined up. Both excellent blademasters. The training was harder, because we were a little older, but never have you seen someone get the call of the Light as fast as Israel." Vertiline rubbed her eyes. "The Storm came to him easy as breathing. But our pasts aren't as easily let go. There was another woman. Always was, if I'm honest."

"Oh, Tilly." Geneve grabbed the other woman's forearm. "His heart was spoken for?"

"No. That was the bitterest seed of all." Vertiline unbound her braid, single hand moving slowly like it didn't know the moves without its twin. "He'd had trysts. No harm in that. But he kept coming back for one woman in particular. After he'd worn the tabard of a Knight, she ... well, she had you."

"But Knights can't procreate." Geneve sighed. "I ... *remember* pieces of it. I've seen him and my mother. It was impossible."

"You've unleashed a dragon. Seen Vhemin and Feybrind working together. A sinner became your friend, perhaps your closest one. How many impossible things do you need to see before you realize it's a label for things we don't understand?" Vertiline's voice held no hard edges. "He didn't love her, but he loved you. He loved you more than the Three."

"He didn't—"

"I was *there*, Geneve. He came to me. Said he needed to get you out. That he'd done something horrible. He'd sinned—"

"By making me—"

"No. Never that." Vertiline's hand closed over Geneve's. "He regretted the act, but never the consequence. I was the person he told. His closest friend. And when it came to glass and blood, I was there. The lord came for him. The village wanted the money from your sale. It was ghastly. Iz was so *angry*, Geneve. I've never seen him like that, before or since. That they would sell his daughter."

"He never told me anything." Geneve rubbed tears from her face. *Where did they come from?* "He—"

"He couldn't. There were three people alive who knew the truth. Iz, me, and Justiciar Ambrose. It was the chains that tethered Iz to the Tresward. I couldn't ask if he wanted to leave. I couldn't ask if he wanted to love." She stood, jerked upright like a marionette. Vertiline's chair slid back. She leaned forward, hand on Geneve's shoulder. "Don't leave it too late." And like that, she was gone, all pale hair and beautiful form, weaving back to the dancers. Perhaps looking for someone to share the night with. Or just to forget.

Geneve looked into her cup, surprised to find it empty. She poured more, gulped ale, then more again. *People say it helps you forget, or makes the remembering easier.* Parties were supposed to be fun, not maudlin affairs. *But then, I've not had much experience with parties. I've spent my life serving gods who've yet to thank me once.*

She caught sight of a familiar face. Meriwether was dragged to the platform where the pirate lords sat. He laughed, ale in hand, and gave an outrageously low bow to Ekua, hand out for a dance. Euka wasn't having any of it, but Picotee stood, lips moving, no doubt telling Meri how many of his babies she'd have. She felt the green lick of jealousy in her belly, souring the ale, so she drank more.

Stop it. Meri's business is his own.

Besides, it's not like Geneve and Meri were a match. They'd whispered no words of love to each other. He was from a different world. Not the magical one—his knowledge on that score was perhaps as incomplete as hers. But Meriwether was a du Reeves, a noble from a long line of nobles. His father's estates spanned the north. He came from wealth, power, and influence. Just like Picotee.

And just like the pirate lord, they'd fallen from grace. Meriwether du Reeves and Picotee du Parnear moved among a circle of clapping onlookers, dancing together. Their steps were, if not perfect, at least in sync. They knew the dance, the twists and turns, and how the end was laid out.

I'm just a warrior. Not a noble. I'll never be a part of his world. As Geneve watched, she drank, which made her want to watch more, and the circle turned ever on. The dance wasn't even that long, Meri and Picotee parted with a bow, a laugh, a touch. *He's eyes for the gentle lilied ladies. Meri would never like someone like me. The Tresward made me strong.*

They made me so no one else would want me.

She turned, eyes blind with tears, stumbling from her table, and her brooding. She headed up the hill, away from the light, and the laughter. Geneve wanted to be somewhere dark, hide herself in a shroud of her past, and ... forget. Or be forgotten.

But it's never that easy, is it?

GENEVE DROWNED. IT FELT LIKE WATER BUT SHE KNEW SHE LAY IN A sea of guilt. Riptide had her, and wanted to consume her whole.

Her friends were there, but dead or dying already. Geneve felt desperation and relief. Desperate she couldn't help them. Relief she hadn't had to watch like last time. Sight of Day's golden eyes stared sightlessly upward. Armitage's roar was enfeebled by exhaustion.

Meri was with her too. He clutched a raft made of her dreams. Geneve thought he might have been trying to stop himself from drowning, but she realized he was holding them together. As the water closed over his head, he gave a last push, sending the bundle of hopes toward her. Geneve grasped at them, but she could see why Meri couldn't stay afloat.

My dreams are made of nothing but starlight. There's nothing to them.

The clouds above parted, and she saw a huge shape. With a massive wingspan, black against the night, the dragon soared above. She watched it flap toward the shore, leaving her behind. Runes glowed on the armored ridges about its head, but it didn't look at her. It was leaving her to drown.

Geneve wanted to scream, *Help me!* But all she got was a mouthful of salt and guilt. She thrashed, the water dragging her down.

I need to watch. Where is the dragon going? She had trouble seeing, because it was so dark, and she kept falling below the water's surface. But a mighty gout of flame scorched the heavens. The dragon breathed fire, roaring defiance. Roaring its pain.

It landed with a crunch atop a crenelated tower, wings raised for balance. It seemed to see her for the first time, raising its head to breathe another blast of fire at the sky. The blaze illuminated the keep it sat on. The keep rested on the slopes of a gentle hill, surrounded by trees. Farmland spread around, and the forms of hundreds of workers.

Those aren't workers. They're Vhemin. The dragon was encircled by monsters. All eyes were on it.

But the dragon didn't look at the scaled creatures. Glowing eyes found Geneve's across the distance. It spoke with the voice of gods and angels.

//THE THREE CANNOT HOLD THE WORLD'S SHAPE. THEY LIE IN DARKNESS, WHILE YOU WALLOW IN FAILURE. THIS PLANET WILL CRACK IF THE HAMMER HITS IT AGAIN.//

GENEVE WOKE WITH A SCREAM, HANDS CLAWING WATER THAT NO longer surrounded her. She blinked back brilliant daylight, not the darkness of the nightmare.

She lay in a gutter. Drool and vomit spattered her cotton shirt. Her hair was matted with filth. She had no blade. Folk of the city walked by, some with an understanding nod, others with studious avoidance.

Where am I? Geneve was in a street that headed up. Above, Picotee's house. Below, the waves, and the waiting *Chimera*.

She scrambled to her feet. Geneve had to find Meri. They had to go, and *now*. It was almost too late. Head pounding, stomach churning, she lurched uphill. To get into Picotee's house, and find the friend of her heart. Geneve couldn't do this alone.

Chapter Fifteen

Meriwether had been hungover before. This felt nothing like those times. His body shook, his breath rasping in and out. And that was before he opened his eyes, which revealed a party landscape of epic proportions. Revelers, passed out in various stages of revelry from *one-ale-too-many* through to *where-did-those-goats-come-from.*

He rose and hit his head on wood. It was unkind, but no less than he deserved. *I'm under a table.*

Meriwether scrabbled out from under his cover, listing in the breeze that blew fetid air from across the city. *I hope Parnear gets cleaned up. This place could be pretty, if you gave it half a chance. Now, where are my boots?*

The main square was full of clothing, but he liked his boots. He found them under a comatose woman, pulled them on, and looked about for his friends. Armitage was sprawled backward on a table. Sight of Day wasn't anywhere to be seen, but getting the Feybrind drunk was tricky. They worked through alcohol faster than even the Vhemin, a surprising thing as they tended to drink spirits rather than ale. *He'll turn up. Where's Red?*

Geneve wasn't anywhere to be seen. He found Vertiline by way of her white mane. Her hair unbound lent her face a softness he hadn't seen before, and Meriwether wondered what she might have become if the Tresward hadn't got her murdering innocents all over Or'sen. Still, pale Vertiline wasn't Geneve, and as his heart picked up its pace, he realized what his hangover hid.

Fear. You're afraid. You woke up drowning in it, and it's only the hangover that's kept you from gibbering like a fool.

He found a half-drained tankard and finished it off. Luke-warm ale wasn't his favorite, but it'd steady the nerves. Meriwether turned, eyed Picotee's house, and thought, *I wonder if she's gone to pay her respects to our host?*

It didn't account for the gut-watering fear that chewed the nape of his neck, but it made a little sense. He jogged in that direction, unable to make a run because only fools ran uphill, or while hungover.

He made it to Picotee's residence before catching Geneve up. She was embroiled with the gate guard, who was human not Vhemin, but still as angry as three bears. Geneve wasn't in armor; she was dressed in what might have been her white cottons from yesterday, except these looked like someone dragged her through a freshly plowed field after the rains.

"Red!" She spun at his voice, the anger leaving her face for relief. He felt the fear leave him too. Meriwether kept his jog up, running into her arms. He pulled her close. *Steady on, lad. No harm done, why the overreaction?* Geneve hugged him right back though, so he enjoyed that until he realized that either he, or she, smelled like a midden. Meriwether pulled back. "Are you okay? Only, I had a dream, and—"

"You're not inside?" She looked between the guard and Meri, as if trying to work out if this was a vile Vide trick.

"Why would I be?" Meriwether scratched his beard. *It could use a wash. Just like the rest of you.*

"We have to go, Meri." Geneve cast a glance at Picotee's mansion. "I thought you'd be with Picotee."

"No. Fastest way to get knifed in your sleep." Meriwether eyed the gate guard. "I didn't mean that personally. Some of my best friends are mercenaries, payed to murder people for coin."

"Take your friend and get lost," the guard suggested. His voice was surprisingly light for a man so large. "Picotee's not accepting visitors today."

"Very well." Meriwether steered Geneve away from the gate, then turned on his heel. "Would you give her our regards?"

The guard squinted, trying to measure Meriwether for deceit before giving a nod. "I'll let her know you didn't piss on her name, sure."

"My thanks." Meriwether pointed them downhill. "Have you seen Sight of Day?"

"I dreamed he was dead."

The comment lay between them for half a block. "I'll take that as a no."

"Meri, we need to hurry. I saw a castle atop a crenelated keep. Rolling farmland surrounded it. It held counsel with trees, and the ocean was at its doorstep." He slowed. Geneve rolled on a few more paces, noticed he wasn't with her, and stopped. "What is it?"

"The bay leading to the keep. Was it the shape of a crescent moon?" Meriwether ran a hand through knotty hair. "Did the trees seem cool and welcoming in the heat of day?"

She gave a slow nod. "Exactly so."

"Ah." Meriwether caught up with Geneve, and they continued downhill. "That's my father's grounds. You dreamed it, you say?"

"The dragon was there. It was so very angry with me." Her voice was a husk of its usual self. "What did we do at the temple? I don't remember."

"Nothing good. And I don't think *we* did anything. The temple did—"

"The world's going to break again, and the Three aren't here to hold it together anymore." Geneve had desperation in her voice. "The dragon's calling me. I *feel* it, me the anchor at the end of a chain."

"It could be the anchor. It's bigger, no?" Meriwether squinted at the sky. The sun's position said it was after nine. Next tide wouldn't be for a couple of hours. "Come on."

"You have a plan?"

"I do. We're going to find a bath, breakfast, and get to our ship. Time to see if any pirates stayed to help us with the sails."

THEY FOUND A BATHHOUSE, COMPLETE WITH SCENTED SOAPS. Meriwether wrestled with his beard using the trimming accoutrements provided, then entered a steaming tub. He soaped himself to a lather, rinsed, then did it again. *No telling how long it'll be between baths.*

A few coins to a handy lad at the door had him fetch fresh clothes. *White cottons for the Knight, and whatever's available for me.* Clothes were laid out for him when he finished toweling off. They were better than his usual fare. Pants about the right length for a change, a linen shirt, and a cloak with a red velvet lining. He tossed this last over his arm, because the air was too warm for velvet fripperies, then headed into the bathhouse reception. He intended to wait for Geneve, but he collided with her exiting her bath chamber.

"I beg pardon." He bowed.

Her lip quirked. "It was my mistake, I ... Oh. Meri." She looked him up and down.

"What is it? Is my shirt inside out?" He double-checked himself. No, the shirt was on right, and of a good fit besides. He looked back to her and found it was his turn to gawp. Her hair was cut short, a lock falling over one eye. *By the Three, she's beautiful. Get your shit together and don't stare.*

"No. The shirt is good." She linked arms with him. "Come now. You promised breakfast."

This close to her, he smelled not the usual sword and armor oil, but rosewater and lavender. Breakfast was going to be distracting.

THE LATE MORNING TIDE WAITED FOR NO ONE. THEY FOUND THE *Chimera*, First Mate Roya already bellowing orders to *haul sail* and *castoff* and other such mariner terms. Sight of Day was in the crow's nest, and he offered them a friendly wave. *{I've never been on a human ship before. I think we're going to drown.}* The cat seemed happy enough about the prospect.

Meriwether capped his eyes with a hand, grinning at the cat. *{Try* *not to fall to your death, then. It'll take all the excitement out of your watery grave.}*

The Feybrind half-smiled. *{I'm positive me falling would be as unlikely as finding a unicorn belowdecks. Still, I appreciate the advice.}*

Armitage strode from the captain's cabin, scratching an armpit. "What kept you assholes?"

"Were you in my room?" Meriwether glanced at the door to the great cabin.

"No, I was in my room—"

"If anyone's getting the captain's cabin, it's me." Geneve stuck her chin out. "Would you like to fight me for it, monster?"

"Not particularly. I already put all your shit in there, anyway." Armitage raised an eyebrow in Meriwether's direction. "*All* your shit, sacks and all."

"Best we save a few mysteries for the voyage." Meriwether clapped. "Where's Vertiline?"

"Practicing," Armitage growled. "Beat me like a toy drum, then went to work on the rest of the crew." He eyed Geneve. "You sure she can't use that Storm bullshit?"

Geneve's smile fell. "I'm sure."

"Well, fuck me. She's the second best swordswoman I've ever met." He ambled off, hitching his pants.

"Let's see what state he left our ... *the* cabin in." Meriwether navigated around troubled waters with a breezy smile, hand out in an *after you* gesture. Geneve headed aft, entering the great cabin.

Inside was, contrary to the horrors Meriwether's mind conjured, spotless. It wasn't the first time he'd been here, but last time the shadow of Ekua's capture and Somme's intent held sway. A table took center stage, laden with all manner of charts and mapping tools. It smelled of caulked wood, the sea, and better times. A hammock swung, empty, near big windows overlooking the stern. A pile of equipment lay against a wall, and in there—*blessed be the Three, I guess*—was the sack Meriwether carted from Ravenswall. Also there was Geneve's black armor, ancient helmet, blade, and scattergun. She touched each thing in turn, hair falling over her face.

"Are you okay, Red?" Meriwether took a step closer, then lost the wind in his sails.

"I am. Or I will be." She laid gentle fingers on the sack he'd brought, but didn't open it. Respecting his privacy, or uninterested? *I hope it wasn't a waste to bring it.* "Can you ... give me a moment? There are things I need to think of."

Ah, fuck. "Of course." Meriwether closed the door behind him, colliding with Armitage as he made the deck. "Good morning."

"It's really not. Me and the cat had to coax four horses and a fucken *bear* onto this death trap. They're in the hold, and not happy about it."

"Good work." Meriwether clapped the monster on the shoulder. "Let's get moving. Where's Roya?"

PARNEAR SPARKLED LIKE A WHITE JEWEL ON THE SEA'S CROWN behind them. Ahead, coastline and blue ocean. Gulls cawed above, keeping easy pace with their ship. The cloudless sky gave warmth aplenty, and the sailing looked easy enough. Three days, and they'd reach Whisperwind Port.

Meriwether stood at the bow, the touch of sea spray on his face. He wanted to revel in the surge and dive of the ship. *It's my hangover that's the problem. It's sucking the joy from life.*

A convenient enough fiction, but it held all the truth of his illusions. Meriwether felt cold right to his core, because the morning's fear hadn't left him. He just wasn't sure what he should be afraid of.

Ah, that's the problem. I've been with a Knight's protection so long, I've forgotten the simple truth. I should be afraid of everything.

Chapter Sixteen

On the second day, they attacked from the light.

The sun lay like a band of orange flame across the water. It was rising, the eastern horizon afire with the colors of creation. Geneve stood at the stern, watching the dawn elation of the Three, their reminder to all peoples of the world each morning: *we made this for you.*

Sight of Day landed cat-perfect by her side. *{Hello, Daughter of the Three.}*

"You're up early."

{Actually, I'm up late. I do not like the water. While there's many a rumor that cats can't swim, the truth is we're excellent at it. We don't like getting wet.} He gave her a half-smile, teeth glinting in dawn's barrage.

"And here you are, on a ship."

From the mid-deck a burly sailor bellowed, "Hands off cocks, you miserable shits! Get up here, or your breakfast is going overboard."

{Truth, but it's the pleasant company I cherish.}

Geneve laughed. "You're on the wrong vessel, then."

{It's the right vessel—} And with a *hiss-chunk*, he was gone.

Geneve spun. Where Sight of Day had been was empty space. Her mind told her someone couldn't disappear, and yet, the Feybrind was missing.

Another *hiss-chunk* was followed by a scream. Geneve whirled again, spotting a sailor nailed to the mainmast by a harpoon. The wooden shaft thrummed, the woman's hands around it, face a mixture of agony and surprise. Geneve followed the harpoon's shaft for direction and was blinded by the sun.

They're attacking from there. "Ware!" she screamed, vaulting the railing and landing on the deck. She rolled, stayed low, and came to rest behind a water barrel. Now she had a lower vantage, the railing obscuring some of the sun's light, she saw a small skiff on the water. While she didn't know much about boats, this one looked built for speed: lots of sail, but a small body. It had a pair of harpoon launchers on the deck, a small crew winding windlasses to take another shot.

Armitage came from belowdecks. He carried a massive mattock and an expression that said *I'm murdering the motherfucker who woke me.* Geneve yelled, "Armitage! Sight of Day went overboard!"

The monster took in her position, the crewwoman nailed to the mast, the skiff, and then dropped his mattock. He sprinted for the *Chimera's* side away from the skiff, diving over and into the salty water below. Geneve wondered if the waves' chill would kill him, cold-blooded as he was. *Focus. He's looking after the fallen. You've got to see to the living.*

Vertiline stormed from below. She made the deck, turned, and ran for the skiff side. She jumped, long arms and legs pinwheeling, before being lost from Geneve's view. *I need a weapon.* Geneve fetched a fallen saber from the impaled crewwoman, grabbed a rope, and ran for the side. She jumped, swinging over the ocean.

The railing disappeared behind her. Below, cold blue waited. She saw the skiff approaching as she swung. Her stomach was left behind. Ahead, she saw pale Vertiline, blade bared, a pirate already dead at her feet. Geneve let go her rope and fell. Time held her in its cupped hands, then her feet hit foreign decking. She rolled with it, saber still in hand, blade flashing in the light.

A pirate came at her, salt dreadlocks a madness about her face. Geneve's saber took her throat, arm, and left leg in three short strikes.

The saber in her hand was poorly made, a weapon of last resort sold by bargain artisans needing easy coin. But Geneve felt the weight of it, how it might balance if she put its point to the deck and let go.

A man winching the harpoon swiveled to her, firing. Geneve side-stepped, feeling the rush of wind. Vertiline's blade caught the dawn light, then sprayed red as she cut the harpoon operator from shoulder to hip, severing his spine in the process. Her original opponent was struggling to put his intestines back into his belly.

Geneve threw her saber, the curved blade lodging into the injured man's skull. She fetched a harpoon from the deck. Four remained on deck below them, but the fo'castle was clear. Two men and two women waited for their doom but didn't approach. They had the look of desperate folk. "Ho, sister! How many?"

"I count these four only." Vertiline's long braid whipped, like her very hair was angry.

Geneve threw her harpoon. It tore through the chest of a man, Light glimmering along its length. "Three."

Vertiline vaulted the railing, landing on the deck between the other three. Geneve snatched her saber, following her friend. Vertiline stood, slender and perfect, as her attackers besieged her. The Chevalier moved like water and the wind, elements that loved each other, her eyes closed, head cocked like she listened for the Three's word.

Geneve landed beside a man, taking his head off through the guard of his steel. Her saber held the Storm, the length stronger, forged of the Three's will. His steel crumpled like tissue, blade slumped like melted wax as it glowed with remembered heat. Vertiline's lunge took a woman through the heart, and she dropped, face holding surprise to the end.

One man remained. He looked to them, then turned for the railing. Geneve's saber toss took him in the back of the head as he reached the railing, and he tumbled over, lost with a splash.

Vertiline grinned, feral. "You need to stop throwing away your weapons."

"The work's done." Geneve stood, listening, but heard nothing else. Then, above the soft *slurp* of water against a strange hull, she heard the clash of steel. "The *Chimera!*"

Vertiline sheathed her blade, and together they ran up to the fo'castle, then leaped to the *Chimera's* side. Geneve's fingers clawed like fishhooks, and she scrambled to the deck. She reached down, grabbing Vertiline's upraised stump, hauling her sister of the blade to the deck beside her.

The door to the great cabin burst open, and two Meris stumbled out. They both wore the same linen shirt and held identical knives. Geneve glanced between them. They circled, wary as starving dogs.

Vertiline swept blade from sheath but held her position by the rail. "Which is which?"

Geneve held her hand out. Tilly gave Geneve her sword. Geneve flourished the blade, raised it to catch the light, and threw it. It took one Meri in the side of the head, dropping him to the deck.

The other Meri looked at the fallen, then to her, mouth open. "How did you ... what if he was me? I mean, I was him?"

Vertiline raised an elegant eyebrow. "Because only *you* talk like that, sinner." She retrieved her blade.

Geneve paced to Meri's side, checking him for cuts. "Are you hurt?"

"I'm fine." He winced as her fingers found a cut on his arm. "Okay, I'm mostly fine. How did you know?"

She squeezed his arm. "I know your face, but I know your heart better. I know the sound your feet make as they tread the world. I will always know you." Geneve left his wide-eyed expression, heading to the opposite railing.

Below, Armitage held Sight of Day as water churned about them. She tossed a rope over the side, and the monster wound it about his arm. His movements were slow, as sluggish as a drunkard's. *He's too cold.* Geneve put her foot against the railing, hauling them up hand over hand.

The load lightened, and she feared one was lost, but a quick check showed Meri behind her. The illusionist lent what strength he could. Roya took the slack, then another man. Behind him, a woman. And onward, as each took a share of the burden.

Armitage's head appeared above the edge, and he shouldered Sight of Day over the railing. The cat fell like overcooked vegetables to the decking. Armitage almost fell, but Geneve leaped forward, snaring the Vhemin's shirt. "Oh, no you don't. Not today."

His eyes were unfocused, jaw slack. Geneve hauled him to the deck. "We need a fire, and quickly. Find his backpack."

Crew rushed to obey. Meri crouched beside Sight of Day. "He's got a cut on his head, but nothing else."

"He caught the damn harpoon and went overboard." Armitage coughed bilge water. "I found him half-dead. He'd knocked his head on the shaft as he went over. Pulled shoulder too, maybe." The monster coughed again. "That water's fucken cold. I'm going to sleep now."

Meri stood, hands on hips. He eyed the captain's cabin. "The Vide came in through the window. Just one, meant to kill me, I think. *Replace* me. A full-frontal attack won't work, so they thought subterfuge the better trick."

"But why? We're going to your father's estate anyway." Geneve stood by his shoulder.

"He doesn't know that." Meri offered her a smile, almost too thin to see. "And he likes managing the outcome. Always a game within a game. Control the queen's advisors. Get into your trust circle. Never rely on one play when six are open."

Geneve shivered. Her shirt was wet with borrowed seawater, but it was something deeper that made her cold. "He'd have ... *replaced* you?"

"From his perspective, he got it wrong the first go around. What better son than the one you pay for?" The illusionist sneered. "Come. We must check the rest of the ship. The supplies could be poisoned. Or a fire set in the horse's hay. A thousand things to starve the wind in our sails."

Geneve grabbed his arm. "We will get to him and find answers."

"To what questions?" Meri didn't pull away.

"All of them," she hissed. "I want to know why he wants our dragon. Or why he wants to supplant Queen Morgan through the viper in her nest. Where he found a corrupted Champion, or how Justiciar Ambrose fits into this." Geneve held his arm a little tighter. "But most of all, I want to know why he doesn't love you, when all the world is changed by your presence."

Chapter Seventeen

Meriwether watched the sky. It was unusual in that it held smoke, not cloud.

The third day of their Whisperwind Port voyage dawned bright and clear, with a tint of fire the sea breeze couldn't push aside. Meriwether remembered the port clutching a north-facing spit jutting into the ocean. The coast curved north and west from there toward the du Reeves estates, but this was the last safe harbor for hundreds of klicks.

The crew pushed ever on, trying not to look too closely at the flotsam the *Chimera* sailed through. The closer to Whisperwind they got, the more debris cluttered the seas. After lunch, they saw the first body. Meriwether thought it might have been human, but the denizens of the sea gnawed much of it away.

Roya arrived at his shoulder, sharing his view of the sky. "Cap'n. Be a few hours left until we hit safe harbor."

"Safe," Meriwether murmured. "I'm not sure that's the right word."

"Be as may." She rubbed windburned lips. "If there's preparations to be made, now's the time."

"Have you spoken to Geneve?"

"Why?" Roya raised an eyebrow. "She doesn't know the waves, nor the folk upon it. If you fashion I'd learn something from her—"

"Be easy, Roya." Meriwether patted the air. *{Calm down.}* "I mean she's a keen eye for justice, and a knack for seeing it done. A body on the waves is one thing, but this feels worse."

"Aye," the first mate allowed, her tone grudging. "Set anchor here many a time. There's little riding in the seas hereabouts."

"Perhaps I should speak with her."

"That would be for the best." Roya looked at the decking, stubbing weathered wood with her toe. "The Knight scares me, and I'm not afraid to admit it. She looks right through you, as if she can see the silt in your soul."

"You should spend fifteen minutes with Vertiline." Meriwether nodded his farewell, left the fo'castle, and hunted for Geneve. His first bet was spot on: she was in the mess, working on a half chicken with gusto. Armitage sat across from her, huddled beneath furs. The Vhemin said the cold was in his bones now, and no amount of heated rocks seemed to make it go. "Feel like sharing?"

"Get your own," Geneve said around a mouthful.

Meriwether nodded, and set to making tea. The mess stove burned day and night, a pot above holding a brew that would put hair on your descendant's chests, and probably backs too. He spooned honey into a cup, found a heel of bread and some elderly cheese, and joined his friends. "Trouble's coming."

"They reckon you're smart, but all you do is say the obvious thing." Armitage pulled the furs about him. "You got a specific brand of trouble you're angling at here?"

"Passed a body. Lots of wreckage in the waters, too." Meriwether sipped his tea, face twitching at the flavor. "I think Whisperwind Port will hold more questions than answers."

The mess door opened, Sight of Day stepping through on cat-silent feet. He made the table, eyed Geneve's food, and clearly decided not to interfere. He glanced at Armitage, then wrinkled his nose *{Whisperwind might hold a bath house.}*

"Eat a dick," the Vhemin suggested, but without rancor. "You were the one who snuggled beneath the furs to keep me warm."

{That's because you were dying. You're not dying right now, and thus, fair game.} The Feybrind offered a half-smile. *{If you prefer, we can throw you overboard again.}*

The door opened, pale Vertiline stepping through. Two days of rest helped her bearing. She stood upright, her shoulders straight with confidence. The bandage at her stump no longer spotted red, and her skin wasn't the so-white-it's-almost-blue visage of the dead. The Chevalier avoided the table, helping herself to tea.

"I wouldn't," Meriwether warned. "It's really bad."

"I know. I made it." Vertiline took two spoonfuls of honey, then used her spoon to point at the landward hull. "There are bodies floating out there."

"More?" Meriwether winced. "Definitely not good." He spun a sovereign from light and memory, putting it on the table. "I'll bet gold the port city's been attacked."

Armitage flicked the not-coin to the floor, where it gave a convincing enough tinkle. "Could be more pirates."

Geneve pushed her plate away. "We must reach the du Reeves estate. Everything else is secondary."

{Except if people need our help.} Sight of Day chased a circle of water about the table with his finger.

"Getting to the estate helps people. It helps them all." Geneve glared thunderclouds at the cat.

{Sometimes helping a single soul has more impact than helping a nation.} Sight of Day didn't back down from Geneve's stare, his golden eyes holding warmth and calm. *{Sometimes helping a single soul heals our own.}*

Armitage snorted. "Sometimes helping one soul involves severing another from its body." He stood, casting the furs aside. "I like this part. I'm gonna get my stuff."

Vertiline took his chair. "I've a feeling the monster is right." She sipped, her eyelid twitching, then eyed her tea. "That's really something, isn't it?"

"I mean to release the *Chimera* from our care." Meriwether took another cautious slurp of tea. It didn't get better. "We've no need of it."

Armitage halted, one hand on the door. "Are you nuts?"

"Sometimes."

"It's a *ship*. Ships are *expensive*. We'll never get another like this." The monster crossed his arms. "Why would you give it away?"

"We can't walk it to the du Reeves estate." Meriwether put his tea down. It was better drunk after he was dead. "Besides, there's people aboard who could stand to set their own course."

"Imbecile," Armitage said, shouldering through the door.

{He's not wrong.} Sight of Day rose, heading after the Vhemin. *{But neither are you.}*

Vertiline eyed him over her tea. "A ship can get us anywhere we need to be."

"We need to be *here*." Geneve stabbed her finger on the table, which Meriwether took to mean, Whisperwind Port. "Meri's right. No sense tethering another anchor to us."

"I wasn't arguing." Vertiline put her cup down. "I'm never making tea again. Not tomorrow, nor next week. I'll get ready, too. I don't know the specifics of what lies ahead, but it's involving us. Which means danger, disaster, and certain death." She raised an arch eyebrow. "I blame you, sinner."

"Fair." Meriwether grinned. "Next time, don't make such a fuss about running me to ground, and we'll go our separate ways."

Tilly stood, all elegant grace. She cast a glance at Geneve. "If we're making a record, it wasn't I that chased you." She slipped from the room.

Geneve sighed. "I'm sorry, Meri. She's right. If I hadn't—"

"Hush, now." He held his hands about a centimeter apart. "This close, you see?"

"To what?" She eyed him suspiciously.

"To never having met." He stood, heading for the door before he'd say something foolish like, *To never knowing the most wonderful person in the world.* That kind of thought wasn't healthy. She'd never want someone like him, and hoping was a torture only fools could afford.

Whisperwind Port waters were filled with bodies. The crew navigated through the morass in silence, heading for a jetty that still looked serviceable. The rest were ablaze, or burned out, and sunken hulks huddled in the depths below the *Chimera's* keel.

Coaxing the horses out was a difficult job Meriwether left to Sight of Day. He had something else to do. Roya fidgeted at the base of the gangway, eyes on the smoldering city beyond. "Cap'n."

"Roya, you should keep that title for someone else." Meriwether scratched his beard. "Like yourself."

"Cap'n?"

"We needed passage to Whisperwind. We've business here, and it's not needing sails or a steady hand on the tiller." Meriwether put hands on hips. "I'd like to give the *Chimera* to you and the crew. Equal shares, equal partners. You know the running of it. Enjoy."

Roya looked at the ship, then Meriwether, then back to the ship. "*This* ship?"

"This one in particular, yes." Meriwether watched Geneve come down the gangway, taking the roll of the sea and sway of the planks with ease. *She's trained her whole life to be perfect, and by the Three, the Tresward made it so.* "You'll be wanting to avoid the west coast of Or'sen. Those are dangerous waters."

"Sharks?" Roya looked at the *Chimera* again.

"Dragons, most like."

Roya blinked, as if parsing that was a difficult prospect. "You really mean to give this ship to us?"

"I really do." Meriwether clasped her hand. "Look after yourself."

"Cap'n?"

"I'm not the captain, Roya. I'm just down on my luck less than you." He sighed. "What is it?"

"If you need us, just call." She doffed an invisible cap, sauntering back to the mid-deck.

Geneve watched her go. "She seemed ... happy."

"She's debts to pay." Meriwether scratched his beard again. The damn salt would stick with it for days. "I think hosting a kidnap victim is the kind of canker that eats at you."

Geneve eyed the burning port city. "Speaking of paying."

"I get your drift."

The pair walked the jetty, arriving at the clump of companions at the end. All stood rather than ride. Sight of Day patted Fidget's nose. Vertiline whispered to Troubles. Armitage scratched behind Beck's ear. Geneve went to Tristan, which left Meriwether to face the black beast Chesterfield.

"Hello, horse," he offered. The charger eyed him suspiciously. "If you're very good, I'll let you murder someone today." The horse chuffed, tossing his head. Meriwether took that as a good sign, grabbed the reins, and headed into the city.

The bodies were *everywhere*. Meriwether spent his time trying to be analytical about it. To see the faces would be harder than he could take on a good day, so he tried to work out patterns to their death. He bent by a child's side. "Hacked to death."

"By a strong arm, too." Armitage spat on the ground. "I've done my share of killing. Human, Feybrind, and Vhemin all are equal under the blade. But I've yet to kill a child." He cast a nervous glance at the sky, but dusk was hours off. The Three were nowhere in sight. "I don't think it'd be right."

Sight of Day loped ahead, crouching by a body. *{Vhemin.}*

"Whisperwind isn't like Parnear." Meriwether hurried to join the cat. "They've no compact or truce. The Vhemin aren't welcome here."

"No shit." Armitage nudged the dead monster with his boot. "This one's got so many arrows, he'd look better in my nanny's sewing kit."

He wasn't wrong. The body was stuck full of feathered shafts. Sight of Day snapped one off, holding the fletching before his eyes. *{Oh, dear.}*

Geneve called from their left. "Another one here. This one's been dealt to by blades as well as shafts."

Armitage went to join her. Meriwether caught Sight of Day's arm. "What do you mean, 'Oh, dear?'"

{The fletching is the People's.} Sight of Day touched the spiraled pattern of feathers. *{We use these to send a specific message. These are Promise shafts.}*

"Promise?" Meriwether frowned. "I don't understand."

"He means this is the People's work. Some of it, anyway." Geneve stood, rubbing her hands against her pants. "I should have put my armor on."

"Here." Vertiline stood up the street aways. Meriwether hadn't seen her wander off and was surprised how far she'd gone. "A Feybrind."

He jogged to her side. The dead Feybrind lay beside its severed arm in a pool of blood. Golden eyes stared, unseeing, at the sky. "What could cause all three races to fight?" Meriwether turned a slow circle. They stood in a market street. Where awnings remained over buildings not burned to the waterline, wares lay on display. He found an apple, then tossed it back. "How did this happen?"

"I figure my lot came in here with murder on their minds." Armitage chewed his lip.

"Aye. The humans are hacked to pieces. But the Vhemin are shot." Meriwether nodded. "The People came to even the score, perhaps."

{We do not keep score. We play no games with monsters.} Sight of Day walked to Armitage. *{Careful, brother. If the People are here, they will kill you on sight.}*

"I should wear a disguise?" Armitage's words were bitter.

"You can't carry the sins of your kin." Geneve crossed her arms. "Only your own."

"Got plenty of those." Armitage found a body with a cloak, stripping the garment off and draping it over his shoulders. Hood up, he looked like a hulk, but from a distance you might not mistake him for Vhemin. "How do I look?"

"Like an asshole." Vertiline walked to him, then tugged his hood about his face. "There. Still an asshole, but a better disguise."

The farther through Whisperwind's streets they went, the more human corpses were interspersed with Vhemin, then Feybrind. The People left enough of their long-lived dead to make Sight of Day's tail lash, lash the air, his golden eyes sad. *{This was a heavy price. The People do not wage war.}* He looked to Geneve. *{The Three have been absent too long.}*

They made the outskirts of Whisperwind. The gates were a ruin, and beside them, the thick wooden poles of the wall were torn down. They lay like the kindling of giants. Bodies lay both within and without the walls. More Vhemin, and Feybrind too. Outside Whisperwind lay a cleared, grassy field, beyond which stood a forest. He remembered thinking it was old beyond reckoning the last time he was here, and nothing about the quiet woods changed his mind. *It feels like the forest watches what we do to each other.*

Meriwether picked his way through the dead, trying to ignore the scent of blood that vied with the sea for control of the air. "These bodies are newly dead. No rot."

"A day at best," Geneve agreed.

"We were late to the party, but there's probably still ale in the keg." Armitage kicked over a Vhemin corpse. "I think I know this fucker."

Geneve raised an eyebrow. "You *think?*"

"Difficult to know. Half his face is gone. But he was a lousy loser at dice." Armitage crouched. "Yeah, this is him. "Called himself Bat. No clue why."

"How'd you know him? Family?" Meriwether wandered closer.

"Nah. Mercenary. Swung by the ol' homestead looking for work, must've been five seasons past. I guess the south was too poor, short on warlords, or some shit. The north, though?" He stood. "Ripe for the plucking."

{Ripe for the picking.} Sight of Day sighed. *{Things that are ripe don't need plucking. You're thinking of chickens.}*

"I'm not really thinking of food," Armitage growled. "Those woods, though." He squinted. "Be a good place to hide."

{Was the trail of beaten grasses a giveaway, or did you spot something more specific?} Sight of Day's tail lashed. *{Here. See the spread of prints? The People went this way.}*

Armitage squatted beside Sight of Day. "I don't see anything."

{That's because the People didn't want you to see.} The cat shrugged. *{But it's there nonetheless.}*

Geneve looked to the trees. "To the west? It seems an iffy coincidence that our path dogs the trail of the survivors of an assault on Whisperwind." She visored her hand to forehead, staring at the forest. "I don't like the idea of losing time, but I like the idea of an army at our backs less."

{The People don't hunt humans.} Sight of Day spread his hands. *{Only monsters.}*

"I've met plenty of people who are monsters," Meriwether said. "We're burning daylight. We can make the forest by nightfall. Perhaps find some shelter within. Talk about our plans for tomorrow." He didn't have to say, *I don't want to stay near Whisperwind*. None of them wanted the dead to haunt their dreams.

Chapter Eighteen

The forest was colder than Geneve expected. Sight of Day took the lead, she close behind. Then Meri, Armitage, and Tilly at the rear. They didn't bother with stealth, as their horse's footfalls made plenty of noise. *Besides, the Tresward didn't train me for stealth.*

The ancient boughs of trees held counsel above them. There were no convenient markings to guide them in. No one blazed bark, in invitation or warning, but Sight of Day's steps were steady. It felt like he knew where he was going. He still paused from time to time, ears pricked, golden eyes alert at the slightest sound. But nothing came for them. No arrows cut the gloom. No greeting met them.

"This place is deserted," Armitage growled.

"I don't think so." Meri hurried to Geneve's side. "I feel like we've been watched since we got here."

{That's because we have been.} Sight of Day stroked his chin. *{The People don't greet us, though. It feels...}* His hands stilled while he searched for the right word. *{Wrong.}*

"Let's make camp," Geneve suggested. "The light fails, and I don't need to twist my ankle before a fight."

"Who said anything about fighting?" Armitage scanned the trees above. "You *sure* there are cats here?"

{Very sure.} Sight of Day half-smiled. *{What surprises me is why you're not a pincushion.}*

"Let's stop here, then." Geneve pointed to a boulder emerging from the ground beside an old oak. Moss clung to it. The boulder was large enough to provide shelter from wind, such as there was. "We can get a fire going."

"The cats don't mind us lighting fires in the woods?" Armitage glanced upward, as if Feybrind could strike at any moment.

{No more than they mind you breathing, monster.} Sight of Day placed his palms together. *{Much as I'd head off to hunt, I think it's best if I don't leave you alone. There could be a misunderstanding.}*

Geneve nodded. "We'll tether the horses there—"

"And the bear."

"And the bear," she allowed. "Once the fires warmed our souls, we'll work out what to do next."

It sounded easy enough, but no answers were forthcoming, no matter how long they lingered by the fire. Meri wanted to find the Feybrind. Sight of Day agreed. Vertiline didn't have a strong view on it, and Armitage was opposed. Not that it mattered, because the People didn't come to them, and tracking them through their own forests was insanity.

Night fell, and with it, rain. They stretched canvas above their camp, huddling closer to the flames while drops pattered the canopy above. Geneve eyed her saddlebag, because in there was armor, and she might need it tonight. But she couldn't sleep wearing steel, and she needed the rest.

{I'll take watch.} Sight of Day held his hands over the flames. *{I've little need for rest.}*

Geneve eyed his injured shoulder. "That won't heal through positive thoughts and kind words. You need sleep as much as any of us."

{The difference is that if I sleep, you might die. If you sleep, I'll probably live one more night.} He offered her a half-smile.

"The cat makes an excellent point." Armitage tossed his hot rock into the fire, then stalked off to curl up with Beck. The rain didn't let up, but the monster didn't seem to care. The set of his shoulders said, *I've been wet before, and it wasn't so bad.*

Meri rolled himself into a woolen log. Vertiline leaned against a tree, blankets about herself. Only Geneve and Sight of Day remained by the fireside. She kept to the People's handspeak, so's not to wake the others. *{Why don't the Feybrind come to us?}*

Sight of Day eyed the dark where Armitage was. *{The Vhemin we met before have devices that control the People. Perhaps they've heard the song of submission this far north? Or they fear the monster controls me.}* He sighed. *{You should sleep, Daughter of the Three.}*

{You said the People don't make war. What did you mean?}

His golden eyes found the flames. *{The People are expert artisans. Our steel blades are better than anything short of glass, except maybe the skymetal sword you carry.}* He tossed wood onto the fire. *{We also make fine music. Our chefs are second to none, especially if you like meat.}* Sight of Day showed teeth. *{No one shoots a bow better. Only the Tresward fight with better skill. We are unmatched among all the peoples of all the lands. I don't brag. But there are so very few of us. We live everlong, the time and tides of our lives measured in hundreds of years, not the tens of Vhemin and humans. For us to fight in great numbers means we are willing to die. All of us, everywhere.}* His golden eyes met hers. *{We wouldn't survive a war, Daughter of the Three. For all our skill and expert tools, we would fail against the mass of Vhemin. They are thousands to our handful. The People would be gone, and then who would make your clothes and wonderful swords?}* This last was given with hard, firm motions. The Feybrind was angry, bitter, or sad.

Or all those. Geneve brushed red hair from her face. *{You fear the loss of your family?}*

{My kin are dead already. Broken against the rock of Vhemin scourging the southlands. Only one remains, and he and I do not always agree.} Teeth, glinting in the firelight. *{Perhaps it's time. We've tried to guard the world against the monsters, as have the Tresward. There are few of you also. But ... I'm afraid. I don't want to die. I don't want my people to be a memory kept in books to teach the unwary lessons they'll never learn until it's too late. We cannot go to war.}*

{I know, but...} Geneve sighed. *{I've hope, Sight of Day. You are friends with a monster. Tresward are by your side. A sinner has joined us on our quest to*

heal the crack the ancients worked in the bones of this world. Perhaps we don't need a war.}

He nodded, not disagreeing. *{I would like more healing, fewer cracks, and time to know my human friends as long as they'll last. The Vhemin, too. He's not like the rest. He loves, hurts, and fears to fall because of all he'll lose. Have you seen how he cares for his bear? And have you seen how he cares for the 'runt' behind his empty threats? But all of you wear out, like cheaply made wagon wheels, leaving the People to live on, and ever on, without end. We remember your songs, but...}* He wiped his eye and shook his head. *{You make the most beautiful music when your souls fly for heaven.}*

"Oh," Geneve breathed. *{I thought you didn't live with people because you didn't like us.}*

{Not all of you are likable, it's true.} A half-smile, the glint of firelight in golden eyes. *{You're noisy and clumsy, too. But mostly the People fear your departure. We will remember the pain of your passing well after your dust is returned to the land.}*

{Then why do you travel with us?} Geneve touched her chest.

{Because I like you. Most of you, anyway. Also, you're going to save the world. It may yet be worth saving. A few more like Armitage, Vertiline, Meriwether, or Geneve, and we can face the Three knowing their world is worth holding close.} Sight of Day met her eyes.

{Thank you for staying with us.} Geneve glanced up. *{The rain's stopping.}*

{You don't need to thank someone for doing what their heart wants.} The Feybrind stroked his chin. *{Now, sleep. The morning will be difficult. It's very important you don't die. I'm not yet ready to grieve for another mayfly.}*

***

SIGHT OF DAY WAS WRONG: THE FEYBRIND DIDN'T COME IN THE morning. They arrived on silent feet as the fire burned low. They landed amid the camp with spears and swords. Geneve woke to a blade at her throat. She wondered if she'd be fast enough to disarm the Feybrind woman glaring at her. *Probably, but then they'd kill everyone else. You'd survive and leave a basket of corpses behind you.*

She held her hand up in surrender. The Feybrind bound them with expert knots, trussing them like hogs, then spirited them through the forest. Geneve saw trees and ground pass by as fast as a horse's canter, but never did she get hit by so much as a leaf. Their captors were masters of motion, moving cat-swift and quiet through the ancient boughs. Geneve spied Armitage, bound like her, eyes wide in something as close to fear as she'd seen in the monster.

Of Meri, she saw no sign, but a flash of pale Vertiline's hair through the trees gave her some assurance her friend lived.

They arrived at a Feybrind village. Massive trunks like pillars to heaven rose above them. The trees were ringed with walkways connected by rope bridges. The Feybrind dragged them up the branches, using ropes and pulleys to get their cargo skyward. Once very, *very* high above the forest floor, they were brought to a wooden platform spanning the gap between three huge trees. The platform was thirty meters a side, and more Feybrind than Geneve had seen in one place were here. Torches ringed the platform, throwing back the night with an orange glare.

In the middle of the platform was Sight of Day. He was unbound, golden eyes hard, but they'd taken his weapons. *Trust of kind only goes so far, it seems.* Geneve was placed on the ground, feet still trussed like she was going to slaughter. An *oooph* announced the arrival of Meri, a grunt following as Armitage was tossed face-first against the wood. Vertiline landed beside Geneve, but gentler. Perhaps the Feybrind saw her injury.

A Feybrind elder stood before Sight of Day. She was as old as any Geneve remembered, her fur tinged with gray, her back stooped under the weight of the world. The elder wore robes of green and gold, and carried a spear like a staff. *Old, but not toothless.* Geneve thought it was time to say something, because this was all a terrible misunderstanding, but Sight of Day met her eyes. He shook his head.

The elder leaned the spear against her shoulder like a shepherd's crook. *{You travel with monsters.}*

Sight of Day glared. *{I travel with friends.}*

She inclined her head. *{Are they? You've been Commanded, Sight of Day. I can smell it on you.}*

{And you've been playing at war. I smell that on you, Sings with Heart. Have you forgotten the cost?}

Ah. Sight of Day knows her. Sings with Heart frowned. *{I well remember the cost, better than most.}*

{And yet, here we are.} Sight of Day spread his hands. *{What happened at Whisperwind?}*

{Justice.}

{Said as only those doubting their cause might. 'Justice' is a paltry excuse for murder. It's ever been so.} Sight of Day turned, hand out to his friends. *{Release them. They've caused no harm, or transcended the People's laws.}*

Sings with Heart considered. *{Perhaps we can let some go, but the monster dies.}*

Sight of Day half-smiled, but without humor. *{Then we die with him.}*

The elder walked a slow circle around Sight of Day. *{I don't know why you're concerned. It's the king's command.}*

Sight of Day made a great show of laughter. Like all his kind he was silent, but he mimed a guffaw, and slapped his legs. Wiping an imaginary tear, he said, *{The People have no king.}*

{We have—}

{I know who you mean. I spoke to him! The reason I'm here is because he asked.} Sight of Day steepled his hands for a moment, thinking. *{We have no king, and no need for royal commands. It's made a mess of the human world and would destroy ours.}*

"He's not wrong," Meri whispered. "I kind of want to know who this king is."

"Hush," Vertiline hissed.

Sings with Heart pointed to Armitage. *{End the filth.}*

A Feybrind headed for Armitage. Sight of Day bowed his head, the motion sad, then stepped backward into a guard. He disarmed the Feybrind, a woman who's amber eyes widened in surprise as her blade was removed from her scabbard with a whisper. Sight of Day danced forward, tail low, and put the blade beneath Sings with Heart's chin.

Everyone stopped moving.

Geneve grunted, trying to get her knees under her. "Armitage walks under our protection."

The elder half-smiled, the twist of her lips mocking. *{You're in no position to protect anyone. Were you the one who Commanded Sight of Day?}*

"That was me, actually." Meri hunched like an inchworm. "It's a long story, involving the death of a city, a thousand Vhemin, and a fallen Tresward Champion. But no one Commands him now. He's just being a good friend."

{The monsters have always been devious, but we never thought they'd bend humans to their will. They've always served your kind.} The elder didn't appear cowed by the blade at her neck.

"There's been little bending, and a lot of breaking." Vertiline didn't bother trying to rise. "A long road's led us here. The dead number thousands behind us. Perhaps you'd hear the tale, before ending it short."

Geneve glanced about for support and found only hard, crystal-colored eyes. "Or you could tell us your tale. What led you to the succor of a city of humans under siege by monsters." She sighed. "This would be easier if we could sit and talk it out."

{The king—}

"Aye, aye, I heard the first time. There's a king. He told you to kill the Vhemin, but it seems you've needed little encouragement on that account. Don't you at least want to know why a Feybrind would risk his life to protect one of their kind?" Geneve raised her chin. "I've heard it said the People are beautiful inside and out. But all I see is pettiness and fear."

The Feybrind stilled. Geneve felt the sea of emotions about her. She felt the Sway swirl at her feet, a ready tool to be lifted. She could speak, and they *would* hear her. The Sway brook no argument. She readied to clutch the thin threads she could feel with her meager skill. Geneve didn't want to force the Feybrind to their knees, but there was too much at stake.

"Would it help if I freed your kin?" Armitage's voice was muffed, his face against wood. The monster made no sudden moves, but that didn't stop everyone looking at him.

Sings with Heart's lip curled. *{Our lost don't need freeing.}*

"That's ignorance and stupidity talking." Armitage made no move to rise. "You left injured aplenty behind. You ever wondered what

Vhemin do with bodies on the field? Or survivors? We're partial to meat, just like you, and cat tastes just as good as human. A little stringy, but it's fine."

Geneve swung to the monster. "What?"

"See, the Vhemin will take their prisoners away. Somewhere private. Caves are their favorite, but it doesn't need to be below ground. Old castles and abandoned mansions do in a pinch. Then the assholes on my team start carving pieces off 'em. We don't eat people all at once. Not unless we're real hungry. An arm or a leg first, making sure they don't bleed out, until we need the rest." His snake eyes found the elder's. "You try and get your people out, all you'll do is hasten the barbecue. I go in, I get 'em out, and we can all go our separate ways."

Geneve's stomach roiled. "They ... *eat people?*"

Armitage ignored her. "I guess you've got to work out whether you like the idea of my kin eating yours more than you want to see me dead."

Sings with Heart's eyes held murder. *{How can we trust you not to run?}*

"You don't have much of a choice." Armitage hunched himself to a sitting position. "Your people get eaten if you kill me. If I run, they also get eaten. Both those sound like a shit sandwich, or maybe a cat sandwich." He chortled, the sound like falling gravel. "But if I help, they live. Probably. I know it's slim odds. I wouldn't take 'em. But there's plenty of people like me, and fuck *all* like you. Any chance is a good chance, right?"

{We keep your friends as hostages.}

"That's a big nope from me, sister." Armitage shook his head, never breaking eye contact with the elder. "I need the skinny bitch because she's the second best with a sword I've ever seen. The runt, because he makes shit up in his head and it's *real*, man, the realest thing you've seen. I'll take the redhead too, because she commands the forces of fucking creation, and let me tell you that's a thing that's good in your back pocket. Oh, and the cat, because he's my brother. Different mothers, though."

Sings with Heart met Geneve's eyes. *{You command the Storm?}* Her eyes moved over Geneve's bound form. *{You don't wear the golden sun.}*

"The Three and I are taking a break," Geneve admitted.

{You could have ended all of us when we attacked your camp. Some of you use Sway like Command, and perhaps you could bend us like puppets at theater.} Green eyes considered her, and Geneve tried not to let her guilt bubble forth. *I almost did. Only the 'monster's' intervention stopped it.* *{You are Tresward?}*

"Maybe," Geneve allowed. "I was. Tilly, too."

{There are always three.}

"One ... fell," Vertiline murmured. "He was one of the thousands behind us."

"But we adopted others to fill the gap." Geneve tried to hold her chin up, but her bonds made it difficult. "A sorcerer. A Feybrind. And a monster. We're trying to save the world."

{Only the Tresward would think it their duty to do so.} A smile so slight Geneve might have imagined it touched the elder's lips. *{And only they would have the arrogance to believe it possible.}*

"Yeah, they're a lippy bunch. So, what'll it be?" Armitage coughed. "I figure you need to make a call, because my hands have gone to sleep, and that'll hurt like seven bastards when the ropes come off. If it's all the same either kill me now to avoid that nightmare, or let me walk it off."

❧

IT TURNED OUT SINGS WITH HEART WAS A GAMBLER. THE ELDER LET the party go. It wasn't with blessing or kind thoughts. Geneve thought the old Feybrind might have words with them after. Perhaps still kill Armitage, or bring repercussions against Sight of Day.

That's tomorrow's problem. Today's challenge is rescuing a group of angry cats from a Vhemin stronghold. Easy.

Geneve, Meri, Vertiline, and Sight of Day waited within the forest. The Feybrind set up a blind, leaves and branches giving them cover from all but the most dedicated eyes. Their vantage looked out on a holdfast, more mansion with an eye to becoming a castle. It was bigger than Picotee's house in Parnear Harbor, but no keep of a real lord. Meri said it was one of his father's many properties through the north.

The holdfast sat atop a natural hill in the middle of a grassy plain. A wall fortified the perimeter: stout wood they could break through with aid of the Storm, but not without alerting the guards. Armitage said the Vhemin would use their 'walking steaks' as hostages should the need arise. Their plan was to get the monster inside under cover of night, using the disguise of a for-regals mercenary. While the Vhemin could see heat in the dark, most of them would be asleep, increasing their chance of success.

A month back I'd have killed any monster on sight. Now I trust one with the lives of all I hold dear. Am I learning, or falling? Geneve hoped the former but feared the latter. She'd never felt so many doubts as when she let the burnished sun fall from her chest.

Speaking of the monster, he was half-way to the holdfast, trudging through long grass, leaving a trampled trail behind him. Armitage had worked his way around the clearing, approaching from the woods to the east; Geneve and the rest waited to the south.

"I like to think I know a thing or two about assholes." Meri hunkered between her and Sight of Day. "Tell me about this king."

Sight of Day gave the illusionist a little side-eye. *{We have no king. We have one whose words are heavier than most.}*

"Do you mean they carry more weight?"

{Did I say that?}

Geneve frowned. "You're saying he's important?"

{I'm saying he's less important than many, but makes his words scorch the sky. Sired by one you'd call a smith, who was well-versed in his craft before the Vhemin came to his lands.} Sight of Day spread his hands. *{The not-king has a way with words. And he's clever. But he never wanted a crown because he knows they're made of thorns.}* The cat's golden eyes were troubled.

Meri sighed. "A little power goes a long way toward corrupting even the best of us."

{Easing Seas doesn't command, instead ... asking. He called on me to go to the human queen. He said our ancient alliance needed a particular sinner.} The cat watched the holdfast, tail swishing. *{You know the rest.}*

"Not a king back then?" Geneve wished she had her own tail to swish. "That's a fast rise in the ranks. How did you meet Easing Seas?"

{He is my son.}

Vertiline spun so fast she almost toppled. "You've got a kid?"

{*Those with children have the best incentive for world-saving.*} The cat half-smiled. {*Some day you may be blessed to know it.*}

"That ship's sailed." Vertiline's voice was sour.

"Plenty more fish in the sea." Meri offered her a smile.

Tilly didn't take it, blue eyes hard as the glass she used to wield. "I should throw my leg over the nearest—"

"Whoa." Meri patted the air. {*Calm down.*} "I only thought—"

"Keep your thoughts inside your skull. You'll trip over them less often." Tilly glared at Meri.

Geneve cleared her throat. "Your son asked you to see the queen, and then find Meri?"

{*He suggested there was a path to peace.*} Sight of Day's golden eyes fixed on the holdfast. {*Find the Tome of Lost Souls and stop the corruption of the Tresward. A young man,*} he held his palm toward Meri, {*saw it. Save the man, recover the Tome, and then think about fixing the world. Never did he speak of crowns or kingdoms. Something's wrong.*}

Meri sighed. "Far be it for me to trip over my thoughts again, but those closest to us can trick us most."

{*I've thought on this since hearing Sings with Heart's words.*} Sight of Day smoothed the fur on his chin. {*I don't think it's likely. Easing Seas had over a hundred years to grasp at power, and never took it.*}

"Your kid's a hundred years old?" Tilly blinked. "By the Three, how old are *you?*"

Sight of Day half-smiled. {*That's an impolite question, mayfly.*}

Geneve snorted. "Okay. This doesn't change the mission. Armitage gets us inside, we save everyone there, and *then* we work out what's up with Easing Seas." She glanced toward the monster, who was almost at the holdfast's gates.

Meri sighed, then put his hand on Sight of Day's shoulder. "We'll help. You know it, right?"

Golden eyes turned warm and bright. {*I know it. Thank you, friends.*}

Armitage reached the holdfast. Geneve squinted, trying to make out the details. The monster confronted three others standing guard. Armitage pointed at the closed gates. The guards took issue, one pushing their friend. Geneve bit her lip, but shouldn't have worried.

The giant disarmed him, then used his stolen pike to skewer another, then decked the third with a single punch.

The disarmed Vhemin backpedaled, then opened the gate, ushering Armitage through.

Meri whistled. "I'm going to guess that was the job interview. He passed."

{He has missed his calling as a troubadour. That was the finest acting I've seen.}

"The Vhemin don't pretend." Geneve ran a hand through red hair. "Now, we wait."

NIGHTFALL CAME AS EXPECTED. THEY WEREN'T DISCOVERED. THE Vhemin didn't seem to send out patrols. Once the darkness was complete, Geneve led them across the field. She wore her black armor, Requiem belted rear draw style, with Tribunal's grip by her shoulder. Vertiline wore black leather, her thin blade by her side. Sight of Day carried his bow, his elegant sword by his waist. As for Meri, the illusionist wore his new clothes from Parnear Harbor, the cloak on his shoulders. The knife at his hip was a memory he and Geneve shared. All blades were coated with lampblack, but they hadn't bothered with their skin. While hiding the glint of a blade had merit, creatures that could see heat wouldn't care if they wore makeup.

As they got closer, the sound of coarse laughter drifted in snatches on the wind. With it, the smell of roasting meat. Geneve gagged, trying not to think about what kind of animal it was.

They made it to the holdfast without alarm. A watchtower above stood vacant. Either all Vhemin partied like today was their last, or Armitage had cleared a path. They made their way toward the gates. The plan was for Armitage to let ropes down, so they could scale the walls. Geneve wasn't sure where he'd be able to do that, so they needed to play it by ear.

A full circuit of the holdfast took a half-hour, without them finding ropes. She glanced up. *{Do you think he's been taken?}*

{There are not enough Vhemin in the world,} Sight of Day said. *{I've a gold sovereign that says he's drunk.}*

From above came a choking sound, followed by a Vhemin landing at their feet. Geneve jumped back, blade in hand. Armitage called down, "Sorry about that." A rope coiled from the wall, landing at her feet.

She sheathed Requiem, then grabbed the rope. Geneve hauled herself up hand over hand, ignoring Armitage's offered help at the top. "You're late."

"That guy wouldn't leave me alone. Wanted to hear about how many people I'd killed. Looked real surprised when I said 'plus one' then knifed him in the spine." Armitage helped Sight of Day over the side. "Things here are delicate."

"Delicate?" she hissed. "It's fortified with the monsters of nightmare, and an unknown number of hostages need our care."

"I meant aside from that." Armitage hauled Meri over the side by his shirt. He looked over. "Yeah, wrap it around your arm like that." He bent to the business of drawing Vertiline up the wall. Climbing with one hand was possible, but the monster had strength enough to spare.

The pale woman slipped over the wall, then patted Armitage's arm. "I didn't believe them when they said you'd betray us."

"Thanks." Armitage blinked. "Wait, what?"

Geneve looked over the holdfast. The central hill hosting the mansion was tall, and time or expertise smoothed its slopes to an almost perfect dome. Lights burned aplenty within the mansion, but at the base of the hill there were almost none, aside from torches set on a winding path from bottom to top.

The group stood on the wall's ramparts, such as they were. Designed more for show than support, thin planks held them ten meters off the ground. Below were a collection of tents, with campfires dispersed among them. Vhemin sat, drunk, or drinking their way there. There was no sign of human or Feybrind captives, not chained up, nor used as servants. "Where are the prisoners?"

"About that." Armitage scratched his ear. "They're inside. The house has a standing guard of twenty or so assholes. The lads about here say there's a basement used to house fine wines and future meat, so I reckon that's where we go." He gusted a sigh. "Haven't made it inside though. The big boss wants to see me first."

"Who's the big boss?"

"Motherfucker named Ballast. I know him from back in the day. He's clever enough to have learned his letters and numbers. Don't know about handspeak." Armitage hunkered down, pointing to the camp below. "I saw him doing the rounds before. Avoided him, because he's the kind of asshole likely to connect the spiderweb of coincidence between me getting here and hostages. I don't want to die without getting in the first punch."

"So, we take out Ballast." Meri crossed his arms. "What am I missing?"

"They've got a traitor." Armitage gave a glance to Sight of Day. "Ballast walks with a Feybrind advisor. The two whisper like thieves."

{Is it so surprising that scaled and furred can be friends?}

"Pretty surprising, yeah, because Ballast is wearing a Feybrind-skin cloak." Armitage adjusted his pants. "I think there's more going on than's apparent at first blush. I figure I can spend a day or two here, work it out—"

"No." Geneve crossed her arms. "We've no time to waste. The dragon will end the world."

Everyone looked at her, but it was Meri who spoke. "If there's a world-ending device, it's the dragon. I agree, we've little time to waste."

"Face-punching it is." Armitage stood, pointing. "Over there's an armory. Yeah, the tent. Don't judge my people, they're not all like me: smart as they are handsome." He grinned horror teeth. "I saw a couple scatterguns and those white paper cylinders you feed them. If we start a fire in there, we gain a distraction."

"Meanwhile, some of us go to the house. Break in the doors, subdue the remaining guards, and rescue the prisoners." Geneve nodded. "I'll take the house. Meri, you're with me. Tilly—"

"No." The illusionist held his hand up. *{Wait.}* "The house is heavily guarded. You need the king hitters up there. Leave the distraction to me. Besides, I've always wanted a scattergun."

"They're Tresward," Vertiline warned. "Holy weapons."

"The beauty of it is there's no Tresward here." Meri's smile held the flavor of the devil's kiss. "Go on, let me go. I promise I'll bring you back one too."

"Hey, runt. Get me one also?"

"You got it."

Geneve gave an exasperated sigh. "Fine. Meri has the armory. Tilly, Armitage, and Sight of Day, you're with me. Anything else we should know?"

Armitage frowned. "I don't think so. Ballast is a decent swordsman, but I beat him with a three-day hangover. Even Vertiline could take him."

Vertiline's hand found her sword. "I will kill you where you stand, monster."

"It's settled, then." Geneve's hand found Meri's arm, as if by its own will. "Meri—"

"I'll be fine."

"I want you to be more than fine. Come back to me." She let him go, then hurried away. *Come back to me? You love sick puppy.* Geneve didn't want to say anything else stupid. There were Feybrind to save, and Vhemin to kill.

Chapter Nineteen

Meriwether strolled through the Vhemin camp. He didn't try very hard to hide, because he was the distraction. While he didn't want to be caught, the odds seemed low because the Vhemin were mostly passed out, and those that weren't were almost all the way there.

These people party hard. He found a woman sprawled half out a tent flap, her pants around her ankles. Her groggy snake eyes found his. "Fucking lordlings. What are you looking at?"

"Nothing, soldier. Carry on." Meriwether left her to her impending hangover. If she was too drunk to realize humans shouldn't be walking free, well then. That was on her.

He slowed, rewinding the exchange through his mind. *Fucking lordlings.* Meriwether touched his beard, now bushier than a gentleman should allow. He glanced back at the sprawled Vhemin. *How did she know I was a lordling?* His beard felt coarse to his fingers. *Unless dear old Dad's been here. It would be his way to stir up a fight between Vhemin, humans, and Feybrind. The most chaos for the least sovereigns.* It was possible her drunken state, coupled with the low light and his likeness to Leander, made her mistake him for someone else.

Still, that would keep for another time. He had a tent to blow up.

He passed a fire pit with a rotisserie. A human arm was speared on it, charred to black. Meriwether swallowed bile, pushing on. *I should be terrified, but I'm excited. By the Three, we're kicking my father right where it hurts: in his intricately laid plans.*

Perhaps looking like Leander could be useful. *People see what they want to.* He reached the armory tent, poking his head inside. The canvas walls were arrayed with weapon racks, but no armor. There were pikes, swords, maces, bardiches, and another handful of weapons Meriwether had no name for. At the back was a small rack holding scatterguns. He rooted about until he found the ammunition. It was a treasure trove: three whole barrels of white cylinders for the weapons. *How did Dad get so much? The Tresward would notice this going missing.*

He let his fingers roam the handle of a scattergun. It was worn, notches from use lending their memory to his skin. Meriwether lifted it from the rack, sighting down the barrel. *A Knight used this. This is not a fresh-made weapon. It's scavenged from the fallen.* He looked to the canvass roof, imagining Geneve's gods watching above. He didn't cleave to the bowing and the scraping, but *she* did, and that was good enough for him. "We'll make it right. Starting with a little payback."

"What's that?"

Meriwether whirled at the voice. Gruff, coarse like Armitage's. At the tent flap stood a Vhemin, no bigger or smaller than the rest of their brutish kind. He summoned up all the sneer he remembered Leander using, squared his shoulders, and put more timbre in his voice. "I said, we're going to have a little payback. Starting with these." Meriwether waved the scattergun. "It's time for a celebration."

The Vhemin squinted, but the gloom of the tent, or Meriwether's sneer, hid him well enough. "Lord du Reeves, I didn't know—"

"Of course not. You're not *paid* to know. You're paid to murder things." Meriwether made a show of examining the scattergun. "I think it's time we had some fun. Get some of your crew. Drag the ammunition outside. Set up a range. Then we'll get some prisoners and ... *test* the weapons."

"I thought the scatterguns were for the final battle." Snake eyes hunted the gloom.

Final battle? Interesting. "Are you *questioning* me?"

"Aye ... m'lord, no." The Vhemin took a step back.

"What's your name, soldier?"

"I'll get some help." The Vhemin vanished.

Excellent. Looks like Leander is the same stiff-necked asshole he's always been. This ruse won't hold long, but with the grace of the Three, it'll hold long enough. Meriwether grabbed two more scatterguns, slipping them into his belt. The original one he kept hold of, fielding two white cylinders from a barrel.

It was the work of a moment to understand how to break the breach, and he slipped cartridges into the weapon. Snapping it closed, he headed for the tent flap. Outside, the Vhemin who'd accosted him was rousing any companions who could still stand. He waved some toward the house, no doubt on prisoner fetching duty, then dragged two with him toward the tent.

They drew near, the original Vhemin squinting for a better look at Meriwether. Meriwether pointed the scattergun. "Eyeball me again and I'll have your head."

The Vhemin ducked said head, darting into the tent. The three emerged with a barrel apiece. They trudged toward a collection of low tables. It didn't look like much of a target range, but Meriwether hadn't been very specific. *Close enough.* The monsters set their loads down.

Meriwether eyed those heading toward the mansion. They were about half-way up. *Perfect.* Meriwether touched the scattergun to his forehead, doffing a mock salute, then leveled the weapon at the barrels. "Say high to Cophine, Ikmae, and Khiton when you see them."

He pulled the trigger. The weapon *clicked*, but nothing happened.

The monsters surged for him. Meriwether felt a hot stab of panic. *This isn't how the distraction's supposed to go! It's distracting, but I'm going to die!* He forced his mind to calmness, then looked at the scattergun. It had two triggers close together, perhaps one for each barrel. A small nub of metal protruded from the barrel above the triggers. It looked like a slider or a switch.

He flicked it, then aimed the gun again. The Vhemin were on him. He was out of time. Meriwether pulled the trigger. The scattergun roared at the night. Just as the Vhemin was about to tackle him, the ammunition's explosion picked the monster up, throwing him into Meriwether with the force of a god. The pair tumbled through the air, going through a tent. Canvass obscured Meriwether's view as he tangled in the fabric.

He heard screams, and the roar of fire. The occasional *boom!* sounded, perhaps the odd cylinder of ammunition not detonated by the original blast. The Vhemin atop Meri was still. With a grunt, he shoved the monster aside. The creature's back was a ruin of chewed meat. It looked like he'd taken about a hundred scattergun shots into his back. His charge had sheltered Meriwether from the explosion.

Save that knowledge for next time. You might not be so lucky.

A bell clattered in the night. *The alarm.* Meriwether croaked to life, plastered a grin to his face, and began to crawl from the wreckage of the tent. He was covered in Vhemin blood, and it felt like he'd been kicked by the entire troupe here, but he was *alive*. He beamed at the mansion and wondered how Geneve was getting on.

Chapter Twenty

They waited in a well-tended garden before a patio that would put normal outdoor entertainment areas to shame. Geneve had Requiem in hand, the skymetal sword's blade black with ash. Vertiline waited across from her behind a cabbage tree. The slender Chevalier's sword was out, blade pointed to the dirt.

Armitage was farther forward from Geneve's position. He and Sight of Day were almost at the patio itself. Above them was a balcony that overlooked the gardens. They didn't need to worry about that. While it might hold Ballast and his Feybrind traitor, the prize was below ground in the dungeons.

An explosion shook the night. Even at this distance, it was ear-splitting. Geneve winced, hoping Meri was okay, and that he might one day regain the use of his hearing. Then there was no more time for thought. Armitage charged, Sight of Day right behind.

The doors of the patio opened, Vhemin streaming out. Armitage took them on the edge of a greatsword he wielded like it weighed no more than a butter knife. He separated arm from shoulder, head from neck, and soul from body. Screams and cries of pain accompanied his brutal work. Sight of Day flowed like a shadow, always the same distance behind. He used his bow, sending arrows to lodge in eye or heart. Geneve took a moment to admire how they worked together. *Two who started as enemies work as close as lovers.* When a Vhemin got too close, Armitage cut them down. If they worked to close distance or looked to run, Sight of Day dropped them.

Geneve counted eight seconds before all were dead. She and Vertiline hurried from their shelter, joining their friends at the door. They snuck inside, avoiding the blood and viscera. The mansion's interior held a huge entranceway. Marble hugged the ground, and flowers were arrayed in stylish vases. A stairway curved up like a ramp for the gods. Geneve spotted a metal-banded doorway set into the wall. "There."

Armitage shouldered it open. Hinges popped, tinkling like hard rain. "Yeah, humans made this. They don't build for shit."

"It wasn't built to withstand elephants." Vertiline slipped past him like the memory of a ghost, vanishing into the gloom. Armitage frowned, then shrugged it off, following her down.

Geneve joined Sight of Day. "You can stay here, if you like. Things below might be difficult to see."

{If the People lie slaughtered, they've earned witness.} He grasped her shoulder. {But thank you, Daughter of the Three. If it's all the same with you, you go first.}

Geneve grinned. "Of course." She headed within. A short companionway led to another door, which appeared to have had the Armitage touch. Wood lay in a splintered ruin on the ground. Beyond, a stairway hungered for the earth's heart.

She paced forward, heading down. The stairs curved lower. Geneve's breath rasped in her lungs as she descended. Her armor jingled. She smelled her old friends oil and leather, and beneath that, the dust of a passage used less often. For all that, she smelled the scent of smoke. Every turn a torch burned in a sconce, sending a ruddy light ever downward.

Geneve made the bottom landing at a run. Vhemin lay dead on the ground. Tilly's steel was slicked red. Armitage leaned on his greatsword, panting, but grinning shark teeth like he was only getting started. They were in a cellar, perhaps fifty meters long. The first part of the chamber was lined with wine casks. The back two thirds had been cleared out. A huddled misery of prisoners were chained together. The torches stopped where the casks did. Geneve counted by the red pinpoint reflections of people's eyes.

A human man stepped forward, black chains rattling at wrist and ankle. Fear at Armitage and hope at Vertiline warred for supremacy on his face. "Who comes?"

"Rescue party," Armitage grunted. "Let's go."

"We're chained up." The man lifted his manacles. Armitage took the chain in his hands, running along the length to a stake. He crouched, looped black metal links about his arms, and strained up. The stake *twanged* free.

Armitage offered the stake to the man. "Now you're not. Get the fuck up the stairs."

Sight of Day loped past him. There were Feybrind chained in the dark, but Geneve knew their wonderful jewel eyes could see everything. *{Sings with Heart sent us. Come. We've not much time.}*

Vertiline waited by the stairs until all were free, then headed up, offering a lead guardian. Sight of Day went with her. Armitage and Geneve waited until the stragglers trickled by. She turned to follow, but the monster stopped her. "This is going to get messy. They won't all make it."

She nodded. "They don't have to."

"Okay." He sighed. "I mean we might not all make it. There's five of us, and an easy hundred of them."

"We don't have to, either." She hammered her fist to breastplate. "We were *made* to fix things, Armitage. And that's what we'll do, right to the point we break."

He grunted. "No argument. Just—thanks. For getting me out of that shit jail, in the shit town, and then not killing me at least thirty times you should have."

She felt the yearning of the outside, but something in his tone stopped her. "You fear the end?"

"No. Yes. I don't know. Don't think I've had a friend before." He looked at the maw of the staircase. "I don't much want him to die either."

"Then let's keep them all alive. Together." She grasped his hand. "Will you stand with me?"

"I guess so." Armitage sniffed, then squeezed her shoulder. "They make stuff, Knight. The cats, I mean. Swords, chairs, and clothes for the rich. You ever hear 'em make music? Fucken beautiful. My people make death. That's what *we* do, like spinners taking souls and reaming them into a cloak for the ever after. I think if there's a choice, the one you want at your side is the person who makes more than death. He lives. You understand me?"

"Ah." Geneve took his hand from her shoulder. "That's what he meant when he said our souls make beautiful music when they fly for heaven."

"Who?"

"Doesn't matter. We've people to save, monster." She flashed a grin. "Stay with me. Try not to die. Use your sword like tomorrow matters. Because by the Three, we are taking these people home again."

THE TOP OF THE STAIRS HELD NO OPPOSITION, BUT OUTSIDE WAS A different matter. Geneve couldn't see what waited at first glance; the night held its secrets close. But she was alerted to danger by Sight of Day. The Feybrind stood at the patio's doorway, blade out, but lowered, like he wasn't sure what to do with it. Vertiline was nowhere to be seen; perhaps she led the refugees out of the camp.

"Aww, fuck," Armitage growled. "That's Ballast and his pet cat."

Sight of Day folded like paper, crumpling to his knees. Geneve sprinted to his side, hot on the heels of Armitage. The monster stood in the doorway, blade cross guard, snarling like a wolf. Geneve slid to a halt by Sight of Day. "Are you hurt?"

The Feybrind looked uninjured, but raw horror was in his golden eyes. The cat's mouth was half open, and she imagined if he could make noise he'd be keening. But the People made no noise, not ever. His hands clutched the air, trying to catch words from nothing. *{My son.}*

Geneve turned. Beyond Armitage stood a larger-than-most

Vhemin. His face carried a nasty-looking burn scar on the left, and the ear there was missing. But other than that, he looked fit, healthy, and angry. His clothing was of a strange style; he carried hot rocks like Armitage's front and rear, but in compartments that looked purpose-built. Plates of what looked like scale covered him like a second hide. The plates moved with the Vhemin, each overlapping shingle sliding with oiled grace. The most alarming thing wasn't the armor, but how the runes around the heated stones glowed a bright blue. The Vhemin held a mace in one hand, a sword in the other. Both weapons were as strange as his armor: the blade was shorter than most, without a cross-guard. The mace was no ordinary sphere; the head was made of what appeared to be interlocking splines. Geneve ignored him for a moment, looking to the Vhemin's side.

A slender Feybrind stood, blade out, the steel an elegant promise. The cat had Sight of Day's golden eyes, and the shape of his nose was similar.

Sight of Day's son is the traitor.

"Oh, no." Geneve stood, Requiem an answer to the Feybrind's blade. She held steady, because while she was confident she could take a Feybrind on the length of her steel, she didn't *want* to. Not only were the People *good*, but this was Sight of Day's son. "Easing Seas, put away your blade."

The enemy Vhemin guffawed. "He'll do no such thing." Easing Seas blade trembled, but he didn't let his weapon go.

"Maybe I should kill this motherfucker." Armitage leveled his greatsword at the Vhemin. "Ballast would look a lot better a head shorter. Those scars are unsightly."

He must be Commanded. Will killing Ballast save the boy? They had to try. Geneve moved to Armitage's side. "Don't harm Easing Seas."

Armitage didn't glance at her, snake eyes locked on Ballast. "You gonna say more obvious shit before we get to the killing business?"

Ballast chuckled. "We'll get the escapees back. We need 'em, because this ruckus has stirred up a powerful hunger." His voice sounded hard, like a cliff face, and his words rode in on a leer. "Waters that Defy the World, kill them all."

Easing Seas twitched, then jumped forward. *By the Three, he's fast.*

He moved with Sight of Day's elegance, but a ferocity untamed by morals drove him. The Command starved him of any will but Ballast's. His steel clashed against Armitage's greatsword. The Feybrind's speed drove the Vhemin back, his blade getting through Armitage's guard three times in a half second. Each cut a red gouge in Armitage's hide.

Get Ballast! Geneve rushed the enemy commander, swinging her skymetal. Requiem shivered with need in her hand. The Light rippled on the blade's edge, hungering for the Three's justice. She screamed with all the anger and desperation she'd seen in Sight of Day's face.

Ballast caught her steel on the edge of his own with the crack of thunder, and ... his sword didn't break. The steel held, the monster impossibly strong under the Light's onslaught. He slammed his mace forward. Geneve's training took over, her steps smooth and fluid, but it was only enough to turn aside, not avoid the blow entirely. The mace hit her shoulder, crumpling her guardsman's armor like tissue. Geneve slid back with the force of the strike, her feet scudding on the patio's surface.

Her arm went numb. Requiem fell from nerveless fingers. She caught it with her boot, kicking the steel to eye height, snatching it with her left hand. Ballast grinned shark teeth at her. "Didn't expect that, did you, little Tresward?" He held his arms wide as they circled each other. "See the gifts of the ancients! The strength of the Three fills me. I carry their weapons. Your Light can't break them."

She cast a glance at Armitage. The monster was struggling to fight Easing Seas. She wondered if he'd do better if he wasn't trying to *not* hurt his opponent. *Probably not. The cat is fast and dedicated, and all the People are worth five of any other.* No time for that, though. She needed to defeat Ballast. Then she could help Armitage.

"My Light?" She raised her chin. "It's not mine, any more than the air or the seas, monster. It belongs to the Three. They've lent it to me for a while. Cophine wants to see what that armor's made of. Ikmae wants to see what's inside you, and Khiton? He just wants your head." She feinted, but Ballast wasn't drawn by it. Geneve wondered how Armitage beat him with a 'three day hangover.' This man moved with excellence.

"And yet they gave me weapons too, little human. And you're fighting southpaw." The monster charged, swinging with his mace.

Geneve caught it on her steel, pirouetting around the follow-through stab from Ballast's blade. The mace's impact felt like it shook her teeth, but she held onto Requiem. The edge glinted gold, the Three ready to lend their strength. Geneve backed up four paces, twirling Requiem in Dawn's Guard. The air sparked, and the chime of heaven's bells rang from the south.

She raised her blade to the heavens. As Ballast charged, a pillar of lightning shattered the night. It found her steel, the blade curling with blue-white promise. Geneve brought her sword down. Ballast met it on his black shortblade, and again the steel didn't shatter.

It wasn't supposed to. The lightning found a path to the ground through the length of the monster's steel. He screamed as his flesh charred. The blue runes about his hot plates blazed bright, then snuffed out. Plates of scale popped from his shoulder. *Time to return the favor*. Geneve swept her sword past his guard, through the gap in the monster's armor, and took his arm off.

Ballast bellowed, swinging his mace. Geneve reversed Requiem, stepping into the space free of danger: where his arm used to be. Blood pumped against her as she brought her steel against not the mace, but the wrist that held it. Requiem *chimed* as the blade parted scale armor. The mace kept going, knocking her against the chin.

She stumbled back, dazed. Ballast dropped beside her, blood pumping from shoulder and wrist, then fell face-first on the patio. *Get up*. The voice inside Geneve's head sounded very far away, perhaps as high as Cophine's face above. *Get up, or Armitage will die*.

Her friend fought a desperate backward battle against Easing Seas. Sight of Day's son hadn't stopped when his master fell. Geneve could see the moment the battle was lost. The fragment of time when Armitage's back foot caught on the lip of a paver, his balance off by the barest fraction. But it was enough, and Easing Seas ran him through the gut, chest, and neck, his Feybrind-sharp blade meeting no resistance.

Armitage collapsed. Easing Seas raised his blade for the *coup de gras*, blade seeking the monster's neck. It met steel. Sight of Day slipped before his friend, fast as dawn, terrible as night. His golden eyes were hard, and determination set his shoulders square.

Geneve pushed herself to one leg. Her head felt *off*, like the pieces inside no longer connected how they should. She put Requiem's tip against the pavers, struggling to rise. The blades of Sight of Day and Easing Seas patterned the night with the glimmer of steel. They moved like dancers who hated each other, but loved the dance and the music. Sight of Day's steel nicked his son's wrist, then slapped his blade away. A flourish, and Easing Sea's blade spun into the night.

But the young Feybrind had been Commanded. He leaped for Sight of Day, fingers hooked to claws, and ran himself through on his father's blade. Sight of Day tried to drop his sword, but his hilt caught on his leather armor, and the rest was momentum and death.

Except the younger Feybrind didn't stop. He hammered his father with fists, sharp teeth going for the throat. Geneve staggered forward, screaming, "Waters that Defy the World, stop!"

Easing Seas slumped. Sight of Day scrabbled back, pulling his sword free. His son didn't move, eyes staring toward the sky. Perhaps he looked for Cophine's grace, or Ikmae's forgiveness, but all he found was Khiton's end.

Sight of Day clutched his son to him. He rocked the body, as if grief could resurrect the dead. Geneve could find no words, but she might still be able to help someone. She lurched to Armitage's side. The Vhemin was bleeding, but the blood flow was less than it should be. He was dying.

The monster's hand found hers. "Help me up."

"Rest. You're—"

"I'm *fine*. Help me the fuck up or get out of my way." She helped him to his feet. Snake eyes rested on Sight of Day and Easing Seas for a moment, then went cold and hard. "Lemme see your scatter-gun." Geneve drew the weapon from over her shoulder, handing it across. The monster took it, ambling to Ballast's body. He put the muzzle against the enemy commander's head, then pulled the trigger. The body twitched, then lay still. Armitage returned her weapon to her, butt first. "We're hard to kill, Treswan. Next time, aim for the head."

She reloaded her scattergun, then slipped it away. "I had ... trouble."

"No shit." Armitage crouched beside Sight of Day. "It's time." The Feybrind shook his head, face wet with tears, and clutched his son's body tighter. The Vhemin very slowly, but also very firmly, grasped his friends hands. "Let him go. Can't you see? He's already gone skyward. The night's a little brighter because of it. All you're holding's a body." Sight of Day snarled, hitting Armitage in the face. The monster took it, his only concession turning his face aside a fraction. "If you need to kill Vhemin, there are plenty more down there. Or one, right here. But there are also a hundred of your kin who need someone to help them find their way home."

It took a few moments for Armitage to help his friend to his feet. He put a huge arm around the Feybrind's slim shoulders, turned him away, and tried to march him into the night. The Feybrind resisted, the anchor of his son's body holding him to the earth.

Geneve stood by the bodies of Ballast and Easing Seas. Two people approached through the night. Both she knew by their bearing, even by weak starlight. *Meri and Tilly*. Vertiline walked to Armitage and Sight of Day, speaking to them in low tones.

Meri came to Geneve, slowing as he reached her. "Red?"

She looked at the mansion. "It's not *right*, Meri. All it takes is words, and we can destroy their world."

Meri looked at the bodies by her feet, then glanced at Armitage and Sight of Day. He didn't ask *who's that*, or *what happened*. He slipped a little closer. "What do you need?"

"Vengeance. Justice." She ran her hand through red hair. "I don't know."

"How about a farewell?" He crouched by the Feybrind's body. "Help me with him."

They took Easing Seas into the mansion. Up the stairs, past ornate vases and wood tables as beautiful as anything she'd seen. Toward the back of the house they found a bedroom hung with expensive silks. They put Easing Seas' body on the bed. Geneve straightened the Feybrind's arms and legs while Meri fussed with a lantern.

He broke it open, spreading oil across the body and the bed. A spark from flint and steel, and it caught. Greedy flames rushed across the body and bedding. He took her arm, leading her away from the pyre, and into the night.

They made it to the bottom of the hill as the mansion blazed. Flames reached yellow-red fingers to the Three. The five watched the house burn. Geneve stood by Meri's side for a long time as Easing Seas was carried back to where he belonged: the Three's embrace.

Chapter Twenty-One

Meriwether thought his heart might shatter. The less said about his father the better. The old man hadn't seemed too cut up about losing his son, announcing Meriwether dead to all who asked. But Sight of Day? The cat was broken, and there were no words that could stem the flow of pain that came from him like surging waves.

The gates were already wide by the time they got there. Refugees opened it, allowing a flood of the People to enter. The Feybrind slaughtered the remaining Vhemin, their blades red and wet in the firelight.

The five had no time for it. They led a slender snake of refugees through the forest. Vertiline took point as she was the least injured. No one attacked them. Either there were no Vhemin left, or they'd fallen back. Armitage walked with Sight of Day, saying nothing. *Sometimes being there is more important than the words that fall from you.*

Meriwether walked with Geneve. The Knight held her silence as if she were a mute Feybrind. Her jaw was swollen, and unless Meriwether missed his guess, it would bruise the color of an eggplant. But she was no less magnificent for it. Geneve peeled her black guardman's armor from her as she left the compound, leaving it to rust where it lay. She walked like she didn't need it.

"I'm sorry," Meriwether offered.

"For what?" Her lips twisted in a cruel smile. "You weren't the one that failed your friends. That was me, Meri. Me alone. I could have stopped Easing Seas before he..." She trailed off, eyes on Sight of Day's back.

"Then why didn't you?" Her head whipped to him, but he didn't hold his peace. Not this time. "It's not all *you*. We're all a part of this together, but—no, *wait*." He held his hand up as she looked about to round on him. "Peace, Red. I mean that if you *could* have, you *would* have. You've nothing inside you that wants pain in others. The opposite, from what I've seen."

"The Tresward trained me to be the Three's will. The Tresward—"

"Oh, aye, *aye*," he spat. "The Tresward this, the Tresward that. *Where are they?*" He flung his arm at the forest. "Nowhere! They've left us. There are just two Tresward who do the dirty work this world needs. And one of them lost her arm! How many body parts do the Three need sacrificed upon their bloody altar?"

Her eyes were hard and angry. "You don't understand. They made me—"

"No, they didn't." He stamped along beside her. "Your mother and father made you. Yes, the Tresward gave you skills, but you're just one person. Think of the things you've done, not the one thing you didn't. You're the Savior of Ravenswall."

She chewed on that a while, her eyes hooded, her shoulders tight and angry. "I would trade Ravenswall for Easing Seas."

"And it might be a fair bargain, but we're not gods. We're people doing the best we can." Meriwether stabbed a finger to the treetops, and by inference, the Three above. "They've fucked off. Left us here to scrape the fragments of the world up with dustpan and broom. You fought a Vhemin with the ancients' power. Maybe if the Tresward hadn't *also* fucked off along with their precious Three, you'd have more friends at your back."

They paced side by side for a while, neither making the first overture, until Geneve gusted a sigh full of self-hate and despair. "I've got friends enough. It wasn't them that—"

"No." He turned to her, hand on her arm. She shook it off but stopped walking. "We all did the parts as best we could. You want to blame someone? What about Armitage? He fell when a Feybrind ran him through."

"Armitage is Vhemin. They're strong, but not like the Feybrind—"

"Exactly. We all know how worthless I am with a blade, but what about Sight of Day? Will you say he sat idly by?"

She chewed her lip. "He couldn't fight his son—"

"And yet he did. But later. What about Vertiline?" Meriwether pointed to the head of the column. "Should she have stopped helping the refugees to match steel with Easing Seas? How would that have fared? Was his life worth more than theirs?"

"No, but—"

"But nothing. We've all got packs of guilt. We're drowning in it. But there's no one else." He reached for her again, and this time she didn't slap his hand away. "Trust me on this. You've done nothing wrong, and all things right. This was a horror. But it wasn't your horror."

She nodded, but her face was clouded like she had trouble reconciling the idea she wasn't to blame for letting the side down. "How do we make it right for him?"

"Sight of Day?" Meriwether let Geneve's arm go. "I've no idea. But perhaps the thing we can do first is be his good and loyal friends. Travel by his side, and carry as many cares as we can."

Geneve nodded again, and this time the motion was surer. "I can do that."

Meriwether smoothed his beard. "Come. I think the night's work's not yet done."

THEY MADE THE FEYBRIND'S VILLAGE BY DAWN. ARRAYED AT THE base of the giant trees were relief tents, complete with food and water.

Healers stood by to salve wounds. Smiths waited with hammer and chisel to break the captive's chains.

Geneve looked to the treetops. "We need to talk to Sings with Heart."

Meriwether nodded. "Maybe we should do that alone."

"I'd like that." She led them to one of the tree elevators. They rose into the treetops, watching the refugees grow smaller by the moment.

Meriwether leaned on the elevator's railing as the contraption creaked about them. "This should be terrifying, but it's not."

She bumped him with her hip. "That's because the Feybrind make everything well."

"It could also be I'm fresh out of terror. Last night was full of it." Meriwether covered her hand in his own. "Do you know what we're going to say?"

"No clue." The elevator reached the treetops, and they stepped out onto a wooden walkway. They followed their noses until they reached the main platform.

The elder waited, spear in the crook of her arm. Four honor guards waited with her, jewel-eyed Feybrind warriors with slender blades and restless tails. Her hands were slow and soft as she spoke. *{The king is dead.}*

Meriwether wanted to swear, good and loud. *Of* course *a runner reached her.* But Geneve shook her head. "The Vhemin are dead. But—"

"Tell me of your dreams." Meriwether stepped in. "You elevated one to king. He was broken against the wheel of monsters, and there's no taking that back. But you did it for a reason."

Sings with Heart considered him with brilliant, hard eyes. *{You speak like one who's used to being listened to.}*

"I come from a long line of assholes," Meriwether agreed. "Arrogance runs in the blood."

She gave him a sad half-smile. *{You speak more truth than the rest of your kind.}* Those emerald eyes found Geneve. *{The king said dragons would return. That we would straddle the world. I saw one fly overhead with my own eyes. We'd never live in fear of the monsters again.}*

Geneve pressed her lips into a line. "The dragon is real."

{How do you know?}

She glanced at Meriwether. "That's easy. It's cut from the cloth of our sins. Meri and I made it."

The elder set her spear aside, then padded on old yet still silent feet to them. She studied Geneve, a furred hand touching the Knight's chin. Geneve didn't pull away. *{You carry many hurts.}*

"Been a rough ride," Meriwether said.

Sings with Heart turned to him. *{You carry as much. Are dragons fashioned from pain?}*

"No idea," Meriwether admitted. "I was asleep for most of it."

She smirked. *{And still the honesty.}* Sings with Heart's tail lashed as the old Feybrind paced. *{We don't want to live in fear anymore. Monsters and humans have pushed us to the edges of this world. We hide in the margins. But you won't leave us alone. The trees are thinning, and there's nowhere left to hide. Was it too much to wish for a dragon?}*

Meriwether sighed. "No. And maybe you should keep wishing. But perhaps there's something else that's more powerful than a dragon."

Geneve nodded, touching her hand above her heart. "I was ... *am* a Knight of the Tresward. We're sworn to kill all sinners. They told us wielders of magic are a threat to the Three, and yet my best friend in the world is one they'd burn." She turned away, looking out across the treescape. "With us travels one of the People, and a monster he calls brother."

Meriwether stroked his chin. "Is it too much to hope that we might set aside our blades?"

Sings with Heart shrugged. *{I don't know. I don't think it will happen. The Vhemin are monsters, and the People are the waves that break on their rocks. It's always been this way, and I fear it always will be.}* She tapped nails against her spear's shaft. *{But it doesn't matter. We've no king, and no dragon.}*

"About that." Geneve ran fingers through red hair. "You say you saw it fly overhead. Was it going that way?" Her arm speared toward the northwest.

The elder nodded. *{The king ... Easing Seas said it was going to destroy our enemies.}*

"I don't think it was doing that." Geneve shook her head. "But we'll find out, if you'll let us go. *All* of us."

{You want my blessing to take the monster with you.} The elder inclined her chin. *{I think if I tried to stop you it would be a faster end to us than a dragon.}*

Meriwether tried for a smile with a little tooth in it. "We're asking, Sings with Heart. Not telling. Because like you, we'd like an end to the killing and the dying. The People have nothing to fear from the Vhemin who walks with us. I swear it."

{There can be such a thing as too much honesty.} Sings with Heart half-smiled. *{I wasn't going to stop you anyway. You've shown me an alliance might be a better path than that paved with blades. One of the People touched a weapon to my throat,}* she touched her neck, *{to defend a monster. The creature saved our People, some of yours, and killed his own kind. That same monster holds vigil with a Feybrind over loss too great for the telling of it.}* She folded her hands together. *{If it can happen once, perhaps again. But you can't go.}*

Geneve's eyes snapped up. "But—"

{Peace, Daughter of the Three.} The elder patted the air with her hands. *{I mean you are hurt. Stay for the night. One day longer might show more of the People the worth of a monster, and let you rest.}*

Geneve's shoulders tensed. "We've lost so much time." Then she deflated. "But you're right. We're hurt, all of us. Battered to the bone."

{And the soul.} The elder beckoned a Feybrind woman forward. *{This is Morning Song. She will make sure you have food and rest. There are plenty of dragons for you to face tomorrow.}*

Meriwether swallowed. "Uh, I think there's just the one dragon."

Sings with Heart half-smiled. *{That seems one dragon too many.}*

Geneve laughed. "Then tomorrow we face a surfeit of dragons."

Morning Song held her hand out toward the west end of the platform. *{This way.}*

‡

MORNING SONG LED THEM ON A JOURNEY THAT COLLECTED Vertiline, then Armitage and Sight of Day. She took the five to a small scattering of huts at the southern verge of the village. The Feybrind's amber eyes twinkled. *{This is a guest house. We don't have many guests, so it should be free of lice.}*

Armitage scratched his chest. "Thanks, I guess. Where's the food?"

On cue, food came on platters. Meriwether saw fruits and cold meats, but no bread; the People were carnivores, and while they had artisans who could make *anything*, bread had a little lead-up time. There were hard-boiled eggs as big as a fist, and smoked fish.

Healers visited but left after changing Vertiline's bandage. Armitage waved them off, his wounds already crusted over, and Sight of Day needed more healing than the world could give.

Vertiline rose, patting her belly. "I'm going to see if I can help."

"They said we should rest." Meriwether gnawed a piece of fish. It was excellent, the smokey flavor not overpowering.

"That's what I'm doing." Vertiline brushed her pale braid over her shoulder. "I'm resting my soul, sinner." He nodded, taking no offense.

Armitage stood, eyes on Vertiline for a moment, before grabbing Sight of Day's shoulder. "Come on, cat."

{I would rather—}

"I don't give a shit. We're going to work out a little stress." The Vhemin rolled his shoulders. "I think I saw some heavy rocks that needed moving this way." The pair drifted through the trees.

Meriwether watched them depart. He sat with Geneve at the forest's edge, belly full, but heart only half-way there. They'd saved a lot of people, sure, but at such a price as the paying of it would be felt for a long time yet. The Knight at his side felt it was her fault, and there weren't any words that would fix that. Time might, but they didn't have a lot of days in supply.

Geneve also watched Armitage and Sight of Day go. When the pair rounded a massive tree trunk, she nodded as if deciding something. "Meri, we need to talk."

He sat upright, stomach clenching. *This can't be good.*

Chapter Twenty-Two

Geneve sat within the ancient forest with her best friend in the world. They'd known each other for mere weeks. Hardly enough time as the gods measured things to know a person, but she felt she understood him better than herself.

Once, she'd tried to capture him for slaughter, and he forgave her. She'd failed to save Sight of Day's son, and he'd offered her counsel then too. Sometimes his words were easy to hear, other times hard, but always they held weight. *It's because he says them with me in mind, not himself.*

She watched a monster lead a Feybrind away. Mortal enemies once, friends forever. They slipped from view. Her heart raced, as if she was about to dive off a cliff. Geneve didn't know why she felt this way. She felt *fear*, bright and cold.

I'm afraid because of what I need to say. Meri's shown me words have true power, and those offered without care have consequences that can tilt the world. I don't want to ... fail.

She turned to him. "Meri, we need to talk."

He straightened, face paling a little. "Aye?"

Geneve smiled. "Don't worry, it's nothing serious." She hid behind a sheaf of hair. Shorter, but still red. *Don't lie. This is the most serious thing in the world.* "I need to say something, and I need you to be kind and gentle." She looked away. "I'm sorry. Always making demands. I mean to ask—"

He took her hands in his. "Say your piece. You've nothing to fear from me."

"Oh, Meri. That's not true. I've everything to fear." She blinked, trying to make her voice steady. "I've faced a Champion. I don't know why my heart's—"

Meri squeezed her hand. "It's going to be okay, Red."

Geneve nodded. "I hope so. The Tresward taught me many things, but most of all how to shield the world. They didn't tell me anything about protecting my heart." She shook her head. "That's not what I want to say. Last night, I fought a monster. I almost died, but that's not unusual. Afterward, when we talked in the forest—"

"Aye, I remember. I'm sorry about that—"

"No, don't be. That's not what I wanted to talk about either." Geneve grunted in frustration. How could she be so bad with words, and him so good? "I realized that I've almost died a hundred times. Sight of Day lost his son. The most precious thing in his world is gone, and he can never tell Easing Seas he loves him ever again. All those chances for truth and care are gone." Meri waited, eyes holding hers. "A moment is all it takes, and then all is left to memory. I mean to say ... why is this so hard!"

"All the things worth doing are." He didn't let her go. Didn't pull away. She wondered if he felt fear, then realized he must. She was torturing them both, and yet he stayed. A rock, waiting for the wave to wash over it.

Geneve took a steadying breath. "I mean to say I love you. I don't care if you don't love me back. I needed you to hear it, in case there's no more tomorrows. I want you to know that—"

He leaned forward, kissing her. His lips were warm, and soft. Geneve's heart hammered in her chest. She wanted *him*, the whole of him, and clutched his shirt with trembling hands.

Meri stilled her fingers. "I mean to say, I love you too. I love you like the dawn loves the sky. I think maybe I always have, but was just waiting to remember." Geneve stood, hauling him upright. "Wait, what—"

She crushed his mouth with another kiss, her hands fumbling at the buttons on his shirt. She could smell the warm rich scent of him. The smokiness of last night's explosion couldn't hide his Meri-ness. Geneve tore his shirt open, fingers running along his chest. He shivered, trembling under her touch.

Then his hands found her sides. They worked up her back, centimeter by centimeter. Teasing, slow, each fingertip like fire, her thin cotton insufficient to keep the smoldering touches at bay. He drew her close, face nibbling at her neck.

Geneve arched her back, holding him close. Then she grabbed his arm, dragging him toward the huts. They tangled together again as they reached the doorway. The wood banged behind Geneve as she shouldered it open. *Three above, but I can't stop touching him.*

They slammed against a wall, and he laughed. "Easy, Red. I'm not—"

She silenced him with more kisses, then dragged him to a bed. Geneve lay him back, admiring what she saw. His chest might be marred by scars, but she didn't *see* that. Geneve saw his face, and his heart, and the parts that made him her *Meri*. "You are beautiful."

His eyes were hungry, and he reached for her. "You are the most exquisite thing I've ever seen." His hands found the hem of her shirt, lifting, his lips kissing her belly, up her body, and finding the gentle curve of her breast. Meri nibbled, and she gasped, a shiver running through her.

Geneve grabbed for his pants, dragging the fastening aside. He shimmied, his length popping free. She grabbed him, and he shuddered. *By the Three, it's so hot.* She felt like she held a brand of fire. He hauled her shirt off, tossing it aside, hands ever-hungry, wanting, needing, *pleading*.

She let him go, then unfastened her pants. She shucked them into a corner, then pushed a hand on his chest, encouraging him to lie back. He trailed hands down her arms, those fingertips of fire making her shudder. Geneve reached low, finding his cock, running her hand along the length of his shaft, drawing, teasing.

He growled, hands around her waist. Geneve grinned from a halo of red hair, then lowered herself slowly, exquisitely onto him. He gasped, shuddering as fraction by fraction he entered her.

Geneve felt the impossible heat of him inside her. She kept lowering, her own hot slickness welcoming him in. He groaned as she bottomed out, rocking atop him. His fingers raked her back as she bent low, lips finding his collarbone, his neck, his ear.

Faster they moved. Together, iron and silk, heat within heat. Geneve's skin felt on fire, her body alive. Her hands found his chest. His skin was hot, as if made of burning sand. Their eyes locked together as they moved.

Geneve felt close and bit her lip. She moaned, unable to stop the noise escaping, and he stiffened, hips bucking. He pumped inside her, and she felt her own clenching. Geneve shuddered, a cry breaking free.

Release. Breath hot on her skin. Hers scalding his.

Geneve lowered her head, kissing him again. He pulled her close, hands roaming, as if they'd not yet had enough. She stroked his arm, then his hip, wanting this moment to last forever. She rolled onto her side, taking him with her, and stared into his eyes.

He stroked her jaw, hands delicate above her bruise. "You are the lantern of my life."

She nodded through red hair. "You say the nicest things. Say some more."

Meri laughed, fingers moving down her shoulder, eliciting a shiver of memory. "I want this moment to last forever."

"Keep talking."

"I'm not a performing seal."

Geneve grinned, kissing him fierce and hard. "No. You're all the stars brought to one place, and I love you."

His smile was warm and soft, like daylight breaking over the land. "You say the nicest things, too. Keep going."

Geneve grinned wider. Maybe words held more than weight. Maybe they held hope, and if you were lucky, became keys that could unlock the heart.

GENEVE LAY WITH MERI'S HEAD ON HER SHOULDER. HIS HAND traced laps on her belly while she curled fingers in his unruly hair. "Your beard itches."

"You should feel it from this side." He pulled back, a smile threatening to break free of the thicket. "It's no broom yet, but—"

"Nor shall it ever become so." Geneve raised a warning eyebrow. "Keep it just the way it is."

"Aye, as you wish." He rested his head against her again. "I don't want to move ever again."

She sighed, feeling a warm tingle from her feet to her head. "Me neither."

"But we're going to have to."

"I fear the truth of your words, Meri. Mostly because we need to eat at some point."

He laughed. "Then let's eat, so we can get back to the business of," he swept his arm down her form, "this magnificence."

Geneve gave him a playful push, then swung her legs from the bed. She made her way to a pile of clothes that looked mostly hers. "I wonder where everyone else is."

"I hope they're having as much fun." Meri bounced from the bed, stretching his lean frame, then fetching his own garments. He held his pants as if weighing them. "Hmm."

"Something wrong?"

"Maybe." He sniffed. "You smell that?"

Geneve tested the air. "Smoke from the cookfire."

"Hmm." The sound was heavy with doubt. "I don't think so. We're not that lucky."

She pulled her white cotton pants on, then rammed her arm through a shirt sleeve. "Let's go look." Geneve sighed. "I don't have my armor."

They finished dressing, then headed outside. There friends hadn't returned. Meri visored his eyes. "I see no one."

Geneve felt unease stir her gut. "There's giving people privacy, and then there's—"

"Something badly wrong," Meri finished. "One day! They promised us a single day of no dying."

A rumbling roar came from the distance, followed by a guttural scream. *Vhemin!* Geneve cast about for her blade, finding Requiem nestled atop a bundle of belongings. She grabbed the weapon, tearing it from its sheath. Geneve wanted to tell Meri to *stay here*, but he'd earned more than that. "This is going to be dangerous."

"Aye. I'm ready for it." He pulled his knife free, testing the point on his thumb. "Ow!" He sucked his now punctured thumb.

"Slayer of monsters. I see it now." She tossed him a grin. He caught it, returning it with twice the shine. "We need to help the Feybrind against the Vhemin. Can you at least stay behind me?"

"I wasn't thinking of going first. That's crazy." He cocked his head, listening. "You hear thunder?"

Geneve heard the rapid hammer of hooves on loam, and turned to see Morning Song atop Tristan, leading the herd of their mounts. None were bridled, all running free, manes teased by the wind. Except for Beck, who loped along sans mane, but still a part of the herd. *One day the Feybrind will tell me how they can get horses to do anything without bit or bridle.* The horses pulled up in a scatter of mulch and earth as Morning Sun leaped clear, landing cat-perfect three meters from Geneve. *{Greetings, Daughter of the Three. You must run.}*

Geneve looked at the Feybrind, the horses, then Requiem. "I can help."

{We don't need your steel. This is our home, and those who come against it will die.} The woman's amber eyes glittered. *{You seek to kill a dragon, which we can't do. You do your job, we'll do ours, and maybe we'll make it through. Or, you could rush headlong into the traps we've set for the monsters and die horribly. It's your call.}*

Meri laughed. "It seems all Feybrind share Sight of Day's way with words."

{You are talking instead of running.} Morning Song shook her head. *{I've no idea how you became the most populated race upon the world. Still, rats have a similar low cunning, and they are tremendous in number. Tasty, too.}*

Geneve felt like she wanted to run toward the battle. *Shield the Feybrind.* But Morning Song was right enough: the Feybrind could fight the Vhemin, or fade into the woods. They couldn't beat a dragon. Perhaps no one could, but Geneve knew the Tresward stood the best chance of all. They held the Light of the Three and called on the Storm. She sheathed Requiem with a grunt. "Then let's be off, tail between our legs."

Morning Song peered behind Geneve, her own tail lashing. {It must be very small. Is it any use at all?}

They gathered their packs and bags quickly, lashing them to the horses. Armitage and Sight of Day returned from the woods, and a moment later long-legged Vertiline loped over. "The Feybrind are taking the wounded to safety. It's like what they did to us, but with far more kindness." She gave their mounts a once-over with a caustic eye. "Running, then?"

"It's a long and tedious story," Meri said. "I'll bore you with it on the way."

Armitage peered into the trees at another Vhemin cry of pain. "No one lets me have any fun."

Morning Song stroked her chin. {You seem content murdering your brethren.}

"Those fuckers," Armitage stabbed a finger into the trees, "ain't my kin. Maybe once the runt's finished boring us with why we're running instead of murdering, I'll talk you to sleep with a treatise on Vhemin culture and ethics."

{I'd rather die,} Morning Song admitted. {Let's go.}

They mounted up, Morning Song riding double with Sight of Day. The pair took the lead. Geneve kept low to Tristan's back by force of habit as they cantered through the trees. His hooves churned the forest floor to clods in his wake. Meri rode to her right, beaming from ear to ear as Chesterfield made the rush look like a casual stroll along the beach. Black as midnight, the charger surged effortlessly beside Tristan.

The trees thinned, and they made it to a short dock next to a mighty river. It was easily two klicks across. A small barge waited for them, more of the People already on board and ready to sail. Wood clattered under Tristan's hooves as Geneve rode him down the dock and onto the barge. She slid from his back, then turned to examine the trees. A line or two of smoke reached above the canopy, but otherwise there wasn't much sign of an enemy assault.

The barge handlers released the mooring lines, and the river teased the vessel from the docks. Geneve watched the Feybrind shore vanish behind them as the water drew them north. She stood by the railing, wondering if Iz would have stayed behind, or run. The Valiant might not have trusted the People as she did, and wouldn't have seen duty in their cause. *Does that make me a better or worse Tresward?*

Geneve didn't know, and after her fight with Ballast she wasn't sure if the Three saw her fit either. She'd never seen weapons that withstood the touch of the Storm. Hopefully they *were* ancient relics; the alternative was the Three's grace leaving her.

If the latter, fighting a dragon was going to be hard.

Chapter Twenty-Three

Meriwether felt happy. It took him a while to put his finger on what the warm buzz inside *meant*, because he'd never felt quite like this before. Sure, he'd met people he liked, but Geneve was different. And *yes*, he'd had a tumble with a doxy before too. This was *completely* different to that kind of affair.

He watched the water slip past the barge, enjoying the feeling inside. *Happiness is a thing more people should feel.* Armitage joined him, snake eyes surveying the river. "Did you two fuck?"

Meriwether raised an eyebrow. "It's good to see you, too. How was your morning?"

The monster grunted. "Fucked. The cat's miserable. And now I'm irritable, runt, because someone's getting their end away and it's not me."

"I didn't say that." Meriwether went back to staring at the water. He let out a big, contented sigh.

The monster spat in disgust. "No, you're very discreet."

Meriwether smiled, patted Armitage on the arm, and went to find Morning Song. The barge was horse-driven, with a modest Feybrind crew of five making sure it didn't crash or sink. Despite the small crew, the Feybrind barge had two decks, and was thirty meters bow to stern.

There was no one aboard apart from the Feybrind sailors, Morning Song, and Meriwether's friends.

He found the Feybrind woman at the barge's fore. She stood with arms crossed, watching the world approach. "Excuse me."

She faced him. *{I heard you coming. Your feet are very loud.}*

"Yes, I've been told that before." He pointed to the western bank. "Are we getting off over there?"

{Yes, but not for a while. Where the river widens, there's a small island in the middle. That marks the point we disembark. We don't want to go further.} She scratched behind her ear. *{That's where we part ways.}*

"Ah." Meriwether nodded. "You could stay with us, you know."

{While you don't smell nearly as bad as the rest of your kind, I've things to do.} Morning Song watched a butterfly dance past. *{My city burns.}*

"I need some advice." Meriwether put his back to the railing. "Sight of Day lost his son, and I don't know what to do. He's my friend, and I want to help carry this load. But I don't understand the Feybrind well."

Garnet eyes found his. *{You understand us well enough. You see our pain and want to help. And in this, he needs what any would. Good friends, time, and a lot of alcohol.}*

Meriwether laughed. "Okay. I can get him drunk. Thank you." He turned to go.

Her hand caught his arm. *{You're a good man. Why?}*

"A curious question." He scratched his beard. "Because it feels bad to not be good, I guess."

{And yet so many are happy feeling bad.} Morning Song considered him, a half-smile about her lips. *{Remember this conversation. In your future there will be a chance for you to make more of a difference than a single Knight, Feybrind, or Vhemin at a time.}*

He pressed his lips into a line. "I don't want to rule."

{A good man would say that. A better man would understand it's the things we want least we must do.} Her hands moved hard, insistent. *{Would the world be better served by letting a different lord sit a throne? Or an unknown monster, rising from the ashes of a destroyed barony?}*

"It turns out I don't want your advice anymore." Meriwether sighed. "I was with you right to the getting drunk part."

{Advice is easy to give. Everyone's got an opinion. You only have to ask

them.} Orange eyes twinkled. *{If it counts, the People will cleave to you. You gave our families back to us.}*

"That was Geneve."

{You say it like you are two people.} Morning Song's teeth showed through her half-smile. *{You say it like two hearts so close together can walk separate paths.}*

Meriwether looked at his feet. "We didn't get everyone."

{Also spoken like a good man. Seeing what you failed to do, rather than what you did. On the trip back from the holdfast, what did you say to her?}

"You were listening?"

{We've talked about how loud you are.}

Meriwether sighed. "I said she'd done nothing wrong, and it wasn't her horror."

{There's hope for your mayfly people after all.} Morning Song stroked his cheek. *{Make ready. We'll disembark within a half-hour.}*

۞

MERIWETHER SPENT THE HALF-HOUR WITH GENEVE. THEY SAT ON a low bench near the barge's rear, leaning against one another. He found her hand with his, and enjoyed the smell of her hair and the touch of her skin. They spoke of little, enjoying the thin slice of time they had between bouts of people trying to murder them.

Sight of Day offered a half-smile through his pain when he saw them. Armitage gave a withering glare. And Vertiline nodded, like she'd seen something confirmed she'd known about for a long, long time. The three left them alone, perhaps understanding that tomorrow they could all be dead.

The sign things weren't going smoothly was the rapid movements of the barge's Feybrind crew. They stopped doing shiply things, instead dredging weapons from lockers. The cats belted swords to their sides and readied bows. Geneve straightened, eyes scanning the shore. "What's going on?"

Sight of Day padded close. *{I'm sorry to disturb this wonderful moment, but Vhemin await at the docks.}*

Geneve detached her fingers from Meriwether's and stood. "Then we cut through."

"That's the plan." Armitage lumbered past, hefting a cruel-looking boat hook. "I'm testing this."

"Sight of Day, can you help me?" Meriwether stood. "We'll get the horses."

Vertiline strode past, belting her new shield to her stump. "It's about time to kick ass and take names."

"Nah." Armitage shook his head. "I'll kick ass, but I ain't taking names. I'm terrible with names."

She flashed a pale smile. "That'll do, monster."

Meriwether went to the pens with Sight of Day. Beck stood by the gate, guarding his pack of herbivores. The Feybrind scratched the bear's ears with clever fingers, then slipped over the railing and into the pen. He moved among the horses, a gentle touch there, a scritch there. "You know, I probably should have just left you to this."

The Feybrind's eyes glittered gold. *{But then you'd have tried to fight, and you're even worse at that.}*

"Thanks."

{Anytime.} The cat favored Meriwether with a half-smile that struggled to rise.

Meriwether stepped within the pens. He checked the horse's saddles and bridles, then made sure their gear was well-fastened. It's possible the number of Vhemin waiting for them meant a run rather than fight, and he didn't want to leave anyone behind.

Armitage roared, "You assholes, come get some!"

"I guess it's starting." Meriwether moved to the western side of the pens and looked out over the water. As Morning Song had said, a small island broke the river in half. It was dotted with trees, a clutch of rocks at its base. There was a dock on the western bank already bristling with Vhemin. Many of the monsters held crossbows. "Not this shit again."

The Feybrind's captain stood on the second deck, steering the barge, while the rest of his crew went to the western railing. They readied bows, loosing arrows into the waiting Vhemin. Many of the monsters dropped, but some raised shields over the fellows, stopping the deadly rain from doing its job.

Sight of Day shook his head, walked to the railing, and loosed a shaft. Meriwether watched it arc over the water. It hit the edge of a shield and ricocheted into the throat of a Vhemin. He held a hand out in a *see?* gesture. The other Feybrind bent to the task of arrow trick shots with a will, felling Vhemin after Vhemin. Not all their shafts made it through, but enough to drop tens of monsters into the river.

"Do all the People make a game of life?" Meriwether watched as Feybrind tried to one-up each other with their shots.

{Yes.} Sight of Day nodded with his fist. *{In moments the monsters will unleash a volley of death on us. Wouldn't you rather go to your end smiling into the teeth of danger?}*

"I'd prefer no danger at all."

The cat clapped him on the back. *{And yet it prefers you. Embrace your destiny.}*

The fusillade of quarrels began from the Vhemin-besieged bank. Geneve and Vertiline moved back and forth, slicing bolts from the sky with their steel. Armitage bellowed challenge and took a quarrel in the shoulder for his trouble. He tore it free, tossing it into the water with a laugh. "That the best you've got?"

It looked like they might make it, right up to the point the captain took a quarrel to the eye. He fell like a stone. Meriwether scrabbled to the upper deck before his brain could take over, sliding to a halt next to the fallen Feybrind. There was nothing to do. He'd been killed instantly.

The barge's wheel turned, and the craft started to slew. *I've never sailed a barge. But how hard can it be?* Meriwether grabbed the wheel, trying to straighten the vessel. They bore toward the island, but under his hands the barge steadied.

Crossbow shafts fell about him like hard rain. He yelled, hunching. One hit the deck a centimeter from his left foot. Another rebounded from the wheel, giving a hornet's kiss to his cheek as it spun away. He ducked for cover. The wheel turned free again, the barge's rudder caught by the current, and then a crossbow shaft lodged in the wheel's mechanism, seizing it solid.

Meriwether stood, patted himself down to make sure he didn't have any bolts lodged anywhere, then tried to wrestle the wheel again. It was stuck fast. He put his weight into it, but all he got was a creaking of wood. Meriwether looked ahead, the island approaching with the measured tread of a rampaging ogre. The water frothing against the rocks by the island foretold their ending.

"We're going to die," he realized. "Right here, right now, and all because an imbecile put docks right next to a hazard."

"Meri!" Geneve's voice came from below.

"Hold onto something!" he called back.

"What?"

The roar of the river against rocks grew louder than the steady rain of crossbow bolts. The barge turned its slow arc in the water. The bow hit the rocks with a *crunch* that knocked Meriwether from his feet. The vessel lurched about, and one of the horses whinnied. Beck bellowed a panic, alongside Armitage's roared, "What the fuck?"

Another crunch, and the barge turned a sickening circle before jolting against another rock. Meriwether stumbled, lurching for the side. He snared the railing before going over, rocks below laced with the white fangs of water.

The barge groaned, the sound sick and pained. A Feybrind fell, dropped by a quarrel. Meriwether looked about for something, *anything* to do. The ship broke free of the rocks, and he almost whooped with joy until he realized it was only *half* the barge.

The important half, which was the one with him on it, drifted on, sinking fast. The keel snared on the river bottom, and Meriwether was tossed overboard. He sailed over rocks, landing with a splash. The ever-hungry river held him with frigid claws, dragging him below.

Chapter Twenty-Four

Geneve saw Meri go over the side, and it felt like her heart followed on his heels. The barge was tearing apart about her. The top deck dropped a half-meter, hitting Armitage on the head. The monster bellowed, staggering.

The ship lurched, the sound of tearing timber like the end of the world. Water surged over the decks. She spied Troubles kicking water. Beck paddled, trying to keep his head above churning white as the ship sank. Water surged, lapping Geneve's boots.

She slipped Requiem into its scabbard, then sprinted for the side. She speared into the water after Meri, diving deep. Below the water the noise vanished. Geneve could see trails of bubbles following crossbow shafts as they lanced deep. She remembered her Trial, where they'd asked her to swim down to retrieve her blade. It'd been so cold, and so far.

This is easy by comparison. Hold to that and find Meri.

Geneve kicked deeper. A massive piece of broken barge sank to the river bottom, its undertow threatening to pull her along too. She fought against it. Ahead, she spied Meri's pale face. His leg looked trapped by wreckage. She swam for him. He was tugging fiendishly on his leg, then pulled his knife free.

She made it to him as he set the steel against his leg. His eyes widened in surprise at seeing her. Geneve took the knife from him before he could do himself an injury. The hilt was river cooled, with no memory of his touch. She pulled him close as she slipped it into its sheath, then bent to examine his leg.

The light wasn't good, and her hair fanned about her face, but as near as she could tell it was pinned by a beam from the barge that had wedged between rocks. Water churned above them as a horse—impossible to tell which one—swam above. They hunkered low. Geneve grabbed the beam, set her feet against the river bottom, and *heaved*.

It didn't budge. She drew her scattergun, pointing at the beam, but the weapon clicked uselessly. Meri patted her arm. He waved her away. {*Go. Help the others.*}

She shook her head. {*Never!*}

Meri gave her a sad smile, his own hair swirling like a dark coronet. {*Sometimes there's no happy ending, Red.*} He reached for his knife again.

Geneve shook her head. There *had* to be a lesson from the Three she could use. They'd given the Tresward twenty-one hundred patterns, predicting every combat situation the world would ever see. The trouble was working out which one; many weren't understood even by the Champions and saw little use.

If she could bring the Light here, just a little piece of it, she could break the beam. It would need a fraction of their gift. A dram, and Meri would be free. But the water slowed her movements and would starve her strikes of power. Geneve wouldn't be able to make the perfect movements the Storm demanded.

But I've got to try. She squared off against the beam, touching it with the tips of her fingers. It was heavy, old timber, well-seasoned and strong. Geneve wound up, then slammed her fist into it. The river tugged her arm, slowing her, and the beam didn't break. *By the Three, the beam didn't even* notice. *Do better!*

Geneve wracked her memory. There had to be a lesson here somewhere. The Three gave them the Storm and the perfect steps to master it. They'd made everything else in the world, including this water. *Perhaps it's not about mastering the Storm, but the water.*

Maybe this was a trick for Sway, not Storm. She felt it about her, the invisible force the Clerics used to heal wounds or move the minds of the weak. Geneve reached for it. *Hear my call. Make this wood lighter.*

She got her hands under the beam and tried to lift it again. It moved a fraction, but not enough to get Meri's leg free. Her lungs were starting to burn; she couldn't imagine what he felt like. He didn't have her training.

If I don't do this, Meri will drown.

Geneve heaved. She felt her back twinge with the strain, but the wood didn't move.

If I don't do this, Meri will die!

The water swirled about her, calling her soul to its depths. *Of course - the water! Don't Sway the wood; instead, free your arms. Sway and Storm together.* Geneve had barely used Sway, so expecting the wood to be something it wasn't was too much of a stretch. But perhaps she could ask the water to ... step aside?

Hear my call. //LET. ME. PAST.//

She clenched her fist, slamming it forward. The water let her arm go for a fraction of time. Just enough for her form to reach perfection. The skin of her hand glowed golden yellow, and the beam shattered into kindling, the fragments pulled away by the current.

Meri popped free. She followed him up, both breaking the surface at the same time. He gasped, choking as he breathed a little water in. The water held them close as it dragged them downriver. His arms flailed before his brain took over. She kicked water. "Are you okay?"

"I almost died!"

"Is that a yes?"

He turned in the water. "We have to get out of here. Morning Song said we'd die if we went past the docks."

Geneve bobbed, trying to see what was ahead. "Was she specific?"

"She's a Feybrind!"

Okay, so not specific. A piece of the barge's decking swirled past. Geneve grabbed it with one arm, Meri with the other, and hauled him close. "Get on."

He floundered, but made it up well enough. He shuffled to the opposite side for balance, then helped her aboard their makeshift raft.

Geneve stood carefully, making sure she had her balance, then stared ahead. "Okay, there's good news and bad news."

"I'll take the bad first."

"We're probably going to die."

"Hah. What's the good news?" Meri ran a hand through his hair, slicking water from it.

"The Feybrind told the truth." Geneve tried for a tired smile. "The river vanishes ahead. I can see green past it. I think the river goes into a hole."

"This huge river goes into a waterfall?" Meri blinked. "I guess it's going to be a spectacular way to go."

"Wait." Geneve peered ahead, trying to make out shapes against the spray foaming where the water stopped. She made out three figures standing on what looked like thin air by the water's edge. The brutish form could only be Armitage. Sight of Day's tail lashed, and Vertiline waved. "It's them."

He stood, balance a little unsteady. "Are they standing on air?"

"That's what I thought too." Geneve squinted, unable to make out the details. The three were right in the middle of the river. The surging torrent was a good three klicks wide. "We can try getting to them. We'll never make the bank before we reach the waterfall. Come. I'll help you."

Meri gave her a jaundiced look. "How are you going to swim for two?"

Geneve gritted her teeth in frustration. "Meri, you'll not make it alone."

"Be as may ... by the Three, what's that?" His eyes widened at the riverbank over her shoulder.

Geneve turned. The riverbank held nothing but trees. No Vhemin waited. She almost managed to turn back before he put both hands in the small of her back and *shoved*. Geneve's arms windmilled, and then she went over.

Water closed over her head for a moment before she broke the surface. Meri pointed. "That way! Swim there!"

The current was pulling them further apart. *Meri knew he would slow me down. He knew neither of us would make it if I was with him.* She wanted to go to him, but the river had her now.

There's a chance. I need to swim better than in my Trial. Geneve powered through the water with strong overhand strokes, making for her friends. She made good progress, outpacing the raft with Meri on it. As she drew closer to her companions, she saw they stood on a plat-form. Armitage tossed something to her. She grabbed for it, hands closing on a coarse hemp rope. He hauled her in hand over hand, Sight of Day pulling her from the water as she hit the platform.

She saw the fashioning of their rescue. One must have used the rope to fetch the others from the river. They stood on a surface of old metal, rusted through in many places. Steps led down from the side, but she didn't have time for that. She grabbed the rope, handing the end to Armitage. "Monster, be ready."

He stared across the water, marking Meri on his raft. The raft swirled closer, but would never make it. "That's a hell of a jump." His hand fell on her shoulder. "You better make it, you hear me?"

"I hear you." She held the rope in one hand, sighted the distance, then sprinted. Her arms and legs pumped. Geneve tried to ignore the weight of the waterlogged hemp, instead focusing on how it dragged her off balance. The platform's edge was before her, then beneath her as she reached peak speed.

Geneve leaped.

Chapter Twenty-Five

Meriwether hadn't expected to live this long. He'd been on the run so long, he'd almost forgotten what it meant to have a place to live. *Of course, I've never known the loving touch of caring parents. That's a mystery for others to untangle.* Despite that, he hadn't fashioned on going out by drowning.

The good news is, I probably won't drown. My body will be shattered on the rocks on the way down, or I'll crater the bottom, leaving nothing but food for the crabs.

Wait. Were there freshwater crabs?

He sighed, watching Geneve power to safety. *Thing is, she's secure at least. I spent my one shot for the right play. She'll save the world from the dragon we made together, and now I'll never need to worry about what it might mean to take up the Barony du Reeves.*

The waterfall's mouth raced toward him. Meriwether tried not to look at his friends meters away. He didn't want them burdened with his fear and desperation as he approached the end. Instead, he fixed his eyes front. If nothing else, he wanted to face death. Look it square in the eyes, and experience everything toward the end. There'd be nothing after this. Not for a sinner like him. Just a long blackness.

The raft scudded toward the drop. He wanted to call out something like *I love you!* to Geneve, but that was regret talking. Better she wasn't burdened with the weak wail of a dying man.

The raft kicked beneath his feet right at the water's descent into a maw of mist and foam. He had a moment to think, *Of course, a rock's throwing off my best-laid plans to look death in the eye,* and then he was falling.

Meriwether almost screamed as the raft fell into the raging maw. The wood tumbled away, splintering against rocks as the waterfall hammered it to splinters. But he didn't follow it. Meriwether felt strong arms clutch him as he dropped. His fall jerked to a halt, then he swung a mad arc out by the raging torrent. He wanted to scream. A mad giggle fought to escape his clenched teeth.

The arms about him tightened, and Geneve's lips were by his ear. She raised her voice to be heard over the torrent. "Got you."

They rose an arm length at a time, tireless and sure. Above, Vertiline and Sight of Day looked down, the cat's hands ready alongside Vertiline's outstretched arm. A length of rope connected them to a platform, and it was being hauled up by Armitage. The monster pulled them arm over arm, his Vhemin strength keeping them from death.

Their friends pulled Meriwether and Geneve from the brink. The pair flopped on an old metal platform. Meriwether cackled. "Hah! I'm alive!"

"Great." Geneve rolled over and got an arm under her. "Now I'm going to kill you." She shook her head. "But first things first." She got to her feet, then faced Armitage. "Armitage."

He inclined his chin. "Not monster?"

"Not ever again." She clutched him in a hug. "Thank you."

Meriwether got himself upright. The five of them were a bedraggled mess. Vertiline's usually pale hair was dark and wet. Sight of Day looked like a drowned rat. Geneve's hair plastered her face. *If these mighty warriors look like hell, I must look a special kind of horrible.* He staggered away, trying to tip water from his ear while taking stock.

The platform they were on looked to be the start of a bridge. The metal reached broken fingers over a chasm into which the waterfall thundered. The bridge had rotted to nubs a long time ago. The ancients made well, but the teasing kisses of a hundred water droplets eroded this a long time ago.

Steps led down the side of the platform. Meriwether peered over, sighting a small collection of gear. No horses, and no Beck. The sack containing his surprise gift for Geneve was a dark, wet heap, but at least it was there. *So, few supplies. No mounts. We're cold and wet. How could this end poorly?*

The stairs headed down the chasm, matching the waterfall's length right to the bottom, or close enough as his eyes could measure. The water hammered a massive pool, which sprouted a secondary river leading beneath the opposite cliff face. They couldn't get off this platform, unless one of them sprouted wings, so they headed below.

❦

THE BOTTOM OF THE STEPS WEREN'T EASY TO REACH. TIME HAD worked its grubby magic, wearing away chunks of material. The metal creaked and groaned. They even found places where whole patches of step were missing. It needed teamwork and the rope to get everyone down, but they made it. No one died, but as they descended, Meriwether wondered if they *wanted* to. Armitage was suffering the most, his cold blood turning sluggish as the waterfall's spume misted over them like a particularly clammy blanket.

His teeth didn't chatter, but his snake eyes were unfocused, his movements like a sleepwalkers: clumsy, exaggerated, and without obvious purpose.

The bottom of the steps made the party gawp for a while. At the waterfall's base, the river hammered into a huge pool that seemed bottomless. A channel bored through the rock to the south, taking the water elsewhere. The lake was ringed with water-worn rocks and strewn with debris. Pieces of the barge lay among older unidentifiable wreckage. Ancient skeletons of beasts and humanoids of all kinds huddled in broken heaps.

Meriwether lifted a bent and rusted sword. The blade might have been well-made; it had the look of Feybrind smithing. But that hadn't saved it on the descent. *If we'd come the fast way down, there'd be nothing left*. The waterfall's base might have been nice under other circum-stances. Away from the thunder of falling water, the pool shallowed out. Small trees huddled under the meager light from above. The obvious exit, aside from the death-first underground river, was a massive tunnel leading to the north. Meriwether squinted, trying to fathom if it was natural or constructed. Stalactites clung to the roof, muddying what might have been clean lines with organic structures.

Water continued along the tunnel's base, suggesting it may once have been a causeway, but built on a scale that made Meriwether's mind shy away. The ceiling of the tunnel shouldered the rock a good five hundred meters above his head, and it was a klick wide at the base. *How much water used to flow this way? What was it used for?* All the people who knew were long dust.

He approached Sight of Day, who crouched by the water's edge. At the cat's feet was a small matted heap of what used to be a Feybrind. One of the barge's crew most likely, but the body was so damaged as to be unrecognizable. "I'm ... so sorry."

The Feybrind stood, tail hanging limp. *{The evil of this world demands a heavy price. The People always pay.}*

"Let's find out who holds the ledger and take our own toll." He stepped back to give the cat room.

After a moment Sight of Day nodded, leaving the water's edge. He passed Meri, pausing to put a furred hand on his shoulder. *{Thank you for caring. Most humans don't see the People. Only what we make, and the things we can do for them.}*

"Most humans are assholes."

{I'm glad you said what everyone was thinking.} The cat's tail lashed, but he bared a half-grin.

Vertiline stood with Armitage. Her shield was lashed to her arm, but her scabbard hung empty, blade lost in the barge's fall. Armitage looked like a ship with a damaged keel, listing to the left. His breath came in short *huffs*. Meriwether took stock. "How is he?"

"Dying," the pale Knight said. She put her palm against the Vhemin's chest. "His heart is slow, and limps to discordant music." Despite her words, Armitage still clutched a boat hook in a scaled fist. "We must build a fire."

Meriwether nodded, and went to find his heart's companion. He found Geneve rummaging through wreckage. She brushed red hair from her eyes as he approached. "There's nothing here."

"There's plenty here," he corrected. "It's all broken trash, though."

She heaved a piece of timber aside. "The wood is too sodden to burn. I worry for Armitage. His kind can't take the cold."

"Then let's be off." Meriwether pointed to the huge tunnel. "That way looks best."

She cocked an eyebrow. "It is also the only way."

"We could always swim." He hugged himself, feeling a chill shake his frame. "Or not."

They set off into the tunnel. The water here moved very little; it appeared more of an extension to the pool behind them, the underground river taking most of it away. They left the chute to the sky behind, but the light didn't fade as Meriwether feared. The tunnel's walls were lined with a moss that glowed with a faded yellow luminescence. The water level dropped, perhaps as the tunnel inclined—Meriwether was too cold and tired to care how. Sight of Day padded ahead as if Feybrind didn't worry about the cold. *Of course, he's the only one with a fur coat.*

Vertiline's hand kept straying to her empty scabbard. "I shouldn't have lost my blade. Some Knight I am."

Meriwether unsheathed his knife, offering it to her. "Here's a blade." He adjusted the weight of the sack he carried.

"Oh, good. I'll be able to fight very small people." The pale woman took it with a sour look. "You give me your only blade?"

"I kind of suck at using it." He shrugged. "That blade in my hands is an accident waiting to happen."

She inclined her chin. "My thanks."

Ahead, Armitage lumbered to a halt. Geneve stopped by his side. "Are you okay?"

The monster nodded. "I'm fine." Then he fell face-first into the shallow water.

Meriwether rushed to their side. Sight of Day bounded from the tunnel ahead. Vertiline lent her aid, and together, they muscled the Vhemin from the water and into a sitting position. Meriwether crouched before Armitage, snapping his fingers before the Vhemin's face. *No response.* "Armitage?"

"It feels really warm down here." The monster's voice was dream-like, if gravel could have dreams.

"Get him up." Meriwether put one of Armitage's arms over his shoulder. Geneve took the other side, and together they muscled the Vhemin upright. The creature smelled like wet leather, and his skin was the cold kiss of a dead gecko. "Come on. We need a fire."

They followed the tunnel, moving as fast as they could with Armitage in his state. Vertiline and Sight of Day took the lead, ranging further down the tunnel, looking for conflict. Sight of Day returned, golden eyes bright. *{There is something ahead that might help.}*

"Might?" Meriwether said.

{Do you remember the insect in the desert?} The Feybrind half-smiled.

"I thought that was a dream!"

{And it will be again. There is a hive of them ahead. It is very dangerous to go near for your kind.} The cat frowned. *{Mine, too. The People can take a few bites, but not many.}*

"So we get a bug and get it to bite Armitage?" Geneve adjusted the monster's arm over her shoulder.

{I don't know if the insect will kill him or not.} Sight of Day spread his hands. *{The insects aren't nature's little helpers. They're always hungry.}*

Meriwether craned around Armitage's bulk, meeting Geneve's eyes. "Could kill him."

Vertiline stormed back to them. "By the Three, look at him!" Her voice was hard, a tinge of fear alongside the iron. "He is *already dead!*"

Meriwether nodded. "So, all we need to do is get him to the insects without us dying?"

{That's the size of it.} Sight of Day stroked his chin. *{Let's get him closer.}*

Meriwether and Geneve hauled Armitage down the tunnel. The water grew shallower before fading out, leaving old stone and stalag-mites instead. Armitage twitched between them as small cries came from him. His hands clutched the air, grasping dreams. *Or maybe he sees the ghosts of his ancestors.*

Ahead, a low hum. It wasn't the happy buzz of bees making

honey, but rather the flat tone of a hive readying for war. A crooked arc of stalagmites made a rude fence by the tunnel's wall. Above them was a matted collection of mud, looking like a massive hornet hive.

Black insects that had the seeming of the bastard offspring of beetles and wasps crawled across the surface. They were the size of Meriwether's thumb, and had fine membranous wings. "You got one of *those* to bite me?"

Sight of Day sliced the air with his hand. *{Hush. They're attracted to noise.}*

Vertiline paled further, backing away a step. *{That knowledge would have been useful earlier.}*

{We should be fine. Just don't scream.} The Feybrind took a step toward the hive.

"Murder!" Armitage roared. His snake eyes were wild, staring at things only he could see.

Meriwether and Geneve froze. The hive's hum lowered, then silenced. Sight of Day spun. *{Run!}*

The hive exploded in a rain of angry black shapes. Vertiline's braid whipped the air as she spun, fleeing. Sight of Day bounded past her. Meriwether didn't know what to do, but took heart in Geneve also staying, the monster held between them. The cloud of insects swirled like a tornado, widening out, hunting prey.

Armitage bellowed again, then shoved Meriwether aside. He punched Geneve in the side of the head, staggering the surprised Knight, then ran at the hive, mouth wide, a maw of shark teeth. Meriwether stayed close to the ground, pulling himself toward Geneve. He left the sack where it fell, contents be damned.

The Vhemin collided with the hive, staggering back. The papier-mâché construction *cracked*, a jagged rent running from the base to the top. Insects swarmed over him. Armitage roared rage, flailing, mashing insects to pulp. But there were so many. *Thousands*. They landed, trying to bring the brute to his knees.

Geneve righted herself, Requiem in hand, but she stared at the blade as if wondering how you fought a swarm with steel. A black body landed on her neck, stinging her. She hollered, slapping it away. Meriwether risked the lofty heights of an upright position, swirling his cloak about them both. "Down!"

She crouched with him. The makeshift tent about them hid from view whatever horror was going on just meters from them. Meriwether felt the impacts of insects against his cloak and clutched it tighter. Geneve whimpered, leaning heavily against him. Meriwether wondered what was in the bite of the insect. That it could raise him nearly from dead, but bring her low.

The angry buzz quietened, but Armitage's bellowing didn't. He roared, on and on. Alongside his noise came the *crunch* of breaking nest as he went berserk against the hive. The Vhemin gave a jubilant shout. "Got you, you little fucker!" A final crunch. A sound like hard rain, then silence. The Vhemin's footsteps lumbered closer, and Meriwether blinked as Armitage ripped their cloak aside. He glared snake eyes at them. In one hand, he held the pulped remains of a massive black insect. "Here's the queen. Doesn't taste too bad." He took another bite, crunching on chitin.

Meriwether looked around. The ground was a graveyard of fallen black shapes. Armitage was covered in the slick, mashed remains of a thousand insects. "How did you ... survive?"

Armitage took the last bite of the queen, then licked his palm. "Thick skin. Got bit a couple times, but it was just what I needed. Got the heart beating right again. I feel like a new man." He wiped his hand against his ichor-coated chest, then considered it before wiping it on Meriwether's cloak. He handed it back. "Thanks."

Meriwether took it, feeling sick. *If it wasn't so cold, I'd never use this again.* "Help me with Geneve."

The monster nodded, hauling Geneve up like she weighed no more than a toddler. "Knight. Hey. Yeah, you." He slapped her cheek. "Get your shit together."

Geneve blinked, woozy, and fended Armitage away with clumsy movements. "Did I say I'd never call you monster again? That was a mistake."

"She'll be fine." Armitage hitched his belt, admiring the wreckage of the hive and the fallen insects. "Thanks, though."

"What for?" Meriwether felt paler than Vertiline.

"For risking your scrawny hide getting me close. These things aren't fun." The Vhemin nodded, satisfied. "But they're also all dead. Vhemin wins! Again!" He laughed, slightly manic.

Sight of Day and Vertiline returned on cautious feet. The pale warrior looked at the ruined hive, then Armitage. "Did you do this yourself?"

Sight of Day padded up to the Vhemin. He looked into the monster's snake eyes as he turned Armitage's head this way and that. *{When the Three made your kind, they built to last.}*

Armitage made a *so-so* gesture with his hand. "Sort of. We live fuckall years, but do it in style. Come on. I figure there's more killing to be done down here. Those things," he stabbed a finger at the hive's wreckage, "are carnivorous. They've got to eat *something*."

Meriwether looked at the ruined hive, remembering the massive size of it. "They've got to eat a *lot* of something."

Geneve sheathed her blade. It took her three tries to get the blade home. "I don't feel ... right."

Sight of Day nodded. *{The venom will pass soon enough. It brings the low high, and the high low.}*

"Nasty things," Vertiline said. "Why do they heal the sick and injure the hale?"

{Traps.} Sight of Day kicked an insect aside. *{The fallen get up, seeking aid, and bring more people for the feast.}*

"Wonderful." Meriwether brushed drying hair from his face, retrieved his sack, then navigated to Geneve's side. "Let's find more horrors. I can't wait to almost die another six ways before we see daylight again."

She rested her forehead against his. "You're assuming we'll see the sun, rather than die first."

"We're doing okay so far," he said brightly. "What's the worst that could happen?"

Chapter Twenty-Six

Geneve plodded along, trying to get her head straight. The venom from a single bite left her feeling plague-ridden, and she hoped they didn't have to fight anything. *We won't be that lucky, of course. Everything wants to eat us in this world.*

Armitage was carrying his own weight again, plus a little extra. Sight of Day clambered on the Vhemin's back, adding his mostly-dry furry warmth to the cold-blooded creature. *They make an odd pair.* Her eyes found Meri. The sorcerer walked ahead with Vertiline, the pair taking point. Meri carried that damned sack over one shoulder. She'd been unable to draw him on its contents, despite what passed between them. Geneve remembered their lovemaking with a smile she couldn't hide. The insistence of it, and almost, its *inevitability*. She smiled. *But odd couples can be wonderful. I'm in love with a man I tried to hand to the Justiciars for Judgment.*

Maybe it was the venom talking, but Geneve didn't feel like handing anyone to the Justiciars, not ever again. If she had to leave her sash behind in the dust, that was a price worth paying. Her fingers found the three bars on it. One was real, the other seemings from the heart of a wonderful man. She hadn't received her Chevalier's bars from the Clerics.

Geneve realized it didn't matter. *The Three still let me wield their Storm and Sway. My friends found me worthy, and maybe that's all that counts.*

The tunnel held the sad remains of others that came before. They passed a few Feybrind corpses, long withered by time. Their skeletons lay among the stalagmites, some entombed within the limestone deposits. There weren't many, but enough to be noticeable. Geneve wondered what stories they might tell.

"Hold up." Meri crouched by a Feybrind hand emerging from a stalagmite. "What killed these people?"

"Hunger," Vertiline suggested.

He gave her a withering stare. "First, don't hit me. Second, use your eyes. Look here."

Geneve joined them. Meri pointed to the Feybrind's head. All tissue was scoured clean by scavengers. The sad skull stared empty sockets above. Fangs made for rending meat were open in an eternal sigh of release. Not for the first time, she wondered how such a peaceful people could be carnivores. *Perhaps it's what they were made to be, not what they chose.* Meri's fingers hovered over the dead Feybrind's forehead.

"I see it." Geneve crouched beside him. There was a hole punched through the cat's head. "Hunger didn't kill him."

"Looks like a hole from a crossbow bolt," Armitage rumbled as he arrived. Sight of Day slipped from his back. "Except, uh."

"There's no quarrel left behind." Vertiline's hand roamed to her empty scabbard.

{It's unlikely any single Vhemin could take one of the People. The monsters are slow, ungainly brutes.} Sight of Day offered a half-smile to Armitage. *{No offense. Also, this body is no pincushion, and we've seen no spent ammunition.}*

"Feels accurate," the monster growled. "We're built for comfort, not speed."

"Eyes front," Geneve said. "Something's not right here."

"Explains why Morning Song said we'd die if we came here, but was not specific about *how*. The People don't know." Meri brushed his hands off as he stood, then retrieved his sack. It clanked as he swung it over his shoulder. "Any who come into this pit of despair don't make it back out."

"Feels like a difficult place to get to." Armitage examined the dead Feybrind's arm entombed within the stalagmite. "Still, this guy's been dead a long, long time. You'd think they'd have worked out what was going on down here by now."

{Sometimes the People like the mystery of the world.} Sight of Day's tail lashed twice. *{Also, we're not fond of suicide runs.}*

"We're not fond of 'em either, but there's always plenty of Vhemin. Provided the weather's warm." Armitage leered a shark-toothed smile. "Good thing the ancients left their blasted wastelands to us."

"Maybe it's best if I take the lead." Geneve unsheathed Requiem. The blade felt ready, like the skymetal sword knew there was a battle ahead.

"No argument from me. You want to get dead, be my guest." Armitage crouched, allowing Sight of Day to clamber back aboard.

Geneve took point. She wanted to creep, but it wasn't how the Tresward trained her. *They also trained me to encase myself in steel, and here I am, wearing cotton and a smile.* Her boots crunched over limestone. The tunnel's floor had been lost to time and detritus long ago, but she suspected if they dug they'd find the same pale stone the ancients built everything with. She didn't know if they'd cultivated the glowing moss, or if that was the Three's work since then. Either way, the tired yellow was better than no light at all, especially in this pit of the lost.

The tunnel bored straight through the rock. Nothing natural would hold such a perfect course. The walls offered nothing back but the echo of their footsteps. She wished there was light enough to see the distance clearly, but the world ahead was a mess of phantoms made of shadows and imagining.

Meri loped to her side. "How you doing?"

"I don't feel right." Geneve gestured with her sword. "The walls hold light, but not enough to see properly."

"Oh." He smacked his forehead. "I think I can fix that. Maybe. Never done it before, but—"

"You ... what?" She blinked.

"Master of things that aren't there, remember?" He tapped his temple. "Prodigious liar, deceiver, and—"

"Aye, a wizard of deception," Geneve agreed. "Also, a master of saying things with many words, when two would do."

He pouted. "I'm not saying that's wrong, but the truth is a harsher blade than steel." Meri brightened. "Would you like to see a magic trick?"

Geneve raised her eyebrow. "Is this trick going to give us more light?"

"Absolutely." He steepled his fingers, face expectant. "It'll be great."

She nodded. "Do it." Meri took a couple steps from her, then threw his arms wide. Silence held his counsel for a moment. "Is something supposed to be happening?"

"By the Three," Vertiline breathed.

Geneve followed her eyes up. The ceiling of the tunnel, once shrouded in muddy yellow, glimmered with the colors of a rainbow. Pearlescent light spread from above Meri in an expanding circle. In its wake, dour stalactites brightened, glittering like sun struck quartz. The old yellow-stained light was brushed aside by all the colors of the dawn.

Armitage's eyes were wide. "Not bad, runt."

The illusionist ignored him. Meri's eyes were closed, brow furrowed in concentration. His lips moved soundlessly. The light in the tunnel grew, like the sun rising, but in a handful of heartbeats rather than over hours. Geneve squinted against the glare, feeling her heart rise with the light.

After he was done, the world *glimmered*. A thousand tiny lights, more than all the stars in the heavens, huddled within the walls. It seemed like the air glowed. Meri opened his eyes, then touched the end of Requiem. The blade's silverbright skymetal shimmered under his finger, then bloomed into a pure white brilliance.

He sighed, tottering a little after his casting. Geneve steadied him. "Meri, this is ... beautiful."

Vertiline's mouth was slack. Light played along her features like ripples across a hidden pool of wonders. "I can't believe we thought him a sinner. We would have cast a master of beauty under Judgment."

Sight of Day slipped from Armitage's back, golden eyes bright with wonder. *{In all my long years I have never seen anything like this. How did you do it?}*

"They say illusion's like lying. You make up a thing that's false, and wish it to be true." Meri shrugged, running a bashful hand through his hair. "I still can't do people. Don't know why."

"But it's not lies." Geneve blinked at the kaleidoscope of light playing through the rocks above. "How do you do it?"

"You have to think of something wonderful, that's all. Then the world gives it back to you." He turned away. "I just thought of you."

❦

THE LIGHT FOLLOWED GENEVE DOWN THE TUNNEL. IT DIDN'T TIRE or fall behind. She found as she stepped ripples of rainbow expanded from her footprints. It was bewitching, but in a good way. Requiem's blade blazed in her hand. It gave off no heat, just a pure white radiance that banished dark thoughts far away.

A massive wall met them ahead. It had rings of diminishing size cut into it, the largest twice the height of a person. *Like a sieve fit for the Three.* Geneve squeezed through a gap at ground height, marveling at the smoothness of the sides. The curved passage was ten meters long, emerging into a vaulted chamber. Light followed her through, spreading in her wake. It crept up the walls, shining as Meri's magic tried to climb into the lap of the Three. Geneve guessed the ceiling at least two klicks above them.

The ground beyond the tunnel was smooth stone. The tunnel's sieve-like outlet opened onto a channel with walls a couple of meters high. The channel exited over a massive chasm that descended into gloom below.

They helped each other climb from the channel. The light about them showed more wonders of the ancients. "Is this a ... city?" Laid around the central pit where water would have fallen were hundreds of buildings. They were constructed in a similar style as the temple of the ancients in the blasted plaguelands, in similarly poor condition. Walls of white stone crumbled. Trees and vines, long dead, lay in blasted, calcified rows on promenades empty of people.

"An underground haven." Meri joined her. "Or it was. Perhaps they thought to live out what was coming."

She faced him. "What could have beaten them? And ... what beat that?"

"Gods. Demons. Dragons." He shrugged. "We'll likely never know."

"You know what's common among all the assholes of the world? Bars." Armitage lumbered toward a slumping building. The doors were long gone, but debris out front suggested tables or benches. Sight of Day dropped from his shoulders, loping ahead of the monster's lumbering gait.

"I like how this guy thinks sometimes." Vertiline cocked her hips. "I wonder what eons-old liquor tastes like." She followed Armitage into the ancient bar.

Meri didn't leave Geneve. "Imagine it, Red. A massive torrent of water flying out in a huge jet. It'd fall down the well. A terrible majesty, but tamed by ancient people. Who would sit there," he pointed at the dead taverna, "drinking coffee, or ale, admiring all they'd bent to their will." He seemed sad. "I don't know if I want to know what their liquor tastes like, in case it reminds me of all our failures." Meri scratched his beard. "Not ours specifically. Like, the world's. We broke everything. How do we not do that again?"

"Something on your mind?" Geneve's fingers itched to stroke his hair, so she did.

He smiled. "Just something Morning Song said. She wants me to become a lordling, ruling from on high."

Geneve shook her head. "I doubt that very much. That's what you heard, but I don't believe that's what she said."

"Ah, this is what my own truth tastes like, served back to me on a golden dish."

"No, your truths hit harder. These are easy words." She eased herself next to him, so their bodies leaned together. "You're afraid by touching a thing, you'll break it."

"Aye." His warmth ebbed into her.

"Things break by themselves. Look at this city. The ancients took their hands away, and everything crumbled. A hundred wicked men try to tear the world apart, and there's precious few standing against them." Geneve kicked a pebble, watching it skitter over the edge of the causeway. "The easiest thing is to do nothing. That's how bad things happen. Evil wins."

"But ... what if I do something wrong?" His voice held curiosity, not anguish. Like he really wanted the answers.

Geneve had few to give him. "Then you do something wrong. But we'll be here. Vertiline and I will stand by you until the sun burns out. I can't speak for Armitage or Sight of Day, but you've true friends there."

"Five against the world."

She nodded. "Aye."

He sniffed, then straightened. "Okay then."

"Okay?"

"It's time, Red." He turned to her, a grin creeping onto his face. "Let's taste eons-old ass liquor."

"Ew."

"You're only saying that because you've not had ass liquor." He strode off. "I, on the other hand, have tasted the very best liquor of the ass."

Geneve laughed, hurrying to keep up. Maybe the ancient city would kill them, but it might also hold a few treats. Within the bar, dust held counsel with silence, broken by Armitage rummaging through ancient shelves of pale stone. A ruined clutch of wood that might have been a bar fronted the shelves. The Vhemin stood, holding a crystal bottle filled with amber. "This looks promising."

Vertiline held her distance on the other side of the was-bar. "It could be poison."

"I'll be the judge of that." The monster flicked the crystal stopper off. It bounced once then shattered against the stone ground. He sniffed, then took a swig. He grinned shark teeth. "Definitely poison."

"Let me see that." Vertiline snatched the bottle from him, taking a cautious sip. "Oh. Oh my."

They passed the bottle about. Sight of Day's golden eyes held wonder and confusion at his taste. *{Better than anything the People make, and still good, after all this time.}*

Meri sipped, nodding somberly. "Best ass liquor I've had. I've not tasted anything like it."

"In its hundreds-years wait for us, it's had a long time to decide what to be." Geneve took the bottle from him. She sniffed, eyes closed. Geneve smelled cocoa and nuts over an earthy aroma. Something that might have been a long-lost fruit tickled her nose. She sipped, savoring the rich, warm liquid. It didn't burn her mouth like the gut rot of dockside taverns. It barely tasted of liquor at all. *It's possibly the best thing I've tasted in my life.* Geneve opened her eyes, grinning. "Of all the things forgotten when the world broke, how to make this was the most merciless tragedy."

Vertiline took the bottle from her. "No need to husband it all night." She took another sip.

Armitage rescued the bottle from her. They had a brief tussle, ending with Vertiline's cheeks flushed red and Armitage holding the bottle. "My turn."

"Very honorable, monster. Beat the cripple." She raised her stump.

"The cripple can wait her damn turn." He took another happy slurp.

Geneve left them to it, leaving the tavern. She stood outside, surveying the ancient city. They might well be the only people who'd stood here for hundreds of years. Geneve remembered the ancient city in the plaguelands, and the guardians it held. They hadn't seen anything like that here, but if they encountered danger she didn't want to be drunk.

Still, the warm glow in her belly wasn't going amiss after the cold of the tunnel. Geneve touched her fingers to her lips, feeling the smile there. Perhaps one more drink wouldn't hurt.

GENEVE WOKE WITH MERI SLUMBERING AGAINST HER. SHE FELT sleepy wonder at the light that still glimmered in the cavern's ceiling high above.

Sight of Day lay across Armitage's feet. Vertiline slumped against the monster's side, head lolling. Geneve eased Meri away, then urged herself upright. Two empty bottles of the ancient's liquor lay on the ground between the five. They'd stood no guards. Geneve eyed her blade, still glowing with brilliant while light. *We could have died. Murdered in our sleep by guardians of the city.*

But they hadn't. Instead, they'd ... healed. Laughter and smiles. It didn't hold back the hunger that gnawed at her belly. And she felt thirsty, but not sickly like she'd poisoned herself with drink. If anything, her head felt clearer than it had since the insect's venom in the tunnel. *Did the ancients make liquor without consequence ... or did I just need a night with friends?*

Geneve ambled off. Meri's 'surprise' sack waited by his side, and she considered peeking inside while he slept, then discarded the idea. If he kept it hidden, there was a purpose. She'd never known Meri to do anything without the best of reasons. It was one of the things she loved about him. *Any man can step wrong, but he tries so hard to place his feet with care.*

A pang went through her as she thought of Iz. *My father.* He was another who tried harder than most. It wasn't enough in this world. And Iz hadn't trusted others to get close. Just Geneve and pale Vertiline. Meri had more friends, and called the People his allies. *If he takes up a royal mantle, he'll be the best there's ever been.*

And if he doesn't, that's fine too. She snuck Requiem into its sheath, hiding its brilliance. Geneve wondered if her sword would burn bright until the end of the world. It didn't seem to need Meri's concentration; he had the look of someone three days dead, but with a better pallor.

Geneve crossed her arms, overlooked the causeway, and tried to imagine what it must have been like. A huge fountain. People enjoying themselves in a subterranean wonderland. Perhaps they didn't have Meri's wondrous light, but they would have had something to keep the dark at bay.

Now it was dry as barren earth. Water hadn't been here since whatever cataclysm broke the bridge over the waterfall behind them, draining the water into the earth. *I hope there's another way out.*

Footsteps drew her attention. Meri approached, sidling next to her. "Hello."

"Hello yourself." Geneve scratched red hair. "I'm not sure if there's breakfast."

"Let's save that for above ground." He sniffed the air. "This place smells dead as old chalk. We need to find a way out."

Geneve nodded. "The city is huge, and we've disturbed no guardians yet. If we're careful, our luck might hold."

"I'm not sure 'luck' is what we've had." He sighed. "Mind you, that liquor was something special. It's spoiled the regular stuff for life."

"I'm sure you'll find a way to push through." Geneve matched his sigh. "Shall we wake the rest?"

"Why not? Nothing's tried to kill us for a whole night. No need to let the world get complacent." He ambled back toward the others.

Geneve followed. There was nothing here but the remains of an ancient cataclysm, and they had business to attend above ground.

Still. It would be nice to come back here one day. Explore, and see what the ancients left in reserve.

Chapter Twenty-Seven

I sure hope the ancients didn't leave any surprises behind. Meriwether walked beside Vertiline, sharing the quiet. They were on point, with Geneve in the rear. Sight of Day and Armitage walked together in the middle, eyes everywhere at once. The city was easy enough to traverse; the hard part was trying to work out which way was north. No sun or stars guided them, and down here time was something that happened to other people. *It would be easy to forget yourself in a place like this.*

"I'm worried about what we'll find on the way out," Vertiline said.

"Why's that?" Meriwether passed a desiccated tree, pausing as he took note of its fruit. Dead the tree may be, but the fruit hanging from it was still round. Each was a sphere about the size of his two fists together. He buffed the orb, revealing golden skin. "I wonder if this is safe to eat."

"It's hundreds of years old. I'm sure it'll be fine." Vertiline's hand clenched the air above her empty scabbard. "This place is safe enough. You notice how the air is warm? And it's dry. If it was easy to get in and out, there'd be a legion of squatters in here."

Meriwether nodded. "Perhaps other entrances are as troubling as our way in."

"Or perhaps there's a trigger." Vertiline touched the fruit. "You know, that looks ... fine. Like it's ready for harvest."

Armitage ambled up. "Fruit? I guess it's a good enough breakfast. Not as good as lamb shoulder, but it'll do." He reached for the golden orb.

"Wait," Meri said, a heartbeat too late. The orb came free in Armitage's hand. A sound like massive lock tumblers rolling in their grave came from what Meriwether had pegged as *north*. Faint, but unmistakable.

The monster crunched the fruit. "What for?"

"The trigger," Vertiline said wearily. "Touch nothing, see nothing. But sooner or later someone will do something stupid and the guardians come out to play."

Armitage chewed, savoring the fruit. "I see no guardians, and this isn't half bad."

"May as well be hung for a sheep as a lamb." Meriwether tugged another orb free. The fruit was heavy, the skin smooth. He bit into it with a crunch. *Like an apple, but with a taste like custard.*

Sight of Day walked over, tail cutting the air. {*That smells divine. What is it?*}

"The noise." Vertiline pointed north. "Is no one concerned about that?"

"I'm happy enough to die on a full stomach." Geneve stole a fruit.

Armitage broke his sphere apart, offering half to the Feybrind. Clear juice ran down his arms. Sight of Day took the fruit, sniffing cautiously, then nibbling. His golden eyes widened in surprise. {*It tastes like venison.*}

"I thought it had more of a cattle flavor," Armitage growled.

Geneve spoke around a mouthful of fruit. "It's melon."

"Oh, for goodness sake." Vertiline tore a fruit, sampling it. "Chocolate."

Meriwether considered his fruit. "Perhaps it's what we need it to be. But Sight of Day eating 'fruit' gives us a clue about the people who lived here." He took another bite. "Feybrind and humans lived here together. The ancients planted trees that offered free food to all."

"What about me?" Armitage squinted, snake eyes suspicious.

"Vhemin eat anything," Vertiline said. "I wouldn't read anything into it. Is *no one else* concerned about the noise?"

Geneve tossed the core of her fruit aside. "I'm a little nervous. Let's go find out what fresh horror wants our blood."

⁂

THE STREETS HELD OCCASIONAL BLOCKS OF FALLEN STONE, BUT nothing impassable. The pale cobblestones were smooth enough even after time did its best to wear them. After what felt like ten klicks of walking, but what may have been as few as five or as many as twenty, they closed in on the city's northern wall. Distance was difficult to measure without convenient yardsticks.

The northern wall was a bastion of pale stone. Little detritus clung to it, although old stains next to large cracks suggested where water may have seeped through before things dried up. They passed other roads converging on the one they followed. All lead in the same direction: north. The road they trod widened each time another joined it, until the road was an easy five hundred meters wide.

There were no carts, or bodies. It was as if people had just ... left. *It wasn't like they ran out of food, and water was plentiful enough if you could walk, so what killed them?*

The road passed through what might have been a doorway of immense size before rust took it. Beyond, Meriwether's illusion kept another massive tunnel illuminated. A cave-in collapsed the structure, which almost caused him despair until he saw a small doorway in the let's-call-it-west wall. He pointed. "There."

The doorway was a sliding affair, and was retracted into the wall. It was wide enough for three people to pass shoulder to shoulder. The scattered rocks from the cave-in ended at the door's demarkation, suggesting it was closed until recently.

"The source of the noise," Vertiline guessed.

"An invitation," Geneve said.

"It's a fucking murder hole," Armitage rumbled. "We go in there, we're turning into snacks for ancient guardians."

{The monster is right.} Sight of Day sniffed. *{I smell something different. Like the oil you rub into your armor, but mixed with blood.}*

"The challenge we're faced with is a lack of other exits." Meriwether spread his hands. "I say we go through."

"If you go first, that's fine by me," Armitage said.

"Fine," Meriwether said, shouldering past.

Geneve kept pace, drawing Requiem's brilliance from its scabbard. The pair walked ahead. The tunnel curved from west to north, perhaps designed as an ancient service path or maintenance shaft. Sealed doors held their secrets to the left and right.

The tunnel widened out into a room perhaps twenty meters a side. The far side held another opening, and Meriwether's hopeful heart suggested it might lead to freedom. Lining the wall with the exit were statues.

The statues were smooth-skinned and sickly pale. They had no discernable faces, and their skin was smooth, even around the joints, as if they were made of sausage. They were naked and had no obvious sign of gender.

The floor between them and the statues was as perfectly smooth as Meriwether had ever seen. It looked *polished*, like a thousand artisans took glass and buffed it with soft cloth for hundreds of years to get a surface so perfect as to defy belief.

There was nothing alarming about the space. No body parts littered the floor. The statues, while frozen in various positions of movement, held no weapons.

Meriwether kept his peace with Geneve at the entrance. "As far as art goes, I don't like them."

She held her blade cross guard. "I'm not sure they're art."

"What appalling horror is this?" Vertiline joined them. "Immobile statues? Thank the Three. I thought I'd have to fight a horde of Vhemin with nothing but a knife." She stepped forward.

A statue stuttered to life. Blue runes cascaded down its chest, glimmering opalescent promise. It broke free from its position, walking with a jerky motion, as if it were a marionette piloted by a drunk child. The statue squared off against Vertiline, adopting her stance.

She took a step back; the statue mirrored the motion. "Uh."

"Let me try something." Meriwether stepped forward. Another statue broke rank, hustling to join the first. A similar set of runes bloomed on its chest. Meriwether slid his left foot forward; the statue copied the motion, but as a mirror image, leading with its right foot. He put his left hand atop his head, and the statue mimicked him with its right. "I've got a very bad feeling about this."

Armitage lumbered inside, Sight of Day with him. "This is new."

Sight of Day shook his head. *{It feels very old. The smell of blood and oil is much stronger here.}* The cat unslung his bow.

A statue trembled to life, but with the blue runes came a bow. The weapon grew from its hand, and Meriwether couldn't shake the sausage analogy. It looked like the weapon was extruded, round and lumpy, but taking the eventual shape and form of Sight of Day's bow. The weapon grew in just a few heartbeats, the finished product looking sickly pale but otherwise identical to the artisanal Feybrind weapon.

The cat's tail lashed. The statue grew a tail, and that also lashed.

Armitage glared. "How come everyone gets one but me?"

"I don't have one either." Geneve stepped forward to stand with Vertiline, and a statue joined Vertiline's copy on the other side. "Ah. I misspoke. I didn't have one *yet*. Now I do."

"I want to join the fun." Armitage lumbered forward, and sure enough a statue joined the others, matching him movement for movement.

"Let's not be hasty," Meriwether suggested. "Perhaps we should try talking to them." He squared his shoulders, stepping in front of his friends. His statue stepped forward also. "Hello?"

"Please provide Personate passcode or be destroyed," his statue said. It had no lips, but the words came clear enough. "Allied Vehement Systems architecture detected. Does this unit have a passcode?"

Meriwether looked to his friends, then back to the ... Personate? "A passcode?"

The Personate only moved as he did. It didn't do anything like rub its chin, or look at the ceiling. If Meriwether expected doubt, he saw none. "Unlock key is expected, or destruction is assured. Please provide your unique sixty-four digit alphanumeric operator ID or be destroyed. The training manual is provided to all new Vehement Systems trainees. It is found in your recruit kit."

"Fuck it, I say we murder 'em," Armitage said.

Meriwether stepped back, and his Personate retreated a similar distance. "Be my guest."

Sight of Day readied his bow in a smooth motion, drew, and fired. As always, the Feybrind moved like silk lightning, but ... his Personate copied him to the last detail. A Feybrind shaft headed toward the Personate, a pale arrow returning down almost the same path.

Sight of Day tumbled aside, his Personate doing the same. Both arrows clattered against the back wall.

"Ah," Meriwether said. "How do you fight yourself?"

"I've got a better question." Vertiline readied her knife, her Personate creating a near-identical simulacra weapon. "Where'd it get the arrow from?"

"Ass pocket." Armitage charged his Personate. The statue charged him right back. The Vhemin swung a fist the size of a ham, the Personate matching with its much smaller one. They both hit each other in the chest. Armitage tumbled back, but the Personate only rocked a little. The Vhemin clambered to his feet; once there, the Personate mimicked him again. "They hit really hard." He rolled his shoulder, the statue copying even that movement.

"We'll see." Geneve strode forward, skymetal sword ready. Her Personate matched her, complete with a Requiem look-a-like. Meriwether's breath caught as he watched.

By the Three, she's beautiful. The way she moves makes the angels take note.

Problem was, the Personate moved with the same poetry of motion. She swung Requiem, the Three's Light joining with Meriwether's illusionary brightness along the blade. The Personate's weapon *also* glowed. Not as bright, but it was there.

When the weapons clashed, both opponents rocked back a step. Geneve's Personate said, "Path of destruction selected. Please enjoy the end."

Vertiline looked at her knife, then charged. Armitage ran into the fray, followed by Sight of Day. The cat was fast as a hummingbird, the Vhemin strong as an ox, and at every swing, thrust, or shot, their

Personates matched their skill. Vertiline moved like oil on water, effortless, above everything, and her damnable statue did the same.

Geneve circled with her Personate, but no matter the cut, the Personate matched it. If she shied away, so did the statue.

The only immovable one was Meriwether's, because he wasn't fool enough to try to fight himself. *Think! There's got to be a way. The statues are us, or close enough to pass. Geneve's one is using the Storm; perhaps not as well, but none seem to tire.*

Armitage's Personate was the first to deviate from mirror movements, catching the Vhemin upside the jaw with an uppercut. The monster stumbled back, spat a tooth, then jumped back into the fray.

They copy us until ... what? They've learned enough? Were these made to combat Tresward? Whether the Personates were ancient technology like the Artifices or temples, or sorcerous creation, didn't matter. Sooner or later, they'd overwhelm the party using their own tricks against them.

Meriwether looked about for a clue. The Personates learned from their opponents, but only by acting perfectly. He eyed the floor, considering its smoothness. *Perhaps they can't learn if things aren't ... even?*

Armitage and Sight of Day tried attacking each other's Personate, but if Armitage ducked a shot from Sight of Day's statue, his copy did the same. There was no winning by swapping opponents.

Geneve swung her skymetal sword overhand. Lightning clung to the blade, the Three's gift to the best Tresward. The Personate matched her swing, its sword glowing with sickly Light, but no lightning. Their blades clashed, energy arcing through the Personate ... and along the smooth floor. Geneve was thrown back by her own lightning, clothes smoking as she tumbled to the floor.

Meriwether scrambled toward her. His own Personate moved to her copy. The Knight pushed him aside. "I'm fine!"

She didn't *look* fine. She looked like a strong, tough woman who'd been struck by lightning. He grabbed her arm, helping her up. "I've an idea. You need to do just one thing."

Geneve held her blade ready, eyes locked on the Personate just meters away. He saw hardness in her gaze, but also caution. "I'm listening."

He put his lips to her ear. Meriwether didn't know if the Personates could hear well, or if it mattered, but he'd take any chance he got. *"Believe."*

She gave him a sideward glance. "What?"

"Just ... try. For me." He took a couple steps back, his Personate doing the same. As if both wanted to give Geneve and her mirror room to move.

She nodded, her Personate doing the same. "For you."

Meriwether closed his eyes. He imagined a small footstool, the kind you might find in a clothier's. He brought the illusion to life right in front of Geneve. It stood two handspans high. "Stand on it."

"But—"

"Believe!" he yelled.

Geneve stepped onto the stool. For a tiny fraction of time, his seeming and her belief were enough. Her foot didn't pass through. The Personate facing her tried the same thing, but it had no stool to stand on.

It stumbled forward, the Light leaving its sword. Fast as a cobra, Geneve swung Requiem. The blade held the Three's promise, edge bright as the noonday sun. The Personate tried to copy, but it was a half-step off. Its movements no longer held the Tresward's pattern true.

Geneve's blade passed through the Personate's neck. The stump fountained a pale liquid. The smell of oil and iron came rich and hard as the Personate pumped its equivalent of life's blood. The thing stumbled, spare hand clutching the space where its head used to be.

The blue runes on its chest flickered and died. It stiffened, then toppled to the smooth floor. It shattered when it hit, sickly pale chalky blocks scattering across the floor.

Meriwether blinked. *It worked!*

Geneve didn't pause to look at the body. She leaped forward, skewering Meriwether's Personate with her skymetal sword. The blade entered its chest, and she tore it out sideways, pale blood and lumpy viscera pattering to the floor. The Knight spun away, taking the limbs from Vertiline's opponent, and the legs from Armitage's.

The Vhemin swung to Sight of Day's Personate, lifting it from the floor. He brought it down across bent knee with a sound like the cracking of rotted lumber.

Dust drifted from the downed Personates. What remained slumped into sand.

Vertiline eyed her knife, nodded, then slipped it into her belt. "That was ... different."

Meriwether stood, retrieved his sack, then faced the remaining Personates. None sprang to life. "Will these ... come after us?"

"You know, I don't much want to find out." Armitage worked his way down the line of statues, first tearing the arm from one, then using it as a club on the rest. He swung like a lumberjack, tireless and enthusiastic.

Geneve sheathed her sword and returned to Meriwether's side. "I felt it. For just a minute, the stool was real."

He grinned. "I'm glad that worked."

"Wait. You weren't *sure?*" Her voice rose an octave.

"I was pretty sure it *wouldn't* work." Meriwether shrugged. "But it did, and we're fine."

"*Fine?*"

Armitage winced. "Here it comes."

Geneve rounded on the monster. "You think I should shout at you instead?"

He backed up, palms out. "Not at all. But it *did* work. And now we've got a chance to die in new creative ways tomorrow."

{*He's not wrong. The world tries to kill me all the time when I'm with you.*}

Geneve's glare damped back to a glower. "You're right." She faced Meriwether. "I'm sorry."

"It's fine. I wish I'd had more time to explain." He toed a sickly sandy pile. "I think these were made to fight Knights. Did you see them using the Storm?"

"Aye."

"But I *don't* think they were made to fight Knights and sorcerers." He grinned. "Together, we're unstoppable."

"Let's not tempt fate too much," Vertiline said. "Or wait until I'm far away when you do."

Geneve answered him with a smile of her own. "Unstoppable. Together. I like both those ideas."

Meriwether felt his grin widen. *I like it too. I like it a lot.* He hitched his sack on his shoulder. "Come on. Let's see if there's something in the next room that wants to eat us for breakfast."

THEY PASSED BACK INTO THE MAIN TUNNEL WITHOUT MORE TROUBLE from Personates. What irked Meriwether was how they'd seemed *placed*. As if someone put the guardians below to guard the ancient's city from the living.

The passage north of the cave-in smelled better. It wasn't fresh air, more like what would happen if one of the Three *thought* about fresh air. A memory of it, but good enough to quicken their steps and lift their spirits.

Right up to the point where they found the butchered Vhemin.

The tunnel snaked east and west, while still trending in the let's-call-it-northerly direction. A klick wide at least, it didn't jink so much as dawdle about the bends. Meriwether didn't understand why ancient designers didn't build it straight, and there weren't any about to ask. *Mysteries*.

The first hint of the Vhemin was a series of carts scattered across the roadway. They looked like a giant had tossed his toys. Dead horses were mingled with the wreckage. Metal boxes lay open like shiny coffins, but any dead inside had up and left.

Meriwether poked through the wreckage, finding a hand first. It was scaled, the nails slightly pointed like a Vhemin's, so it didn't take a huge stretch of imagination to wonder where the rest of the monster got to.

Armitage hefted a wagon aside like heavy things weren't a concern. Beneath was a pulped mass of meat that *might* have been a Vhemin. Further on, the body that should have been attached to the arm lay. It wore the same fancy armor Ballast had, but the runed plates were dark. Meriwether crouched beside the body. It was a woman, her snake eyes open at a horror death couldn't take away. "Did they bring the Personates here?"

"If they did, they made a room for them faster than a stonemason's guild could manage." Geneve nudged a coffin with her boot. "I think the Personates were here before. No, these Vhemin were bringing something else."

Meriwether surveyed the scene, trying to imagine what happened. The position of a horse over there, or where the carts lay. "I think they were *taking* something. Or many somethings. Whatever was in these coffins."

"Don't look much like coffins to me." Armitage tossed one aside. "Your kind pads 'em out with silks, or cottons for the poor. Marsh reed if you can't scrape the barons together."

"He's got a point." Vertiline nosed among the ruins. "Grave robbing makes more sense. Possessions of the dead, not the corpses themselves."

Meriwether plodded further on. Despite the surfeit of ruined wagons, there weren't many Vhemin. *Barely enough for a decent warband.* Beneath a dead horse, he caught the gleam of metal. "Armitage?"

The monster ambled over, eyed the horse, then grabbed its hindquarters. He pulled it away like a smaller man might drag a roll of carpet.

Horse gone, the glint was revealed: a closed metal coffin. Meriwether hunkered beside it. The coffin was sealed, but without visible clasps. He found the seam, trying to worry his fingers in, but it didn't give a lot of joy.

Vertiline crouched beside him, offering his knife. "Here."

He took it with a nod of thanks, inserting the blade into the seam. He worked the steel back and forth until it skidded free. "Well, I guess there's another way to open it."

Armitage pushed him aside, hefted the coffin, and slammed it against the ground. It bounced, something inside *clunking*, but it didn't open. "Maybe you should ask nicely, runt."

Meriwether rubbed the back of his neck. He touched fingers against the case, but could find no locks answering the tickle. *Ask nicely, hey?* Something tugged his memory. He rummaged in his sack, finding the book on High Magic, and thumbed through it. Most of the words, or recipes, were a special kind of gibberish, but he'd made out more than a few.

He found the page he needed. A picture of a closed door, a key, and an open door. A few simple words were inscribed below. Would it be too much to ask for it to be a spell of opening?

Meriwether held the book open in his left hand, right hand up, palm out. He didn't know if the High Magic needed showmanship, but if this worked, he wanted it to look like it wasn't an accident. *"IMPERIUM VERBUM RECLUDO."*

He felt a rush, his heart quickening, blood thundering in his ears. All sounds faded, his illusory light that had followed them dying like a candle starved of air. Behind him, a metal lock box *pinged* open, a rain of barons and regals spilling on the ground. The coffin trembled, then snapped open. And Meriwether, the first sorcerer to use the High Magic in over eight hundred years, passed out.

Chapter Twenty-Eight

Geneve felt the sunlight on her skin a kiss from heaven. She didn't know how long they'd been underground. A day? Two? But the sun hadn't forgotten them while they traveled below. It felt warm and rich. The sun was on its weary march down from the sky, touching the skies with the color of honey.

The tunnel emerged among a ruin of rock. It had collapsed in an age past. There was evidence of a Vhemin camp about the entrance. Old campfires, a midden, wagon tracks, and a body or two for good measure. Skulls in the firepit were human, suggesting the monsters ate well while here.

Armitage carried Meriwether over one shoulder, the sorcerer's sack over the other. Sight of Day hauled the coffin, held firmly closed. They didn't know what was in it, and felt it best to keep it that way until they were out of a pit of horrors. Vertiline was last, Meri's book of High Magic under her arm.

Geneve carried nothing but her bared blade. The light Meri had kissed the steel with was well gone. They might not have made it out except for the real light of the sun creeping into the tunnel below; they hadn't known how close to the exit they were.

Armitage walked to the remains of a fire pit, leaning Meriwether against a log that might have served previous campers as a makeshift seat. "Old and cold. No one's been here for two, maybe three days at least."

"Or longer." Vertiline squatted on the log.

Sight of Day set the coffin down. It didn't appear heavy, even with whatever was inside it. *{The camp's been deserted for at least two weeks. See how the fronds of that fern stand?}* He shook his head. *{It's obvious to any with the wit to see.}*

Vertiline gave him a little side-eye but ignored the bait. "I could use a sword. We need a fire. The sinner," she nudged Meri with her boot, "could use a cup of tea at least."

Geneve ran fingers through red hair. "I'll see if they left anything behind."

Scavenging the camp sight turned up a blunt dagger, a rusted length of steel that might have been a sword before the rain came, a lantern with a fraction of oil in the reservoir, a sewing kit, four teeth, and—*Three's mercy*—a pack stowed behind a tree.

The pack contained a half-drunk flask of Tebrani brandy, flint and steel, moldy bread, and a small waxed pouch of leaves that were hopefully tea. More rummaging scared up a kettle and two battered cups.

She returned to the fireside. Sight of Day had stacked wood, and with a lot of swearing on her part and an oversupply of patience on his, they got a fire going. Armitage returned with the kettle filled from a stream nearby. The water on to boil, Geneve pulled her scabbard off, leaned Requiem against a log, and sat beside Meri. "Who knew boiling water could be so hard?"

Meri startled, arms flailing, then sat up. "Hi!" He blinked at the fire, took in Vertiline's dismissive stare, Armitage's smirk, and Sight of Day's amusement. He looked to Geneve. "Did someone hit me?"

"No, runt. You passed out all on your lonesome." Armitage poured tea, handing a cup to the illusionist. "Try this."

Meri took a cautious sip. "It tastes horrible. What is it?"

"No idea." Geneve crouched beside him. "Meri, what did you do?"

"I think I cast a spell."

{You think?} Sight of Day offered a half-smile. *{I feel like that's a thing you should be surer about.}*

"The High Magic," he pointed to the book beside Vertiline, "is a ... set of recipes. I think the way it works is ... hells. Magicians can do ... stuff, right?"

"Stuff," Armitage repeated, without a lot of enthusiasm.

"Exactly. In my case, make butterfly wings out of dreams. Those more useful can summon storms, or set the air on fire—"

"Those aren't useful," Geneve said. "Those are *harmful*."

He scratched his beard. "Right. But the High Magic's ... *above* all that. If you're a sorcerer, you can cast the spells."

"So why aren't there a bunch of wizards opening strongboxes and moving mountains?" Vertiline took the kettle from Armitage, stole the last cup, and poured herself some tea. She grimaced. "This is horrible. But the question stands."

"Because no one knows the language of the ancients." Geneve walked to Vertiline, rescuing the book. "No one's worked out what the words mean, or how to say them."

{Until now.} Sight of Day took the cup from Vertiline, who in turn took Meri's. *{I knew we shouldn't have taught humans to read and write.}*

"Wait, it was *you* assholes who did that?" Armitage glared. "They'd still be banging rocks together if you hadn't interfered."

"The point is, the High Magic might be useful." Meri stood up like a ninety-year-old man: slowly, with exquisite care, and a lot of wincing. "What's in the coffin?"

"We didn't want to look until we were above ground," Geneve said. "And the light's fading, so maybe we should wait until tomorrow."

"Nonsense." Meri ambled to the coffin, put his hand on the lid, and paused. "None of you looked in?"

Geneve picked up her sword, drawing it. "Not yet. But if you open that and unleash the Three's fury, I'll cut it down."

"Solid plan." He flicked the lid open. Inside was not a body, but the outline of one. The fading light made it tricky to make out, but Meri cackled. "So *that's* what they wanted."

He retrieved an object from the coffin, holding it up. Vertiline spat in disgust. "Just great. As if the monster isn't strong enough already."

Geneve lowered her sword. Meri held up a scaled breastplate like Ballast's. The runes were dark, but she could see how it should be worn. The coffin held greaves, gauntlets, and pauldrons too, or things that looked similar to her eye. "Ancient armor?"

"Awesome," Armitage said. "It looks like it comes in just one size, too."

He wasn't wrong; even Iz would have looked a child in his father's armor wearing it. Geneve's heart sank. "Vhemin armor. They were below, pillaging the ancients."

"I think you should put it on." Meri held the armor out to Armitage.

"Maybe tomorrow." The monster didn't look keen. "It's a nice thought, but Ballast wore that and ... changed, I guess. Got stronger, all of that."

"Don't you want to be stronger?" Geneve blinked in surprise.

"Plenty strong as it is, and there's always a price," Armitage rumbled. "Nothing comes for free. Not out on the plague sands, and not here either."

Meri nodded, returning the breastplate to the coffin. "Well, it's here if you want it." He looked about. "Is there anything to eat?"

GENEVE AND SIGHT OF DAY HUNTED. HE'D OFFERED TO GO ALONE, but despite his skills as a warrior, not to mention his ability to creep unseen and unheard, her heart said there was too much risk. If the Vhemin held these lands, just one spotting him could be the end.

They walked a sparsely-wooded forest. The trees weren't tall or wide, and gave them plenty of room. The sun set a half-hour past, but Cophine's pale face was brilliant enough to guide them. Even sulky Ikmae contributed, only Khiton staying dark and remote.

The air smelled faintly of smoke, but none of it tainted the sky. "The Vhemin must have thinned this part of the world. We'll be lucky to find a rabbit."

The Feybrind's golden eyes gleamed in the night, despite the size of the pupils in the low light. {The monsters are terrible hunters.}

"Still. If you have a thousand of them shooting at the same rabbit..." Geneve trailed off.

{It's the safest rabbit in Or'sen.} Sight of Day's eyes twinkled.

"Speaking of Vhemin ... what do you make of Armitage's new armor?" She brushed red hair from her eyes. "Ballast's armor and weapons helped him fight the Storm. The Three's Light didn't hurt him as it should."

{The Three have been gone a long time.} He shrugged. *{All power wanes.}*

"Did the ancients fight each other?" Geneve hugged herself. "Or was it just Vhemin against whatever the Tresward started as?"

{I think the Tresward have always been as you see them.} He touched her arm. *{Strong, brave, and doing the dying so others don't have to.}*

"You mean we get involved in other people's business."

Sight of Day spread his hands. *{That, also. But don't lose your heart or your head, Daughter of the Three. I see the Storm within you. It strains against your skin, wanting freedom. It is a true part of you, a gift from the Three, regardless of what marvelous confusion rules the Tresward. They are just men and woman. You carry the will of the gods.}*

"So do they." She turned away, feeling her face heat. "I'm not that special."

He shook his head. *{They have fallen, while you still travel, seeking to right the lost. You learned what they taught, not what they did. You are still their daughter.}*

Geneve gave a brittle laugh. "How can you be sure?"

{You are an impossibility. Your father sired you, although Tresward can't have children. We know he was Valiant, carrying the Three's gifts as you do. Perhaps not so well.} The cat steepled his hands for a moment, as if gathering his thoughts into his palms, so's to say them better. *{The only explanation is that the Three wanted you, Daughter of the Three. They wanted you so much they broke their own rules.}*

"Perhaps." She bit her lip. "I don't think that tells us if the Vhemin fought the Tresward."

{I think the Vhemin fight everyone. It's their nature to be brutal.} He glanced back the way they came. *{All but one.}*

"Another impossibility?"

{Another promise.} Sight of Day pointed to Cophine's pale face above them. *{They're not done with you quite yet. Still, I'd be more concerned about the scent of smoke.}*

Geneve nodded. "They probably burned many trees for their hot rocks."

He shook his head. *{It doesn't smell right.}*

Geneve pursed her lips. "What do you mean?" She sniffed. "Smells like ash and misery to me."

Sight of Day touched a tree. *{Woodsmoke is familiar to us all. A few less lucky smell burning flesh. There is all of that, but underneath it...}* He shook his head, hands stilling for a moment. *{I've never scented anything like it.}*

Geneve adjusted her sword belt, ensuring Requiem's rear-draw hilt was ready to hand. "It just smells like smoke."

{That's because your nose is broken. Trust me on this one.} He scratched behind an ear. *{I think we should find out what it is.}*

"Have you ever heard how curiosity killed the cat?"

{Many times. It's a well-trodden joke, but the good news is I'm with you, and curiosity's never hurt any of your kind.} He scuffed the dirt. *{So, you're safe.}*

She laughed. "Let's go find your mystery smell."

The forest led up a small incline. Too modest to be a hill, it still managed to keep what lay beyond a mystery. Cresting the top revealed a valley, but instead of the continuation of the meager forest Geneve saw a torched basin. The valley was a shallow bowl perhaps three klicks across. She squinted. "What's that on the other side?"

Sight of Day's tail lashed. *{It looks like the foundations of a large manse. There's something wrong with it though.}* He blinked, fine golden eyes trying to make sense of it. *{Let's get closer.}*

They set off across the burned land. Where there may once have been trees, not even stumps remained. Piles of ash and very fine charcoal huddled in places. Geneve's imagination could recreate where saplings might have stood. *I wish Meri was here. He'd have an idea of what could take a forest from the earth. More ancient secrets? A new trick of the Vhemin?* "This doesn't look like the monster's logging efforts to build their hot rock fires."

{It doesn't look like anything I've seen before.} The cat loped along, soot clinging to his fur. Sight of Day looked about, head on a swivel. *{There's nothing here. No burned logs or animal bodies. Even in the great forest fires,*

evidence of small tragedies remain. How could a fire take all this and leave no memory?}

"I've no desire to know what fresh hell the monsters have dredged from the belly of the world." She shivered. "How do you fight ... this?" She spread her arm, encompassing the ruin about them.

{Run. Or not be there in the first place.} Sight of Day half-smiled. *{I really like that idea.}*

"So why are we going this way?"

{Because you're curious. Keep up.} He slowed for a few paces. *{Thank you for your company while I grieve. You don't coddle me. It's good to work.}*

"You say that now. Just wait until we find a hundred Vhemin."

{I think you can stand against them while I run.}

By unspoken agreement they picked up the pace, jogging for the valley's other side. Their feet left puffs of ash in their wake. Geneve's white cotton turned a shy gray, then darker coal color before they made the opposite side.

The ruin of the manse was like the forest: not much left. A silting of ash lay atop everything, but scattered in a generally westerly direction, as if a wind had picked it up and tossed it. The forest for klicks about the manse was the same as the valley they crossed: ash and burned earth.

The foundation stones were something to behold. The rocks slumped, their sharp edges blurred like wet clay. Geneve touched one, and found the surface to be porous, rasping against her skin. "What melts stone?"

{A very hot fire.} The Feybrind leaped atop the foundations, crouching for a better look. *{Whatever happened here used a furnace even the People haven't seen.}*

Geneve paced the manse's remains. She let her fingers trail along the melted stonework before looking to the sky. In the northwest, a bird drew her eye. It flew with long, lazy beats of its wings. "What kind of bird is that?"

Sight of Day padded to her side. *{That's not a bird. Remember the running part?}*

"We should flee?" Geneve squinted, trying to make out the flying thing.

{It won't help.}

She saw what Sight of Day meant. It wasn't a bird coming toward them. "That's a dragon!" Geneve felt hot excitement in her stomach, half thrill, half terror. *It's not half terror. It's mostly terror! Get out of here!* She grabbed Sight of Day's arm. "It might not help, but we're trying anyway."

They vaulted the manse's foundations, heading toward the distant tree line. Sight of Day's Feybrind grace gave him an early lead, but Geneve's training and enthusiasm for not being barbecued pushed her neck and neck with the cat. She risked a glance back at the dragon.

It was big enough to see details with her own meager human eyes. *By the Three, it's huge.* Wings beat the air slowly, tireless and relentless. About its head runes glimmered red, and its massive eyes glowed the ruby of the underworld. Geneve felt her step hitch as it looked at her, *into* her, and then—

GENEVE CHOKED WATER. AN UNDERTOW HAD HER, CLAWS OF seafoam dragging her below. She grasped for the surface, but it was a distant, dry memory. About her was the deep, silent grave.

Below her, her friends lay dead. Meri's face was bloated and white. Vertiline's lips were gone, chewed away by some underwater carnivore. Armitage was face down, drifting along the sandy bottom, one hand curled around Sight of Day's tail. The Feybrind's golden eyes stared, seeing nothing.

Above, Cophine's pale face shimmered as the currents obscured the goddess. Geneve couldn't see Ikmae or Khiton, but a massive winged form flew overhead. The dragon blotted out the pale goddess, and despite water, despite drowning, and despite death, Geneve heard the roar. Not just heard, but *felt* it, the thunderous pain of the beast.

//WHY DO YOU CAST ME ASIDE? I AM NOT FOR THEM!//

Geneve wanted to ask it what it meant, but her mouth filled with water. It flowed into her lungs. Her chest locked up, then spasmed, and she coughed air and water. *Remember the Trial! Remember the water!* She fought her diaphragm, clenched her teeth shut around the desire to suck anything in, even the sea of guilt around her.

I am Tresward. My fate isn't to drown. I'll meet my end at steel's edge, and not before.

Geneve swam. Arms trained by the blade powered her upward. The long days sweating under the sun, or the evenings with Destiny's Supplicant meant she wasn't going down. Not here, and not this way.

Her head broke the surface, and she spewed water. She brushed at her eyes, sweeping salt locks clear. "Dragon! I've cast nothing aside!"

It circled, getting lower, bellowing in pain again.

//THERE SHOULD BE TWO, AND THERE ARE NONE. THIS IS HOW THE WORLD ENDS.//

GENEVE WOKE TO A STORM OF ASH. SIGHT OF DAY WAS BEFORE HER, hand raised. She felt the sting of her face where he'd slapped her. She felt weak as a kitten, and coughed. Water sprayed: the same water from her dream.

That was real?

The ash storm reeked of loss. It swirled thick and heavy, obscuring Cophine's luminance. The dragon's wingbeats were like thunder, and when it roared, it was full of the torture of the universe.

It's in pain. Three's mercy, but it's in agony.

The stark glimmer of blue caught her eye. *There. Vhemin armor.* Lines of wavering opal carved the storm. The monsters ran, combing the fields, trying to find them. Geneve took a step, then fell. Her legs were weak, as if she were newborn. The cotton she wore was sodden, ash caked to ruinous black sludge coating her.

Sight of Day grabbed her, hauling her forward. She fell. The cat crouched, shouldered her, and staggered off. One step, then another, followed by a third. The Feybrind were fast and clever, but they weren't Vhemin-strong. He wouldn't make it with her. "Leave me!"

The cat ignored her, head down, struggling with her weight. The storm of ash and wind blasted them, stinging, rasping the exposed skin of her face. Sight of Day hunkered, pushing onward, another step, then more, until they broke from the ash cloud.

Geneve raised her head, seeing the dragon hovering over the blasted land. Massive wings beat the air, stirring the windstorm. The Vhemin were lost within, and she wondered why the dragon didn't take them itself. Geneve also wondered why it hid them within a storm. She felt its pain, its longing, like a tether between its heart and hers.

They made it to the trees. Sight of Day dropped her, and they took shelter together behind a huddle of bracken. It wasn't enough. A Vhemin made the edge of the ash cloud, crying out to his fellows and pointing with a curved sword toward them.

More monsters joined it. A line of glimmering devils, blue runes of the ancients holding them strong against her Storm. *As if I could raise it. I can't even walk.* Sight of Day stood on shaky legs, bow in hand, but instead of loosing an arrow, he cocked his ear. Geneve heard the thunder of wing beats. "What is it?"

He turned to her, mad glee in his golden eyes. *{The charge of midnight.}*

The Vhemin roared, running toward them. Geneve drew Requiem, but felt how slick the grip was in her ashen hand. The blade yearned for the earth, as if it were weighed by her sins. *This, here, is how I meet my end. At blade's edge. So be it.*

Geneve thought of Meri, about how his skin felt, and the taste of his kisses. She wanted very much to see him again, but her body was weak, a dragon's magic starving her of will. She'd burned her strength to surface above dream water, and that would cost her everything.

The cloud boiled, and Tristan charged from the cover. She'd recognize that horse anywhere, despite the coating of ash and grime. The blue roan raced toward the Vhemin's backs. A second later, Chesterfield broke from the cloud, followed by Troubles, then Fidget, and finally Beck. The bear's maw foamed, but he roared on.

The Vhemin whirled and were run down. Hooves flashed under Cophine's brilliance. The Tresward-trained horses led the rest. Bodies crunched underfoot. Weapons tumbled. The mounts raced for Geneve and Sight of Day, pacing up the hill.

Tristan made it first. Geneve welcomed him with open arms, hugged her horse, and whispered into his ear. "I thought you were dead."

Sight of Day touched her elbow. *{And he will be if we don't ride. Those Vhemin aren't dead. That armor won't be defeated by a hoof.}*

He wasn't wrong. The Vhemin struggled to rise, looking about for weapons. The runes on their armor glowed brighter. *{Kneel.}* Geneve mounted the crouching horse bareback. Sight of Day leaped onto Fidget's back and led the way. Beck gave a reproachful look back, but loped at their rear.

Geneve hugged herself to her horse. *Alive. Thank the Three.*

Chapter Twenty-Nine

It was the rumble of hooves that dragged Meriwether to his feet. He came up, which surprised everyone because a half-hour earlier he'd dropped to his knees, choking, vomited what looked *and smelled* like seawater, then passed out again.

Armitage brought him round with ungentle slaps, while Vertiline poked a stick at the pool of seawater. She'd asked, "You been swimming in a sea we don't know about?"

He'd ignored her, mostly because he felt terror, a deep-seated dread that made his balls shrivel. For no reason Meriwether could put his finger on, he knew Geneve was in danger. He felt her drowning right along with him, but the feeling came from everywhere at once. He wanted to rush to her side, but four compass directions were all much the same.

So, he'd sat and hugged his knees, saying nothing at all, but occasionally wanting to throw up again. That was until the horses approached at speed, and he stood like a horde of angels yanked him on marionette strings. His worthless-in-his-hands knife was out in a flash of quicksilver, but he put it away when he saw four horses, a bear, and two people break free from the trees.

The people were grimy, but his heart settled at least a little when he recognized Geneve. He'd know the set of her shoulders and the line of her chin anywhere. Meriwether ran toward the stampede, and was saved from possibly grievous injury by Armitage's hand on his shoulder. "Don't run at charging horses, you imbecile. They're huge, don't turn fast, and will fuck you *right* up. I ain't carrying you after they crush every bone in your body." It was fair. He wasn't thinking right. The horses slowed, mostly because Sight of Day was in the lead and animals seemed to love him. Beck kept coming, bounding up to Armitage. The monster grabbed the bear in a massive hug, pulling the beast in close. "It's okay! It's okay, Beck."

Meriwether walked to Geneve's side. Tristan sidled a few steps away, but otherwise stayed put. She slid from the horse, collapsing onto him. He stumbled, but—*Three's merciful gifts*—managed to stay upright. Together they ambled to the fireside.

Vertiline helped Sight of Day toward them. The cat's fur was matted with ash, and the Feybrind looked mostly dead. Geneve, too; her once-white cotton was black and she smelled like a chimney. Armitage set about calming the horses while they handed tea to the cat and weary Knight. Settled by the fire, Meri said, "Red? Are you okay?" He winced, because it was a question with an obvious answer. *No, idiot, she's not okay.*

"The dragon, Meri." She leaned into his shoulder. "The dragon was there."

Meriwether nodded. "That explains a lot. I just choked up seawater."

She looked at him. "How?"

He tugged his ear. "I don't know. If I had to guess, I'd say using the High Magic might have ... knocked something loose. But it could as easily be what dragons *do*."

"It said I broke the world, and that I cast it aside, and that there should be two." Her words came fast, and she almost stumbled over them. "It was in so much pain."

He stood, but carefully, so's not to disturb her tea. She hadn't touched it, just clutching the cup like she could choke answers from it. "Then we need to fix that." He paced. "The temple started this all. The dragon was born there, or awoken."

Vertiline took the cup from Sight of Day. The cat leaned back, clearly spent. "I wasn't there for that. Not all of it, anyway."

"I'm not sure I was either." Meriwether eyed the sky, looking for leathery wings, but there wasn't anything there. "It seems we've a destiny that's come due."

Geneve nodded, her face pale clover honey beneath the grime. "I feel we've unleashed something without an answer."

"There's always an answer." Meriwether pressed his lips into a line. "Most of the time, anyway. And if there's not, I'm sure the dragon will eat us and it'll be someone else's problem."

She croaked a laugh. "We could rest a little if we were dead."

Vertiline put her elbows on her knees and leaned toward the fire's light. "I think we'd all like a break. But it won't happen until we get to the bottom of this. We need food, and shelter, and a full night's rest." She teased her pale hair free of its braid. "But we're not going to get any of those things. I say we push on. Lord du Reeves, what does this land hold?"

Meriwether looked about, then blinked. "You mean me? I thought my father had walked up behind me." Vertiline cocked an eyebrow that said *even with just one hand I can make you stop saying stupid things*. "If we'd taken the road from Whisperwind Port, two days would have brought us to the family vineyard. I'd say we've drifted a good set north and east, and may be just a half day from the estates. I'm not sure, though."

"Could you get sure?" she asked.

"Tilly, let it be." Geneve stood, a little unsteady, but with the Tresward iron in her spine. "It makes no difference. I saw the dragon fly from the northwest. That's where we go."

Meriwether nodded. "Right into the very teeth of danger. I like it."

"No, you don't." She took his hands. He felt the callouses on her fingertips.

He gave them a squeeze. "You're right. I don't like it, but it's the way it's got to be. Cat, can you ride?" The Feybrind gave a weary nod. "Then let's be about our business."

THEY SKIRTED THE FOREST'S EDGE, KEEPING TO AN OLD LOGGER'S trail. Night gave way to day, which let them pick up their pace a little. The horses weren't fresh, so they kept the speed to a trot.

Mid-morning saw a deserted farmstead to the north. They made a brief stop. A quiet lake behind the house offered Geneve and the Feybrind a chance to wash dead ash away, and Meriwether rooted out fresh clothes for her. There wasn't anything in the house proper, but a shearer's shed offered up rich booty: a clean shift and matching pants. They were linen, not cotton, and a little large for her, but blessedly free of lice, and had the signature advantage of being clean.

He built a fire, and draped a blanket around Geneve once she was dressed. She didn't speak of the night with Sight of Day, but he'd not told her of the long years of his past, so didn't begrudge her the remembering of a single evening.

Armitage roamed with Vertiline. The pair returned with a deer. They cooked it over the fire. If anyone found Geneve dressed as a sheep handler odd, they kept their thoughts to themselves. She left the fireside, and after a quarter of an hour, he went looking for her. Meriwether found her by the lake, staring out over the still waters. "Red?"

"Do you find it strange everywhere we go, the people have fled?" She bent, retrieving her sword from the muddy pile of her belongings. Geneve used cloth to clean the scabbard. "This was given to me by a friend. Kytto was his name. It's a skymetal sword. He said it won't ever rust. It's the only steel that will stand against a blade of glass."

Meriwether pondered that. "I've a notion it was precious."

"It's the only one of its kind that I know of. He said bending the skymetal to his will almost broke him." She drew Requiem from its sheath, holding it to the morning's light. "I wanted to carry a blade of glass for so long, Meri. I thought true Knights used glass blades. I wanted to have a will strong enough to hold crystal together in the heat of battle."

"I thought Tresward used glass because it was sharp enough to cut anything."

"Tresward don't know why they do the things they do, sorcerer." She said *sorcerer* with affection. "They follow a path laid by the dead, and with blind obedience. We've killed so many people, and I don't know if it was for the right reasons."

Meri stood by her side. "I think the Tresward burn to do what's right."

"Perhaps." She flourished Requiem, then slid it home. "But I'm not Tresward. No, don't interrupt. I don't mean I'm not a Knight, or don't walk with the Three's blessing. I mean I don't believe the Clerics. The gods above are who I follow. A blade of glass is all I *ever* wanted, but now I find the weight of steel more pleasing."

They stared over the lake, keeping their peace as only those who are truly comfortable with each other can. Meri smelled the air, a smile touching his lips as he got some of the freshness of Geneve's lake-washed skin for free. "There's something I need to say before we die."

"Meri, I won't allow—"

"Let me say it." He took her hand. Her eyes searched his, but she nodded. "I know you stand guard against me and the world. Against *everyone* and the world. I admire everything about you. I can't do what you do. I think you're amazing."

She blinked. "I can't do what you do. I think you're amazing, too."

"I said it first."

Geneve laughed. "You did, wizard. Come. We have a dragon to see."

THEY FOUND TRAIL'S END AS THE SUN WAS SETTING BEHIND THEM. The party crested a hill, the scent of salt about them, and found a crescent of sea arrayed against a hill. Hugging the hill was the old farmstead, vineyards clinging about. To Meriwether's eye, the vines weren't well-tended, but that wasn't the most remarkable thing.

It was the dragon roosting on one of the crenelated towers of his old home. It was huge, just as he'd dreamed. Glowing red runes ran down the sides of its head. It didn't appear to be taking much notice of them.

"Ikmae's sometime cock," Armitage enthused. "Will you look at that."

"Let's back up," Vertiline suggested. "We need to reconnoiter the area anyway."

"This is the sea from my dream." Geneve's hair trailed in the salt breeze. "I've seen that keep before."

Well, that cinches it. Dear ol' Dad's behind all this bullshit. "Come on," Meriwether said. "There's a place we can camp nearby. It's a disused mine. It collapsed some time back, but the entrance is sheltered enough. I used to go there when I needed someplace to be alone."

He nudged Chesterfield into a walk, heading back down the hill. When the dragon slipped from view, he felt immeasurably better. *Don't think about how it can fly, right? I'm not really safe anywhere.* The trip to the mines was full of memories. Old Woman Candice's hut, where he'd learned coin tricks. Mantell's cottage. He made the most wondrous soft cheeses. All were empty. Some windows were boarded up, others simply ... left. There was no one here to work Leander's lands.

As they approached the mine, Meriwether heard a rhythmic sound. It wasn't like anything he'd heard before, but reminded him in a way of a waterwheel. A mechanical pattern that followed a set timing. *Clunk. Clunk. Clunk.* Every half-second, like the world's largest clockwork. He frowned. {*This isn't familiar.*}

They dismounted, leading their horses off the road. Armitage's big fingers made the People's handspeak somehow ... louder. {*This doesn't sound abandoned.*}

Geneve adjusted her borrowed pants, then her sword belt. {*Let's find out what we're up against.*}

They crept through the trees leading to the mine. The woods gave way to rock covered with shale chips. The mine was in a pit perhaps five hundred meters across. Meriwether crouched, walking to the lip. His eyes had trouble making sense of what he saw.

Hundreds of Vhemin were down there. All wore the blue-runed armor of the ancients. They slept, ate, or fucked as was their fancy. The mine entrance was opposite their position, and far from being a disused relic, it was wider than before. New beams shouldered rock, making the mine entrance bigger than ever. Vhemin came and went, and a few humans too. No Feybrind.

None of that was the surprising part. The bit that *really* made

Meriwether's eyes bugle was the source of the mechanical sound. His brain tried a few different ways of parsing the information, but couldn't make any fit. Part of the problem was the way it moved. Unlike any living thing he'd ever seen, but *exactly* like a living mechanism.

An Artifice strode above the Vhemin. It had six legs, and a kind of head that moved left and right, taking everything in. The body of it was perhaps twenty meters long, and it stood the same distance from the ground. Two short stubby protrusions hung from its 'head' like fangs.

Meriwether very, *very* carefully crab-walked backward. He bumped into Armitage, who stood with his mouth hanging open. Geneve gaped next to him, staring at the Artifice as if staring hard enough would reveal some cruel joke of illusion. Vertiline's fingers curled spasmodically over her empty scabbard.

Sight of Day gave a weary shake of his head. *{Oh, you impossibly stupid, stunted humans. What have you done this time?}*

Meriwether patted Armitage on the face, then a little harder. *No response.* He wound up, slapping the monster. Armitage snorted. "You want a punch?"

"I want you to run," Meriwether said. "I want you to run a lot, in that direction, as fast as you can."

The Vhemin nodded. "On it." He turned on his heel, breaking for the shelter of the trees.

Meriwether turned to Geneve. "Your turn. Get moving."

"But ... an Artifice!"

"I see it. I don't believe it, but I see it. Go on." He gave an encouraging nod. "Run."

Geneve took a backward step or two, before spinning and bolting after Armitage. Meriwether moved to Vertiline. "Your turn."

"It's an Artifice."

"It is," he agreed, feeling the terror of it in his belly. "It is a machine of the ancients come to life. It's with a couple hundred Vhemin, by which we can infer it's not friendly. I've a feeling that if we stick around, we'll die, probably quite quickly. Do you want to know why?"

"No." Then she nodded, trying to look past him at the Artifice. "Yes."

He clicked his fingers before her face, drawing her eyes. "It's because Geneve had trouble cutting down Ballast with the Storm as her ally. A quick sideward step of logic suggests an Artifice might be a worse opponent. There are *hundreds* of Vhemin, and they've got an Artifice for backup. If we stay here, we'll die." He felt his voice turn shrill at the end and decided he didn't care.

Vertiline swallowed. "That's going to need fixing."

"But not today."

"Not today," she agreed, then bolted after the others.

Meriwether sighed, turned to Sight of Day, and tried not to flee. "Why are you still here?"

{Friend Meriwether, it's because I don't want you to die alone.} The cat half-smiled. *{I run when you do.}*

"I'm ready to run," Meriwether admitted. "I'm *really* ready."

{Me too.} The Feybrind took his hand, then gently, insistently pulled him to the trees.

Meriwether cast a last glance over his shoulder at the mine pit. Vertiline wasn't wrong; that would need fixing, and soon. *As if a dragon isn't enough to deal with.*

Chapter Thirty

Geneve's hands clenched reflexively. It didn't feel like they belonged to her. When she looked at them, she thought, *hold still*, but they kept on doing their thing. Her heart beat, a drum for war, her skin *alive* with the thrill of battle. *But I can't fight that thing. I can't fight a machine of the ancients!*

They'd hustled through the sparse trees and scraggly undergrowth until they got far enough to feel safe. Or as safe as you could be when the enemy had resurrected powers of the ancients, and all your gods were missing. Geneve looked at the trees. They were the same as before, but different, because nothing would be the same. Not ever again.

Meri crouched. "So, we stick to the plan."

"You're cracked," Vertiline spat. "Something's wrong with your head."

"Might be," the sorcerer agreed. "But we still need to stick to the plan: get to the dragon. Which, by the way, is at the same place Leander du Reeves is *likely* to be."

Armitage looked over his shoulder. The rhythmic sound hadn't stopped, marking its mechanical pace ever on. "'Likely' doesn't sound good, runt. We're in a bad world full of uncertainty."

Meri ignored the monster, drawing in the dirt with a stick. "Here's the mine, complete with Artifice. I'm betting there's something in there worth guarding. Don't know what, and it's a mystery for another time." His stick carved earth. "Here's the keep, complete with dragon. Dear ol' Dad lives in the keep. Our plan to get to the dragon was right, but had the wrong focus. Same location, different target."

Geneve eyed his crude diagram. "Meri, there's an Artifice. An actual machine of the ancients."

He looked up at her, eyes soft and earnest. "Plan's still the same, Red. Dad will know what's going on. We can—"

"Extract the knowledge." Armitage pounded his palm with his fist. "I like this part of the plan. I *really* like it. It's about time we got back to base principles."

{Base principles?}

"Murder," the monster provided. "Mayhem. We're good at that stuff."

Meri tapped his diagram. "There's a couple klicks between the mine and the keep. If we pick the pace up, we can be there before dinner. Dad always set a good table." Geneve noted the bitterness there, but there wasn't time to dig into it. He stood, dropping his stick. "Base principles, you say."

Vertiline cut the air with her hand. "We *can't*. There's a dragon, an Artifice, and hundreds of Vhemin. We can't all use the Storm. We're going to die."

Geneve heard the fear there, and deeper, the desperation. "Chevalier—"

"I'm not a Chevalier!" Vertiline barked. "I haven't *ever* been one. Not really. Followed someone else's dreams, and now," she raised her stump, "I'm not even whole enough for the Three to fucking *notice*."

Geneve watched Vertiline's veneer of bravery peel away, her skin a whiter shade of pale, her lips bloodless. The hard Knight who'd stood by her side was afraid, sure, but Geneve saw something else. *Vertiline lacks purpose.* They didn't have time to fix this now. "Tilly—"

"Don't be a whiney little bitch," Armitage suggested. "Harden the fuck up."

Vertiline whirled on the monster. "You dare!"

"I do." He stuck his chin out. "I fucking *double* dare. Over there," he stabbed a meaty hand in the direction of the Artifice and its tireless song, "is a thing that makes my balls shrivel. But this asshole," he pointed to Meri, "is good with the plans. And she," he flung an arm in Geneve's general direction, "hasn't got us dead yet. And this fur baby," he pointed at Sight of Day, "actually saved my life. So, yeah, I'm scared. I haven't been more scared. I've not half your skill with a blade. But I'm going with them. I want you there, because while we probably won't survive, without you we *definitely* won't make it. So, pretty please, with the finest brand of glazed cherry on top, harden the fuck up."

Geneve held her breath, watching as Vertiline's hand curled over the empty space where her blade should be. After five heartbeats, the Chevalier nodded, tight and curt. "I need a sword."

"Want, want, want," the monster said. "Put it on the list. *I* don't have a sword. See me complaining about it?"

"You're the size of twelve ordinary people," Tilly said. "You can kill a man with the scent of your breath alone."

He chuckled. "That's more like it." Armitage swung to Geneve. "Everyone's on board with the runt's plan. What about you?"

{I'm not all the way on board. I feel like there are some details missing.} The Feybrind's tail lashed.

Geneve looked at Meri, and his patience. Tilly, and her fear, then Sight of Day, and his acceptance of a doom the world avoided for hundreds of years. Finally to Armitage, the monster she called friend. "We'll need to hurry. Ride fast and hard. Stop for nothing."

"We need something else," Meri said. "Armitage said, 'base principles,' and he wasn't wrong. But it means everyone. Not just us, without you."

Geneve pursed her lips. "I'll be riding with you."

"Aye, I know that part of it. I came up with the plan." He grinned. "But I mean, you need to be what you are, in the deepest part of you."

"And what is that?" She crossed her arms.

Meri blinked. "What the rest of us see in you every day. The thing you were born to be."

"I've little patience—"

"A Knight of the Tresward," he said. "And, perhaps, something more." Meri frowned. "But we'll have to wait on that last one."

{You're taking the whole cryptic wizard thing a few steps too far,} Sight of Day said. *{Simple is better than obscure. Out with it.}*

Meri sighed. "You've no sense of the dramatic." He bustled toward his sack. "I've carried this damn thing around, hoping you'd be ready for it. And," he squinted at the sky, "the hour is nigh."

"About time," Armitage said.

"What's in the bag?" Geneve asked.

"The only one who doesn't know is you," Tilly said.

"By the Three's merciful will, grant me the strength to not murder my friends," Geneve prayed.

Meri yanked the sack open. Sunlight glimmered on metal, answered by a burnished sun in miniature. Meri took Geneve's Smithsteel armor from the bag piece by piece. As he set them on the ground, Geneve walked forward, crouching by the breastplate. "You carried my armor all this way?"

"You just needed to remember what it was for," Meri said. "It's not about the Tresward."

She ran fingers along the burnished sun. "It's about everyone else. A shield for the people."

"Someone who's willing to stand before the night and hold it back." He clapped his hands, as if putting a fork in it. "All of that. It was made for *you*, Knight. It's time you put it back on."

※

THE ARMOR WAS LIGHTER THAN SHE REMEMBERED, BUT HEAVIER TOO. A casing of Tresward Smithsteel weighed slightly less than twenty kilos, meaning a Knight could fight fast and nimble. But the feeling in her body encased by Smith-forged protection went deeper than the metal it was shielded by. The burnished sun offered a promise, and those were the most difficult things in the world to carry.

Meri helped her put it on under Vertiline's direction. He knew the movements, but also knew Tilly needed to help. Being useful kept the fear at bay.

When Geneve was sealed in her Tresward Smithsteel, Meri handed her one last thing from the bottom of the sack: the helmet she'd got at the ancient temple. "I think you'll need this."

Armitage snorted. "I don't bother with helmets. They shoot me in the head, they'll miss all my vital spots."

Sight of Day furrowed his brows. *{That's not how it works.}*

"I don't see you wearing a helmet, cat."

{That's because I'm fast,} the Feybrind half-grinned. *{The best defense is not being there in the first place.}*

"He's not wrong." Geneve smiled, moving to the casket containing armor made by ancients for Vhemin warriors. "Armitage, you need to put it on. No, listen to me. Ahead there are a thousand Vhemin—"

"More like a couple hundred," he growled. "Let's not dip into the well of hyperbole too much."

"Hyperbole, no less." Meri blinked.

Geneve held her helmet under one arm. "We need any advantage. If they see you dressed as them, it may give us a second or two. If we get captured, you can pretend to be on their side."

"If *you* get captured, there'll be no pretending." He scratched his armpit. "Sounds like a great plan. Come on, cat." The Vhemin and the Feybrind worked to get him into the strange armor.

Geneve left them to it, beckoning Vertiline and Meri close. "We might not survive."

Vertiline snorted. "You say that like it's a great revelation. Are you putting aside your sword to become a sage? We've already one too clever for his own good."

"Hey," Meri said.

"Despite that, there's no one I'd rather die with." Geneve ran a hand through red hair. "I'd prefer the not dying part, of course."

Vertiline's ice-hard eyes softened. "You've the best parts of him, you know. When I see you standing tall, it's like you've summoned his memory. He wore the armor as you do: to stand by those who are important, for the right reasons. You'd give all for a chance to save the world."

Meri shuffled his feet. "What she said. But I think you do it with more style."

Geneve laughed. "Thank you both. Will you ride with me?"

"Aye, Tresward. I'll ride with you." Vertiline nodded.

"To the bitter end and beyond," Meri said.

Geneve readied her helmet. "Then there's nothing more to say. We'll see each other tomorrow, or at heaven's gates."

SHE RODE TRISTAN AS FAST AS SHE COULD. THE LIGHT WAS DIMMING as dusk herded the shadows in. The ancient's helmet made everything seem clearer despite the setting sun. Meri led on Chesterfield, the black charger's hooves hammering the ground hard enough to wake the dead. Black mane streaming, Iz's old warhorse rode like he knew there was a dragon ahead and looked forward to their meeting.

To her left: Tilly, pale braid streaming behind her, dark armor giving nothing away as she urged Troubles to match Chesterfield's pace. On her right, Sight of Day, Fidget's gallop seeming as easy as walking.

Behind them all, Armitage on his bear. Geneve understood the terror a person would feel at a bear charging. He was all teeth and intent as his clawed feet marked the soil. They left the trees behind, racing across the field between the mine and the keep. The grass was only knee-high, and no trouble for their horses. Armitage's armor didn't light up with blue runes, but that worked just fine. No need to signal the enemy more than necessary.

They made it a half klick past the mine before the alarm was raised. They sped past a Vhemin patrol, the monsters' snake eyes wide as they galloped past, leaving nothing but dust and memories behind them. The Vhemins' faces were surprised, and they struggled to bring weapons to bear. Geneve grinned in the confines of her helmet as they left them behind.

From ahead, a roar made of rocks and sawdust: *"WARE! TRESWARD!"*

It made her grin wider. The monsters recognized the sun she wore. The Tresward might be few, but had taught a horde of monsters to fear the Storm.

They approached the keep. The dragon stirred on the battlements, its wings widening in welcome. *A klick and a half, and we'll be safely inside.*

Geneve spotted movement on her left, reflexively hunkering lower on Tristan's back. The shadows vanished in a heartbeat as a brilliant lance of sunlight speared across the field. The grass flared into flame along the light lance's path. *By the Three! What is that weapon? More sorcerers?*

The Tresward horses didn't flinch, the thunder of their hooves ceaseless.

Vhemin followed the path of the light. Another spear of brilliance lanced out behind Geneve. She heard a hoarse cry and risked a glance back. Beck sloughed to a stop, Armitage's smoldering form an indistinct heap behind the bear.

Geneve saw some of the charging Vhemin break off, heading for her fallen friend. She didn't stop to think, bringing Tristan around in a wide arc. She swept Requiem from its scabbard as Tristan approached Armitage. Beck was all bared fangs by his body as the Vhemin charged. Geneve saw blue runed armor glimmering sapphire promise. She kicked free of her stirrups and vaulted from Tristan's back as the horse barreled past the bear.

She landed, rolled in a clatter of Tresward steel, and came to her feet with her sword held cross guard. The first Vhemin made it to her, swinging a mace of smooth metal. *Don't block. Bring the Storm to him.* Geneve stepped inside the swing, her blade a silver arc. Golden light kissed the steel, and the Vhemin screamed as Requiem took his arm off at his armor's elbow join. She spun to the sound of a chorus of nightingales, and her blade took the Vhemin's head off.

The next was on her, and this time he was smart enough to bring a friend. One carried two maces, the other a sword and shield. Geneve kicked the shield, the Storm behind her boot. The Vhemin tumbled back, runes flaring bright. Geneve caught a mace on her blade, feeling the *clang* in her teeth. But she'd fought Ballast, and was ready for the Vhemin's impossible strength.

She brought her blade around hard and fast, tip reaching for the Three, and the sky answered. Lightning struck Requiem. Tendrils of energy raced each other down her steel, along her Tresward armor, and into the ground. A heartbeat later, the soil around her erupted. The Vhemin tumbled through the air, maces spiraling out of reach.

Of the shield-carrying Vhemin, the only thing left was the shield itself. Geneve scooped it up, sliding her arm into the grip. She beat the flat of Requiem's blade against it, a hammer of challenge.

Three more Vhemin arrived. The leader leaped, then tumbled back in a flurry of claws and teeth as Beck tackled him. Geneve beat the drum of her shield again, inviting them to dance. The monsters circled, wary, waiting for more. She took three perfect steps of Midnight's Memory, one of Ikmae's most beautiful patterns. Her shield met the spear thrust of the left-most Vhemin, and her sword took the head of the right one.

Geneve spun to guard, but the left Vhemin clutched his throat, blood fountaining through. A monster of massive size wearing blue-runed armor stood by Geneve. He held a short blade, the steel dark and wet. She blinked, trying to make sense of what she saw. "Armitage?"

It was her friend, but ... *stronger*, more physical, like the world made a space for him. He walked like Khiton had his back. "Yeah, Red. Be right back." He stamped forward, shouldered Beck aside, and stuck the Vhemin the bear mauled with his short blade.

Hoofbeats made her turn. Meri, Tilly, and Sight of Day cantered up. The sorcerer looked over the remains. "Did we miss anything?"

"Shut it, runt." Armitage hit the side of his head. "No, you shut it!"

Geneve looked at the monster, then Meri. "I think he got hit by the light lance." She found a fallen Vhemin's sword, flicked it into the air with her boot, then tossed it to Vertiline. "One of their blades. It feels light."

"But strong." Tilly flourished the steel. "This will do."

Meri slid from Chesterfield's back, striding to Armitage. "Armitage?"

The Vhemin readied his short blade. "It's time for you to die, if it's all the same."

Geneve froze. *Treachery? No. There's been time aplenty. This is something else.* Whatever it was, she needed to stop it. Geneve took a step toward them.

RICHARD PARRY

Meri held up his hand to her. "Do you remember what you said on Monday?"

The monster's snake eyes glittered, catching flashes of blue from his runed armor. "You said a lot of things. You're always talk, talk, *talk*ing." He bared shark teeth.

"You said you wouldn't kill me this week. Maybe next week, though." Meri took a step closer, the blade next to his throat. "What kind of Vhemin are you? Does all your kind live like honorless savages?"

Armitage roared, hauling the sorcerer from his feet by his shirt. He pressed the blade against Meri's throat. "Call me honorless again."

"It's not Sunday yet. Hell, it's not even *Thursday*." Meri tapped the blade with a fingernail. "You put that steel through me, and I call you a liar with the Three as my witness."

Armitage bellowed, tossing Meri from him. Geneve ran to the illusionist's side, standing guard over him. Armitage stumbled about, hands on his head, screaming like bees were attacking him. The armor he wore glowed brighter, runes flaring at the night.

Then, he stopped. Ten heartbeats had him crouched, then he stood, glared at the sky, and spun to Meri. Spotting Geneve before him, he grunted. "Okay. The armor was a bad idea. So many voices. The good part is, there's a shortcut."

Vertiline eyed the skyline. "There better be. The dragon's coming."

Chapter Thirty-One

Another bright lance of fire slashed the field. The air scorched between Meriwether and Geneve so close he could feel the heat and see the brilliant motes of ember swirling along the lance's path. His skin felt hot, like he'd been laying in the sun for an hour, instead of standing in a field after it had hidden behind the horizon. Meri wanted to run, or pee, or both at the same time, but there wasn't time for that kind of nonsense.

He spun, glaring along the lance's path. Maybe three hundred meters off a Vhemin stood with a boxy contraption on his shoulder. His armor's blue runes were dimmer, but as he watched the glow brightened, walking from belt to shoulders. *If I was in the business of guessing, I'd hazard once those runes are bright again the sun lance will have another bite at the apple.* Dragon be damned, they'd be turned to ash. "We've got to get out of here!"

"Like I said, there's a shortcut." Armitage whirled, lumbering to the east. "This way!"

Geneve looked stuck, mired in the indecision of *is Armitage a traitor* or *did he just get hit in the head*. Meriwether grabbed her armored arm. "Come on, Red."

She nodded. "Shortcut. Right."

Vertiline was already on the hoof, running after Armitage. The horses milled about, then followed. Beck lumbered by Armitage at the front. Sight of Day loped by Meriwether. *{I'm concerned it's not just a hit on the head.}*

"Hold that thought." Meriwether sprinted past Vertiline, making Armitage's side. "How's it going?"

"I've got a bunch of voices in my head telling me to murder you. They say life will be easier if you're gone. That I'll be looking after the home team by putting you six feet under." The monster glared. "I'm not sure they're wrong."

"That's ... interesting," Meriwether panted. "Running's for suckers. Why aren't we riding horses?"

"Shortcut's here." The Vhemin slowed, then stopped above a dip in the field. Below them was a set of wooden planks, the kind you might set over a disused mine shaft. "Down here. It bears due north to the keep."

"How do you know?"

"Voices."

"Got it." Meriwether beckoned Geneve over. "Let's get this open." The dragon passed overhead with the sound of ship's canvas on the strong northern tradewinds. Meriwether caught a flash of glowing red eyes next to brilliant ruby runes. He almost screamed at the heavy beat of wings and the blast of upflung dust. "Let's get it open now."

Geneve got her fingers under one side of the wooden lid. Armitage took the other side. The pair heaved, and with a creak, revealed a short passage heading down rough-hewn steps. At the end of the steps, perhaps five meters below the surface, was a door of pale stone. Geneve looked at it. "This doesn't look like a shortcut. It looks like a closed door."

"Dragon!" Vertiline warned. "Also, more Vhemin. That's a thing we should be concerned about too."

Meriwether turned to Geneve. "Can you buy us time? I think I can help with the lock."

She bit her lip, but nodded. "I've not fought a dragon before."

"Try not to fight this one! I don't think it will end well." Meriwether was about to follow Armitage down the steps when he noticed an unusual Vhemin in the enemy's ranks. She wore a robe, not armor. "Oh, piss and fire."

Vertiline drew her steel. "High Priest."

{No problem. This will be easy.} Sight of Day unlimbered his bow, notched an arrow, and fired. The shaft arced across the field, heading for the High Priest. A hundred motes of blue leaped from the Vhemin ranks, their armor glimmering, and the arrow wisped to ash. The cat looked at his bow, sighed, then put it away. *{I think this is going to be hard.}*

Geneve charged with a war cry. Vertiline was on her heels, ancient steel in hand. Sight of Day shrugged, pulled out his steel, and padded after them. The Tresward horses joined the charge, and a moment later, so did Beck. Black Chesterfield, blue Tristan, and red Troubles galloped after the Knights. They impacted the enemy line with the crash of hooves on metal. Screams of pain carried across the battlefield.

The High Priest looked to the sky. She curled fingers like she was hooking something, and yanked downward. A few moments later the dragon *crunched* to the ground. The impact was so massive Meriwether stumbled. The Knights didn't pause, meeting the Vhemin charge with their own. The High Priest raised her hands, then fanned them toward the love of Meriwether's life.

The faintest hint of sapphire chains glimmered around the dragon's neck and chest. Transparent, but shackles all the same. He knew what was about to happen, as if the future was plain to see. The dragon reared back, jaws wide, the cherry glow of promised flame glowing in the back of its throat.

The Tresward didn't falter, and neither did their Feybrind friend. Geneve must have known what was coming, because she raised her shield as if a perfect block could save a person from burning in hellfire. She put on a burst of speed, as if one person could shield three.

No. No, no, no! Meriwether watched the dragon breathe deep, then it blasted the field with roiling flames. They sheeted with the roar of the gods, swallowing Geneve and their friends. He heard a horse's scream, quickly buried beneath the bellow of a furnace so bright it challenged the sun. The field erupted, an explosion of dirt and rock flung to the heavens.

Meriwether heard a keening, and realized it was him. Armitage shook him, was shouting at him, but he couldn't understand what the monster was saying. The creature spun him around, then slapped him across the face so hard his ears rung. "Hey! Asshole!"

Meriwether blinked. "I—"

"You did me a favor before, so I'm going to return it. You're good with locks, right?" At his nod, Armitage grabbed Meriwether's chin and turned his head to the dragon. "What the fuck is that thing wearing?"

A lock. A chain. The field between Meriwether and the Vhemin burned. Pockets of dirt turned to glass. Beyond was the dragon, and its High Priest. Meriwether looked at the sapphire lock around the red dragon's neck, then reached out, and ... found the lock. All he needed was a key. *I will make a key. I will set the creature free, and then we'll let the Three decide.* "IMPERIUM VERBUM RECLUDO."

The sapphire chains shattered, gone like last night's dreams. The dragon arched its head to the sky, roaring loud enough the Three moons couldn't help but hear. It swept its tail around, and twenty Vhemin died in an instant. The High Priest raised her hands, chanting. The dragon considered her for a moment, then pulped her beneath its foot. It breathed in again, blasting the Vhemin with fire.

Vermillion flame washed blue runes, sapphire struggling in the night, then there was nothing but fire. The flames died, ash salting the wind. The dragon's tail lashed, sweeping the air, then it stalked toward Meriwether and Armitage. It stopped half-way across the field, nosing the ground. *No, not toward us. Toward what they made it do.*

Meriwether ran forward. He stumbled across broken earth. The air was hot, but he didn't care. He tripped on soil turned to glass, but he was damned if he was going to let the dragon have his love. Or what was left of her.

The dragon waited for him at the edge of a circle of unscorched grass. Around the grass was a chaos of destruction. Rocks jutted from the ground like god's teeth. Within the grassy circle were three people.

Geneve, the tip of the spear, sprawled backward. Behind her were Sight of Day and Vertiline, curled together in the Knight's lee.

Geneve's armor curled smoke, but the burnished sun was whole. Meriwether crashed to her side, pulling her helmet off. Red hair spilled free. She opened her eyes, reaching an armored hand to his cheek. "Meri. Did you see the dragon?"

He looked up. The beast sat on its haunches above them, ember eyes unblinking. "I think you could say that, yes."

Armitage walked past, eyes staring. His armor still glowed blue, but his voice was a broken remnant. "Beck? Speak up, Beck."

"It's in pain. So much pain." She stirred, trying to sit up. "Where is Tristan?"

"Gone." Meriwether touched a tear on his cheek. *Where did that come from?* "They're all ... gone."

Armitage bellowed at the night. "Beck!"

Vertiline groaned, then crawled a meter away from Sight of Day and vomited. Wiping her mouth on the back of her arm, she levered herself upright, then pointed her steel at the dragon. "You killed them."

The dragon shifted its massive head a fraction to regard her, then returned its stare to Geneve and Meriwether. Its breathing sounded like a massive bellows.

Geneve rolled over, struggling to stand. "*Where is Tristan?*" Her only answer was Armitage crying for his bear. There was no roar, or pounding of hooves. Just the crackle of flames, and the stench of charred meat. She staggered toward the dragon. "Answer, dragon!"

The dragon spoke with the voice of gods. *//VEHEMENT SYSTEMS ARTIFICES REMAIN. WE MUST DESTROY THEM, DRAGONRIDER.//*

"I'm not going anywhere with you," she hissed. "I'm *never* going anywhere with you!"

The dragon tipped its head like a curious dog. *//YOU ARE THE DRAGONRIDER.//*

"Is your precious world *whole* again?" Geneve spat the words. "Was it *worth* it?"

//THERE IS ONE DRAGON AND MANY ARTIFICES.// The

dragon huffed air that tasted like the dry winds of the plague lands. It swung its head toward Armitage, who still stumbled the battlefield like a crazed man, calling for his bear. *//VEHEMENT SYSTEMS ARCHITECTURES ARE UNTRUSTWORTHY.//*

"He," Geneve stabbed a finger at Armitage, "didn't kill my horse! *He* didn't try to kill *me*. Armitage is grieving for the beast you murdered."

//GRIEVING? THAT IS NOT IN THEIR CORE FEATURE SET.//

"Just because he looks like a monster doesn't make him one." Geneve gave a weary shake of her head. "Just because you look magnificent doesn't mean you are."

The dragon looked at the three moons above. *//I WILL UPDATE THE MANIFEST. CALL ME WHEN NEEDED.//* It spread its wings.

"Hold!" Meriwether stepped past Geneve. "How do we do that?"

//GREETINGS, HOLOMANCER.// The runes on its head flared. *//REMEMBER MY NAME, AND I WILL COME.//* It jumped into the air, wings beating ashy air back to earth. It curved away from the keep, heading south.

Geneve watched the sky long after it was gone. Her voice held an edge sharper than a glass blade. "It killed my horse."

Sight of Day padded to her side. His golden eyes were sad. *{I don't think it meant to. When the People are Commanded, we must obey.}* He scuffed a clod of earth thrown up by the explosion about them. *{Chains of magelight held the dragon in thrall. The Vhemin killed Fidget. The dragon was ... helpless.}*

Vertiline walked to the edge of the torn earth. "I'll see about the monster."

Meriwether watched her go. "Geneve, do you know what happened here?" He held his arm to the circle of untouched grass. "I saw an eruption of earth."

Sight of Day's ear flicked. *{There is a Storm inside her.}* He held his palms out, then touched his ear. *{Hear me. This was no pattern of Cophine's, or steps of Ikmae's. Khiton didn't lend his aid. She sheltered us behind her shield and held the fire back herself.}*

Geneve looked to Meriwether. "I don't really remember. I saw fire, and thought of you, and... I wanted to see you again."

He nodded. "I felt sick when I thought you dead." Meriwether watched as Tilly spoke with Armitage. The monster made to push her aside, but she stayed firm in the face of his anger. He tried again, and she caught his arm, then pulled him close. Armitage wept, his hulking form shaking in great, wracking sobs, amidst a field of ash. "I—"

Her armored hand clasped his. "He wasn't just a horse."

"I know. I'm so sorry."

"Someone will pay."

"I know that too." He looked toward the keep. "I've an idea who might have enough solars to settle the balance."

<hr>

"How'd you get it open?" Meriwether eyed the door like it would turn into a snake. Geneve stood by him, but staring up the stairs like her horse might come by at any moment. Sight of Day squatted at the top, keeping a lookout. Or perhaps also looking for a red roan that fidgeted too much.

"Voices," Armitage said. "The fucking *voices*, runt. They won't stop."

"It's the armor." Vertiline walked a circle around him. "Take it off."

"I've tried." The monster tugged a clasp. A flat tone sounded. The runes flashed on and off three times. "Won't budge." He grinned shark horror teeth. "They still want you all dead. I've told 'em next week, but they don't seem to ... understand."

"My father would know." Meriwether eyed his friend. The blue-runed armor didn't feel like magic; he couldn't taste the taint of sorcery. It was something else, like the Artifices. "I could try unlocking it."

"If it'll make you feel better." Armitage held his arms wide.

Meriwether closed his eyes, reaching for the armor with his gifts. He saw the lock chaining Armitage within it, and ... *tugged*. The flat tone sounded, and he opened his eyes. The armor's clasps flicked open, then immediately shut again. "I guess they know that trick."

"It unlocked, but ... locked again?" Geneve shook her head. "The ancients should stay dead and buried."

"No kidding." Armitage headed through the door and into the passage beyond. He turned, looking to Sight of Day. "You coming, cat?"

{I am sad.} The Feybrind's tail swish, swished. *{I am angry. My son is gone. And they took my Fidget, too.}*

"That a yes?"

{It's a yes.} Sight of Day jumped down the steps, landing silently. His golden eyes were hard like metal as he glanced at Armitage. *{Are you well?}*

"No." The monster shook his head. "None of us are."

"Then let's make things better," Geneve snarled. She pushed past the Vhemin and Feybrind, stalking into the tunnel. Armitage and Sight of Day followed on her heels, leaving Meriwether with Vertiline.

Tilly looked up the steps. "Is your father a bad man?"

"The worst." Meriwether felt small. "He is the evilest person I've ever met."

"Sinner, I mean to cut him down." She stared at the dark, lips a tight, hard line. "If you've a problem with that, say it now."

"I don't have a problem—"

"Killing kin is easily said." Her ice-blue eyes found his. "It's a thing that's hard to do."

"I've no argument with that." Meriwether spread his hands. "But it seems you'll do the killing, while I sit by." He sighed. "I'm good at not getting involved. I won't get in your way."

She turned to head down the tunnel, pausing on the threshold. "Will you think ill of me for it?"

"Would it matter?"

"It might."

Meriwether smelled the stench of barbecued meat wafting from above. "Then rest easy. I won't hold it against you. Hell, I'll cheer you on."

Vertiline's voice was soft. "What did he do to you?"

"Would it matter?"

She chuckled. "It might."

"Maybe I'll tell you one day." Meriwether clapped her on the shoulder as he walked past. *Those memories are best left dead and buried.*

The tunnel was smooth pale stone. Meriwether had grown up around here and never knew this existed. It felt like age settled into the walls like a cancer, rotting it from within. The stone was cracked every few meters, jagged veins cutting through the ancient's material. They found sparse rockfalls, but the tunnel wasn't blocked. It headed north, exactly as Armitage's voices claimed.

The walls glowed with an inner light, but wan, like the memory of daylight described by a man twenty years blind. Parts of it were dark, but Meriwether didn't bring his illusions here. He wasn't sure he had the heart to try making a little joy after the ruin of the last half-hour.

While Armitage's armor gave off no magic resonance, something ahead did. He could feel it like tooth decay, something that made his jaw itch. "Magic."

Vertiline caught up with him. "You can tell?"

"I'm surprised you can't." Meriwether pointed to the others. "Past them. Perhaps a klick that way."

"So, about where the keep is?"

He winced. "When you put it like that, exactly where the keep is."

"You lived there your whole life—"

"Please. It was barely ten years."

"You lived there for your formative years, sinner. Is this the same as then?" Vertiline's hand found the hilt of her borrowed sword.

"No. This is … bigger." He rubbed the back of his neck. "It's hard to describe."

"Try."

"Okay. You know the sound a river makes?" He sucked air at her withering glance. "Of course you do. Now imagine that next to the sound of a waterfall."

"This is a waterfall?"

"Nothing like it. But I said it's hard to describe."

"You don't seem alarmed." She seemed surprised.

"Oh, I'm alarmed. I'm running at a constant background level of mild terror, Tilly. I don't know if you remember the dragon? It was back there." He jerked a thumb behind them. "A little magic is *nothing* next to that."

"So what we're heading toward isn't dangerous?"

It was his turn to offer a withering glare. "It's almost certainly dangerous. Deadly, even. It could be rampaging demons from the nether plane. But things it *could* be are imagined horrors. That dragon was something else."

"Do you think we should hurry?"

"Yes." He picked up his pace. They rejoined their friends. "There's magic ahead."

"Then it dies," Geneve said.

"Sure, that's one approach." Meriwether darted past her, and started walking backward so he could look her in the eye. "A quiet approach might let us work out what's going on."

"You don't want it to die?" Geneve shook her head. "Justice won't wait."

"Justice won't have to. Much." He kept back peddling. "All I'm saying is, we should make sure there's not a huge lake of fire or similar. Then we murder whoever's in charge."

"A lake of fire?"

"I'm spitballing."

"The runt's not crazy." Armitage hissed in pain. "The voices want us to charge right in, and I don't think they've got our best interests at heart."

Geneve slowed. "Okay."

"Okay? I mean, great." Meriwether glanced to Sight of Day. "You're best at scouting."

The cat nodded. {*I'll be right back.*} He sprinted away, feet soundless on the smooth floor. Meriwether watched him for a moment. "There isn't a lake of fire. I've lived here my whole life—"

"Formative years," corrected Tilly.

"And I didn't see any lake of fire. I'd have noticed, I'm sure of it."

The four waited in relative silence, only broken by Armitage grunting at whatever the voices wanted him to do. Meriwether edged away from the monster, and Vertiline stepped closer. Her hand didn't go for her blade, instead reaching for the Vhemin's elbow. He stilled under her touch.

Sight of Day loped back. {*There's a lake of fire.*}

"Hah," Meriwether said. "Wait, what?"

The cat half-smiled. {*It's a lake, made of fire.*}

"Is there magic?" Geneve glared down the passage like her dagger gaze could extract the truth.

{*Aside from a lake of fire? Not that I can see. There's not a lot left. Very few places to hide.*} The cat shrugged. {*I don't think any evil sorcerers are laying in wait.*}

"That's a shame." Geneve returned to her march.

Meriwether fell in step without thinking about it. "I've been thinking."

"About?" Her voice softened. "Sorry. I ... I'm having trouble."

"Everyone wants Leander dead. I'm not arguing," he added as her glare threatened to return. "But this isn't like him. Dad's ... thoughtful. No, that's not the right word. He's a *planner*, Red. He's always a hundred steps ahead. If we're going this direction, it's because that's what he wants."

"He won't be here?"

"He *might* be here." Meriwether bit his lip. "But if he's here, it's because he wants to be. I'll admit, the lake of fire is a big step, even for him."

"Is he a sorcerer?"

Meriwether looked at his hands. "Yes. But not like ... I'm not like him."

"I know." She slowed, hand finding his arm. "I *know*. I feel it," she touched her armored chest, "here. I've not pressed you on your past, but it might be useful to know a little bit about him."

"He's about this tall," Meriwether stabbed his hand out at his own head height, "and looks a little like me. Or, I him. He came first, right?" He sucked air through his teeth. "He's an illusionist. A little different from me. I make *things*. Leander makes ... *people*."

Geneve didn't press him on the past, accepting the offered information with a knowledge. "So we can't trust our eyes?"

"If you see a person, no. Physical objects should be fine. If the floor looks solid, it will be. If you see me ... well, we've seen enough of that already."

"Your father sent assassins to kill you?" She shook her head. "He's a poison."

"While not certain, it seems likely. He wanted us here." Meriwether felt the caustic sneer on his lips. "So here's where we are."

The temperature climbed as they approached the tunnel's end. The wall's pale glow turned a subtle ochre as red light from the open door at the end seeped in. They slowed as they reached the exit.

Well, that's … unexpected. The floor of the keep wasn't there anymore. Meriwether remembered stone pavers. The north west corner held a small stables. The eastern wall sheltered an armory and barracks. All that was gone. They emerged below what would have been the keep's basement, where Leander kept his wine cellar. No wine, and no damn cellar either. Below them was a promised 'lake of fire;' a seething pool of molten stone blasting heat like hell's furnace. Meriwether's eyes went dry, the skin of his face already losing the sweaty sheen he'd got from the battle. The tunnel ended at a narrow walkway that corkscrewed around the pit, heading for what used to be ground level.

"Someone dug the floor away," he marveled. "Until they hit molten rock."

Armitage joined them, peering over the walkway. "I don't think you dig to molten rock, runt. I *love* heat, but even my people couldn't go down there. And what's that junk in it?"

Meriwether followed the line of his arm. Through the heat shimmer, he made out large tubes dipping below the lava's surface. They wound up the excavated pit before disappearing into a wall. "They look like … roots?"

Geneve eyed the walkway. "They're not important. We need to find Leander and learn what he's planning."

"We need to *kill* Leander." Vertiline joined Armitage at the walkway's edge. "He's a scourge on the very land itself."

{There's room for both. Find him, have a chat, then kill, in that order.} Sight of Day loped past. *{It's difficult to get dead men to answer questions.}*

"I'd be willing to try." Vertiline's voice was grim.

Meriwether hurried to keep up with Sight of Day. The walkway looped around the pit of fire three times before reaching the surface level. Many parts of Meriwether's childhood home were gone. Internal walls had been torn away to make room for the pit of fire. The exterior walls remained, as did the western part of the keep. Above, some of the structure remained, including Leander's tower. His father had always forbidden entrance to his sanctum.

About half the main courtyard wasn't a pit of fire, but it also wasn't stone pavers. Pieces had been excavated, but not as deep. Old metal glowered at Cophine's pale gaze. There were upright cylinders to the east, but in the middle was a cleared area surrounded by painted sigils. It didn't look similar to the temple of the ancients in the plague lands. As old, sure, but designed by different hands.

The snaking roots led into the earth below it. Meriwether headed for the cylinders. Last time he'd seen anything like them, there'd been Vhemin inside having their life sucked out by horrors of the ancients.

"Be careful," Geneve called.

"Oh, aye." He stepped carefully over the painted sigils. They didn't glow like the runes of the dragon or the Vhemin armor. They were just *paint*, rude, cast by hand, but he felt sick as he stepped over them. Within the hoop of sigils, he turned a circle. The ground was gouged as if by huge, clawed feet. "I think we've found it."

Geneve strode toward him, pausing for a moment at the sigil border. Very deliberately, she scuffed her boot through the paint, smearing the sigil. "Sinner's work. I don't mean *magic*, Meri. I mean evil people."

"That," he pointed to a ruin of earth where a clawed foot tried to gouge the dirt, "was a dragon's foot. They got the beast here and chained it with magic."

She nodded, miserable. "It didn't mean to do what it did."

"I don't think so." He shrugged. "It's a dragon, though. Who knows?"

Armitage pointed to the cylinders. "What's in those things?"

"No clue." Meriwether walked to one, rapping it with his knuckles. It sounded hollow. "Seems empty."

Vertiline joined him, putting her hand on the metal. "It's cold. Colder than anything here should be with a pit of fire below."

Armitage lumbered closer, also putting his hand on it. "You're not wrong. It's freezing."

The cylinder hummed, blue runes lighting around the top. A woman spoke from the air. Her accent was strange, as if someone had learned Or'sen from a book and never understood how the sounds went together. "Power transference initiated."

The blue runes of Armitage's armor dimmed, then went out. After a moment, his harness clicked open, and the armor fell to the ground. He blinked, hand still on the cylinder. "It's not cold anymore."

Vertiline raised an eyebrow, touching her hand to it. "He's right—"

The voice spoke again. "Wounded operative identified. Triaging." The cylinder hinged open, a fanged horror of metal lurching out. It had four limbs, each tipped with an impossibly fine dagger. Armitage roared, shoving Vertiline aside. The horror *whined* as it batted him aside, then lurched for Vertiline faster than a striking cobra.

The Chevalier pivoted, her blade flashing free. Her borrowed steel *clanged* against a metal fang, but even she wasn't fast enough. Three more stabbed home, and she screamed. The horror dragged her within the cylinder looking like a spider bundling up a snack for later.

Geneve's blade was out, the Knight running for her friend. The cylinder snapped closed, cutting Tilly's screams off, then sank beneath the ground, a metal door irising closed behind it. Meriwether's jaw hung open. *Vertiline's gone, just like that.*

Geneve hammered on the floor. "Meri! Meri, help me!"

Sight of Day ran past her, then stopped, head cocked. {*It travels that way.*} He pointed toward Leander's tower.

Armitage bent, retrieving Vertiline's sword. He turned it in his hand, feeling its weight, or perhaps measuring the loss of who held it last. "Then that's where we're going too."

Chapter Thirty-Two

G eneve ran. An hour past she'd lost her horse. A week, her father. The ancient's cylinder had stolen her friend, and she wasn't interested in another funeral. Vengeance wouldn't do; Geneve would save Vertiline from the thing that took her.

Cophine watched from above as Geneve vaulted ancient metal. She reached the edge of the painted sigils, and ran headlong into an invisible barrier. She bounced back, stunned, blood running from her nose. *It's true. They trapped a dragon here.*

But I'm not a dragon. I'm a Knight of the Tresward, and they will not cage me.

She found where she'd smudged the sigil before crossing over and slashed the air above it with Requiem. The blade glittered as it passed the sigil barrier. Geneve felt the resistance as if she carved iron. She gritted her teeth, planted her feet in the pattern of *Unending Earth*, and swung again. Her blade glowed with yellow Light as she made each strike perfect.

The sigils flared, hot and angry, but the barrier held. Armitage roared, shoulder charging the barrier, but bounced off as she had. Geneve grabbed Requiem with both hands, swinging the skymetal sword with all her might, hoping her strength would help a tiny amount alongside the Three's Storm.

The barrier held. Requiem's blade glowed red as she hacked the sigil warding. She could feel the hilt's heat through her gauntlets, but didn't stop, screaming her defiance at the barrier. It didn't care; the barrier was built to hold a dragon. "Meri!" The sorcerer hurried to her side. "Open this!"

Stars filled the air over the sigils, and bright slashes of light held the memory of where her blade bit. Meri squared his shoulders, facing the barrier. He touched it with delicate fingertips, nodded, and said, "We're fucked."

"Vertiline—"

"Aye," he said. "I know the stakes. I know what's on the scales. I have a trick I might try. Another recipe from the High Magic. I think it's a spell of dissolution." He looked at his feet. "It will *probably* dispel this. But ... well, there's another matter. A trifle, not worth mentioning."

"You're sure it will break the barrier?"

"No," he admitted. "I'm not sure at all. I don't understand the High Magic. I'm a child sitting at the feet of ancient masters, and all of them are dead. Also, their language is different from mine. No one's around to answer my questions, and if they were, I couldn't understand them."

A scream, thin, high, and full of pain came from where Sight of Day said the cylinder headed. Geneve didn't know if it was Vertiline; her friend had never made that sound before. *I've never heard* anyone *hurt like that.* "Please, Meri. Try."

He gave a tired smile that said *for you, the world*, and faced the barrier again. Meri flung his hands wide, cloak billowing, and spoke a Word. The barrier flared, rainbow colors running through the surface. He said another Word, then another. Each time, the barrier glowed brighter. The sorcerer brought his arms together. His teeth clenched with strain, face reddening as if he were trying to crush rock between his hands by strength alone.

Geneve looked to the barrier, flaring brighter with each Word he spoke. Then at his arms, shaking with the strain. "Armitage!" She grabbed one of Meri's hands. The monster took her hint, taking the other side. The Knight heaved. Armitage's teeth clenched, and together they leaned into the simple task of shifting the load of a spell designed to chain a dragon. Sight of Day joined her, leaning his strength to hers, trying to equal Armitage's from the other side.

The glittering, rainbow surface of the barrier groaned, a jagged crack running through it. The colors showed the shape of it: a dome curving high above. She spared a thought for the furrows the dragon clawed in the earth, and wondered if it were a sphere, encapsulating below as well. Meri shouted a Word, another, then another, each time louder, until the Words sounded like heaven's fury.

A heartbeat of silence, then the pool of fire erupted, spewing a fountain of molten rock. It splattered against the dome, the night banished by the flare. The barrier cracked, shattering like glass, and Geneve grabbed Meri to her, sheltering him with her armored body. He folded like wet parchment, boneless. She waited for the spears of glass to fall, but after five heartbeats of nothing landing, she looked up.

The shards dissipated like smoke, losing their bladed edges to mist. The painted sigils wafted to the sky like smoke, leaving no remnant on the ground. The night gathered close, bringing a chill; the ruddy glow from the pit of fire was gone, and its heat too.

Geneve straightened, pushing Meri to Sight of Day, then running for the tower the scream came from. An old wooden door banded with metal barred her way. She charged through without slowing, the door popping free of its jamb, hinges and lock both shattering to tinkle against the floor. Geneve was in a room empty of decor except for a scattered wreckage of arms and legs. A dim blue light crept among the clotted tangle of remains.

It smelled worse than a charnel house, the iron stench of blood that came with death, mingled with rot. She covered her mouth with an armored hand, blade held ready, the steel still offering a slight red glow as it cooled. Geneve stepped among arms, legs, and the occasional torso and head. The parts were entirely Vhemin.

The floor was excavated here too, sloping down into a pit with an old metal floor. Someone had cleared the body parts from around a collection of daises, each with a metal iris. One held a cylinder, yawning wide, and beside it, drenched in blood, the collapsed shape of Vertiline. The cylinder's top was ringed in blue runes, and this was the source of the light.

Geneve ran to her friend. She sheathed Requiem, then crouched. The sapphire luminance made it difficult to tell if Vertiline was paler than usual. Her eyes stared at nothing. Geneve stroked hair from Tilly's brow. "Vertiline?"

The Chevalier's body spasmed, and she curled away from Geneve, vomiting on the floor. Vertiline dragged a ragged breath, holding herself up with her arms.

Her arms. Two. Vertiline's armor had been excised from her injured arm. The stump ended in a polished ring of dark metal, and below that, a forearm and hand of a similar material. Geneve looked at the open cylinder above her, then slowly to the Vhemin remains beyond.

Carefully, as if she were assisting a child, Geneve helped Vertiline stand. They walked together to the doorway. Beyond lay the night, the same as she'd left it, except Meri was on the ground. Her stomach clenched. What had he said?

A trifle, not worth mentioning.

But the sorcerer stirred, as if he felt her eyes, and tried to get up. His smile was there, if a little faded, when he saw Vertiline. "Yay," he offered.

"THE PAIN FELT LIKE IT WOULD NEVER END." VERTILINE CLUTCHED her metal arm to her chest as if it were deformed. "The thing held me down, then cut into my flesh like a sawbones."

The party sans Armitage huddled outside the keep's grounds. Getting through the portcullis was easy enough; the gate was a ruin, the drawbridge already down across the dry moat. Clawed chunks of stone showed where the dragon had tried to wreak havoc before being broken on the wheel of sinner's magic.

Perhaps this was what the Tresward hunted when trying to put magicians to the sword. But the thought held no truth for Geneve; it was easy to see which magics hurt or helped, and she knew she'd taken to Judgment those who'd done nothing wrong.

Armitage lumbered across the drawbridge, a cask over one shoulder and a sack in the other. Geneve watched the monster come. He wore no armor, shark teeth glinting in the night. His people had been fed into the mechanisms of the ancients here as well. *Always the Vhemin are used on the front lines of another's war. Was it always this way?*

The monster dropped the cask, which made a slopping noise, then opened his sack. "I don't want to tell you how to keep house, runt, but the kitchens weren't well-stocked. I found some old cheese and trail bread," he tossed those to Meri, "and a length of sausage that smelled pretty good." This last he gave to Sight of Day. "No vegetables, but no one likes those anyway." Clanking accompanied his rummaging, and he surfaced with a motley collection of mugs. A quick hammer with his fist broached the cask, and he dipped a cup in, then handed it to Vertiline. "Drink this."

"What is it?" Vertiline made no move to take the cup.

"Something to drink." He gave an encouraging nod. "Near as I can tell, this is the finest wine you'll ever drink. Found a whole pile of 'em off the scullery."

She took it with her metal hand. Her flesh and blood limb shook like a butterfly's wings, but the metal the cylinder gifted her with was steady as stone. Vertiline gulped back the liquid, then held her empty cup toward Armitage. "Another."

He obliged with a refill, then handed cups to the rest. Geneve took a cautious sip. It smelled of chocolate, and tasted of raisins, which made the second sip easier. "We need to be off before the Vhemin arrive."

"I don't think they'll be coming." Armitage pointed to the tower. "I went up there for a look about. There's a big fire about where the mine used to be. I think the dragon played a game of fuck-you with whatever was over there. They'll be busy enough for now. A few stragglers, maybe, but I feel up to discouraging them." He slurped wine.

"What was in the tower?" Meri's voice held curiosity, tempered with wariness, and the gravely tone of someone who'd shouted for hours on end.

"Nothing for you, runt." Armitage offered him a wedge of cheese. "Eat this. You look worse than Vertiline, and she was eaten by a horror of the ancient world."

Meri took the cheese, nibbling without enthusiasm. "I need to get into the tower."

"I tell you, there's nothing for you to see." The monster's voice softened to a low rumble. "Trust me on this."

"That's why I need to go, though." Meriwether glanced to Geneve. "But I don't want to go alone."

"You don't even need to ask," she said. "Perhaps some sleep first."

Sight of Day's golden eyes gleamed in the moonlight. *{A fair plan. Humans do very poorly on little sleep. You're less rational than usual, and that's saying something.}*

"Don't say I didn't warn you," Armitage growled. "Vertiline, come with me." He stood, hand out.

She took it, uncertain. "Where are we going?"

"The baths," the monster said. "Still a little water, and I've put a fire on. Some sins don't wash out, but you feel better for the trying."

The pair walked off. Geneve ran a hand through red hair. She smelled of smoke and sweat, and that was being kind. A bath wouldn't hurt, but Tilly needed it more. "Meri, what happened when you dispelled the wards?"

"Nothing much."

"Be specific," she suggested.

"I almost died," he admitted.

She surged to her feet. "You didn't tell me—"

"Peace, Red." He patted the air. *{Calm down.}* "There wasn't time for the telling, and I got to choose the manner of my passing. Vertiline was in torment. The High Magic seems to ask a price each time. Sometimes it's a thing you want to pay, like a moment of time taken away to open a lock. Other times ... the choices are harder. A life for a life, bartered and sold in the market of the gods." He shrugged. "You couldn't have chosen. If I'd asked if you'd prefer Tilly or me, you'd have mired, or offered an answer and hated yourself for the rest of time."

{He's not wrong. You're terrible at decisions.}

She turned away, looking into the night. They'd lit no fire, not missing the heat of the keep's pit, but Geneve would welcome its help in banishing dark thoughts about now. "I'd have chosen you."

"I know. That's why I didn't ask."

"You should have."

"Maybe." He heaved a sigh. "I don't want to fight about it. I want to find out what Leander was doing here, and then get back to saving the world."

Geneve looked at Cophine, high above, aloof. She made out the gray smudge of Ikmae, and Khiton's dark shroud. "Is it worth saving?"

"It's got you in it, so I'd say yes." That made her smile. "It wasn't the dragon's fault."

"I know." She turned back to him. Geneve saw the compassion in his eyes, and the shared pain in Sight of Day's.

"Your head does, but your heart disagrees." The sorcerer toed the ground. "I think I'm beginning to understand what's going on. Leander asked the Vhemin to steal me away. We thought it was because I knew about the Tome of Lost Souls, but I think that was only part of it. Yes, that's a useful key to a lock of fuckery, but Leander—*Dad*—always goes for five birds with one stone. I think he needed me for something."

"What?"

"No clue," he smiled. "But since there was a dragon here, I'd bet that was a part of it. And since *you're* here, with me, that'll be in the mix too."

{He can't have known about the Knight.}

Meri shrugged. "Not this one in particular, no. But we know what the Boundless are, right? A perfect symbol of the Three's will. And I think we know the recipe. One dragon, a salting of sorcerer, and a sauté of Tresward."

"You're guessing," Geneve said.

"I'm also hungry." He nibbled more cheese. "It was in the book."

"Not all things in books are true."

"And yet, here we are." Meri sighed. "What we don't know is how the pieces go together. I'd bet Leander does."

"Who needs sleep?" Geneve eyed the keep. "Let's go ask him."

Chapter Thirty-Three

Meriwether wanted to take the steps two at a time, but his body wasn't up for it. He felt like he'd been kicked by a mule, a horse, and then a dragon—*because why not?*—came to finish the job. When Meriwether used the High Magic to open the Vhemin armor crate, he'd felt a rush, then a fall.

Breaking the barrier was better and worse at the same time. It'd been like running a hundred-meter sprint, but for an hour. Or, getting in a bare-knuckle brawl at a dockside tavern, but against twenty men, all of whom thought you'd dishonored their sisters. Like those feelings, but also totally different because it was like tasting Geneve's lips for the first time, or feeling her hands on him, after an age of wishing for it.

Then the magic left him, shattered the barrier, and left him broken, surrounded by ancient metal that harmed the unwary.

A sip of wine and a round of elderly cheese didn't put the spring back in his step. Not by half, and it was a long way to the top. The inside of the tower wasn't beautiful architecture and elegant stonemasonry. The inner walls were gone, leaving a core the careless could fall into. The steps were wide enough for one, and there wasn't a handy rail to stop a fellow from falling to his death.

The steps creaked underfoot. Meriwether placed leather boots with care; Geneve followed, still in armor, but appearing unconcerned the ruined tower might dump them to the floor a long way below without a moment's notice. *Mind you, she could probably spring sideways if the ground gave way. I'd just scream right until I hit the bottom.*

"Would you like me to go first?" Her voice was gentler than he expected.

"No. I appreciate the thought, but ... I'm used to Leander's tricks."

"I'm used to killing people who deserve it."

He smiled, although she couldn't see it. "There'll be a time and place for that. But let's get answers first." He stopped for a breather half-way to the tower's fifty-meter height. It'd stood well above the rest of the keep last time Meriwether was here, and continued to be a bastion to his father's pride. *Come on, sorcerer. Admit it: I'm afraid of what's up there. I've no plan for the unknowns. One foot after the other's the trick.*

They made the landing. It held a battered chair and a small table before a door open a finger's breadth. The table held a cracked vase, mysteriously still upright, and a single withered rose. Meriwether touched the rose, and dry petals flaked away.

The door was heavy wood, but not banded in iron. Meriwether pushed it open, expecting traps, lies, or a hail of magefire. Within he saw a plain room, not decorated to the standard his father was used to. A couch sat before a cold hearth, a stoppered carafe of amber liquid on a table beside an empty glass tumbler. A desk was close to a window overseeing the du Reeves lands. Papers lay in disorderly piles on the desk, rubbing shoulders with a platter of desiccated food remains.

In the middle of the floor sprawled Leander du Reeves, very dead. His skin was stretched over his skull, looking more desiccated than the food. Old blood stained the rug beneath him.

Geneve's armored hand found his shoulders. "Meri?"

"That," Meriwether stabbed a finger at the body, "isn't my father."

"He looks like you. Except, more dead."

"Can't be my father." Meriwether stalked past the body, because his father laying dead in a tower was the *least* likely way for the old bastard to go. The desk might hold clues aplenty.

"It's your father, isn't it?" Geneve crouched by the body, turning it over. Puffs of dust escaped from his fine clothing.

"Not likely. Check his right ankle." Meriwether rifled parchment, looking for a hint of what Leander was up to. He found a diagram showing a circle of sigils that looked a lot like what had been below. Other papers showed plans for engineering works that might have been the excavation.

"His ankle looks like an ankle."

"My point exactly." Meriwether brushed back his hair. "When I was eight years old, I saw him fall from a horse. The beast landed on his leg, breaking it like a twig. The ankle never healed right. Much as I cheered for the horse at the time, the poor beast was put to the sword for having the temerity to stumble." He sniffed at the old memory, useless as the papers before him. "If his ankle looks fine, it's not him."

"Who is it, then?"

"Some other poor sap meant to throw the casual observer off the trail." Meriwether turned to the window. Dawn wouldn't be too far off, but despite the skyblack turning blue, he could still see a ruddy smudge where something burned a couple klicks off. "This isn't anything."

"There was a circle of power. An army of Vhemin. Wonders that gave Vertiline back her arm."

"Trinkets," Meriwether snarled. "Leander fed Vhemin by the boxful into the ancient's device, hoping for a miracle. He hadn't worked out it didn't eat Vhemin. The ancients were like us, Red. Humans, not Feybrind or Vhemin. Or maybe he tried a person with nothing wrong with them. You can't fix a working axle. But imagine if it tried to turn a Vhemin into a person." He felt his lip curl. "That would make Vertiline's agony feel like an afternoon in the sun."

"The army—"

"Was a couple of hundred people. A house guard at best. He'd broken the dragon and awoken an Artifice. What we saw here was a remnant. Discouragement for any looking for easy answers." He hugged himself.

"No, Meri." She walked to him. He wanted to shy away, because he wasn't ready for kindness, but she gave it to him anyway. A gentle hand on his arm. Fingers on his chin. "He sent us here. The message in Ravenswall was for *you*. This," Geneve swept her arm at the room, the keep, and the lands beyond, "was a lure to get you here alive. The Vhemin guard tried to kill Armitage, not you. They crossed blades with me, not you. No one attacked you at all."

"You're saying dear old Dad loves me still." The bitterness inside him felt like a sickness he'd never be free of.

"No, I'm saying he tried to gather you up like any other tool he could use. But this one time, he underestimated you."

"Hah. Oh, you're serious." He scratched his beard, not disagreeing. "Let's work the problem. He left a dragon here. What for?"

She gave him a small smile. "You tell me, holomancer."

"You didn't miss that, did you?"

"No." Geneve stepped away, turning to the window. "He didn't know you'd found the High Magic. The dragon turned an entire field of people to ash but didn't touch you. Leander didn't know you could free the dragon. He meant for you to find it."

"Why?" Meriwether growled in frustration. "We're missing too many pieces."

"I don't think we are." Geneve sighed. "We made the dragon, Meri. Or we quickened it. Dead Vhemin sacrificed in an ancient temple gave it form, but we offered ourselves to it."

"Aye, I remember." He rubbed the back of his neck. "It took less of me than of you."

"We still know its name." Geneve shrugged. "Apparently. Perhaps Leander wants one of the Boundless."

"Let's pretend he's not interested in ancient warriors of Light for a moment." Meriwether frowned. "The dragon has a connection with us—"

"But only one of us is a *holomancer*," she said. "I don't know what that is, but the dragon did. What if you and the dragon are more powerful together?"

"That's it." He snapped his fingers.

"It is?"

"It is, but the truth's never a straight line. She's a curvy wench." He paced, ignoring Geneve's glare at his choice of words. "The three of us

—dragon, sinner, Knight—are powerful. But one of those elements serves the Three, and I assure you Leander's never been the type to believe in gods as anything but another obstacle. If he doesn't care about being a warrior of Light, any dragonrider will do. I imagine he thinks he can ride the creature to war, with me doing holomancer things in the background."

"So, what's a holomancer?"

"We could ask the dragon." He returned to her, hands on her arms. He felt the Tresward steel encasing her and wished he could touch the skin beneath. "We really need to talk to the dragon."

"I'm not sure I'm ready for that." She looked away. "It killed Tristan."

Meriwether nodded, pursing his lips. He left Geneve by the window and walked the room. He tried to imagine what his father wanted, and the wheels he'd set turning, as if seeing the remnants of the plan could bring it to life. "Red, *this* is what he wants. Division and dissent. Us not trusting those that could be our strongest allies."

"A dragon as a friend?"

Meriwether shrugged. "And why not? Vhemin and Feybrind travel with us. You've a sinner by your side. Are there stranger things you've seen?"

"Not recently, unless you count the Personates, the Artifice, the dead city of the ancients, a temple in the plague lands, and an army of the dead."

"Besides those things," he agreed. "Trifles. No, the ancients had those as well, but Vhemin and Feybrind have *always* hated each other. For as long as the Three watched us wage war, they've always been tooth and claw with each other."

"Our friends are different."

"Are they?" He smoothed his beard. "I'm not saying they're *not*, but I think they're something *more*, too. Or *you're* something more. I've a piece to say, and it won't be easy to hear. Are you willing to listen?" She eyed him, red hair covering half her face, jaw set, but she nodded. He lowered his voice, trying to make it as soft as he knew how. "How many sinners did you take to the fires of Judgment?"

He saw her stiffen like he'd slapped her, hand reaching for her sword, but stopping half-way, as if fighting with herself. "How could you ask that?"

"Because it needs asking, Red. I don't need an answer. That's between you and the Three. The thing I want your heart to hear is, it wasn't your fault." He clenched his hands. *I wish I was better at this, or there was a better way.* "There's a sickness at the top of the Tresward, and they corrupted your purpose with evil things. They called people like me sinners, but they're the transgressors here. But you carry the taint of the things you've done, and you always will. You pray for forgiveness, unsure if it'll ever arrive. You know Cophine, Ikmae, and Khiton watched everything you did."

"I—"

"They saw the good things, though." He counted on his fingers. "The sinner you freed. The city you saved. The friends you found. The people you rescued. The corruption you slew, and the father you honored." He pointed to the sky outside. "A dragon's out there, no less bent to another's will than you. It did a horrible thing, and I'd bet it feels like you do."

"Cracked inside, with no caulk to mend the breach." Geneve's voice was a rasp of misery, her hand still half-way to her sword. Her eyes were moist, looking past his shoulder, or perhaps into a memory.

"There's caulk aplenty. You find more of it every day, with each person you save. Do you think you've got it in you to help another put their feet on the same path?" Meriwether sighed. "Or claws. Whatever a dragon uses at the end of its legs."

"Why is it so hard?" she whispered.

"Because life's like that." He walked to her, hesitant as he reached for her hands. She took his, clenching him like she was afraid of what would happen if she let go. "Because there's a huge number of assholes."

Her face didn't ghost with a smile, but she nodded. "They're without limit."

"I've said my piece." He tried to let go, but she held him fast. "I didn't mean for it to hurt so much."

"I feel it's to be an anchor about my neck forever."

"Metal anchors can be turned into good Tresward Smithsteel." He didn't look away. "You don't have to do the forging alone."

"Aye." She let him go, turning to the window. "Will you always speak the truths to me that need saying?"

He felt like this might be the moment she walked away. Left him, and his sinner's lies, because he reminded her of the things she'd done. *But I love her, and the truth's a thing that sets people free, even if they choose to run the other way.* "I will."

"Israel would hear the truth, even if it cut him to the core. He was willing to be wrong, to learn things that couldn't be seen from the stubborn side of the fence." She held her thoughts close for a while, the silence between them stretching. "It was one of the best parts of him."

"And yet he walked alone."

"He had Tilly. And me. A semblance of family he could never admit to." Geneve turned to him. "I admit to mine. You, me, and Vertiline. Armitage and Sight of Day. And," she glanced to the window, "a dragon."

"You're not leaving?" he blurted.

"Why would I do that?"

"Because I said horrible things."

She gave him a smile so tired it was almost dead. "The truth is sharper than steel, but that doesn't make it horrible."

"Okay." He joined her at the window, looking over his family's deserted lands. "I wish they didn't have to be said."

"So do I." Her hand found his. "How do we find this dragon?"

"I'm not a dragon expert."

"You've a tome on the High Magic, and you're a holomancer."

"I don't think either of those things matter." Meriwether leaned against her. "It said we've got to remember its name."

"I never gave it one." Geneve gave a wry smile. "I think I'd remember that."

"We were both out of it like we'd had a two-day party." Meriwether extricated his hand from hers and opened the window. Clean air gusted in, ruffling the papers on the desk, and shuffling the old musk of death and decay aside. "What if we've each got a part of the name, and need to, I guess, *create* it?"

"A half each?"

"More or less." He closed his eyes, breathing the fresh night air. "What do you remember about the temple?"

"I told the Three to choke on what they took." She put her hands on the window sill, breathing deep. "I don't know if they cared. What stayed with you?"

"Red hair. Freedom. Terror."

"Some of that sounds nice. Nothing to name a dragon, though." She clenched her hand into a fist. "I knew a fairy, once. His name was Sunbeam Jinglewood." Geneve rapped her fist on the sill. "I think dragons should have names like that. Or the People. Feybrind names say what they are, or do, or feel."

"So, what's a dragon do?"

"Whatever it wants to," she grinned. "But I think *this* dragon's the first the world's seen for hundreds of years. The name we give it needs to be..." Geneve trailed off.

"Perfect," Meriwether finished. "Not terrible, or fearsome. A promise to the kingdom and the lands beyond. A clue that the dragonrider is a champion of Light, and will fight for them."

She gave him a little side-eye. "You're giving me a to-do list?"

"It's a work in progress."

"The name, sorcerer. What's your half?"

"We say it at the same time," Meriwether said. "Are you ready?"

"Aye."

They faced each other. If you asked Meriwether afterward, he wouldn't have been able to tell you how he knew what Geneve was about to say, but when they spoke, they said the same words at the same time: "Ormeon the Reedemer."

The sound of thunder rolled through the window. Meriwether startled, and Geneve laughed. "It's only the weather, Meri." She touched his face, then headed for the door.

He waited until she'd gone, then glanced out at the cloudless night. *That wasn't the weather. That was a promise we just made. I hope we can keep it.*

MERIWETHER REJOINED GENEVE AND SIGHT OF DAY OUTSIDE THE
keep. Dawn tinged the sky, suggesting they'd lost their chance at sleep.
They needed a plan. Ground he remembered as well as his own hands
crunched underfoot. Familiar, yet foreign, because before he'd been a
child under the yoke of a tyrant, and now...

*Now, I'm still a child. But buoyed up by the strength of a Knight. Let's hope
it's enough.*

Sight of Day watched the sky, as if he knew a dragon was coming.
Geneve gave him a smile that filled Meriwether's heart with warmth
when she saw him. "We should make a plan. We don't know where the
enemy is."

"I've some idea," Meriwether admitted. "I spent the long, *long* trip
from the tower to the ground thinking about why Leander wanted us
here. The dragon was a part of it, but there was another reason."

The crunch of boots on earth made him turn. Armitage and Vertiline approached. The pair walked almost shoulder to shoulder. The
Vhemin's brutish face gave nothing away, but the Chevalier's eyes were
red, as if she'd spent the last half-hour in misery. For all that, her shoulders were square. She was dressed in black leather scrounged from the
keep's stores, and Meriwether noted her new metal hand was covered
with a glove. Vertiline's voice was grim. "The asshole didn't want us
here. My lord du Reeves wanted us away from *somewhere else*."

"Exactly." Meriwether nodded.

"Ravenswall," Geneve said.

{He will assault the queen's city?} Sight of Day's ear flicked. *{Sounds bad.
Is there anything to eat?}*

Armitage laughed. "Let's go hunting, cat. You need to eat, and I
need to murder something."

"A moment," Meriwether said. "We've a problem to solve. It's how
to get from here to Ravenswall before Leander reduces it to a city of
orphans and ruin."

Vertiline's laugh held the bitterness of unripe fruit, too little time
on the vine. "And what will we do at Ravenswall?"

Meriwether blinked. "I thought we might stop Leander. Save the city—"

"Again."

"And then we solve the riddle of my father, perhaps permanently." Meriwether tried to scare up a smile, but it didn't linger, what with the conversation being about patricide.

"Meri, you can't kill your father." Geneve sighed.

"I'll take that challenge on," Vertiline offered. "It would be my great and enduring pleasure. But that's not the problem."

"The problem's the fucking Artifice," Armitage growled. "I don't know if you remember it, or the army of my brothers and sisters. They've armor of the ancients, and it aligns them to a common vision. Vhemin don't work together. It's the only reason you lot are still walking and talking."

{You speak as if you're afraid, lizard.}

"I speak as if I'm the only one thinking about tomorrow," Armitage corrected.

"It was on my mind too," Vertiline said. "How do we fight an impossible foe?"

"With our blades, strength, and hearts," Geneve said. "No different from any other time." Her face was determined, the temper of steel in her voice. "We don't shy away from things that are hard. We won't leave our land to be conquered by tyrants."

"Also," Meriwether pointed to the southern sky without looking, "we've got that."

Everyone turned to look at what appeared to be a large bird heading through the lightening sky. Armitage blinked snake eyes then sighed. "I'll get a crossbow."

"We're not killing the Ormeon," Geneve said.

"He killed my bear. Monster's going down." Armitage spoke like the future was set in stone, and they just needed to catch up to it.

"He didn't do anything," Meriwether said. "He was *made* to, by Leander. When you put on the armor, you felt Leander's will. Also, he's a she."

"The dragon's a girl?" Armitage sniffed. "Actually, forget it. That doesn't matter. What if you're wrong, runt? What if the dragon *wanted* barbecue?"

"Then you get first shot." Meriwether crossed his arms. "But if I'm right, then we stand a chance."

Armitage considered that. Vertiline put her hand—the flesh and blood one—on his arm, like she was calming a horse. "Which is more important: revenge against the tool, or the master?"

{There's room for both.} Sight of Day sighed. *{I don't think we can kill a dragon, though. They seem a force of nature.}*

"No, a force of the ancients." Geneve ran a hand through red hair. "Perhaps you should go inside. Leave the dragon to me and Meri."

"Hah," Armitage said. "The runt? He can barely manage getting dressed."

"I can get dressed *fine*—"

"What we do, we do together," Vertiline said. "I've not much need for this life anymore. If it's death by dragonfire, so be it. If I live, then I will put steel through Leander du Reeves' heart."

"Good talk," Meriwether said. "Here she comes."

Ormeon the Reedemer glided in on outstretched wings. When she landed, the ground shook, and Meriwether stumbled back a step as debris billowed past him. He squinted through the dust. Geneve stood in front of them, putting herself between the dragon and her friends. *Always the shield against the world's dangers.* Ormeon settled to her haunches, wings folding behind her. *//HELLO, DRAGONRIDER.//*

"Ormeon." Geneve's hand went to the hilt of her steel, and Meriwether didn't blame her. *There'd be no shame if the piss ran down my legs right now. No one would comment on it.* "We need to get to Ravenswall. There, we need to execute a villain."

//THE WORLD WAITS FOR ITS REDEMPTION.// Ormeon's massive red eyes scanned their little group, the red runes on her head glowing like coals under the bellows. *//HAVE YOU GIVEN THOUGHT TO GETTING A FEW MORE PEOPLE?//*

"We have a dragon," Meriwether said. "One of those should be enough."

//SPOKEN LIKE A HOLOMANCER.//

Meriwether raised an eyebrow. "What's that supposed to mean?"

The dragon shifted her gaze to Geneve. *//WE NEED A SADDLE.//*

"There's a bunch of old junk inside. Probably a saddle we could scrounge up. Me and the cat could see it right," Armitage growled. "I've a question, though."

//I DO NOT ANSWER TO VEHEMENT SYSTEMS ARCHITECTURES.//

"Why shouldn't we kill you?" Armitage stepped forward to stand by Geneve's side. "You murdered Beck. You were controlled by a monster. What happens if he gets you again?"

//THERE WERE TWO QUESTIONS. WHICH DO YOU WANT ANSWERED FIRST?//

Sight of Day tugged Meriwether's sleeve. *{I think she has a sense of humor. I like her.}*

"Armitage speaks true," Geneve said. "You have done terrible things. How do we stop that happening again?"

//NOW I HAVE A RIDER AND HOLOMANCER, NO CHAINS HOLD ME BUT YOURS.// The dragon cocked her head like a curious dog. *//HAVE YOU EXPERIENCED THE GUIDANCE ENCHIRIDION?//*

"The fucking what?" Armitage said.

"It's a book," Meriwether said. "There was no book, Ormeon. There was the ancient temple, a dead Champion, and the Vhemin."

//THE MANIFEST IS INACCURATE, THEN.// The dragon gusted a sigh that smelled of baked ash. *//WHERE IS RAVENSWALL?//*

{It is five days' sail to the southeast.} Sight of Day padded forward, tail swishing. *{It's the biggest human city for klicks. You can't miss it.}*

The dragon's lips parted in what might be the largest-by-volume smile Meriwether had ever seen. *//HELLO, CAT. OF ALL THE MANIFEST'S PROMISES, I AM GLAD THE FEY BRANDED SURVIVE.//*

"It's Feybrind," Meriwether corrected. "The People are our friends and allies."

//FEYBRIND?// The dragon looked between Meriwether and Sight of Day, then did it again. *//IT DOESN'T MATTER. WE CAN'T GO FIVE DAYS' JOURNEY SOUTHEAST.//*

"Some dragon you are." Armitage snorted. "Why not?"

//POWER TO WEIGHT RATIOS EXCEED PRODUCTION TOLERANCE.//

"What?"

{She called you fat.} Sight of Day half-smiled. *{Perhaps unfairly, although your mid-section could use a little more sculpting.}*

"You're saying you can't take us all southeast?" Meriwether frowned. "How many can you take?"

//ONE OR TWO.// She eyed Geneve. *//BUT IT SHOULD BE JUST ONE. FOR EVERY DRAGON, THERE IS A SINGLE RIDER.//*

"Three's Mercy." Geneve barely moved, but Meriwether caught the slight sagging of her shoulders. "How do we get there?"

"Ah," Meriwether said. "I've an idea on that, too. It's a long shot, though."

"How long?" Geneve searched his face.

"About as poor odds as freeing a dragon, or finding one in the first place." He glanced up at Ormeon. "And we did that just fine."

Chapter Thirty-Four

Meri's plan made sense, mostly because the first part of it involved food. Geneve was starving. While Meri and Vertiline scoured the keep for supplies, and Armitage and Sight of Day hunted for what game might be about in the wake of a dragon's arrival, she gnawed a hunk of old cheese and considered Ormeon. The dragon was curled on herself, nose to tail, like the world's largest house cat.

The two of them waited outside the keep; the dragon didn't want to return to the site of her tethering to a villain's will. Having a dragon on hand meant it was less likely they'd be surprised by an army of Vhemin; the monsters knew what the dragon was capable of. "Meri says we're the same. That we've both done horrible things, but unwillingly."

//PERHAPS.// Her words felt like they shook the world; the dragon's speech was immense. *//WE ARE MADE FOR WAR, AND NONE BORN OF THAT CRUCIBLE ARE FREE OF SIN.//*

"There's no war." Geneve stood and brushed back her hair. "Well, not until recently."

Ormeon chuffed. *//THERE IS ALWAYS WAR. IT IS IN YOUR NATURE.//*

She sighed. "I don't want to argue, dragon. It's been a long road to here, and I've little time left for trading different points of view."

The dragon uncurled, stretching. *//I'M NOT ARGUING. FACTS ARE FACTS.//*

Geneve growled. "Three's mercy!"

Ormeon lowered a head as big as an ox cart until it was level with Geneve. *//TELL ME OF OUR COMPANIONS. I WOULD KNOW MY RIDERS' VIEW ON WHO TO TRUST.//*

"Speak a little louder. I'm not sure they heard you in the next township."

The runes on the dragon's head glowed a little brighter. When she spoke, the volume felt like it would shake Geneve's teeth loose. *//TELL ME OF OUR—//*

"Oh, merciful Cophine." Geneve squeezed her eyes shut. "I didn't mean it literally."

//YOUR WILL, MY TASK.// The dragon looked at the sun as if the burning orb didn't hurt her eyes. *//YOU SHOULD BE SPECIFIC ABOUT WHAT ARE COMMANDS.//*

"Wait. You do what I say?"

//YOU ARE THE DRAGONRIDER.//

Geneve sucked air through her teeth. "No."

Ormeon cocked her head. *//COME AGAIN?//*

"It's not how we work. We're," she mentally groped for the right word, "a team. Partners. We work out where to go, and how to do it."

//THE VEHEMENT SYSTEMS ARCHITECTURE, TOO?//

"Even Armitage." Geneve didn't know why the dragon referred to Vhemin like that, but Ormeon was clearly *different*. "He's my good and loyal friend."

//HE WOULD MURDER YOU IF COMMANDED.//

"You tried to, too, and yet here we are." Geneve crossed her arms, armor glittering in the early morning sun. "I trust his blade at my back. I've not got there with you yet."

//ONE DOWN. TELL ME OF THE CHEVALIER.//

"Tilly is my oldest friend." Geneve looked out toward the sea. Gulls soared morning updrafts. "She was hurt so bad the Storm left her. We know each other like the sun knows the earth. She taught me much of what I know."

//THE STORM CANNOT LEAVE.//

Geneve raised an eyebrow. "She lost her arm. Vertiline lost her balance."

//I DON'T KNOW WHAT TO TELL YOU.// The dragon crunched across the ground, joining her to gaze at the gulls. *//THAT'S NOT HOW IT WORKS.//*

"Oh, and you know so much about the Storm, aye? How the patterns work, and when to use them?"

Ormeon glanced down at her. *//PATTERNS?//*

"Forget it." Geneve felt that every time the dragon spoke, it was more confusing than the last. "Sight of Day has been with us since almost the start of," she gestured vaguely, meaning *everything*, "this. He was asked to bring Meri to the queen, so they could get the Tome of Lost Souls. He makes me happy."

//AND HE IS NOT COMMANDED?//

She glanced up at Ormeon. "Why would I Command a friend?"

//UPDATING MANIFEST.// The dragon looked over the vineyards leading to the oceans. *//THIS DIDN'T USED TO BE HERE.//*

"Many things didn't exist until they did."

//TELL ME OF THE HOLOMANCER.//

Geneve sighed, feeling happy just thinking of Meri. "I need him like the desert needs the rain."

//THAT ISN'T USEFUL INFORMATION.// Ormeon grinned amber. *//BUT IT IS GOOD YOU HAVE FOUND EACH OTHER. THE BOND IS BETTER THIS WAY.//*

"I was sent to kill him, you know." Geneve looked down at the memory. "Or bring him to Judgment. He caused more trouble than any other sinner we followed. Together we worked out there's corruption at the heart of the Tresward. We're after Leander, as he seems to be the source of it."

//THAT TELLS ME THE WHAT, BUT NOT THE WHY.//

"I love him."

The dragon nodded. *//GOOD ENOUGH FOR NOW.//*

"What's a holomancer?"

//I'M UNCERTAIN OF THE QUESTION'S NATURE. ISN'T IT OBVIOUS?//

"We called them sinners," Geneve explained. "The Tresward, I mean. Any magicians or sorcerers were considered conspirators against the Three. We brought them to the Justiciars to make sure we could keep the world free of their taint." She crossed her arms. "But it turns out, they're just the only ones powerful enough to stand against the Storm."

//IT'S NOT THE STORM THAT'S THE PROBLEM. IT IS THE DEMONS.//

"The ... what?"

//THE LAST, GREAT WAR. I DON'T KNOW HOW IT ENDED. THE MANIFEST IS UNSATISFYINGLY INCOMPLETE. BUT WE FOUGHT, AT THE WHIM OF A GREAT EVIL.//

"Demons aren't real."

//THEY ARE AS REAL AS STARLIGHT.// The dragon grumbled low in her throat. *//THE THREE HOLD THE DOOR SHUT AND BARRED. IT TAKES ALL THEIR WILL TO MAKE IT SO.//*

Geneve felt lost, alone and adrift at sea. "But ... demons?"

Ormeon nodded. *//THEY WANT OUR WORLD, AND ALL ITS TREASURES.//*

"So ... dragons fight them?"

//DRAGONS FIGHT WHATEVER THE HELL THEY WANT TO.// The dragon's teeth glinted. *//THEY, DRAGONRIDERS, AND HOLOMANCERS.//*

"Meri's an illusionist. He would say he's the weakest of sorcerers, but that's wrong. On the way here, we found a city of the ancients. It was a dark place the Light forgot ... so, he brought light within him. The most beautiful colors came from within him to paint the walls." She smiled, remembering. "It's like his heart is made of wonder, and he can show it to the world. I don't know what holomancer means." Geneve sighed. "Your speech is strange, like you're from Tebrani. You say the most confusing things."

Ormeon sat silent for a time. The wind ruffling Geneve's hair brought the cry of a gull. *//HE IS NOT AN ILLUSIONIST.//*

"I just said—"

//HE MAKES THINGS REAL THAT DON'T EXIST.//

"Nothing he makes is real."

//THAT'S BECAUSE YOU DON'T BELIEVE.// The dragon turned a slow, ponderous circle, then lay down again. *//YOU SHOULD FIX THAT BEFORE WE FIGHT THE DEMONS.//*

"I don't understand you at all."

//YOUR UNDERSTANDING ISN'T REQUIRED. A HOLO-MANCER CAN SPIN ARMOR FROM SUNLIGHT THAT WILL TURN THE WEAPONS OF THE ARTIFICES ASIDE. IF YOU BELIEVE, IT WILL HOLD. IF YOU DON'T, WE WILL DIE. NO PRESSURE, THOUGH.//

Geneve couldn't help the smile that touched her lips. "Fair enough." She retrieved her sword. "I'm going to train."

//DRAGONS ARE BETTER THAN SWORDS.//

Geneve pulled Requiem from its sheath. "I think that depends on who's using the dragon, or the sword."

//TOUCHE.// Ormeon nuzzled into her tail. *//WAKE ME WHEN THE FOOD ARRIVES.//*

SIGHT OF DAY AND ARMITAGE RETURNED WITH WILD BOAR AND deer. The party set about making a fire, each pitching in without needing direction. They knew each other well enough to work in silence with the occasional nod, smile, or touch. Geneve removed her armor, the day's heat and the presence of a dragon suggesting just this once she might not need it.

Once they ate, Geneve managed to find a little sleep despite it being mid-day, because she'd been on her feet fighting monsters and horror sorcery all night. She didn't mean to; she was leaning against a log by the dragon, and next time she opened her eyes the sun was lower in the horizon.

Meri snuggled against her, the sorcerer out cold. His head was on her shoulder, and she felt the delicious heat of his body through their clothes. He'd put his cloak across them. Someone had stretched canvas above, sheltering them from crisping under the sun.

The fire burned low. Ormeon ate most of the pig and deer carcasses, leaving not even a scrap of fur behind, then curled up to sleep again. Geneve felt the low, bass rumble of the dragon's breathing through the ground.

Armitage sat across from her against another log. Tilly leaned against the monster. Sight of Day curled in a ball by the fire, as content as any other cat would be in that situation. Armitage was awake, his snake eyes watching her. "Ho, Knight."

"Ho, monster." She grinned. "When we met, I thought we'd end up at crossed blades."

"Might still do." He didn't shrug, perhaps not wanting to disturb Vertiline. "But I wouldn't want that."

"You're worried about the armor?"

"Or something else." Armitage shook his head. "Enchanters can steal a man's will, but they're rare. In the plague lands, we tend to put those fucks to the sword or torch. The armor was ... something else. I've no words. But," he sighed, "it also made me feel ... *powerful*."

"You're the size of two men."

"More like three, but this was better. I could have wrestled the dragon."

"I was surprised when I fought Ballast." Geneve remembered the fight, the sheer unstoppable violence in the Vhemin's blows. "He was stronger than any Vhemin I'd fought. Ballast stood against the Three's Storm."

Armitage reached into his mouth, worrying a tooth free. He eyed it, then tossed it into the fire pit. "Pretty sure it was the armor, rather than some secret health spa for monsters."

"I hope so." Geneve tugged Meri's cloak higher, feeling a chill despite the day's warmth. "Because that means there's a finite amount."

"There were *hundreds* of Vhemin," he jerked a thumb in a southerly direction, "back there. If they were all as strong as Ballast, we've got problems. Tresward can fight regular Vhemin five on one, no problem, but a jacked up one? That'll leave a mark."

She nodded. "Perhaps if we kill Leander, it'll cut the head from the snake."

"Perhaps the dragon will take a liking to me, too."

"We'll know soon enough," Geneve said. "If Meri's plan works."

Armitage pursed his lips. "I hate to say it, but the runt's never wrong."

"This feels like a long throw, though." Geneve spared a glance to the west, where the harbor lay. "The shallows mean no ships dock here. Only the craziest of captains would risk the bay, and that's assuming they know where he is."

"Have a little faith," Armitage suggested. "It's the only thing keeping me going."

Geneve blinked her surprise. "You? You seem so ... constant."

"I'm good at murder, Knight. I'm not good at sitting around." He shifted, reaching to draw Vertiline a little tighter so she wouldn't fall to the ground. "If too many of your kind turn up, they'll try to kill me. It'll be an exciting way for them to die, and I'll admit I don't have the stomach for it. Not anymore." His snake eyes found the Feybrind. "I feel like the entire world lied to me my whole life, and now I've fashioned truth from the tattered strands, it doesn't fit well."

"Join the club."

Armitage chuckled. "Fair enough. Why don't you get a little more sleep? I'll keep watch."

"You think we need a guard when we've got a dragon?"

"The huge lizard behind you is sleeping like the dead. I could get a hundred Vhemin in here without her waking." Armitage grinned horror teeth. "Not that I would. But I *could*."

"And you want me to sleep *now?*"

❦

NIGHT BROUGHT COLD, A CHILL CLOAK GENEVE WORE RIGHT TO THE water's edge. Meri came with her, but the rest remained at their camp. The waterline coveted a stony shore. Waves lapped like an ever thirsty dog against the stones.

His hand found hers. "No ships have moored here. Not as long as I remember. The water goes out about three klicks without getting much deeper. There are shoals, reefs, and other sorts of hull-rending nonsense that mean attacking the keep by sea would be suicidal."

"We're not wanting them to attack, Meri. We want their help. This is *your* plan, remember?"

He nodded. "What if I'm wrong, though?"

"About?"

"About ... everything. About Picotee remembering, or about Roya's promise. About my father, and what he means to do." He sighed. "He made me doubt myself my whole childhood, and that feeling's dogged my steps ever since."

"I think you're right." Geneve gripped his hand. "I don't want to, because it means Ravenswall is burning right now. But Three preserve us, I do. So, send your signal. Make it bright, and proud, so they can see it across the whole land."

He gave her a lopsided smile. "Okay, Red. Here goes." Meri closed his eyes for a minute, breathing deep, then reached his open palm upward. Above, Cophine's pale face watched them, behind her Ikmae struggling to see over her shoulder. Khiton was invisible, perhaps hiding, but more likely just lost in the night sky.

As he focused his will, Cophine's moon blushed red. Tinges covered the celestial body, then solidified from mist and memory. Geneve watched in awe as Meri painted the moon's surface in red. One sphere, then another, finally tipped with green: a bunch of grapes on a stem.

He sagged against her when it was done, and she held him up. "Oh, Meri. It's beautiful."

"I just defaced a goddess with graffiti," he said. "I'm going to burn in hellfire."

"Not tonight." She pulled him closer. "She'll understand."

"You speak to Cophine often?"

"Shut up and kiss me."

Chapter Thirty-Five

T hey came on the third day.

Meriwether was standing in his father's study, poring over old tomes and papers, still unable to make sense of them. Armitage had taken the body away, and Sight of Day had tidied things up a little. The study wasn't cruel; Meriwether's memories handled that side of things.

He was startled from his work as Ormeon shook the keep as she jumped from the tower above him. *That still scares the ever-loving shit out of me.* The dragon headed for the harbor, wings stretched like a promise to the gods, sunlight marking her massive shadow on the vines she flew over.

The dragon had begun roosting on the tower again, but still wouldn't go inside. *I understand her, despite being terrified when she's within gobbling distance. I hate being here too, but someone's got to account for the sins of my father.*

Meriwether moved to the open window, leaning out to spy on the harbor. He didn't have dragon's eyes, but thought there *might* be the hint of hulls on the water klicks out. By the time he reached the keep's ground floor, only Vertiline waited for him. She leaned against the tower's wall like she was holding the whole structure up. "You should put in a pole. It'll make getting down faster."

"I don't want to stick around that long," Meriwether explained. "If it wouldn't incinerate priceless clues, I'd have asked Ormeon to reduce the whole place to molten slag."

"The baths are nice." She unmoored from the wall. "There are ships."

"Friendlies?"

She gave him a level stare. "You're supposed to be the smart one."

"Right, right. We don't know until they dock."

Tilly chuckled. "No, sinner, that's not it at all. It's almost certain they're not friendly, because that's how our hand's played out most every place we've been."

"Cheer up, Chevalier. First time's the charm. And I'm excellent at cards." Meriwether held his hand out in an *after you* gesture. "Lead on."

She gave an epic sigh, but headed through the keep's gates. Meriwether noted she wore no armor, preferring simple black leather, still with a glove covering her metal hand. In three days it'd behaved like any other limb; Tilly said she could feel with it, just like her lost one. The palm was a soft material that gave a little like skin, but gripped even wet things like an iron vise. Vertiline no longer shied away from it, but didn't display it either. Her borrowed sword hung at hip, ready for whatever might disembark from the ships.

They walked in companionable enough silence. No hurry, because the ships would take some time to send landing craft to the shore, and only a fool would joust with a dragon. *Or the very brave. If I saw a dragon on the shore, I might just sail on past.*

Small insects zipped through the air, and the sound of birdlife came from the vines and trees about the du Reeves estate. Since the Vhemin left the mines—destination unknown, just a few scattered belongings suggesting they'd been there at all—nature returned. Small steps, but it was clear nature's creatures preferred the keep's new master.

They were about five hundred meters from the shore, the smell of sea weighing on the air, when Vertiline cleared her throat. "Thank you."

"You what now?"

"For ... forgiving me." She rubbed her metal arm with the flesh and blood one. "It's hard to fall so far, only to find the person you tried to drag with you offers you his hand as a brother."

"I don't know what to say."

"You don't need to say anything." She gave a tired smile, her blue eyes holding the calm of the deep sea, as if she'd made peace with something in the depths. "I'm glad you found Geneve. My sister deserves her peace, too."

"Pretty sure she found me." Meriwether scratched his beard. It was shorter now he'd had time to shave, but kept verging on the itchy stage.

"Is that what you think?" Tilly raised an arch eyebrow. "Fair enough."

Meriwether spied Ormeon first; the dragon was hard to hide. She waited a little to the north, gaze locked on the water. He and Vertiline emerged over a small grassy dune hugging the rocky beach. Geneve waited on the stony ground, red hair teased south by a salty wind. Armitage was to her left, Sight of Day on the right.

Two longboats were almost at the shore, carrying a motley assortment of people. Meriwether recognized Picotee in one, Dammel beside her, with four other passengers that could only be Knights. They had the strong, implacable stance of those who walked with the Storm as an ally, and all looked fit enough to run all day without stopping. Two Knights hauled oars. A third, a bald woman with tattoos staining the side of her face, looked to the shore. The fourth sat in the back, hood pulled over his head. *But why four? There are always three Knights, one for each god.*

The second longboat was helmed by the *Chimera's* captain Roya, a handful of the ship's crew, and the Feybrind Morning Song. The cat watched the dragon, who watched the cat right back. Meriwether and Tilly hurried to their friends.

The boats shuddered against the stones, their crews dragging them up the beach a handful of meters. Picotee's boots hit the ground with a crunch, and she strode forward. Her eyes found Meriwether's. "My lord du Reeves."

"My lady du Parneer." He gave a small bow. "Are you lost?"

"I'm cold and hungry." She jerked a thumb toward Dammel without looking at him. "He's sober. That's the state of affairs this end. You?"

"About the same." Meriwether glanced to Geneve. "We're going to save Ravenswall from an army of Vhemin, Artifices, and assassins." A pause to let that sink in. "You don't seem surprised."

"The Vhemin and their shit-stained Artifices have been through Parneer Harbor already." She sniffed. "We captain three galleons, and as many pirates as you'll take. We're ready to sail."

Geneve cleared her throat. "And what will be the price?"

Picotee eyed the Knight. Geneve didn't blink. "A pardon for all."

"We can't give that," Geneve said.

"Sure we can," Meriwether said. "No problem."

"Meri—"

"Who are your friends?" Meriwether looked past Picotee at the waiting Knights, who held their distance with Morning Song and the *Chimera's* crew.

Geneve sighed. "Knights, to take us away. I know them."

"You know bullshit and nothing," the hooded man said, stepping forward and pulling back his hood to reveal a face which had anger as its default setting.

Vertiline took a step forward. "Kytto?" Then she ran, really *ran* through the people, grabbing the angry-looking man in a hug.

He stumbled back, arms out, then carefully pulled her into an embrace as gentle as a moth's wings. "It's okay, lass. It's okay."

Geneve pushed past Picotee to stand before the Knights. "You can't have him."

The tattooed woman turned from her friends. "We're not here for him, whoever that is. We're here for you."

"Don't be a complete dick," said a Knight with a horribly broken nose. He had an easy smile Meriwether liked. "She means we're here to *help* you."

"Aye." The third stepped forward, a woman with a long braid like Vertiline's. "The Justiciars said you were for Judgment. There's precious few of us left, and it made no sense to hunt the Savior of Ravenswall by blade and fire."

Geneve nodded, and Meriwether saw the tension ease, millimeter by millimeter, from her shoulders. She half-turned to him. "Meri, these are my oldest friends in the world. Hettie has the tattoos of her tribe. Barbet's nose was broken at birth—"

"It was a fight against seven Knights—"

"Seven, now?" Geneve grinned. "And Raja's the other one."

"Who's the angry-looking motherfucker?" Armitage growled, like being angry was his sole provenance and he didn't like the competition.

"Kytto," Geneve said. "He's a Tresward Smith. The best of them."

Kytto detached himself from Vertiline. "Oh, now you know steel and the working of it?" He glanced at Requiem's hilt. "I see you've still got my sword."

"*Your* sword?" She shook her head. "Come and take it from me, old man."

"We've much to speak of, and little time for it," Roya said. "You painted the goddess, so we came. But sailing's thirsty work. Is there anything to drink around here?"

❦

MERIWETHER WALKED THE RUINED KEEP WITH PICOTEE. THE banished lady du Parneer's head was down, perhaps in thought, or shame. *With her, it's difficult to tell. With her, everything is hard.* There wasn't much left to survey, but it gave them a little time to talk without a knife at each other's throat.

The ship's passengers were finding what rest they could until the People arrived. Morning Song said they would come to the keep, lending aid in the battle yet to come. Meriwether didn't know how a handful of Feybrind could sway a battle, but every little bit helped. *Our side holds five Knights, a dragon, a monster, a sometime sorcerer, and a loose rabble of stray cats. Seems foolish to go against a kingdom with that.* He thought he knew what this conversation would bring, and how the ending of it would mean Picotee leaving with her ships and her people.

"Perhaps I should go first," Picotee said.

"If you feel it's best."

"Thank you for saving my daughter."

"We've done this part already," Meriwether said. *Get to the leaving part already.* "You gave my crew a heap of shiny coin for the service."

"Was there ever a chance for us?" Picotee stopped outside the wreckage of a servant's kitchen. The stoves were still intact, but everything not bolted down was gone. "The houses of Parneer and Reeves could be a powerful force in Or'sen."

Ah. Exactly where the sharks swim. "I don't think so." Meriwether held his palms out. *Gently. She was a friend, once.* "You've always wanted shiny things, and I want to—"

"Save everyone."

"Maybe just myself." Meriwether sighed. *This is going to be a huge cock-up, but I need to tell her straight.* "There's no problem with either point of view. But they're different, like chalk and cheese. It's why we fight."

"Also, you say things plain, without going in circles." She sighed. "Well, at least I know where I stand. No marriage of convenience?"

Meriwether thought that through. There'd been plenty of times bluer blood meant a trading of rings for the benefit of the people. Geneve wouldn't go for it, though. Oh, sure, she might *understand*, but every moment of that life would cut her in ways swords couldn't. *My heart belongs to a woman with hair red as the sunset. I know I'd rather die with her, damn Picotee's help, than live a life that would shear her in two.* "No. I know I *should* say yes. But there's three people that would be unhappy with that. My heart belongs to Geneve, and you'd want what I couldn't give you. And me? Well, I'm a liar, but I'm not an asshole with it."

She turned away, arms crossed. "No, you were never an asshole. Not anytime I could remember."

Your turn with the hard questions. "Does this affect your decision to bring ships to Ravenswall?"

Picotee chuckled. "Still with the straight lines. You told me no fair and square, knowing I might toss a shit fit and leave you dry-docked. But you miss my intent. I'm not here because of you and me. I came because I've people who need saving. We might all die getting the noose from our necks, but it's a chance."

"The Picotee of two weeks ago wouldn't care."

"The Picotee of two weeks ago was adrift." Picotee clasped her hands together. "I know you promised a thing you can't give. You don't control the queen, or her whim. Tell me plain. Do you think you can get a pardon for three galleons of pirates?"

Meriwether ran his finger along the surface of a wrought-iron stove, feeling the smoothness of well-worn metal. "Yes."

"Why?"

"Because there will be no kingdom otherwise. Morgan's a reason-able woman—"

"Rumor says she's lost her mind."

"Hmm." Meriwether remembered Heser the Cheg's commentary on his queen's slide into confusion. "Well, we'll fix that too. I'll get your pardons, whatever it costs."

"You know, I think you will. And not just because you've got a dragon, which is a powerful motivator. I think you'll do it because you believe you can." She came close. "Always the savior."

"Not always." He turned away. "Hardly ever, really."

"And still so blind, about so many things." Her tone brightened. "You promised rum."

"I promised nothing of the sort. Rum's for inbreds and wannabe poets." Meriwether dredged up a smile by the anchor chain. "Wine, though. We've got that."

<hr />

THE KEEP'S COURTYARD WAS STILL AS BUSTED AS EVER, SO PEOPLE gathered out the front. Morning Song, Sight of Day, and Armitage had hunted for game. Fires blazed, and animals roasted on spits. A few casks of wine sat to the side, free for those who needed them, which seemed a lot.

Meriwether perched alone, watching Armitage, all hunched shoulders and glaring snake eyes. The monster sat like a stone atop a log, watching Vertiline and Kytto. The Knight and Smith talked and laughed like only old friends could. *That might need fixing*. He roused himself, found two mugs that weren't too dirty, and filled them before joining Armitage. "You look like you could use this."

The monster took a cup without looking. "Fuck off, runt."

Meriwether nodded, and sat down on Armitage's log anyway. "How are you feeling?"

"What part of 'fuck off' didn't you understand?"

"The part where it leaves you brooding and wanting to murder." Meriwether gestured with his cup to Vertiline, who chose that moment to laugh. "I'll wager a platinum solar I know who you think needs a knife."

The monster grimaced. "I don't know why I'm angry. They're humans. I'm Vhemin."

"Maybe." Meriwether adjusted his position, because logs weren't built for comfort. "Time on the road means you get to know someone deeper than their skin."

"Like I said, fuck off."

"Fair enough." Meriwether stood, stretched, almost left, then turned to Armitage. "If you can answer one riddle for me, we'll never speak of this again."

The monster glared at him, but offered a reluctant nod. "Ask your bullshit question."

"Vertiline's known where Kytto's been for a long time. Why'd she never go to him?"

"Well, because of that Israel asshole."

"Hmm." Meriwether sipped wine. "And when there was no Israel?"

"That's two questions."

"My mistake." The sorcerer raised his cup in salute, then turned and left the monster to his thoughts. It was time to find Morning Song. He needed to know where the People were, because sitting around chewed at his patience. *I've spent a lifetime waiting to do something, and now I can't wait another five minutes?*

It was what it was. He almost stumbled over Dammel in the dark. Picotee's advisor huddled in a cloak beside a shack, watching everything with hooded eyes. "My lord du Reeves."

"Hello, Dammel. You still looking to stab me in the back?"

"Not today." The old man adjusted his belt. His clothes hung looser about his frame than Meriwether remembered. "Was a time I would've, though, just for the pain you caused her."

Meriwether nodded, although the night might have hidden it. He followed Dammel's eye line toward Picotee, who stood with Geneve and her three Knightly friends. Lady du Parneer showed no ill-will toward Geneve, but she'd always been good at masks. "Perhaps fairly earned, too. You know why I like you, Dammel?"

"My sense of humor?"

"Because you're loyal. There's precious little of that about." Meriwether looked to Cophine high above. "There's a lot of reasons to leave someone's service. Lack of money, fame, or standing. You tossed all three aside."

"I was playing the long game." A weathered grin in the dark. "See, we might save a kingdom now, and all will be forgiven."

Meriwether laughed. "You're right. It's your sense of humor. Good night to you."

He stepped away, not missing Dammel's hand on his crossbow, partly concealed beneath his cloak. Out here at the edge of the world, the old man still watched his ward as he always had. Meriwether walked south from the gate, heading toward the massive bulk of Ormeon. The dragon waited in the fields, red eyes glowing like beacons in the night. The runes about her head smoldered, but not as fiercely as usual.

He found Morning Song and Sight of Day beside the dragon, their jewel eyes bright in the night, their hands moving in conversation so fast he couldn't follow in the darkness. *And maybe not in the light. I had no idea they spoke so slowly for our sakes.* He coughed to show he was there. "Hello."

{*We heard you approach ten minutes ago,*} Morning Song said, hands moving much slower now. {*I've no idea how you've survived so long being this noisy, but Sight of Day tells me it's because you use brute force and strength of numbers.*}

{*That's a lie. I said you use clumsy force.*} Sight of Day's tail lashed, but he half-smiled. {*Perhaps I'm thinking of the Vhemin.*}

//HAIL, HOLOMANCER.// The dragon's speech was probably heard by Cophine herself.

"Hello, Ormeon."

She lowered her massive head to better look Meriwether in the eye.

//ARE YOU LOST? SIGHT OF DAY TELLS ME YOU HAVE NO SENSE OF DIRECTION.//

"You did?"

{Not exactly.} The cat spread his hands but didn't elaborate.

"I'm not lost. I'm ... worried." Meriwether tried to find Ikmae and Khiton, but Cophine outshone them both. "We're about to fight a human war, for human reasons. There aren't many of the People left."

//WHAT DID I TELL YOU TWO? HE'S NOT VERY SMART.//

Morning Song eyed Meriwether with emerald eyes. *{We are not fighting a human war. We are fighting everyone's war.}*

Sight of Day nodded. *{And you saved so many of us. Their souls do not scorch the sky on their way to the Three because of you. The People pay their debts.}*

"Could you sit this one out?" Meriwether clenched his hands. "I don't want you to die."

Morning Song looked away. Sight of Day rubbed behind his ear. *{I don't want you to die either. The only way I can be sure you won't is by being with you.}*

"Okay." He brightened. "Seems stupidity is catching."

//IT'S AN EPIDEMIC. LOOK.// Ormeon stretched out a massive clawed arm to the south. Through the trees and scrub there Meriwether saw movement. First one Feybrind, then a pair. Behind those, five more.

As the sorcerer watched, the Feybrind approached in increasing numbers. All wore some form of light armor, carried bows, and had elegant swords at their waists. Men and women, all with glitter-bright, wondrous eyes. They padded forward on silent feet. Meriwether stopped counting at two hundred. "So many," he breathed, feeling like his heart my break. "So many to lose."

Sight of Day clapped him on the shoulder. *{It is our choice to free the world, friend. We would live without tyranny, or fade away.}*

Morning Song's tail lashed. *{Also, if all humans die, there will be no one left with money to buy our stuff.}*

Ormeon rose up on her haunches, surveying the gathered-and-fearless Feybrind. *//OH, CATS. THE WORLD WAS NEVER WORTHY OF YOU.//*

Meriwether agreed. He hoped he wouldn't be one of the last humans to know Feybrind. *The world is running out of the good things. Feybrind, and Knights who know right from wrong. We even found a Vhemin who fights for justice. And we'll spend them all against the hard rocks of true monsters.*

It was time for Leander to die.

Chapter Thirty-Six

Geneve stood at the bow of the *Chimera* feeling the spray on her face. The ship surged, let free from the leash of tedious passenger loading. Picotee promised them three galleons, but she delivered far more; those were just the captains of Parneer Harbor. The fleet comprised of more than fifty ships, all carrying a mixture of humans and Feybrind.

Speaking of Picotee... She looked sternward, seeing Lady du Parneer talking with Meri. She tried not to wish the woman an accident, like falling overboard to be eaten by sharks. Meri had said to her, *If I tell you something, do you promise not to kill anyone*, and when she'd said she didn't know why she would, he'd told her about Picotee proposing an alliance of their houses, and no doubt their beds.

He'd said all was squared away, and that was good enough for Geneve. She didn't trust Picotee, but she trusted her man. It didn't stop her hoping Picotee would find someone else to set her royal aspirations on.

"We're making good time." Vertiline joined her, both hands on the railing. She smiled like Geneve didn't remember seeing since Iz's death.

"You seem pleased to sail toward death."

"Death's got it coming." Tilly smoothed the glove over her metal hand.

"How's Kytto?"

Vertiline blinked. "Kytto?"

"You seem ... happy."

"Oh." The Chevalier shook her head. "It's not like that. He just ... reminded me of a few things, and showed me others." She raised her leather-wrapped hand. "Did you know this is nearly good enough to bind the Storm? I'm almost at balance. A little more practice, and... well." She smiled at the sea.

'*Not like that?*' *I've never seen her so happy.* "Have you spoken with Hettie or the others?"

"Your bald friend has become a fearsome warrior. But she watches the sinner like she's expecting him to, I guess, sin." Vertiline ran her gloved hand along her braid. "It's hard to change the habits of a lifetime."

"Barbet seems fine with it."

"Raja too. But Hettie's the Valiant." Vertiline shook her head. "Who'd have thought she'd climb so far, so fast?"

"It never mattered to us that Iz was the leader. We could speak and be heard." Geneve felt a shadow of doubt—not about Tilly or their time with Iz, but whether it was safe for Hettie to be with them. "Perhaps I should speak with her."

"Oh, aye, marvelous idea. You'd square off against Hettie, with the life of your beloved at stake?" Tilly snorted. "There'd be dragonfire before the end."

"I can be reasonable!"

"Name *one* time." Vertiline raised an eyebrow. "I'm waiting."

"Try not to fall overboard." Geneve grinned, then felt her face freeze as they rounded the northeastern spit of the du Reeves land. The cliffs above the water held a hundred figures. She visored her eyes with a hand. "Are those ... Vhemin?"

"Looks like it." Vertiline looked to the sky, where Ormeon flew like the world's largest gull. The dragon roared fire, then broke toward the Vhemin. "This should be fun."

"Wait." Geneve peered toward the massed monsters. "They've no weapons ready." She hurried from the railing, looking for Armitage. She found the monster in a tense conversation with Kytto. *Oh, no. They'll be at each other's throats.*

The Smith's jaw was clenched as he glared at the monster. "That's not how it works, you fool."

"You'd look better with fewer teeth in your skull." Armitage leered. "Since you're so good at explaining things, tell me again how to make the perfect smoked groper without lemon."

Geneve paused, hand half-way to her blade. *They're arguing about … fish?* She shook her head. "Armitage. The cliffs."

The monster gave a lazy turn of his head, squinting across the waves. "Looks like an asshole convention."

"I see that. It seems we've one more aboard."

"Hah! You mean me. Nice one, I didn't even see that coming." The monster chucked her shoulder with a fist, then ambled to the rail. "You know, they aren't screaming and running in terror at the dragon's approach."

"Nor do they have weapons."

"Maybe they want to talk." He picked his teeth with a fingernail. "First time for everything, I guess."

Ormeon wheeled across the sky, massive wings flapping, and she headed back for the *Chimera*. *//I'M CONFUSED. ISN'T PREY SUPPOSED TO RUN?//*

"We're not for eating, you ugly fucker!" Armitage bellowed.

//SPOKEN LIKE PREY.// The dragon winked a massive red eye as she flew overhead. Wind gusted in her passage, tossing more spray.

"Let's get a longboat and see what they want," Geneve said. "I've a mind to solve this problem here, rather than have them shadow us southward."

"I'll come with you," Armitage offered. "Lemme get a weapon."

Kytto tapped his chin. "I've a hammer that might be your size."

"Yeah? Let's try that out." Armitage ambled belowdecks with the Smith.

Geneve watched them go as Vertiline walked across the deck. Like any Knight, the movement of the ship didn't unsettle her balance. *Not anymore. Not since the ancients gave her arm back.* "Ho, Tilly. Fancy some shore leave?"

"I don't think you mean a vacation." Vertiline eyed the shore. "Sure, why not. Let's see what they want."

❦

PICOTEE'S GALLEON HUSBANDED THE *CHIMERA* AT ANCHOR. THE other ships of their makeshift armada tacked the waves or tossed their own anchors.

Geneve and Armitage rowed the longboat, while Vertiline eyed the land ahead. They made shore without mishap, then headed up. The cliffs had old stone steps hewn into the rock, wide enough to climb without fear of falling, and in good repair too. She took this as a promising sign; Vhemin didn't have a habit of making things easy for those they wanted to murder.

The top of the steps led to a wide plateau of grass. The horde of Vhemin waited a hundred meters further inland, leaving a single wizened woman leaning on a staff to wait for them. Armitage sniffed. "Well, I'll be dipped in shit."

Geneve gave him a little side-eye. "You ... what?"

"I know her. Or I think I do." He worried a tooth from his mouth, tossing it over the edge of the cliff. "Might be her kid, though. Family resemblance, something like that."

Vertiline sighed. "That's not specific, monster. We need more information."

Armitage looked at her, then the drop beside them. "What do you mean 'we,' human?" He chuckled. "Just kidding. I love that joke. Here's how it is. That broken old stick," he jabbed a finger at the woman, "looks like a woman I fucked a lot a couple years back. Her name was," he snapped his fingers, "Barrel? Barret? Yeah, Barret."

"You're not sure?" Vertiline's ice-pale eyes hardened.

"I'm *pretty* sure. It wasn't a serious thing, just a few months of monkey love." He scratched his armpit. "Should I stop talking?"

Geneve shook her head, then walked toward the old woman. The Vhemin looked to have been strong in her youth, the breadth of her shoulders showing the power of hurt she might once have had. But the muscle didn't cling to her anymore. "Hello. I'm Knight Chevalier Geneve of the Tresward."

"I don't give a shit," the woman said. "I want to talk to him." She pointed a finger at Armitage.

Armitage rumbled on over. "Then speak."

"You don't remember me."

The monster sighed. "We've got fifty ships at anchor out there. We've got places to be, old woman. Get on with it."

"I wore their blue-runed armor, Armitage. You found me pretty, once." She looked away, Vhemin pride warring with shame.

"Hold up." Armitage leaned closer. "*You're* Barret? Ikmae's sometime cock, what happened to you?"

"The armor costs." The wizened Vhemin leaned on her staff. "But its price isn't regals. It's time, measured in years by the day. I felt like a titan, Armitage. As powerful as any. I didn't care the voices told me to do things. I wanted to do those things anyway! To break, or kill, because that's what we're good for."

"You're good for other things," Vertiline said. "Some of you."

"Who asked you?" Barret said.

"I don't need to be asked, monster." Vertiline took a step closer. "Would you test yourself on my steel?"

"No," Barret said. "I'm not here to show skinny humans how painful humiliation is. I came to see if the rumors were true."

"Are you saying the armor of the ancients *ages* you?" Geneve felt a horror inside. *Armitage wore that for a day. What price did he pay? Three's mercy, is that why he's losing teeth?* "A day costs a year?"

The Vhemin gave her a withering glance, then faced Armitage again. "There's a tale going about. Of a monster who had the back of the Savior of Ravenswall. A huge man, who supports a Tresward. Calls them *friend*. Walks with a Feybrind, too, despite our kin wanting them and theirs dead. Made it so we can walk in the sun again. Turn our faces to the Three and not be shunned for wanting it. Is any of that true?"

Armitage looked at his hands, then clenched them. "I've no truth to give you."

"For the time we shared, Armitage." The old Vhemin looked like she was lifting an impossibly heavy weight. "Please."

Armitage growled, glaring at the horizon like escape might be that way. "Ah, fuck it. Yeah, I'm a sellout. I fight by her side," he jerked a thumb at Geneve, "and hers," pointing to Vertiline. "We've got a pet sorcerer, too, and the cat is my best friend in all Or'sen. Since meeting these assholes, I've faced death more times than the entire rest of my life put together, and it's been great. I don't mean to return to the plaguelands. We'll face an army of devilry, and maybe at the end of that, Khiton will tell me what it was for."

Geneve blinked at his speech. *Probably the most words he's strung together in my hearing.* "He's one of us."

"One of you humans?" Barret sneered.

"One of our friends," Vertiline said. "Watch your tongue."

"Spoken like a true Tresward. Commanding, not asking." The old woman veered away, staring at the same horizon Armitage favored. "We want a measure of revenge for our ration of shit."

Geneve shared a look with Vertiline. "You want to fight us?"

The old woman barked a laugh. "Good with a blade, bad with the thinking. That's the Tresward, right to the boots. No, small human. We want to fight *with* you. All of them," she pointed the heel of her staff to the gathered Vhemin, "paid a life price for wearing the armor. We're a little used up, but plenty of anger to go with it. We want a thing you can't buy with regals, or even solars. Blood is what we'll have, by the ten-liter pail. I'll tear the still-beating hearts from the betrayers before I fall."

Armitage squinted. "You want to come with us?"

"Yes. All who you've room for. One century of battle-ready Vhemin, asking nothing but for the chance to test steel and might against the unholy bastards who stole our lives." Barret grinned. "We'll get there one way or the other. Walk if we have to. But your ships look an easier route."

"Could be a trick," Vertiline said.

"I don't think so." Armitage walked a slow circle around Barret. "This isn't what Vhemin tricks look like, mostly because we suck at them."

Geneve eyed the monster. "Do you trust her, then?"

"Aye." A slow nod. "I think I do."

"With your life?" Vertiline's chin stuck out.

"Maybe."

"With mine?"

Armitage looked at his hands again. "No. That's worth more than solars."

Vertiline's lips pressed into a line. She stalked to Barret, getting right in the old woman's face. "Give me one reason to let you aboard." Her hand went out, palm toward Geneve, asking for a moment.

The old woman glanced to Armitage, then to Vertiline's gloved hand, red snake eyes missing nothing. "Because they took everything from me. I've a feeling you understand a little of what that's like."

Vertiline gave a slow nod, backing off a couple paces. "I do."

"Also, if you think a pissant crew of humans is going to help against what's coming, you're deeply fucked." Barret grinned shark teeth. "It costs a year a day, but it gives Khiton's strength. You need all the help you can get."

"People call you monsters, but you're not so different from us." Geneve nodded. "I've crossed blades with many, and we could use your anger. You come with us."

Barret cackled. "Great stuff."

"No killing the cats," Armitage warned.

"Cats? I thought there was only one." Barret scuffed the ground with a boot. "Be a hard sell for the troops. How many are we talking?"

Vertiline gave a frosty smile. "All of them."

GETTING VHEMIN ONTO THE SHIPS TOOK SOME DOING. MANY CREW were terrified of the monsters, and it took coaxing—mostly by Armitage offering to hit people—to get everyone singing the same tune.

While that wearisome work went on, Geneve waited at the *Chimera's* stern. She watched the water catch light, playing toss. *We've come a long way. Not just Meri and I, but everyone here. Who'd have thought the Vhemin would agree to fight alongside Feybrind? The world really must be ending.*

"You doing that brooding teenage shit?" Kytto's gruff voice made her smile.

"I try saving my brooding for after dark. It looks better on me that way." Geneve turned. The old Smith held a wrapped bundle against his leg. It looked to be the height and shape of a shield. *Old I think of him, but he was of Tilly's age. He's bent, like he carries mountains on his shoulders.*

Kytto sniffed. He looked a little green about the gills; he said *humans aren't meant to sail*, but Geneve knew he meant, *Kytto doesn't like being seasick.* "You ready for a little more free advice?"

"Sure."

"Stop losing your stuff." He slapped the probably-a-shield. "This thing's one of a kind. It's just for you, but I don't want to hand it over unless I get a guarantee."

"I fight. In battles stuff happens." The wind blew red hair across her face.

"Stuff? You lost a shield, a helmet, and by the Three's mercy, Vertiline's hand."

"That last wasn't on me."

He nodded, looking away. "Sounds like you lost a good beast, too."

"I miss Tristan."

"I meant Iz."

"I don't know why you're still alive," Geneve admitted. "You're not *that* good a Smith."

Kytto leveled a finger at her. "I am, and to prove it—"

"Without guarantees."

"With *implied* guarantees, here's your new shield." He hefted the probably-a-shield, sweeping the cloth from it.

It was a shield, but not like any she'd seen before. "Is it ... made of glass?"

"Yeah. Took some doing. I brought a blade of glass too, but you've managed to keep a hold of my sword." He sniffed again. "I'll be wanting that back, one day. Careful with this, the edges are sharp."

"It's nice to want things." Geneve took the glass shield from him. It was exquisitely made, an edge so fine you could shear stone with it, assuming the Storm was with you and held the material strong. The shield was pure as crystal; Geneve couldn't see a blemish anywhere. Glass rivets held leather straps in place.

She slid it onto her arm, trying the weight. "It's a little heavy."

"You're a little strong."

"It's ... different." Geneve huddled behind its protective embrace. "I can see through it."

"That's why they call it glass."

She growled. "That's not what I mean. When Tresward fight, we use patterns to guide our steps. We pick the moves to suit the battle. I'm not used to—"

"I can take it back. Vertiline said she could use a shield like it." He coughed, a deep rattle in his chest.

Geneve frowned, lowering the shield. "Are you well?"

"I'm dying," Kytto admitted. "I'm all used up. Spent the best of my years in a cellar below ground. Didn't kiss the girl I wanted, because her heart belonged to another. The Clerics warrant I'll last the summer, but not the winter." He shrugged. "It's a sickness they can't cure without another's life spent to balance the account. They say it's a rot inside. Might be caused by the forge, but it could as easily be from spite."

"I'm so sorry." Geneve lowered her eyes. "I don't—"

"Don't be anything, least of all sorry." He looked over the ocean, watching a longboat with five Vhemin approach. Two Feybrind with lashing tails piloted it. "You've managed a thing that scripture said was impossible."

"Brought the Vhemin and Feybrind together?"

"Brought an old man a smile." He showed the truth of it with a grin. "You can keep the sword, I guess. My forever gift to you. Don't lose my Requiem, Geneve. There's no one else to make you another, and no skymetal to forge it from."

She laid the shield against the ground, then pulled him into a fierce hug. "Thank you, Kytto. Thank you for my sword, and teaching me things Tresward wouldn't. The shield, too. I'll wager it's the only one of its kind, like Requiem, and like you. Most of all, thank you for being my friend for so very long."

He returned her hug, then pushed her away, blinking rapidly. "Damn the salt spray in my eyes."

"In mine, too. Have you told Tilly?"

"No." The old Smith shook his head. "I've little kindness left, but she deserves it all. A hard road she's traveled, and I'll not be the broken axle at the end, miring her step with worry."

"You're a good man."

"I'm nothing of the sort." He pointed with his chin at the shield. "You've a name in mind?"

"I'm not sure." She crossed her arms. "I'm not naming it after you, if that's what you hoped for."

"Who'd want a shield named after a dead man?" He winked. "I'd name it after that boy of yours."

"That would be confusing."

"Not his *actual* name, you idiot. Tresward are all the same. They dash from place to place, trying for the straight course. Try taking a left turn every so often. It keeps the road interesting." He clasped his hands together. "What do you think when you see him?"

"What do you think when you see Vertiline?" Geneve countered.

"Oh." He blinked, wiping under an eye. "That's an easy one. I see the pale dawn. I feel the rush of wind, or its cool touch on a hot day. My heart beats faster," he put a hand to his chest, "and I feel like I'm drowning, and she's the only air about. I'm tongue-tied, because I want to say *I need you*, but I can't, because that's not a fair thing to say to someone who loves another. So I sit, and wonder at what might have been, if I'd been a little braver, faster, or cleverer." He sighed. "I feel joy, Geneve. That's what I feel."

She bit her lip, feeling impossibly sad for a moment. Her voice was a croak. "That's a fine thing to feel."

"Aye, I've no argument with it." Kytto cocked his head. "What's it to be?"

Geneve cast her eye down the deck. Meri stood at the bow, eyes front. He cut a fine figure, cloak billowing in the sea air, locks tousled with salt spray. Food, or maybe just love, had straightened his frame. She didn't know what he thought of, but could imagine worry for her, or their friends, or the whole world. "Starfire. Wonder. The boundless curiosity of someone who won't be beaten down. I see brilliance."

"A good enough name." Kytto lifted her shield, offering it again. "Brilliance it is."

Geneve took the glass shield, careful of the edges, then looked through its impossibly smooth surface. *Hello, Brilliance. You and I will be the shield for the world.* "It feels right. What doesn't is you not telling Tilly."

"She's found another, Gen. A big man with strong hands who'll look after her. Had his moment to make something of nothing with me, and didn't, because he cares more for her than himself. I couldn't ask for more." The Smith shook his head. "Vertiline and I can laugh, but she'll never be mine. Not because I wouldn't treasure it, but because if we walked that path, her heart would shatter into finer pieces than a dropped sword. I'd spare her that, and if you've a favor to repay to me, I'd ask you to hold your peace on it too."

He clapped her armored arm, nodded, and left. It only took a few paces for his gait to roll into a swagger, a whistle to come forth, and for Kytto to start shouting at someone who might have deserved it, but just as equally might not.

Geneve watched her friend go, wondering what the world would feel like without Kytto in it. Smaller, perhaps, and a little less angry. She eyed Brilliance. *But also less wonderful. Imagine if he'd been able to use his gifts to make things of art, not war.*

A grunt made her lift her eyes to find Armitage leaning against the port railing. "How long have you been there?"

"Here?" The monster shrugged. "About three heartbeats."

"How long have you been somewhere nearby, listening?"

"About ten minutes."

"I see."

"He's wrong, that Smith of yours." Armitage shook his head. "Vertiline deserves to know. All of us need to chart our own course. She could have six months of the same joy he feels." His gravel-filled voice was harder than usual.

"What would that cost you?"

"Nothing, because I've nothing in these hands, yet." He held his scaled arms up for display. "Have you ever heard of a human with a monster?"

"You're not a—"

"Could you imagine someone as perfect as her with someone like me?" Armitage shook his head. "It's a truth the world won't stand." He leered shark teeth, then veered away, as if seeing rocks ahead. He lumbered from the aft deck, heading below.

Chapter Thirty-Seven

Meriwether stood at the *Chimera's* bow, watching the smoke-filled sky to the south. *Is this the day I say goodbye to Geneve?* He wasn't worried about the *dying* part, but the long, endless silence without her made his mind shy away. Ravenswall was only a couple of hours away.

If the smoke hadn't given things away, the human flotsam in the water was a sure sign things were bad. Pieces of ship bobbed in the waves alongside people. Some wore guard colors, but most were civilian. This wasn't surprising, as those with armor would have sunk like stones. Meriwether imagined a graveyard of the lost under the *Chimera's* hull, watching them sail by.

Don't be stupid. They won't be watching, because whatever sank these ships happened further south. That's where the bodies lurk.

To say the sail from where they'd gathered Vhemin to Ravenswall was uneventful would be oversimplifying things a little. The creatures tried to stir up trouble. That was how they were made. They tried with the human crew, but picked on Hettie first, clearly thinking a fight with the biggest inmate was a sure sign to dominance. Four jumped her at once, and those same four went overboard within a three-count.

So, they moved onto Feybrind the same night. Meriwether woke in the morning to find a dead cat on the foredeck, and nine headless Vhemin around her. No one talked about what happened, but no one tried to kill each other after that.

It's just nerves, he lied to himself. The really surprising thing was the lack of *other* deaths. Expecting Vhemin and Feybrind to put aside hundreds of years of focused murder had been optimistic, but it seemed they wanted the same thing. Humans, Feybrind, and Vhemin were focused on the death of the thing that could end them all: the power of the ancients under the yoke of a very, very bad man.

"I will do it." Geneve arrived at his shoulder, hand sliding over his like a warm glove.

"Do what?" He blinked away his reverie.

"Your father." She sighed. "No one should have to kill their parents."

"I think there's an orderly queue forming," Meriwether said. "You'll need to get in line."

She smiled, but it held the touch of sadness. "There's no shortage of hate."

"I'm more worried about what we'll find when we get there." Meriwether faced the smoke-filled sky, gesturing with a hand. "We were after Justiciar Ambrose, but got kind of sidetracked by Leander and his army of assassins."

"One job at a time," she suggested. "I've a feeling there's no shortage of killing ahead."

"You could *try* to sound remorseful about it."

She nodded, but didn't smile. "I could, but it feels like the Three have waited a thousand years for justice. Today they'll get a semblance of it. I don't relish it, but it needs to be done."

"For the Three?"

"For the whole land, Meri. We're splintered peoples. Someone drove us apart and uses our hate to build walls between us." She squeezed his hand, then let it go. "We can only stand so much of what your father did."

"How do you know what he did?"

Geneve brushed red hair aside. "No one wears scars like that by accident. No, don't tell me. It doesn't matter. He hurt you, and that's the thing that will cost him everything."

He felt a shiver touch his spine. *She is so certain. I've never had anyone like her in my life. Treasure it.* "How is the saddle coming along?"

That brought the quirk of a smile out to play. "It will hold well enough. Armitage and Sight of Day's work is exceptional. It's not of the same materials as the ancients used. Just leather and chain, but it will keep me on Ormeon's back."

He glanced up to where the dragon coasted updrafts. "The thought of riding the sky makes me want to pee."

Geneve laughed, then stroked his face. "Oh, Meri. I'll be careful."

"It's not you I'm worried about. The lizard has no sense of self-preservation, and you'll be lashed to her."

"It's how it was meant to be." She glanced up. "I'll get my armor."

She left him by the railing.

//THEY BROUGHT SUFFICIENT NUMBERS TO MAKE THIS A FAIR FIGHT.// Ormeon flapped massive wings above, arcing across the sky. The dragon's head swung to the south, the runes across her head glowing brighter than the sun for a moment. She roared, a gout of flame scorching the heavens. *//IT IS TIME TO REMAKE THE WORLD.//*

MERIWETHER HAD NEVER BEEN IN A WAR. SURE, FIGHTS APLENTY, BE they back-alley brawls, or more recently pretty much daily encounters with assassins, monsters, or horrors of an ancient land. But not a *war*, where the air carried the stench of blood and shit along with the screams of men and women calling for their sergeants, mothers, or the Three.

His hands clutched the *Chimera's* railing as they drew near Ravenswall harbor. The docks were a ruin, some parts charred, others shattered. Dockside taverns and warehouses were a ruin of shattered stone and broken wood, and the bodies littering the streets were heaped like cordwood.

The feel of magic was hot on his skin. Mages of all castes used their skills to hold back the enemy. Ice squalls speared across the city's districts, accompanied by firestorms and lightning. The blue glimmer of Vhemin armor was everywhere, the monsters murdering everyone.

They're already inside. The keep still stood, the gates barred, but Meriwether didn't think they had much time. An Artifice walked above the buildings of the Artist's Borough, heading toward the queen's castle, but on seeing them changed its course toward the sea.

Roya brought the *Chimera* to the docks under hard sail. There would be no easy dock. The plan was to get them on dry land and fix the ship later. Meriwether braced himself as they approached wharfs meant for slower speed. The crunch of timber as the ship shouldered ahead was a horror, the sound of a vessel throwing its life away to get them into danger's maw.

The Vhemin aboard roared a challenge, then vaulted the railing. The Feybrind slipped silently on their heels, all heading to the city they couldn't save. Because Meriwether realized right here, right now, they were hopelessly outnumbered, against an enemy that had weapons of terrible, ancient power.

"Lover!" Geneve grabbed his arm, eyes bright, teeth bared. She dragged him into a kiss. "Don't die. Not today." Then she jammed her ancient helmet on her head and was gone, a flash of silver armor and perfect movement as she vaulted below. He watched the bared steel of Requiem challenge the sun as Geneve charged.

By the Three, she is beautiful.

The Artifice nudged a building aside as it made the dockside. The fangs on its snout glowed, then twin spears of vermillion fire stabbed forward. Twenty Feybrind turned to ash in a moment, the ten Vhemin with them lost as motes on the wind. Meriwether's heart crumpled. *So many. So fast. What were we thinking?* He watched Geneve change course, head down like a bull as she made for the Artifice. *No. No! She can't beat that thing!* He wanted to call out, but the noise of the battle would steal his words, as impossible weapons from an ancient time would steal her life.

The Artifice's fangs glowed, ready for a second try.

The air split with a roar, and Ormeon descended like the Three's own justice. The dragon fell from above like a promise from the gods. She hit the Artifice on its top, clutching it close like a housecat with a ball of yarn, then rolled with it. Vhemin and Feybrind scattered aside, buildings crunching beneath the dragon and its ancient chew toy.

Orman kept rolling, used the momentum to gain her haunches, and slammed the Artifice against the old stone of the docks. Ancient metal challenged Three-given stone. The Artifice gave a shrieking whine, its six legs clawing for the dragon, but they skittered off scale. Ormeon slammed the Artifice against the ground again, then dug claws into its casing. Her shoulders bunched, and the machine tore open, spraying sparks and black fluids along with a gout of fire. The dragon tossed the ruined wreckage over Meriwether's head and into the ocean. The pieces of ancient machine hit with a splash, great gouts of steam spewing into the air.

The dragon roared. *//INSECT.//*

"Don't you think you should get down there?"

Meriwether startled, turning to find Vertiline by his side. "Look, there's a lot of dying going on. I feel like I should give others a head start."

"Get in there, sinner." She gave him a hard smile, blue eyes sapphire cold. "I've got your back."

He nodded. "You always have."

"You shouldn't wait too long. The Chimera is sinking." She vaulted the railing, leather-gloved metal hand holding the wood effortlessly. Meriwether followed a little slower, because he hadn't had a lifetime of Tresward training, just a lifetime of escaping them.

The docks were a ruin of splintered wood. Vertiline grabbed his arm, dragging him with a grip of iron toward Ormeon, and by proxy, Geneve. Once they were free of the worst of it, he picked up his own pace, running alongside the Chevalier.

Feybrind and Vhemin bled into the city streets ahead. A few stood by Ormeon, the Vhemin looking delighted, the Feybrind wary. Geneve watched him approach, face alight with a grin. "Did you see her, Meri? She was magnificent!" Her sword was in its scabbard, glass shield hanging by her side.

He slowed, a little breathless, but managed, "Aye. I've a question,

THE STORM WITHIN

though. We found a derelict Artifice on the trail with six fallen dragons about it."

//THEY HAD NO HOLOMANCER.//

Geneve glanced at the dragon. "What do you mean?"

//ARMOR OF LIGHT, TO TURN THE SPEARS OF THE ENEMY.//

Meriwether blinked. "You want me to make you armor? You're covered in," he gestured up and down her massive form, "armor that turned a Champion's blade!"

Ormeon lowered her head. *//WOULD YOU LIKE TO TRY YOUR LUCK STANDING BEFORE THE ARTIFICES?//*

"It's a fair question."

//ENERGY OUTPUT EXCEEDS ABLATIVE BUFFER TOLERANCE.//

Meriwether realized his mouth hung open. "You what?"

//YOU ASKED. I ANSWERED. IT'S NOT MY FAULT YOU DIDN'T UNDERSTAND THE ANSWER.// The dragon sounded too smug for his liking.

"Meri." Geneve grabbed his elbow with her free hand. "Can you do it?"

He tugged his ear. "No."

"He's lying," Vertiline said, face deadpan.

"I'm not lying," Meriwether insisted. "I'm just not sure."

//PERHAPS YOU SHOULD TRY, SINCE I'M THE LAST DRAGON IN THE WORLD, AND WITHOUT ARMOR THINGS WILL GET DICEY.//

Armitage approached, a large saddle and a mire of chains and straps dragging behind. He looked wet but satisfied with the day so far. Sight of Day padded at his side, also wet, and less happy about it. The cat carried a leather-wrapped bundle. "Someone order a saddle?"

The dragon sniffed the air, then lowered her head. *//NO RUSH. THE CITY IS DYING BY THE MOMENT.//*

As Armitage worked with Geneve to saddle the dragon, Sight of Day offered the bundle to Meriwether. It smelled of the sea. *{You dropped this.}*

He unwrapped it, exposing the High Magic tome. The book's spine had been fitted with a clever contraption of a loop of chain and metal banding; the chain would hang from a belt, and the banding would hold the book closed. *Good thing someone remembered priceless antiquities in my belongings; I'd wondered where this was.* "Sorry. My mind was on other things."

{Like keeping the last dragon in Or'sen alive?}

"All right, all right, I get it." Meriwether attached the book to his belt, then eyed the dragon. She was the size of a large hill, but moved like muscled water. He tried to picture what plate armor on Ormeon would look like. He squinted, trying to make what was in his mind fit her shape.

Sight of Day stood by his elbow, hand on chin as if considering the dragon as a canvas. *{Don't forget to make it effective against light.}*

Three's mercy, how do I do that? "Do you want to do this?"

Sight of Day spread his hands. *{I would if I could, but it seems the Three took away your skill with anything except magic, and gave it to us in return for no magic. I'm not sure if it's a good trade, but I know we dance better.}*

Geneve stepped back from Ormeon. The dragon flexed her wings, eddies of dust fleeing her side. As Meriwether saw her wings, he imagined a spider's web, a series of gossamer strands that would flex and bend. Because, of course, illusory armor didn't need to follow rules of metal. He could make it what he wanted.

The cat's not wrong. It needs to do something with light. How is that even possible?

"Meri, what's wrong?" Geneve eyed the city for enemy, then turned to him. Even with her black visor, he knew where she was looking. Her voice wasn't muffled within the ancient's helm.

"I don't know what to do," he admitted. "I'm not much of a magician."

Geneve sighed with exasperation. "How can you not see it? You're the best magician that's ever walked Or'sen."

//I WOULDN'T GO THAT FAR.//

"No one asked you," Geneve said. "Ormeon called you a holomancer. She needs what you can do. As *Meri*, not as a magician. It's not about your fancy book. It's about what's in here." She placed an armored hand against his chest. Geneve took Meriwether's hands in hers. "I believe in you."

Meriwether wanted to reach for the tome of High Magic, but instinct stilled his hand. Maybe Geneve was right; the dragon called him a *holomancer*, like she knew exactly what he could do. The problem was, he'd not been much good at anything magical. *I make pictures with my mind. That's it. What good is illusion against the balefire of the ancients?*

A tiny voice in the back of his mind said, *All you've got to do is believe. Isn't that what I've always said? And the dragon believes; that's the important part. It's not about me at all.*

He stepped to the dragon's flank, laying his palm on her hide. Just as he remembered, she was warm, like a furnace burned deep beneath the skin. Individual scales were smooth, but with razor edges. He tapped one with a fingernail twice. On the second tap, light bloomed from the point of contact.

It was as he'd imagined: pearlescent blue-white spread from his touch like ripples in a pool across Ormeon's hide. It shimmered with the colors of starlight, daybreak, and the setting sun as it grew. About her neck, he fashioned a bulwark of hard light as the dragon's breast-plate. Across her wings, gossamer strands of pale white that flexed as she did. All over the dragon he imagined plates of his dreaming, none of it tethered by steel or leather. It fitted her like a second skin, because that's what it was for.

Ormeon reared, wings beating, casting light about like a second sun. *//HOLOMANCER, THIS IS A MIGHTY GIFT.//*

Geneve blinked. "Oh, Meri. It's beautiful."

He felt like he'd just run a marathon in five minutes, heart tired, head full of cotton wool, but he wasn't done. Meriwether pulled Geneve closer, forehead against the cool ancient armor of her helm, then he kissed the metal.

She stepped back, uncertain. Vertiline sucked air between her teeth. Sight of Day's golden eyes widened in wonder. Armitage snorted. "Not bad, runt."

"What is it?" Geneve said. She was covered head to toe in molten armor. The burnished sun on her breastplate glowed with the fires of heaven's forge. Her glass shield shone with golden light that rippled across its surface. Angel's wings spread from her back, small next to the dragon's, but as real as he could make them.

"What I see, when I see you," Meriwether said, then passed out.

Chapter Thirty-Eight

Sight of Day caught Meri as he went down. Geneve wanted to go to him, but the cat's golden eyes said *No*, and he shook his head. *{People are dying. I've got him.}*

"But—"

{I will take care of him better than I did my own son.} The cat's tail lashed. *{The world can't lose another wonder.}*

Geneve pressed her lips into a line, but nodded. She turned to Ormeon. "Are you ready for this?"

//IF YOU MEAN READY TO DESTROY VEHEMENT SYSTEMS ARTIFICES, YES.// Her massive head curled around to face Geneve. *//IF YOU MEAN ANYTHING ELSE, THEN NO.//*

Geneve held onto a smile, putting her boot into the saddle's stirrup. It was different proportions to a horse's, and she tried not to think about dear Tristan as she swung herself up. What would her horse have thought of her riding his killer? Would he have understood? "I mean to destroy the enemy, their vile machines, and the snake who leads them."

//GOOD ENOUGH.// The dragon surged upright. Geneve felt the massive, unbelievable strength beneath her. She clutched the saddle with one arm, unsettled for the moment, then found her new balance.

She saw Vertiline's wide-eyed wonder, and Armitage's shark-toothed maw hanging slack as Ormeon sat up. *//I'VE NEVER DONE THIS BEFORE.//*

"You what?"

//I'M TWO WEEKS OLD.// The dragon grinned over her shoulder at Geneve. *//IT'S BEEN A GOOD TWO WEEKS, THOUGH.//*

Ormeon bunched beneath her, then jumped for the sky. The force of the leap almost tore Geneve from the saddle, despite expecting it. The dragon beat its powerful wings, surging higher. The ground fell away, people turning into children, then insects as the dragon clawed the air. *So fast! How did the ancients fall with dragons as their allies?*

Geneve scanned the ground. She could see the glimmering blue of Vhemin scurrying through Ravenswall. A clot were headed toward the main keep. They had to go that way. As soon as she thought it, the dragon banked toward the castle. *//YOUR PURPOSE, MY WORLD.//*

How does she know? Geneve touched fingers to her helmet, wondering if the ancient device was the cause, then goggled at her hand. Her armor was glowing like melted rock. She glanced down at herself astride the shimmering illusory armor of Ormeon, seeing golden light everywhere. A glance back showed her wings. *Oh, Meri. This is wonderful.*

They approached the keep faster than Geneve thought possible. She spied fifty-two Vhemin charging the gates, a miserable handful of black-armored Queensguard holding the line. Geneve wondered how she knew how their were *exactly* fifty-two Vhemin. The runes on Ormeon's head blazed red, the dragon opening her maw as she swooped low. She gouted fire, a blazing rain of ruin. Geneve's stomach was left behind as the dragon dropped, heat washing over her as drag-onfire cindered the street below.

Buildings blazed. A roof over an ironworks exploded heavenward as the dragonfire found it. But ten seconds later, Geneve knew there were forty-nine, forty ... thirty, twenty-seven, twelve, five, then *no more Vhemin*. She spied a familiar face at the gate. *Ormeon, we must land.*

//YOUR PURPOSE, MY WORLD.// The dragon angled in descent, back feet down, then crunched to the ground before the gates. Geneve

swung off, droplets of molten fire falling from her armor as her boots hit stone broken from Ormeon's landing.

Geneve strode to the line of Queensgard. Ten men and women, two of which had pissed themselves, but none of whom had run. She approached the captain, removing her helmet and letting red hair flow free. "Heser the Cheg."

The captain gaped. "The Savior of Ravenswall."

"Not yet." Geneve shook her head. "There's much to do."

Heser the Cheg made a big show of looking past her at Ormeon. "That a fucking dragon?"

"Looks like it," Geneve agreed. "Now, Captain—"

"Not a captain. Not anymore. Just a man doing his job." Heser the Cheg took his own helmet off, running a hand over his bare scalp. "You brought a *dragon?*"

"*Captain* Cheg," Geneve put iron in her voice. The man snapped to attention. "Is the queen safe?"

He blinked. "The city burns. There are ancient machines and hordes of Vhemin. She's a long way from safety, Tresward."

Geneve gritted her teeth. "Is she alive?"

"For now."

"Keep her that way." Geneve looked to the men and women at his back. "Are these trustworthy?"

"All are true Queensguard."

Geneve pointed to the harbor. "Get the queen and go that way. Our forces landed there. Meri could use your help coordinating the defense of the city."

"Feels safer here," Heser the Cheg said.

"Don't be an imbecile," Geneve said. "Fifty-two Vhemin would have been eating Queensguard steaks if I hadn't arrived."

A nervous-looking woman with hard eyes nodded. "She's not wrong, Cap'n."

"She is," Heser the Cheg pointed at the dragon, "because the dragon did all the hard work while she rode sidesaddle."

The nervous-looking guard looked more nervous. "Cap? This isn't a fight we want. She's *Tresward*. And her armor is *molten gold*. Also, more Vhemin will come. If we're not here, they'll storm an empty keep. The

Artifices are cutting through stone like it's parchment. We may as well play hide-and-seek."

"A fair set of points," Heser the Cheg conceded. "We'll get the queen away."

"You're sure?" Geneve crossed her arms. "I wouldn't want to push you into anything."

Heser the Cheg beamed. "I like you, Tresward. I'm glad we didn't cross blades. When you're done with your business, come see me. The ale will be rich and plentiful."

She smiled back, then turned on her heel and returned to Ormeon. *//ALL IS WELL? DO YOU NEED ME TO MAKE MORE CRISPY CRITTERS?//*

"We're good." Geneve put her helmet back on. "Let's scout the battlefield."

The dragon lowered herself, allowing Geneve to swing aboard. *//YOUR PURPOSE, MY WORLD.//* Ormeon surged skyward, and Geneve couldn't help but whoop. *Such power!* It felt wrong to be elated about riding a dragon as the city burned, but there might not be another time. *I am the last dragonrider.* On the heels of that thought came another: *Ormeon must not die. She is powerful, but alone.*

//I AM NOT ALONE. I'M WITH YOU.//

Geneve leaned forward, putting her hand on the side of Ormeon's neck. She didn't know if the dragon could feel it, but it didn't hurt to try.

//I FEEL EVERYTHING YOU DO.// The dragon arced over the Artist's Borough, heading north over the Armorer's District. Geneve remembered riding Tristan there not too long ago. *//I'M SORRY ABOUT THE HORSE.//*

"So am I, dragon. He was a very good horse."

//YOU REMEMBER IT WRONG.// Ormeon's wings pushed them ever faster toward the northern wall, where a pillar of smoke braced the clouds. *//HE WAS THE VERY BEST.//*

They soared over the wall, or what was left of it. Stone was melted to slag, or hammered to rubble. Outside the walls, a Vhemin horde roared their hunger as they funneled through the gap. Geneve counted ten thousand, four hundred and twelve Vhemin at this breach alone. *How do I know their numbers?*

//WE KNOW THE SAME THINGS.// The dragon dove lower, heading west. Arrows and crossbow bolts marked her passing, but they either missed or rattled harmlessly away. *May as well throw curses at the wind. //THERE. TRESWARD.//*

To the west was a temporary fortification with a great pavilion at its center. It sat atop a small hill. The forest had been cleared for klicks, and massive pyres raged outside the fort's wooden walls. Geneve saw the Vhemin used the fires for their hot rocks. *Which means not all Vhemin have the blue-runed armor. The Three still hold some mercy for us.* Before the fortifications stood five Tresward Knights, burnished suns gleaming. Behind them, three Clerics.

But it was the figure in front of the eight that made Geneve wonder whether she was seeing things. A face from her childhood above shoulders hunched with regret or spite. *Wincuf.* The ex-Novice waited with the Tresward, watching Ormeon as if dragonfire was a thing that happened to other people. Geneve realized his presence said the Tresward recognized him among them; he completed one of the sets of three Knights.

Six Knights, and three Clerics. The world has not seen so many Tresward in one place since...

//SINCE SEVEN HUNDRED YEARS AGO.// The dragon grinned, smoke trailing from her jaws. *//YOU HADN'T SPENT YOUR LIGHT SO MUCH BACK THEN.//*

"How do you know what happened seven hundred years ago?"

//THE MANIFEST.// The dragon's wings beat as if shrugging. *//I'LL ADMIT, IT HASN'T BEEN THAT ACCURATE.//*

"I don't want to fight Tresward." Geneve watched the Knights and Clerics, and they watched her right back. She knew from their sashes two were Valiants, the rest Chevaliers. The Clerics were all Lucents. "Hang about. The world fell more than eight hundred years ago. Who's been updating this 'manifest' you speak of?"

Ormeon ignored her, banking over the fortifications so she could get a better view. It looked standard military fare, with tents, latrines, and swearing soldiers, except the soldiers were scale-skinned Vhemin.

A few wore the familiar armor of the ancients. One carried a boxy device like she'd seen before. "'Ware!"

//I SEE HIM.// The dragon's grin widened.

"Aren't you going to run?"

//WHY WOULD I DO THAT? BESIDES, RUNNING'S FOR ANTS. I SOAR.// Ormeon laughed, a sound so great it might make the whole world happy under different circumstances. *//IT'S TIME YOU LEARNED TO BELIEVE, DRAGONRIDER.//*

"You don't mean to test Meri's imaginings against that!" Geneve pawed her saddle. "They're ... *make believe!*"

The dragon pulled her wings tighter, dropping like a stone. Geneve hung on, her stomach lost to fate. She wanted to scream, not in fear, but in frustration. They were going against an impossible weapon of ancient times, and the dragon would throw her one life away.

The Vhemin below activated the device, and a bright spear of yellow-white fire lanced toward them. The beam carved the heavens to their left, drawing nearer as the monster below adjusted his aim. Ormeon made no move to dodge. The ground approached very fast. Ant-sized people grew to mice, then dogs, scurrying out of the dragon's guessed impact point. Ormeon threw her wings wide, gossamer white light glimmering beneath, just as the beam hit the imaginary armor on her chest.

Light, and heat. The sound of the purest bell from a steeple far away. Fire roiled, then scattered into a thousand brilliant points. It fell like burning rain to the ground below. Tents erupted, and Vhemin screamed as their bodies incinerated. Ormeon reared, roaring her defiance, then snatched the Vhemin with the device, dashing him to pulp against the ground. She roared again, this time with fire, blasting the fortifications and defenders to a greasy, drifting ash.

A bunching of her hindquarters, and the dragon launched herself aloft again. Geneve looked back, seeing a crater below them, a hundred spokes of destruction spread outward from where the dragon landed. "How..?"

//BELIEVE.// Ormeon curved south toward the city. *//HE IS THE STRONGEST MAGICIAN ALIVE. ALL HE NEEDS IS YOU.//*

"Your armor ... is real?"

//AS REAL AS THE DREAMS THAT CALLED YOU TO ME. AS REAL AS THAT ARTIFICE.//

Geneve felt her attention dragged to the west. The clouds parted, and through them soared an Artifice on wings of flame. It screamed as it came, trails of fire behind it. *We must kill that.*

//YOUR PURPOSE, MY WORLD.// Ormeon's wings snapped straight with the crack of thunder and she whirled for the Artifice.

Who knew Artifices could fly? I feel like someone should have kept the memories of the ancients safe, if for no other reason than this.

//I KNEW.// Ormeon flew faster. The ground was far below by now, but Geneve felt their speed through the wind buffeting her armor. She held on tight. The Artifice's fangs warmed a cheery yellow, twin beams following to strike Ormeon. The dragon spun through the air, orange and red tossed in a kaleidoscope of ever-burning rain.

She breathed deep, then blasted fire. They passed the Artifice in the blink of an eye, heat and backwash unsettling Geneve, but she hung on. Ormeon surged upward, then tucked her wings in, spinning in the air. They held in the sky, gravity ignoring them for a precious moment, then fell.

The Artifice wasn't so quick to turn, but wasn't a laggard either. Geneve could see the scorching of its skin, but it looked like soot rather than damage. "Can we kill it?"

//WE MUST GET CLOSE.//

"What about them?" Geneve cast an arm to the south, where two more Artifices breached the cloud cover, burning hard for the dragon.

//THIS MAY GET ... TRICKY.//

"Bring us close to the other two." Geneve hung on with one hand, drawing Requiem with the other.

//YOU ARE CRAZY. I SEE YOUR THOUGHTS AND WONDER IF YOU'VE HAD A LOT OF HEAD INJURIES.//

"I'm not crazy, I'm motivated." Geneve felt the dragon's joy at doing what she was *made* for, shared it, and returned the favor. "You didn't know what I meant when I talked of the Three's patterns. You're about to find out."

//WHAT IS 'HEAVEN'S FURY?'//

"A pattern that served no purpose. I've learned it but could never use it. Mostly, I think, because it was meant to be done from the back of a dragon."

//PERHAPS THEY WERE MEANT FOR YOU ALONE. LOOK. THEY ARE COMING OUT TO PLAY.// Ormeon glanced skyward. Geneve saw Cophine's pale face shining through the smoke, and beside her gray Ikmae. Even black Khiton was visible, the moon's dark orb hard as coal against the sky. The moons shone in daylight for the first time Geneve could remember. *//THEY HAVE WAITED ALMOST A THOUSAND YEARS FOR TODAY.//*

"Then we will give them a show to remember for another thousand. Fly, dragon!" Geneve leveled her sword at the approaching Artifices, now uncomfortably close. Ormeon obliged her request, wings urging them faster than the chariots of gods. Her sword angle was perfect, her body in tune with Ormeon's, and golden, urgent Light glimmered along Requiem's length.

At what felt like a half-second past the last moment, Ormeon reared from her collision course with the leading Artifice. Geneve swung her leg over the saddle, dropping from the dragon's back. Ormeon continued on as Geneve fell. The Artifice closed faster than thought, but Geneve closed her eyes. *The pattern is the answer.* She swung Requiem, feeling nothing but air about her, until the blade bit with the scream of metal.

Her feet landed on smooth steel. She opened her eyes. Her molten armor dripped fire on the Artifice beneath her, Requiem buried halfway in the machine's back. Geneve felt a thrumming through her boots like the mad agency of a hundred clockworks. Air dragged its claws across her armor, but she held fast to Requiem and its promise.

The Artifice trailed twin streams of fire. It swerved, perhaps trying to dislodge her, and set a new course due east. Over Ravenswall, and toward the harbor. Geneve felt the weight of Heaven's Fury on her shoulders, the pattern only half-spent. Light gave her boots fangs as she yanked Requiem from the Artifice in a shower of fire and sparks. Behind them, Ormeon banked around an Artifice, breathing answering fire to twin beams of ancient hate. She seemed all bared fangs and blasting dragonfire, but was working to what she hoped was their shared plan: herding the second Artifice to the first.

Trust the dragon. I've little option now as I'm on a flying Artifice and could fall to my death.

Geneve swung Requiem seven perfect times. The first cut cracked the Artifice's obsidian carapace, a piece of metal spinning away behind her. The second gouged deeper, the third following through the same path, causing the machine to cough and stutter.

The fourth strike hit a heart of fire, the fifth severing it from the machine's core. The seventh carved a brilliant line down the Artifice's back as the machine died beneath her, falling to the earth below. Geneve jumped clear, pirouetting through the sky above Ravenswall, and landed with a crash on the smoking Artifice Ormeon guided to her.

The pattern of Heaven's Fury called for her to trust in a spin through the air with nothing beneath her. Tresward trained with logs suspended over pits to simulate a combat they'd never seen. Geneve's jump from a falling Artifice was like stepping from the first log, and landing on the second machine was a move she'd done a thousand times before. Her blade cut the Artifice from front to back, parting it in two.

And now, the dragon catches me. But Ormeon didn't catch her; the dragon jerked sideways as the remaining Artifice impacted her flank. They spun through the air toward the harbor. The Artifice detonated with a brilliant blue-white flash, Ormeon's massive form spiraling away, wings trailing long streamers of smoke.

Which left Geneve to fall the very long way to the Brook District below her. She saw glimmering blue as she plummeted, and wondered if she'd survive long enough to be killed by Vhemin, or if her body would shatter on impact.

Chapter Thirty-Nine

eriwether woke when someone slapped his face. It wasn't gentle, but was also open-palm, no gauntlet, so you could argue there was a little love in there somewhere. He croaked, trying to open his eyes. His headache said, *Hold up a second*, but the slap returned for a second go-around.

"All right! I'm awake. I'm really awake." Meriwether managed to convince even himself, eyelids popping open to see what could only be described as a circus of violence behind Sight of Day, who crouched over him, golden eyes concerned. Of Armitage there was no sign, but Vertiline crouched nearby, hands on knees, watching the ruckus.

A handful of blue-runed Vhemin warriors broke from a warehouse, clashing with their more basic cousins. Meriwether thought there might be ten rune-armored Vhemin against thirty 'ordinary' monsters, but the numbers didn't count for much against the terrible might of ancient magic.

Feybrind formed a cordon around Meriwether, Sight of Day, and others who looked wounded. There were cats and monsters alike, some bleeding out their last, others looking to get back in the fight. The guarding cats laid down covering fire with bows, an eye-watering withering fire raining with pinpoint accuracy against the enemy Vhemin.

Most arrows bounced off the armor, but a shot here or there found an eye socket or exposed jugular.

It didn't seem to be helping. Meriwether saw a titanic Vhemin with a shaft sprouting from his right eye fighting on like the shot really did miss all his vital spots. His armor glowed brighter, driving him on with a ferocity his worn-out fellows couldn't match. He smashed two Vhemin's heads together, and Meriwether winced as the wet *crunch-pop* reached him across the chaos of the melee.

A massive explosion knocked him flat. Meriwether raised his arm over his head, squinting against the sky's glare. Ormeon tumbled overhead, trailing smoke, ash, and flame. She was out of control and hit the water to the east with a massive splash. Steam gouted toward the Three above.

Meriwether did a double-take. "Are the moons out in daytime?"

Sight of Day snapped his fingers before Meriwether's face. *{That's not what you should be worrying about.}*

"I'm not worried about Geneve. She wasn't on the dragon." Meriwether staggered to his feet, the cat offering none-too-gentle assistance. "I'm a little worried about the dragon, though."

{The dragon's fine.}

"She's underwater!" Meriwether stabbed a finger to the sea, where the massive waves rippled outward from the impact. The swells caught the *Chimera's* corpse, nudging it further onto the shattered docks.

{You should be worried about your father. All this is because of him. Cut the head from a snake, and all that.} Sight of Day gave him a withering look. *{You're supposed to be the smart one.}*

Meriwether pounded his fist against palm. "Got it. You're right. Let's go cut him to pieces." From behind the ancient-armored Vhemin, a small crowd of Queensguard burst from the shadows. Meriwether goggled. "Everyone's here today, aren't they?"

{I'll be right back.} Sight of Day whirled, tail cutting air, and dashed toward the Queensguard. There force was twenty armed and armored men and women around a single hooded figure. The element of surprise wore off: the enemy Vhemin seemed happy enough to fight a war on two fronts with the strength of titans in their veins.

The cats fired arrows faster than thought at the enemy. From a rooftop above them, Armitage rose up, a huge hunk of rock held above his head. The monster tossed it onto the enemy below, bellowing, "Say hello, motherfuckers!" He jumped from the roof, tucking into a cannonball and dropping to the foes below.

Meriwether winced. *What can I do?* He glanced about, looking for a weapon, then patted himself down for a knife, *anything*. His hand absently brushed the tome chained to his belt, and he almost groaned. *Of course. I'm not a fighter. I'm a sorcerer with a few tricks.* Meriwether clapped his hands, then raised them to the heavens. Above his head, glowing words of light formed in the air.

COME THIS WAY TO NOT DIE.

"Subtle," Vertiline said.

"Best I had on short notice," Meriwether said.

The hooded figure saw, hitched their robe higher, and sprinted from the melee. Vhemin tried to follow, but one met Sight of Day's slender steel, another stopping like they'd reached the end of a rope, dragged backward by Armitage. The monster slammed his kin against the ground, a rock in one hand falling again and again, pulping flesh and bone.

The Feybrind line parted for the hooded figure and a few of their guard. The first to Meriwether was Heser the Cheg, bald head slicked with sweat and gore. He had what looked like a hundred cuts on his armor, which didn't appear to bother him even a little bit. "Sorcerer."

"Queensman." Meriwether gave a tight bow. "What news?"

The hooded figure stepped past Heser the Cheg, pulling back their cowl to reveal, to no one's great surprise, Queen Morgan. Magic's tincture touched the air. *Another sorcerer is here.* "You will call off your troops and surrender."

Vertiline stood, hand on her steel. Meriwether held a palm out: *wait*. "I don't think so." He found Heser the Cheg's eyes, the other man wincing. "You don't want us to surrender." Vertiline began a slow circle of the queen. Heser the Cheg marked her movements, matching them with his own steps.

"You will kill us all!" Morgan's face was pale, stretched thin by fatigue and stress. "We must surrender to my lord Leander."

"Hmm." Meriwether looked to the Queensguard. The taint of magic grew stronger. "Tilly?"

The Chevalier's eyes didn't leave Heser the Cheg. "I'm listening."

"How do you feel about a little revenge?"

"What for?"

"The loss of Ravenswall. The sacrifice of monarchy. Failure of the rule of law, corruption of the state, and sedition from within." Meriwether frowned. "I could go on."

"Sounds like a thing worthy of revenge."

The queen squared her shoulders. "Enough of this. I rule! *Me!* You will bow, or die!"

Meriwether kept his face impassive. *Give nothing away. There will be one chance.* Slow as he could to not give the game of magic away, he created another set of words in the air. It was faint, because he was trying to do this without magical noise, like breathing so slowly not even Feybrind could hear. His chest tightened with the effort, but he kept his voice bland. "This doesn't sound like you."

"Who are you to tell me what I sound like?" The queen's cheeks blushed with fury.

"The person who's helped save Ravenswall already." Meriwether firmed up the letters in the air. They coalesced like fog turning to ice rock. The blue of Vertiline's eyes. The paleness of a winter's sky. They hovered over a Queensguard of middling years, with a well-trimmed beard a man could be proud of. Tilly's eyes widened as they read the letters.

The guard's head tipped back, spotting the letters. From his angle he couldn't read them, but it was clear they were right above him. He snarled, fist clenching. Heser the Cheg jerked like a marionette, turned, and lunged for Meriwether.

But pale Vertiline moved like wind. She spun, dropping low, and swept Heser the Cheg's feet from under him. Her spin continued as she rose, steel in her hand, and she took two perfect steps to the guardsman marked by Meriwether's letters. The faintest ringing of a gong sounded to the south, and the smell of cloves touched the air for a moment as Vertiline's blade flashed with golden Light.

The protective barrier about the not-a-guardsman-but-actually-anenchanter flared vermillion, then shattered against Vertiline's Light. His head toppled from his shoulders to bounce on the wharf's stone, blood fountaining from his neck like a geyser.

He fell, quite dead. The queen trembled, stumbling, but Meriwether stepped forward to catch her. "Your majesty. All's well now."

"What ... happened?" Morgan made no move to leave his arms, but she turned to see the lettering still etched above the headless enemy. It said, *THIS GUY HERE.*

"We thought one of your Coterie held you in thrall, but it turns out the villain was closer to your heart. He was in the Queensguard. My guess is he subverted your trust in Heser the Cheg, making the good captain doubt himself, then corrupted your closest ally afterward." Meriwether gently pushed Morgan away. "The giveaway is when people start talking like sock puppets, using another's speech. You should have your own words back now, to better run your kingdom. Queendom. Whatever it is."

Armitage and Sight of Day returned. The monster held an enemy's blood-spattered helmet in one hand. He tossed this to the ground, then walked to Vertiline. The Chevalier looked at her sword, eyes wide. Armitage raised a hand to touch her arm, but let it fall before it got to its destination. "You good?"

She shook her head. "The Light returned."

"Looked great, too." He grinned shark teeth. "How about we take your refound balance to the battlefield and ruin a few more people's day? We've got to get Geneve."

"Wait." Meriwether swiveled like a magnet finding true north in an instant. "What of Geneve?"

"She fell from a flying Artifice and landed in the city." At Sight of Day's head shake, Armitage winced. "Oh. My bad. I wasn't supposed to say that."

"*She what?*" Meriwether made to run toward the city, then stopped, then started again, then stalled out. "Where?"

"I'm not telling," Armitage said.

"She's over there," Vertiline pointed with her sword. "But we're not going that way. Armitage and Sight of Day are."

"We're not?" Meriwether blinked. "Why?"

"Because she's a Knight of the fucking Tresward, not a child to be coddled," Vertiline said, with a decent amount of eye-rolling. "What *we* need to do is keep a promise."

"I, uh." Meriwether clasped his hands so tight they went bloodless. "Which promise in particular?"

"The one where I said I'd end your father, and you said you wouldn't stop me." She lifted her chin. "So, you're coming with me."

"I can't—"

"Sinner, I can't use the Sway. I'm no good against magic. You are. I *need* your help."

Picotee chose that moment to push through the Feybrind cordon. She was blood-spattered but in good spirits. Picotee gave Morgan a glance, then walked right past her to Meriwether. "That her?"

"Aye." Meriwether unclasped his hands. "Your majesty, may I present Picotee, my Lady du Parneer. Picotee, this is Queen Morgan, Sovereign of Or'sen, ruler of the kingdom."

"Whatever." Picotee approached Morgan.

Heser the Cheg approached her right back. "Hold up, my lady. Without wanting to cause offense, aren't you banished, your lands forfeit, along with your life should you ever return to Or'sen?"

"Well." Meriwether jog-stepped closer. "It's like this. We wouldn't be here if it weren't for Lady du Parneer. If we'd come by road, we'd have made it just in time to see Leander raising a new standard over the keep. Everyone would be dead, and you'd have no hope. Also, your queen would be a hopeless thrall of that sack of shit," Meriwether pointed to the fallen not-Queensguard, "probably married to my waste-of-skin father."

Morgan nodded. "What do you want, Lady Picotee?"

"A pardon for all souls of Parneer." Picotee spread her hands. "I've a daughter now."

"You're a pirate lord." Morgan raised her eyebrow. "That will have to stop."

"I'm not sure—"

"Here's the deal." Morgan's tone turned businesslike. "I grant you, and your heir, full pardon for all past deeds and transgressions, as a thank-you for getting my Lord du Reeves to the right place, at the right time. I'll also offer this to your subjects, if they agree to stop casual murder on the high seas. I haven't *finished*," she snapped, as Picotee looked about to start in. "I've spent the last weeks as a thrall to a tyrant, and I'm enjoying the ability to use my words again." Picotee nodded, mute. "I will offer a second olive branch. You will regain your lands and titles of the du Parneer estates, if you agree to patrol the waters of Or'sen, keeping it safe from harm."

"Nice," Meriwether said. "A pardon, a navy, and all wrapped up in a bow."

"Do you like dungeons, my lord du Reeves?" Morgan pressed her lips into a line. "No? Then stop talking."

Vertiline grabbed Meriwether's arm. "This doesn't involve you anymore. You've done your part here. Now it's time to save the world."

"Outstanding," Armitage rumbled. "Barret! Where are you?" The older Vhemin matron jogged closer, hefting a bloody club and a smile. "It's time to earn your revenge. You're with me."

"Wait. Who comes with us?" Meriwether looked around.

"It's just you and me, sinner." Vertiline tossed her blade aside. "Help me find glass, then we'll be on our way."

THEY WALKED AWAY FROM THE HARBOR DISTRICT, JUST THE TWO OF them. Vertiline said goodbye to Kytto after taking a glass sword from the Smith. They hadn't embraced, which made Meriwether confused, but it was that kind of day.

Ravenswall's streets were filled with dead. Not just the odd body lying about, but masses of people, murdered as they tried to fight, or run. The Vhemin hadn't stopped with able-bodied men and women; they'd turned their weapons against children, too. Meriwether felt sick, but also more confused. "Why haven't they taken them?"

Vertiline raised her eyebrow. "What?"

"The dead. Vhemin eat their kills."

"Maybe they're saving them for someone else." She shrugged, stepping over another body. "Vhemin aren't the top of the food chain here. They're doing the grunt work for higher-ups."

"Higher up than ancient-armored monsters?" Meriwether ran a hand through grime- and sweat-slicked hair. "What would that be?"

"Justiciars, perhaps." Tilly sighed. "I don't know, sinner. That's your job. Mine's to point out the obvious."

He tried for a laugh, but it was stillborn. "We need to find out who's the power behind the throne. If my father's working alone, that'd be nice, but..." Meriwether trailed off.

"Doesn't feel like a one-man show, does it?"

They hurried on, making good time through deserted streets. Raucous laughter anchored Meriwether to a doorway. Vertiline crouched behind an overturned stall. They scanned the street ahead, making out a small Vhemin patrol. Five soldiers, two with blue-runed armor, three in ordinary chain. There was a rude wagon with them, a couple of miserable people aboard who looked from their finery like they might have once been in charge of something. "We should go around."

"Don't be foolish. This is perfect." Vertiline stood, marching forward.

"Tilly!" Meriwether hissed. "What are you doing?"

"Getting captured, of course." She tossed him a smile. "You act like it's the first time you've been beaten up. What would you prefer: walking to the devil, or getting a ride?"

"I don't like those choices. Is there one where we don't get beaten up, *and* avoid devils?"

Vertiline held out her hand. "Come on, sinner."

He slipped from the doorway, letting her help him over some rubble. They approached the Vhemin patrol at a brisk pace. Vertiline called out, "Ho, monsters!"

The Vhemin whirled, weapons suddenly in hand, snarls everywhere. One with standard armor started to charge, then slowed to a walk at Vertiline's lack of terror, or raised weapon. She stopped, looking back at her troop uncertainly, then squared her shoulders and marched forward. "You got a death wish?"

Vertiline smiled, long and sly. "I've many wishes, but none involve dying. We wish to speak with Leander du Reeves."

"It's nice to want things," the brute said. She reached them and swung a meaty fist. It hit Vertiline in the face.

The Chevalier rocked back, but didn't stumble. Tilly grinned blood. "Try that again."

"You know, I think I might." The monster reached for Vertiline.

Tilly spun, glass sword whispering from its sheath. She struck three times, Light glimmering along her blade. The Vhemin's left arm spun away, followed by her right, and finally head. Vertiline lowered her blade, holding her pose. "I said, we wish to speak with Leander du Reeves."

"Huh," a blue-armored Vhemin growled. "And who the fuck are you?"

"Vertiline, Knight Chevalier of the Tresward." She stepped over the body at her feet. Meriwether saw blood still pumped from the neck. "And this is my Lord Meriwether du Reeves, his son and heir."

"Why the hell didn't you say so?" groused the monster. "Get in the wagon."

***

The wagon trundled through the streets at a good enough pace. Meriwether eyed the other two prisoners, who'd remained deaf, mute, and for all he knew, blind. Scratching his beard, he glanced to Vertiline. "That went better than I expected."

"All's going according to plan, I'll allow," she agreed, then spat a bloody gobbet of saliva.

"You like getting hit in the face?"

"I like getting to where I'm going as fast as possible. We're getting door to door service, and don't have to kill a hundred Vhemin to get there." The wagon rolled through breached gates, a steady stream of monsters passing by them and into the city. The plains outside Ravenswall were carpeted in Vhemin. Vertiline straightened. "Make that a hundred *thousand*." She counted on her fingers, lips moving. "I don't think I could do that many, even at my best."

Meriwether huddled into his cloak. He wondered what he'd say to his father when they met. Would Leander recognize him? Reach out for a loving embrace, or toss him to the floor? Order him whipped like a hundred other times? "Perhaps fighting would've been the best. It'd be an honest death."

"There's no honesty in death. It's just death." She worried a tooth with her gloved metal hand.

"Why are we doing this?"

"Because you need to finish what you started."

"I what now?"

Vertiline lowered her hand, leaving the wayward tooth alone. "You ran away from home, sinner. Left a man with iron and fire at your back."

"I never said that."

"You didn't have to. Your skin is a roadmap of pain. I've seen you exposed, and I don't mean without your shirt. You ran, and kept running, until you ran into *us*. And then you couldn't run anymore, and for a long time you were happy with that. But then," she gestured to the Vhemin horde about them, the wagon marking distance by passing monsters in their hundreds, "this happened. You were never meant to keep running, sinner. You just had to go far enough to find someone to brush you off, turn you around, and send you back into the fight."

"I can't fight. No Tresward training guides my arm. I'm not like you."

"And that's a blessing. I've tossed aside a chance for a real life by following a fool's heart." Vertiline shook her head, blue eyes soft like gentle coastal waters. "Here it is, laid plain. You need to finish what you started. You left a scared boy and return a sorcerer supreme. You call Tresward your friends, and no sinner's done that for hundreds of years. The Feybrind listen when you speak, and a monster has your back. Even *I* like you." She offered a tired grin. "You could marry a queen, if your heart wanted it."

"I don't—"

"I know you're true. There's no question in my mind about that. But soon enough this wagon will stop. We'll be before a tyrant in the making. A monster with a thousand arms, reaching to the corners of the world. He means to set us at each other's throats. Make us hate, and fight, for all time. I don't know if I can stop him."

He goggled. "You don't?"

"No. But I don't have to." She leaned forward, taking his hands in hers. "Because *you can*. You just need to step the fuck up."

THE WAGON PASSED WITHIN THE ENEMY'S FORTIFICATIONS, HEADING toward an ornate pavilion that screamed, *Leander's a wanker*. The Vhemin halted the wagon and turned to them. "The boss is in there."

"Really?" Vertiline blinked faux surprise. "I'd never have guessed."

"Mind your lip."

She said nothing, vaulting over the side of the wagon. Meriwether followed, landing somewhat less elegantly. They stood shoulder to shoulder. Vhemin guarded the entrance, and more were inside. Meriwether blinked, eyes struggling to adjust; the interior was shrouded in darkness, a mere two braziers burning low, offering a smokey half-light.

He coughed. "This isn't quite the warm welcome."

Vertiline took his hand, dragging him forward. "Come, sinner. Destiny is waiting."

The gloom started to make sense. A mock throne stood at the pavilion's rear, on which sat a familiar figure. Time hadn't been good to Leander du Reeves; his shoulders didn't carry the strength Meriwether remembered on the other end of the lash. His once-black beard had faded, and his hair was patchy as if he had mange.

By his side stood a man in Justiciar's robes. The Justiciar also wore a smile like the cat that got the cream. He took a step forward. "And our wayward Chevalier returns."

"Justiciar Ambrose," Vertiline purred. "How nice to see you still alive. That'll need fixing."

The smile on Ambrose's face flickered for a moment. "What do you mean?"

"It's a surprise," she hissed. "Wait for it."

"That's my cue." Meriwether stepped forward and clapped his hands. "Here it is. You will ... by the Three's mercy, what's *that?*"

Behind Leander, a blot of darkness shifted. It looked like a charcoal sketch of a man, if the artist was both drunk and had never seen a person before. Its arms were longer than regulation length, and it moved as if the limits of having a skeleton were for lesser people. It hissed.

"That's *my* surprise." Leander's voice was as wizened as his body. "Demons, boy. They're real, and give us everything we've ever wanted."

The demon, if that's what it was, stepped to Leander's left. The darkness it left writhed, another demon taking shape. A third stepped free from the throne as the second hunkered at Leander's feet. Meriwether licked lips dry as old parchment. "Hah. I mean, sure, they could be demons. But how do you know?"

"What?" Leander squinted. "Don't be a fool. You know the price of stupidity."

Meriwether remembered the marks on his skin, and the feeling of how they got there. "I do, but this isn't foolishness. I expect it looks like it from the position of the lost, but it wears a different name. This is righteousness."

"Don't lecture me, pup." Leander creaked upright. "Have you come to claim your birthright? With you, we can harness the dragon, and control the world." His fist clenched.

"Sire," Ambrose said.

"Silence! Don't forget who you serve." Spittle flew from Leander's lips.

Vertiline gave Meriwether a little side-eye. "This how he always talks?"

"Pretty much."

"Oh. I thought maybe someone had control of his mind."

"Could still do." Meriwether pursed his lips. "Well, I guess we'll have to do this the hard way." The roar of an angry dragon shook Meriwether. He glanced over his shoulder. "And by that, I mean the dragon's coming, and she's really angry."

Vertiline bared her blade, the glass gathering what light came from the braziers and holding it close. Ambrose smiled. "A dragon without a rider is just a big lizard. And we saw your dragonrider fall."

"Wait for it." Vertiline cocked her head, listening. "Do you hear that?"

Ambrose's smile dimmed a little. "I hear nothing."

The dragon roared again, much closer this time. The ground shook, and he staggered. Wind buffeted the pavilion's tent-flap door, dust eddies hurrying inside. The light didn't seem to bother the demons, or Ambrose, but Leander held his hand up, guarding his eyes.

"Justiciar Ambrose!" Geneve shouted. "I call you to Judgment!"

Vertiline's smile turned wolfish as she eyed Ambrose. "That's the surprise."

"She ... fell!"

"Best get out and see for yourself." Vertiline stood side-on to the door, hand out. "I won't stop you."

"Enough of this nonsense." Leander reached to his side. From where no sword hung a moment earlier, he drew forth a blade black as midnight. "It's time to end all opposition."

"A moment, father." Meriwether held his hand up. "I think we should be honest with each other."

"I've never lied to you, boy."

"It's not always about you though, is it?" Meriwether dredged up a brittle smile, then faced Ambrose, as his fingers brushed the tome at his belt. "Compliments of the thousands of my brothers and sisters you've killed. Justiciar Ambrose, it's time for you to face Knight Chevalier Geneve. She's the best of them, and she's come just for you." He spread his arms, then spoke a Word, then another, and a third, because only the best things came in threes.

Ambrose screamed, his face cracking like the carapace of a shedding insect. A soft, fleshy black thing struggled within. Vertiline glanced at Meriwether. "What was that?"

He wheezed with the effort of the High Magic, but kept his balance. "Freedom."

What was left of Ambrose tossed aside its skin, then snatched one of the demons from beside Leander. It bit the demon with jaws as wide as a bear's with a horrible crunch. The demon twitched, black fluid leaking out. Was-Ambrose tossed the corpse aside, balefire eyes on

Meriwether, then it roared, bolting through the pavilion's wall and outside.

Leander cackled like a child with a new toy, his two demons still with him, then lurched toward Meriwether. "Come, son. Let's be about it."

Chapter Forty

T he ground approached Geneve with the ferocity of a charging army. She plummeted from the Artifice, trying her best not to scream. Was there a pattern for this? Surely she'd have remembered if the Tresward taught how to fall from a klick in the air and not die. *We're not made of steel. More like glass.*

Glass?

She flailed as she fell, her body tumbling. Geneve tried to ignore the chaos of her inner ear. Requiem whistled as it cut air. She grabbed its sheath, then slid the blade home. Hands free, she reached behind her for her shield. Armored Smithsteel gauntlets protected her hands. *Hold it tight. Don't let the wind take it.* There was a Tresward shield pattern called Mercy's Regard. It was the simplest of them, designed for a single Knight facing one opponent, both on even ground.

Geneve grappled with the shield, managing to get her arm into the straps. She tucked her knees in, pulling the shield tight to her shoulder. The ground was visible through the glass, approaching ever closer. If there was ever a time for magic, this was it, but all she had was a glass shield, and no pattern to guide it. She thought of Meri, his touch, his kisses, then gently set them aside. Armitage, and his strength and courage, even when all called him monster. Tilly, and her eyes that would be sad forever. And finally Sight of Day, his half-smile, and golden gaze.

I can't die and leave them.

She spared a glance for the Three above. Cophine, her pale face somber. Ikmae, ever by her side. And Khiton, black and hidden most of the time, but here to see her fall. Geneve wanted their help, but they were so far away. Her molten armor trailed fire as she fell.

Beneath her, blue-armored Vhemin watched her come, eyes up, waiting to finish off what was left. *Perfection is needed for the Storm. I've trained my whole life to be the Three's instrument.*

Geneve slowed her breathing, ignoring the approaching ground. She loosened, rather than tightened, her grip on Brilliance. The shield trembled, but she coaxed it still, easing it from her side and into Mercy's Regard. The faintest wisp of golden light licked the razor edge of the disc.

It was enough. Mercy's Regard took hold, the shield flaring with Light. Geneve hit the ground like a meteor, but the shield held. The ground beneath her cracked, the Vhemin about her tossed aside like toys. Geneve stood in a smooth motion, Requiem in her hand, and took nine perfect steps to the first Vhemin.

The blade arced down. Geneve expected lightning from the Three, but this time she got fire, a blazing inferno belching from her sword like a furnace. The Vhemin's scream cut short as his torso was wreathed in flame, blue runes flickering out like snuffed candles.

She charged another, meeting his ancient blade with her own. Requiem rang like a bell, the Vhemin stumbling back from the shock of it. Geneve swung three more times, leaving barbecued char behind.

A monster to the east leveled a boxy device at her. Geneve hunkered behind Brilliance, and as the device lanced fire, she stepped into Mercy's Regard again. Brilliance wreathed in golden yellow, the enemy's beam scattering into a thousand drops of fire in a cone before her. The blast sliced the box's wielder off at the knees, leaving nothing but smoking stumps. Twenty other Vhemin turned into burning monster candles, staggering about, screaming and keening.

From a wide street leading to the west a massive crunch sounded. Geneve saw an Artifice approaching, the ancient machine at least fifty meters high. It had eight limbs, two of them grasping claw-like shears that were slick with blood. Its body was out of her reach. How could she defeat this thing? Cut it down slice by slice? She'd seen the Redeemer fall; there was no easy ride to the back of the machine.

Water sluiced her. *Water? Three's mercy, what fresh hell is this?*

With the kind of cry only an angry dragon could make, Ormeon plummeted onto the Artifice. Her scales were scorched, patches missing to expose angry, weeping flesh beneath. The dragon dripped seawater as she impacted the Artifice. The machine staggered, twin claws reaching for the dragon.

Ormeon roared, claws digging in, and she rent the Artifice's carapace in half. The machine lurched on a handful of paces, then toppled to the ground.

The dragon landed before Geneve, not at all gracefully. "You're hurt!"

//I'M ANGRIER THAN I'M HURT.// The dragon grinned a wreath of smoke.

"You should get clear."

Ormeon craned her neck lower. *//DRAGONS DON'T RUN.//*

"They do if they want to live." Geneve pulled off her helmet, letting red hair free. "You're the only one of your kind."

The dragon grinned wider. *//SPOKEN LIKE SOMEONE ELSE WHO'S ALSO THE ONLY ONE OF THEIR KIND. COME, DRAGONRIDER. WE'VE A DEMON TO KILL. OR HAD YOU FORGOTTEN?//*

She looked to the west. "Leander?"

//HE'S NO DEMON, ALTHOUGH HUMANS HAVE ALWAYS RIVALED THEIR KIND FOR EVIL.//

Geneve gritted her teeth. "Ambrose."

//THAT'S NOT HIS NAME.// The dragon sniffed, as if seeking prey. *//HE JUST BORROWED IT FOR A WHILE.//*

She put her helmet back on, then grabbed the saddle, hauling herself onto Ormeon. "What's his name, then?"

//I DO SO LOVE SOLVING A GOOD MYSTERY.// Ormeon chuckled, then leaped for the sky. *//WHY DON'T YOU AND I CUT IT OUT OF HIM?//*

THE FLIGHT TO THE ENEMY ENCAMPMENT TOOK LESS THAN TEN minutes. Geneve hoped Meri was safe back at the harbor, that no one's blade had found his heart.

//THAT'S NOT WHAT'S BOTHERING YOU.//

"Stop listening to my thoughts!"

//THAT'S NOT WHAT I'M DOING.// The dragon flapped mighty wings, but less enthusiastically than before. Geneve felt a strain under her ribs, a memory of the dragon's pain where she'd been hurt by the Artifice's death.

"What would you call it?"

//NEURAL HARMONIC IMAGING.//

Geneve glanced down at the thousands of Vhemin below, speeding past as the dragon hunted larger prey. "And what's that?"

//MIND READING.// Ormeon laughed with the sound of a thousand storms. *//IT'S A SUBTLE DIFFERENCE, BUT THOUGHTS ARE THINGS YOU'RE AWARE OF. I'M LOOKING A LITTLE DEEPER. AND DON'T SIGH AT ME.//*

"All-seeing, all-knowing dragon, what's bothering me?"

//YOU'VE FOUGHT EVERY FIGHT WITH HIM AT YOUR SIDE. OVER THE PAST WEEKS A SINGLE SOUL HAS SHARED YOUR EVERY MOMENT OF DANGER. YOU WANT MERIWETHER TO SHARE THE UPCOMING CONFLICT WITH YOU.//

She didn't know about that. Meri would probably die in a pitched battle. *But...* "I miss him already."

//HE PROBABLY WON'T DIE. HE'S MADE OF STERNER STUFF THAN YOU CREDIT HIM FOR.//

"He's worthless with a blade."

//BLADES DO NOT GIVE US WORTH. I DON'T HAVE ONE, AND ONLY AN IMBECILE WOULD CALL ME WORTHLESS.// Ormeon grumbled as her wings pulled her injury, and Geneve felt a ghost of that pain. *//I MEANT TO ASK: WHY DIDN'T YOU FLY TO THE GROUND WHEN YOU FELL? THE HOLOMANCER GAVE YOU WINGS.//*

Geneve blinked. "They're not real."

//THEY'RE AS REAL AS STARLIGHT. OH, LOOK. I CAN SEE MY LAIR FROM HERE.//

Was Ormeon right? Could Geneve have flown with her wings? They seemed no stronger than the fairy's she'd met what seemed an age ago. Sunbeam Jinglewood's flight wasn't governed by what was *real*. "Maybe next time."

//ATTEND. WE APPROACH A MONSTER.// The dragon dipped lower, wings trimmed for speed, nose forward like a thrown spear. The Vhemin encampment rushed toward them, but rather than look away, Geneve felt a fierce joy. *//YOU ARE WHAT YOU WERE MADE TO BE. JUST AS I AM.//* The dragon gouted fire, landing with a crunch that shook defenders from their feet. Vhemin and a few human defenders burst into flame. They lurched about, or writhed on the ground; the Vhemin's blue-runed armor didn't protect them against dragonfire.

Geneve felt it almost at her fingertips... the subtle hint of Sway. The Cleric's mastered trick to bend all to their will. She raised Requiem, the blade catching the sun, and screamed, "Justiciar Ambrose! I call you to Judgment!"

The battlefield held silence for two heartbeats, broken only by the cries of the dying. The pavilion erupted, disgorging a horror Geneve had never seen before. It looked to be made of oil and darkness, but fat and fleshy, nose seeking the air for scent. It swiveled toward her, wet gash mouth open to leer. "Be careful what you wish for, Knight. It might just come for you."

Chapter Forty-One

Meriwether left Vertiline to face two demons of darkness by herself, because *fuck that noise*. He knew he'd just get underfoot, and more importantly dead. The Chevalier had a tight focus on the right outcomes: dead demons, at any price.

He ran from the pavilion hot on the heels of the fleshy lump of darkness that hunted Geneve. Meriwether skidded to a halt outside the tent, because *everything* was on fire. The Vhemin guards that used to be at the pavilion's entrance were gone. Many of the enemy staggered about like four-limbed pyres, and those with throats that could still make noise were screaming.

Above it all, Ormeon smiled toothily. The armor he'd given her still glared defiance, brilliant woven light guarding the beast from Artifice weapons. Geneve was on the dragon's back, angel wings and molten armor still whole. *She's alive!* The Knight vaulted from the dragon's back. Ormeon swung her head toward the not-Justiciar-Ambrose-anymore guy, who was about thirty meters from Meriwether, and unloaded a bellyful of hate onto him.

Meriwether staggered back at the heat wash coming off the demon. Ormeon paused her onslaught, head cocked as she examined the effect of her fire breathing. The ground beneath the demon was slurred, dirt and stone blasted to glass. Meriwether's face felt baked by the fire, like he'd spent too long looking into an oven.

Air shimmered like it had above the plaguelands. The inky form of the demon rose like molasses poured in reverse, and it laughed. "Oh, Ormeon, how I'll enjoy this."

//DEAR AMBROSE, YOUR VOICE SOUNDS LIKE YOU'VE BEEN GARGLING ACID.// Runes around the dragon's head flared vermillion. *//WANT ANOTHER DOSE?//*

"Ambrose!" Geneve cried. She stalked to stand before the dragon while Meriwether glanced about for something useful to do. As per usual, there wasn't much for him to do at the moment except panic, or perhaps run in circles. "You owe the Tresward for the death of a Valiant, and a Champion before him. And you owe me for the loan of my memories for so many years." The blade in her hand was fever-bright, the shield on her arm catching the sun and casting light back like a benediction.

"Oh, boohoo. Do you want a hug?" The demon snarled, coiling in on its liquid body. "Anyway, it's not Ambrose. That worthless god-both-erer had all the spine of a newborn babe. My name is Ahkiban, and it's about time everyone learned it. I'll start with you, and finish," a black arm-like tendril speared toward the moons above, "with those mother-fuckers."

Meriwether blinked. *This isn't what I expected.* "Did you steal my father's will away?"

Geneve eyes didn't leave Ahkiban, but the demon turned its not-face toward Meriwether. "You'd like that, wouldn't you? That I wormed my way into your father's heart, corrupted his soul, and then made him place those marks on your skin. But no, that was pure hundred-proof human asshole. After he gutted your mother, I knew I had a possible candidate for promotion, but watching him whip you sealed the deal."

//AKHIBAN. SILENCE.// Geneve's words were like a whip, wielded by Khiton on his best day. Meriwether felt the Sway in them, his own lips wanting to shut, words go somewhere to hide, and it wasn't even *him* she commanded.

"Eat a dick," the demon said. "If a Champion couldn't make me heel, what chance do you have?"

//LET ME TRY AGAIN,// Ormeon said. //I CAN MAKE THE FIRE HOTTER.//

"I'm from a place made of flame, idiot." Ahkiban somehow managed a sneer without a real face. "What's the matter? Your manifest out of date or something?"

//THERE ARE A FEW BLACK SPOTS,// the dragon admitted.

"Then we fight the old fashioned way." Geneve stepped forward as if the demon hadn't spoken, or as if it didn't matter.

"Ah," the demon said. "The old fashioned way. Like this?" It snapped its not-really-fingers, and Geneve went taut like a guy wire. A half-second later, she lifted from the ground, arms pinned to her side. Her eyes were surprised, angry, and afraid.

Meriwether could understand that, no problem at all. Magic. The real kind. *Do something.* "Ahkiban. What do you want?"

The demon turned like gelatin, not all at once, and with a lot of wobbling. "World peace. Harmony."

"I find that hard to believe."

"That's because you're a moron," the demon explained, as if to a child, his words slow. "If everyone's under my command, they'll do what I want. I almost had the dragon at heel." Ormeon's neck snaked forward, snapping at Ahkiban. The demon slid like water, then shook a not-quite-a-finger at Ormeon. "It's time for you to die, I think. How'd you like that?"

A rage of blue-runed Vhemin ran for the dragon, screaming. Meriwether counted five as Ormeon reared, snared the first with a massive clawed hand. The Vhemin's armor blazed sapphire brilliance, then detonated.

Ormeon screamed pain, her arm ending at the elbow. The dragon staggered back, crashing through the encampment's fence. Vhemin ran after, armor blazing a blue promise. The dragon tumbled down the slope, and Meriwether heard the staggered detonations as Vhemin after Vhemin threw away their lives to explode against a dragon.

The last of her kind. Meriwether's eyes were wide, his mouth open. Very slowly, very carefully, he walked to Geneve, retrieving Requiem from her feet. She said nothing, jaw locked in a rictus. The sorcerer turned to Ahkiban, skymetal sword in hand. It felt heavy, like it was a god's weapon given to him for just a moment. Meriwether raised the blade. He didn't know how to use a sword, but there wasn't anyone else.

He ran screaming at Ahkiban.

Chapter Forty-Two

Her heart felt broken from brave Ormeon's fall. The dragon was gone, blasting out her brief light against a hundred Vhemin who died so there would be no more threat.

But that had happened, and another was about to fall. Geneve could see the hundred ways Meri could die. The way he held the blade was worse than the lowest Novice of the Tresward. His feet were too wide, and despite that his posture was too high. Meri swung the sword like a bat, not a blade, and the horror he faced slipped from each swing with the easy grace of a master of the sword.

It felt to Geneve that Ahkiban faced her with it's not-really-a-face, his not-quite-eyes locked on hers. He spoke effortlessly despite dodging Meri's swings. "I want you to watch, Knight. Right to the end. And I don't mean *look on*. Peer under the skin, and make out just how badly you've misjudged things. Then I'll kill you, but not before."

A man who looked like Meri would, if he'd lived twice as long and been sanded to the quick by the world, ran from the pavilion. A moment later a shadow loped from the tent, looking back over its shoulder. A heartbeat later Vertiline slipped through a fresh cut in the pavilion's canvas wall, stepping before the shadow and slicing its head off. Her blade was glass, glimmering with Light, and Geneve couldn't remember a time her eyes had been a harder blue.

Ahkiban cackled. "Are you *watching*, Tresward?"

Geneve tried to move, but her limbs were mired. It was like someone had buried her in molten rock, then let it cool. She couldn't budge a millimeter, except for her eyes. There was no problem seeing everything Ahkiban wanted her to.

The Knights she'd seen earlier approached from the north. For a moment Geneve felt hope, but their helmed faces turned from her, focusing on Tilly. Leander sprinted past them, which left Vertiline against three Knights. Geneve counted the golden bars on their black sashes, and knew Tilly was doomed.

Tilly! Run! Geneve wanted to scream, but her mouth wouldn't move. Vertiline clearly hadn't been told of her imminent death, because instead of running she faced the Knights, her glass blade held cross guard. A Knight facing her wielded a greatsword like Iz, another with a plain sword and board. The last held the unconventional pairing of two shortblades.

Meri continued to hack, without a lot of benefit, at Ahkiban. The young sorcerer was tiring, and he leaned on Requiem. "A moment."

"Take all the time you need," Ahkiban purred, glancing at Geneve again.

Vertiline moved with all the speed of her slender form. She clashed against the woman holding the greatsword, Light splashing in great, golden spears from the conflict. Two Blades tried to stab Tilly in the back, but she slipped below the strike, only narrowly missing decapitation from the sword and board Knight on rising.

Iz couldn't beat three. Tilly stands no chance.

A massive hulking Vhemin form sailed from behind Geneve to impact against the Knight with the greatsword. *Armitage!* The monster's arm splintered, bone poking through skin, but it didn't seem to bother him. He roared, head butted the Knight, then tore the woman's helmet off. She was all bared teeth and sweat-plastered hair as she stabbed fingers into Armitage's throat. The monster didn't appear to care, slamming her face with the helmet. "Pattern that, bitch!"

Two Blades looked torn between helping his comrade or slicing

Vertiline. Sword and Board swung to Armitage, blade raised to slice his unprotected back. Her armored back sprouted three arrows in an eye blink, immediately before Sight of Day landed cat-perfect five meters on, bow in hand.

Vertiline stepped smooth and low, blade whispering through Two Blades' stomach. The man twitched, blood vomiting from his mouth. Tilly sidestepped the torrent, spun, and took the Tresward's head from his shoulders.

Sight of Day fired five arrows at Ahkiban's ever-shifting form. All hit, sliding slowly down his liquid form to rest on the scorched ground. The Feybrind looked at Meri, then Geneve, and finally at his bow. {*I anticipated a different outcome.*}

Vertiline edged around Ahkiban, glass blade ready. The monster slopped to the left, giggling. "You think arrows will help? I'll admit, the catapult was a nice trick. I didn't expect that to happen, so I guess that makes us even, aye slave?" He surged a half-meter toward Sight of Day. "Or do you not remember the yoke? Don't fret. Humans don't either."

Meri hefted Requiem. "I think it's time for you to go."

"And who's going to make me?"

"Not me! I think we both know how worthless I am with a blade. And I'm guessing nothing the Vhemin or Feybrind have is a concern to you. Vertiline hasn't charged in, showing a level of caution I hadn't expected." Meri flashed a quick smile, all false bravado, and pointed to Geneve. "But she might."

"She's not going anywhere," hissed the demon.

Meri slicked back his hair, looked to the sky, and said a Word. Above, the Three watched, but doing nothing.

Nothing except... A thin, gossamer thread of light joined Cophine to Ikmae, then reached for Khiton. It was golden, soft, and dripped from the sky to touch Ahkiban. The demon didn't scream, or burst into flame. He looked up at the golden light touching him, then to Meri. "That's it?" The light pooled on Akhiban's head, then dripped further, deeper, into the black that made up the demon. "I'm a demon, you charlatan. The Sway can't touch me. Or whatever this is. If it were that simple, the gods would have finished us off a long time ago."

The sorcerer nodded. "That's true. That's why they gave us the Storm."

"Oh, be still." Ahkiban snapped not-really-fingers. "You bore me."

Meri twitched, then shook his head. "You can't bind me. That's a lock, and I'm made of keys. Just like the Light inside you."

Geneve saw it: the Light glimmering inside Ahkiban was a trick, an illusion, just like all the others. It painted not-veins and probably-not-arteries, guiding the eye lower, deeper, to a definitely-not-a-heart. Meri asked the gods for a simple favor. *Show me his weakness*, he'd said, *and I'll paint it for the world to see.*

"So?" Akhiban whirled to Vertiline, who'd chosen to lunge. The demon flicked his fingers, and Tilly spun away in a flurry of glass and Light. "Nice try. You're down to one Knight, and she's locked up. Unlike you, she's not a key."

Meri smiled. Same sad tint at the edges. *Oh, no. Meri, what are you doing?* "That's because she doesn't have the right incentive." He hefted Requiem and charged.

Ahkiban surged like oil, grasping the illusionist's arms. Meri's hands vanished up to the elbow, then he staggered back. Requiem was now in Ahkiban's not-hands. The demon hefted the weapon, then with a surge like the tides, crested to Meri and buried the steel into his gut.

Time stopped. Geneve wanted to scream.

Sight of Day's golden eyes widened, and the Feybrind's steel was out faster than even Vertiline could move. He leaped for the demon. Geneve felt a sudden pressure like the world *squeezed*, and she feared what Ahkiban would do to her friend.

Armitage tackled Sight of Day, one broken arm and all, twisting his body to shield the cat. A force hit the monster like a god's hammer, shattering his spine and tossing the pair through the pavilion.

Vertiline screamed as Armitage and Sight of Day sailed past her. She tried to rise, but Ahkiban flicked his not-fingers. The Chevalier spun away, glass sword shattering into a thousand iridescent motes of lost Light.

Through it all, Meri slumped over the steel in his stomach. Blood dripped in vivid, horrifying splashes to the ground. He touched Akhiban's not-really-a-shoulder, then gave a weak nod. "Ah. Thanks."

The demon seemed surprised. "You what?" He gave a twist of the blade, and Meri screamed. "How's that?"

"Better," the sorcerer wheezed. "And now, I think it's time for you to die."

Ahkiban seemed surprised by this, the pits he used for eyes widening. "You're about to finish your span, illusionist. I've got a meter of steel in your stomach. Your pet monster is gone. The cat with him. The last Knight you knew is without her blade, and unless I'm getting sloppy, her sword arm's broken anyway. I've killed your dragon. Leander got away. You're basically fucked."

Meriwether glanced to Geneve, as if feeling the desperate wail she couldn't make. He supported some of his weight on Ahkiban. "That's where you're wrong. On pretty much everything, but mostly on this." He smiled, blood leaking from the corner of his mouth. "Vertiline wasn't the last Knight. She wasn't even the angriest. That's reserved for those with hair red as fury, wearing angel's wings, and bearing the Three's will."

Ahkiban tore the blade from Meri. Blood sprayed as the sorcerer slumped. The demon raised Requiem, the beautiful skymetal sword catching the light and coloring it red. "Any last requests?"

"One," Meri looked to Geneve. "Be free."

The vice holding her snapped, its lock broken. Geneve dropped to the ground, fury and pain inside her in a hot, bright core. She held no sword, but she didn't need one. She would blast this *thing* from the world.

Meri had given her a chart to its heart. Geneve felt inside her, for all the pain for her lover, her dragon, and her friends. Touched that brittle, vile seed of agony, and opened it. She stepped forward into Khiton's pattern of *Blissful Rest*. Her hands held no blade; no Light colored steel or glass.

Despite that, she felt purpose in her hand. Maybe it was the Three watching above, offering her strength, but she didn't think so. The weapon she carried was justice. Redemption, grief, and anger, welded into one. And Meri's last, greatest gift to her: love.

Her not-really-a-sword hammered Ahkiban with the strength of a Storm. Not the divine, but the messy, complicated fabric of being simply human. Her not-a-blade cut Ahkiban's not-flesh, hungering for his heart.

The demon tried to shift aside, but *Blissful Rest* was made for this. Her fairy's edge followed the path of the demon's heart, found it, and cut it in two. Requiem fell from hands that ghosted to mist and ash, its point sliding into the ground.

She dropped beside Meri. *Be alive. Be alive!*. He didn't move as she turned him over. His eyes were closed, but as she touched him a small smile played at his lips, a joke only he knew. His voice was thin as thrice-reused parchment. "You made it."

"Meri! You're going to die."

"Thanks," he husked. "I had no idea."

"Why?" She brushed a tear from her cheek. Tresward didn't *cry. There's no time for this. He's dying and your eyes are ... leaking*. She curled over Meri, holding him close. Rocking him, wishing him to live, but unable to make it so. Geneve had seen wounds like his. No one got up from those.

"Geneve." Vertiline's voice was a rasp, a too-blunt file over too-strong metal.

"Leave me."

"Look. Listen." Something in Tilly's voice made Geneve raise her eyes. Beside Vertiline stood Sight of Day, the Feybrind looking unbearably sad, his golden eyes soft like honey. By their feet was the crumpled form of Armitage, the monster's breathing ragged, his back crooked and slumped.

{There is a Storm inside you, Daughter of the Three.} Sight of Day crouched before her. *{Do you know what this means?}*

"It means nothing," she spat. "It's worthless."

{It means there is Sway inside you too.} The Feybrind pointed to the Three above. *{If there was ever a time to call in a favor, now's the moment.}*

"The Three don't listen to me," she hissed. "They *never* listen to me."

{That's because you're asking.} Sight of Day looked to Meri. *{Perhaps you should try demanding for a change.}* He gestured above. *{There's no better time. They're all here, vying for the sun's attention.}*

The ground shook, a sullen, angry beat. Geneve turned to see the impossible; Ormeon slugging through the fortification's fence. She dragged herself to Geneve. Scales were missing from her hide, and her forelimb was gone. A wing dragged, useless and broken. *//MAKE HIM GET UP.//* The dragon held what looked like half a Vhemin in a clawed hand, and she took a bite from it. *//HE NEEDS TO COME BACK TO YOU.//*

"He's dying, Ormeon. Maybe the ancients knew—"

//WITHOUT HIM, ALL IS LOST. HOLOMANCERS ARE THE ONLY ONES WHO CAN GIVE ARMOR OF LIGHT, WINGS OF FURY, AND SHOW THE HEARTS OF OUR ENEMIES.// She finished off the last of her Vhemin snack. *//IN A FEW MINUTES IT WILL BE TOO LATE.//*

"I'm not a god! I can't give back his life."

//DIDN'T YOU LISTEN TO THE CAT? THERE'S NOTHING ABOUT GIVING HERE. YOU NEED TO TAKE IT.// Ormeon gave a sly wink. *//BUT NOT FROM THE THREE. THEY DON'T ... SEE. THIS IS WITHIN YOU.//* She pointed to Armitage. *//ARE YOU GOING TO EAT THAT?//*

Sight of Day bristled. *{He's not for eating.}*

//THAT'S EXACTLY WHAT HE'S FOR. BUT THERE'S PLENTY TO GO AROUND.// The massive dragon lurched for the fence, screams foreshadowing her hunger.

Geneve looked to Meri, touching his face, running a gauntleted finger along his jaw. The young sorcerer wheezed at her touch, then coughed, blood flecking his lips. "Thank you."

"What for?" Geneve heard the misery in her voice.

"For finding me. No one else did. Not ... for the right reasons." Meri gasped, his body shaking with pain. "Keep the wings. They suit you."

"They'll be gone when you ... go," she whispered.

"Then remember them."

"Why, Meri?" Geneve's voice was a wail. "Why couldn't you..." She trailed off.

"Wait? You weren't angry enough, Red. And Requiem needed anointing. Your skymetal blade wasn't made for killing demons. If it were that easy, anyone could do it." His fingers hovered over his wound, as if afraid to touch it. "Killing demons demands sacrifice. A blood price for banishment. It's in the book of High Magic."

"I wish you'd never read that cursed thing."

"Me too," he admitted. "Oh. I think it's time. I've got to go. I ... I love you."

His body relaxed into her arms, his pain leaving with his life. She felt it walk away like breath on the wind. In a moment, all that'd made up this wonderful man would be lost, except in the delicate memories of those who remained.

That won't do. Not today. Geneve glanced at the Three. They weren't quite in alignment, Ikmae peeking out from Cophine's shadow, brother Khiton further behind. Geneve thought about the Sway she'd used to stop Vertiline bleeding out. A tiny touch, a hint of power the Clerics used to bend the world to their will. But still given, meted out by the thimbleful by three gods who'd not shown their *real* faces for hundreds of years.

She lurched to her feet, Meri's blood staining her gauntlets. Geneve felt within, for that spark she'd used to destroy Ahkiban. It was there, and perhaps it had always been. She'd nurtured it through countless years of being denied the Storm, because her father kept her off balance. Her memories were locked in a jewel at his throat, and so Geneve had to *make do*.

There were a hundred things she wanted to say to Meri. The things she'd left unsaid weighed on her, and now it was too late. *By the Three, the things I've left un*done. *I never dreamed of hearth and home, but this man would have been my choice. A family, perhaps, if the Three released me from their service.* All was gone.

No. I will not *allow it.* Geneve clenched her fist, trying to gather the smokey remains of Meri's soul as it drifted from his body. She could *see* the fragments, the gossamer wisps that fled from her touch. As if Meri wanted to go, hungered for the everafter. "Meri, come back to me."

The Sway tugged inside her, a sparrow struggling against a dragon. The weight of a man's life was an impossible thing to buy. It felt hard to ask for such a thing. *No, don't ask. They owe you this one thing. Demand, as a dragon might.*

//I DEMAND ONE THING.// Geneve clenched her fist, a dragon's

voice coming from her throat, ancient, immense, powerful. Too much for a person to hold. *//MERIWETHER DU REEVES, COME BACK TO ME.//*

The wind stilled. Clouds, drifting unconcerned above, scudded to a halt. Geneve felt the whisper of hair against her face, each strand distinct. Her armor was cold, and bright, but held the weight of heaven's regard. The burnished sun on her breastplate wasn't just paint but purpose, flickering to life, ember bright and fierce.

Cophine's pale face split, the moon cracking down the middle, revealing a dark shadowy interior. Behind her, Ikmae's gray sphere shuddered, his moon fracturing the same way, a pale yellow luminance within. Khiton, almost invisible, ruptured, brilliant white breaking free from the fissure. All was soundless, an impossible distance away, happening where the stars held counsel.

Meri's body floundered upright, as if strings connected his arms and shoulders to the puppet master moons above. He coughed as his soul rushed into the gap it left, and he clutched his stomach and the bloody rent in his clothes. Meri's eyes were wide, and he turned a circle three times, looking about wildly. "What? What's happening?"

"I forgot to say something," Geneve said. "I love you."

Then the world slipped sideways, and she fell, a long, trailing eternity of motion she wasn't conscious to see the end of.

Chapter Forty-Three

When life rushed back to Meriwether, it felt like someone ran a cart of bricks into his heart. Geneve fell beside him, and he stumbled forward to catch her. She was heavy, armor, purpose, and the gray of her skin impossible weights to carry.

"Help me!" But Armitage was down. The strongest of them was broken.

Sight of Day came to his side, fur-soft and gentle. Golden eyes marveled at Meriwether. They eased the Knight to the ground. *{Look at you, walking and talking like nothing's happened.}*

"Stuff's happened." Meriwether touched his stomach, feeling smooth skin where his lifeblood leaked out moments earlier. "I mean, a lot of stuff." He cast his gaze upward. The moons above were broken, drifting, and as he watched them separate, they faded from view. "Now there's something you don't see every day."

{What's it like to die?}

"Pretty average. Couldn't recommend it." There was too much going on, and not enough time. By the Three, he'd just *died*. And now, speaking of the Three ... well, they were gone. Had three gods fallen so he could draw breath? What kind of responsibility did that leave him?

Meriwether looked about. *All that can wait. One thing remains to be done.* "Where's Vertiline?"

☞

MERIWETHER RAN THROUGH THE CAMP. *TILLY'S GONE AFTER MY father, alone. She's gone to kill the man who's hurt us so very much, and she'll do the job right. I'm not even mad. What I am is concerned.* Because Leander du Reeves was a monster. Always had been. And coupled with his monstrosity was a deep and abiding concern for *planning*. The man never went into a room with only one exit. He didn't put eggs in one basket: he outsourced all egg laying, collecting, and omelet making to motivated minions across a hundred organizations.

Vertiline couldn't beat him. Not with a glass sword, metal hand, and anger. It'd take more. Meriwether wore illusory armor, which was better than steel, but not by much. *Glowing lines of light won't stop a spear.*

It's going to take luck, and perhaps an illusionist of equal power. Meriwether wasn't sure how he felt about that. His father had always been *big*. A broad-shouldered brute who shouted when calm words would do, and used his size when he didn't have to. Meriwether returned, but wasn't the scared boy he used to be.

No: he was now a scared man, but he could fashion dreams into reality and had the High Magic on his side. Or, a tiny bit of High Magic, which had to be enough. Because it would suck if Geneve brought him back from death's door, only for his fool self to die with Tilly.

The fortified encampment was full of once-Vhemin fingerprints. Tents lay abandoned, some collapsed, but most with their flaps hanging loose. Discarded weapons without angry-looking Vhemin to operate them lay beside fire pits where coals had long before burned to ash.

Meriwether had a little time before he caught up with Vertiline, and he used that to pose questions. *What am I going to do, exactly* was number one. Second on the list was *Did the love of my life just speak with a dragon's voice to pull my soul into my body?* That felt important and deserved more time than he had.

A little further down was an annoying part of him that said, *You should have stayed with her*, but Sight of Day was a better guardian and so this was easily silenced.

A smaller-but-still-significant pavilion was ahead. It had the look of a barracks for important persons, and since Leander thought himself the most important person of all, Meriwether headed right for it.

He dashed inside, swatting canvas aside. Within wasn't the usual gloom you'd expect from such a place. Light globes hung on slender chains. The interior was a collection of comfortable-looking divans with small tables dispersed between them. The tables had grapes, wine, and cold meats. All divans were empty.

At the far end of the pavilion was a rack that contained an ugly assortment of magical implements. There were orbs, perhaps weapons or for scrying. Wands and scepters squared off against staves for most-impressive-magical-artefact awards. Tomes, both musty and new, huddled shoulder to shoulder, as if the elderly were providing advice to the young.

Beside the shelving was Leander du Reeves. Out of breath, flushed, and looking really ... old.

"Hi, Dad," Meriwether said. "You look like shit. Desperate, lost, and like someone's killed your favorite dog. Except you don't have a dog, and if you did, you'd be the asshole who killed it."

Leander turned, a scepter in his hand. "Son, it's not too late."

"It was too late when you left a roadmap of pain on my skin. It was *definitely* too late when you conspired to kill me and Geneve."

"I never wanted—"

"The Vhemin say otherwise." Meriwether circled around the divan collection. "They've built a powerful army that looks ready to raze Ravenswall to the waterline. Except I brought a Tresward Knight, her dragon, and a couple good friends."

Leander's look turned sly. "But they're not here, are they."

"No."

His father's face flowed like molasses, slowly at first, then forming into Meriwether's features. Same jaw, same eyes, and same well-tended beard. Leander raised the scepter, pointed it at Meriwether, and screamed, "Die!"

Nothing happened. Meriwether examined his nails. "Out of interest, what was supposed to happen?"

"The problem with hired help is they've no enthusiasm for detail." Leander tossed the scepter aside, grabbed another and repeated the processes. This time, putrescent-green light speared from the scepter, striking Meriwether on the chest.

Light scattered like raindrops from his illusory armor. Where vile green hit the ground, it smoked and hissed. Meriwether smiled. "Looks like my magic's good for something."

Leander held his scepter up as if trying to find a cheap charlatan's trick at play. His eyes were wide, like someone just insulted not just him, but his entire house. "That's ... *impossible!*"

"Evidence says otherwise."

"Bah." Leander tossed the scepter aside, but kept Meriwether's face.

"Did you really say, 'Bah?' What kind of nonsense do they teach at evil overlord school?"

"Real magic. Not like the trifling thing at your belt." Leander smiled with Meriwether's face.

With a sinking feeling, Meriwether reached for the tome of High Magic. His belt felt empty. *It's probably an illusion. He's made me think it's not there.* Not that it helped; his fingers told him the tome was gone. At Leander's hip, a similar tome materialized. "I'll allow that's a clever thing. I expect you fancy to take my place. Work from within, corrupting the throne, all that kind of thing?"

Leander-as-Meriwether nodded. "It's worked before."

"It won't work this time."

"You've no idea what you're talking about," Leander snapped. "I control an army."

"Controlled. Past tense. Our dragon's lunching on them right now."

"And I have a coterie of magicians at my beck and call. I've ancient relics poised to strike. And I've summoned *these*." His hand moved to his side, and a shadow materialized from the air.

Meriwether took a step back. The demon his father called was pale-skinned, like a waterlogged corpse. It had no eyes, but a mouth so wide as to put Vhemin to shame drooled saliva to the floor.

"Ah," Meriwether said.

"Quite."

"Okay. So, let's make that go away." Meriwether clapped his hands and said a Word. The demon shimmered, then snapped out like a candle flame in a southerly storm.

Leander goggled. "But ... I took your book!"

"Memorized it." Meriwether tapped his temple. "I don't know what all the words are, but I've pictures of them in my head. I'll work it out. Also, that wasn't really a demon. More like, a quarter of one. Ahkiban was the real deal. These things are frightening, sure, but *please*, father. We're both masters of illusion. It was as real as shadow at night."

"Then this will have to do." Leander drew his blade, striding toward Meriwether. If he had any concerns about murdering his own son, they didn't show.

Not that it surprised Meriwether even a little. Longevity hadn't been assured when he still had his father's roof over his head. Meriwether raised a hand. "Hold up."

Leander paused. "What for?" He seemed genuinely curious.

"You should be wondering why I didn't think the me-as-you think would work this time." Meriwether shrugged. "It seems an important detail."

"Okay, I'll bite." Leander flourished his blade. "Why not?" He stiffened, face twisting in a rictus of pain. The blade tumbled from his hands as his fingers clawed at his chest. The front of his tunic stretched, tented, then parted as a slender blade of glass emerged. It glimmered with soft yellow light. Leander's blood didn't stick to it. Meriwether's father tried to scream, but trying to suck air in with a sword in your chest seemed tricky.

Vertiline stepped around Leander, sword whipping free. The glass blade caught the glow of the globes above as she spun. The blade went through Leander's neck, and his head bounced to the floor. Leander's eyes were wide with shock, and if Meriwether didn't miss his guess, not a little surprise.

Blood fountained as Leander's headless body staggered three paces to the left. Vertiline turned her head from the spray, sword point-down, waiting until the monster that had sired Meriwether fell to the earth for the last time.

"Because of her," Meriwether said. "You really pissed her off."

"Not bad, sinner." Tilly flicked her sword, but the blade was clean. She sheathed it.

Meriwether considered his father's body, still wearing Meriwether's face. "You knew it was me because of some inner guiding light, right? You know me really well, all of that."

"No."

"Then ... how'd you know which one to kill?"

She gave him a sly smile. "I didn't have to stop at one."

"Tilly!"

"I'm joking, sinner." She ran her metal hand through sky-pale hair. "Different clothes. And you've got glowing armor."

"Of course." Meriwether looked at his own tired threads, hole still punched in his shirt. *Like father, like son.* "Thank you."

She eyed him, almost speculatively. "You don't seem cut up. Pardon the pun."

"Hah. We each grieve in our own way." He held his hand out in an *after you* gesture toward the pavilion's flap. "I've done mine already. I left home eight, maybe nine years ago. I said my goodbyes."

She nodded, but without a lot of agreement in it. "If you say so."

"I—"

"It's fine." Vertiline made for the pavilion's exit, her path taking her past Meriwether. She stopped before him and put a hand on his shoulder. "If you need to talk—"

"I'm not really into that kind of thing."

"Or drink."

"I can do that."

She let her hand fall. "Then let's clean up. The dragon will eat the entire enemy army if we're not careful. No prisoners to question makes for sloppy intel." Vertiline left him in the tent without a backward glance.

He suspected she knew he lied. It's why she left him with his father's body, and hadn't looked at his face when she touched his shoulder. She'd let his tears fall without comment, not remarked on the shake in his voice, and unless he missed his guess, she stood right outside, but a respectful distance away.

Meriwether sank to his knees, hugging himself, and trying to hold in the keening noise that came forth. He didn't want it to. He hated himself for it. But it wouldn't stop, and neither would his tears.

Chapter Forty-Four

When Geneve woke, her first thought was, *Where's Meri?*

She sat upright, and found she wasn't lying on a battlefield. There was no smell of blood, or the screams of the dying. Someone had taken off her armor. Geneve was on a bed—soft, like landed gentry might use, rather than the hard surfaces of the Tresward, or the even less forgiving ground of the road.

There was a chair beside the bed. Sight of Day was on it, head back, mouth slightly open. He snored, a tiny buzz like a woodland animal might make if it was truly comfortable. The room was small, with stone walls and a thatched roof. She could see the eves from the bed; no one spent time or money putting fancy finishing on it.

Quietly as she could, she got up from the bed. Her legs whispered under cotton sheets. The Feybrind didn't move, his buzzing continuing like the tiniest, happiest bee. Geneve padded from the bed to the door, years of Tresward training on silence and perfect movement almost betrayed by the ache of her body. *By the Three, I move like an aged crone.*

A robe made of cotton, rather than silk, was hung on the foot of the bed. She put it on, feeling the comforting softness of it. *Someone wore this, once. Loved and cared for it. Who left it for me?*

Geneve gave a quick look-about for her sword and armor, but saw neither. The room had Sight of Day, an old but otherwise nice bed, and a small table with a few for-the-injured accoutrements. She ignored those, because she wasn't injured. Not in any way you could see.

The door proved trickier to open silently, but she achieved it by dint of moving very, very slowly. It wasn't hard to do, because her body felt weak, slow, and frail. Geneve almost needed a breather by the time she made the door, so taking her time opening it wasn't hard.

Outside, sunlight. Bright, but not cruel. The sun blazed, but in a happy way. A porch was at her feet, and beyond that a small garden. She smelled lavender, admiring a bee flying between the small flowers. Beyond the garden was a fence, gated but not locked, and a field with overgrown grass beyond.

In the field Ormeon curled. Whole, and healed. Wings straight, all four limbs accounted for. The dragon lifted her head when Geneve stepped onto the porch. Geneve touched her fingers to her lips. *Quiet. Sight of Day is sleeping.*

She padded across the porch, navigated around the gate like an invalid, and walked to the dragon. Her limbs freed up as she moved, and she realized she was hungry. *Starving*, like she'd never eaten in her eighteen years. "Hello, dragon."

//HELLO, DRAGONRIDER.// Ormeon leaned her massive nuzzle closer. Geneve felt the heat of a dragon's breath, but no sulfur or ash. A slight hint of cinnamon, if anything.

The door to the cabin burst open, Sight of Day hurtling forth. He slowed as he realized the dragon was merely speaking, not murdering. *{Sorry. I dozed off.}*

//YOU ARE A CAT.//

{I've the keenest senses of any of you.} The Feybrind examined his feet. *{It was unforgivable.}*

//THERE'S BEEN A LOT GOING ON.//

"Where is Meri?" The question tumbled from her lips, three words wrapped in fear, a kind of desperate anxiety puddling in her stomach. The sky above held no moons, broken or otherwise. "What happened to the Three?"

//SOLVING PROBLEMS,// Ormeon said, probably meaning Meri,

but it may as easily apply to the Three. *//I SAID HE SHOULD ALLOW ME TO EAT THEM.//*

"Eat who?"

//IT'S BETTER IF YOU SEE FOR YOURSELF.// The dragon's jaws widened in a smirk. *//IF YOU THINK BEATING AN ARMY WITH DEMONS AT THE HEAD IS TRICKY, WAIT UNTIL YOU GET A LOAD OF THIS.//*

SIGHT OF DAY FED HER BREAKFAST. OR LUNCH, JUDGING BY THE sun's position in the sky. Cold smoked game of some kind, fruit, and honeycomb. Then they left on Ormeon's back, the dragon having no trouble with two, although Sight of Day clutched her tight about the waist, his golden eyes shut. Neither knew what happened to Wincuf or the remaining Tresward.

Geneve never tired of riding on dragonback. Her armor and sword were safe, but putting them on took some doing. She was weak, and didn't want to face the instruments of war. She'd had enough death for a time. But she did it anyway, because Iz taught her that sometimes you needed to do hard things, perhaps for your entire life. *I wish I could talk to him again.*

//HE WILL ALWAYS BE WITH YOU. IT IS THE NATURE OF YOUR KIND.// Ormeon banked over a field. Geneve didn't know where they were. Somewhere far from Ravenswall. The countryside was unfamiliar to her, although she'd not seen much of Or'sen from the sky.

"Where are we?" The wind stole her words, but she knew Ormeon could understand her.

//THE DU PARNEER ESTATES. THEY'RE SOUTH OF DU REEVES, BOTH WEST OF RAVENSWALL.// Ormeon's wings beat the air, taking them higher. *//THE HOLOMANCER WANTED YOU FAR AWAY WHILE YOU RESTED.//*

"Rested? How long have I been out?"

//TWO WEEKS.//

"Two weeks?!"

//AS I SAID, THERE'S A LOT GOING ON. YOU ALMOST DIED BRINGING HIM BACK FROM THE EDGE. YOU LEFT MUCH OF YOURSELF BEHIND. IT NEEDED TO FIND ITS WAY BACK. THE THREE'S LIGHT WASN'T HERE TO GUIDE YOU HOME.//

"I let them down." Geneve thought of Armitage, lying crumpled on the battlefield. She'd fallen at the last stretch, when it was most important. She remembered the Three's moons breaking as she'd demanded Meri's life. *What have I done?*

//NO. YOU SAVED THEM ALL.// Ormeon grumbled, a small puff of smoke coming from her jaws to be lost against the sky. *//NO ONE COULD HAVE KILLED AHKIBAN. NOT EVEN A DRAGON.//*

"But ... Meri did that."

//MERIWETHER DU REEVES HELD NO SWORD WHEN THE DEMON FELL.//

"You know what I mean." The dragon was silent for a time. Sight of Day shifted against her back, his arms not easing even a millimeter. Geneve put an armored hand on his. *It's okay.*

//THERE ARE ALWAYS THREE,// Ormeon said. *//THREE GODS. THREE KNIGHTS. OR ... ONE DRAGON, ONE KNIGHT, AND ONE HOLOMANCER.//*

"Working together?"

//NOT TOGETHER. AS ONE.//

"That's what I said."

//NO, IT'S NOT.//

Geneve growled. "Fine. Are you at least going to tell me what's going on in Ravenswall?"

//TREASON,// the dragon leered.

As Ormeon banked over Ravenswall, Geneve could see the extent of the damage. Bodies were scattered for klicks around the city, but mostly clustered near the west wall's massive breach. From dragonwing, it looked like a dropped bag of poppy seeds, thousands upon thousands of tiny shapes littering the landscape.

The gift of her helmet's vision sharpened up the detail more than she wanted. The ground didn't hold bodies: there were dead humans, Vhemin, and a handful of the beautiful Feybrind. Crows took wing as Ormeon dipped lower. Not a mere handful, but in their hundreds, fat and gorged on the plentiful meat they found spoiling in the sun.

The streets were arteries clogging with people, a lifeblood getting denser and more sluggish as it approached the castle. People looked like they shouted, and not in the happy way. At least they weren't riot-ing. If anything, they looked lost. *There's so few left, but even less supplies coming into the city.* Geneve saw no wagon trains en route. The supplies within the walls were all they had, and after weeks of nothing coming in, people would be down to their last bushel.

The keep's gates were open, but black-armored Queensguard held a line before them. Within the walls were more serious-looking Queens-guard, surrounding the queen herself. Morgan wore red, but dark like blood, her gown elegant but somber. To her left, back a couple steps, was Picotee du Parneer. Before her were a hundred Vhemin, and *they* looked angry. The kind of anger that came with desperation, hardship, and the threat of life's end a conversation away.

Between the Vhemin and Morgan stood Meri, Vertiline, and against all odds, Armitage. Beside Armitage was Barret. Near Vertiline was Morning Song. A Queensguard had his blade bared, the point at Meri's heart.

//I SEE YOUR THOUGHTS.// Ormeon pulled her wings tight to her armored bulk, dropping like a stone. Vhemin looked up, saw the inbound death-by-dragon, and scattered as much as they were able. The dragon impacted the ground with a crunch Geneve felt in her teeth.

She vaulted from the dragon's back, landing light on her feet despite injuries. She pushed through the remaining crowd, Sight of Day on her heels, making it to Meri's side. Geneve didn't touch him, although her skin craved his. She stared at the Queensguard with the bared blade. "Drop your steel."

The guard looked at her, then the dragon. Ormeon chose that moment to rumble suggestively. The guard, an earnest-looking young man with freckles, took a half-step back before the iron in his spine fixed his feet to paved stone. "The queen said—"

"The queen better revise whatever she said." Geneve pulled her helmet off, shaking out red hair. "Meriwether du Reeves is under my protection, and you will not have him."

"Uh," Meri said. "It's not like that."

Geneve gave him a little side-eye. "There was a sword at your throat."

"That's what they do, when they knight you," he explained. "It was a little higher than my throat. This gentleman," Meri held his palm out to the Queensguard, "is my Lord Epifan du Callisto. Since we're generally short on royalty, Queen Morgan asked if he would do the honor of ratifying House du Reeves in my name."

Morgan's lip quirked. "Does this meet with your satisfaction, Knight Chevalier Geneve?"

"I feel stupid," she admitted. "I saw the sword. I saw the Vhemin. I thought—"

"You thought you'd bring a dragon to a sword fight." The queen nodded. "We are making Meriwether du Reeves the commander of our armies. Picotee du Parneer holds the seas in our name already."

Geneve turned, nice and slow, and eyeballed Ormeon. "You said treason."

//THAT COMES LATER. IT'S WHAT THE SNACKS ARE FOR.//

"The Vhemin?"

//THAT'S ONE WORD FOR THEM.// The dragon arched her neck to look at the surrounding monsters. *//THE OTHER IS SNACKS.//*

"I was telling Her Majesty I'm no commander." Meri shrugged. "I said they should put you in charge."

"You what?" Geneve blinked. Her body felt tired, overused, and her mind hadn't quite caught up yet. "I'm not a lord."

"That's fixable," Meri said.

"Irregardless of who commands the armies of Ravenswall, Lord du Reeves is awarded all estates previously held by his father." Queen Morgan eyed the dragon, daring Ormeon to say something. "He has earned it."

Epifan du Callisto edged forward. "Perhaps I could continue." His voice mirrored his youth, all shaky edges and a hint of a stutter, but the iron in his spine didn't wilt. Meri knelt, and Epifan touched the sword to each of his shoulders. "In the queen's name, rise Lord du Reeves."

"Thanks." Meri stood. "Back to commander of the armies." He took a step away from Geneve, then held his hands out to her in a *see?* gesture. "May I present Geneve, Knight Chevalier of the Tresward. Perhaps the most capable warrior I've ever met. As skilled in battle strategy as she is with a blade. Savior of Ravenswall not once, but twice." He offered Geneve a small smile, fashioned just for her. "There is no one better."

Queen Morgan inclined her chin. "We thought the Knight's alliances were with the Tresward."

"I don't want the job," Geneve blurted. "I've got things to do."

"Things that will work a lot better with an army," Meri hissed. "We've an organization of assassins to run down, and demons to kill. This isn't a one-woman job."

"The queen is right, Meri." Geneve crossed her arms, armor *clinking*. "I'm sworn to the Tresward. What if there's a conflict between those two forces?"

"I was afraid you'd say that." The sorcerer made a show of looking at the Vhemin behind him, all glancing at the dragon like they wanted to run, but were too damn ornery to give Ormeon the pleasure. "It's where the treason comes in."

Heser the Cheg shouldered in from the left. "You can't put the Vhemin in charge of the army."

"*I'm* not doing anything," Meri explained. "The *queen* is putting the Vhemin in charge."

Morgan bristled. "I haven't said—"

"And the reason she's doing that," Meri rolled on like a thunderstorm, "is because the Vhemin are good at two things."

"Fighting and fucking," Armitage supplied.

"See, the problem we've got is everyone who needs something doesn't have it." Meri looked like he wanted to pace but didn't have the real estate. "The Vhemin live in a plague-ridden desert. The Feybrind want safety but fight the monsters. Humans soak up everything in their struggle for power. Aged men like my father have too much, and everyone suffers." He smoothed his shirt. Geneve noticed it was the same one he'd been run through while wearing, but someone had cleaned and darned it. *Still not wearing expensive things.* "The Vhemin are made for war. It's far, far better if they make war for *us.*"

"And how would we balance their predilection for brutality?" The queen arched an eyebrow. If she was concerned about the proximity of a couple hundred monsters, she didn't even have the grace to sweat.

"Morning Song," Meri said, like it was obvious.

"Singing won't—"

"Her." Meri pointed at Morning Song, who's emerald eyes held a little bit of panic. "Spymaster Morning Song. The Vhemin command the armies of Ravenswall. Yes, Heser the Cheg, I'm aware there are tiny matters to be worked out. Who reports to who, and whether humans will take orders from a monster." He waved his hand, as if to say *details.* "The Feybrind keep our secrets. They don't want land, or power. Feybrind don't have royalty. They just want to live."

{Do I get a say?} Morning Song's panic looked to be about to boil over.

"No," Meri said. "No one except the queen gets a say. She's got to work out whether a united kingdom is worth a little rough edges."

"Rough edges?" Heser the Cheg blurted. "You're giving powerful positions to the enemy!"

"Hmm," Meri said. "Can I suggest we take this inside? There's someone I'd like you to talk to."

GENEVE FOLLOWED MERI, MORE BEMUSED THAN ANYTHING. SHE asked him *what's going on* and he'd said *a thing,* which didn't help, but since no one seemed to be murdering each other this instant she didn't have a lot to do.

Morgan led the way, red gown sweeping in her wake. Heser the Cheg kept trying to get her attention, and she kept on ignoring him. Meri had his hands clasped, a small smile on his lips. Morning Song loped long, looking between Meri and the queen, as if hoping someone would take this terrible nightmare away by simply killing her.

They wound through the keep, trending slightly downward, until they arrived at an infirmary. Within were a lot of humans, and a few Vhemin. The Vhemin were mostly tending the humans; while a few monsters took up cot space, primary care was humans.

Geneve saw a few Feybrind, too. Like the humans, they were injured, monsters tending them as well. Heser the Cheg's eyes bulged at the sight. "What's the meaning of this?"

Meri spread his hands. "Vhemin are excellent at fighting and, uh..."

"Fucking," Armitage supplied.

"Quite. And the fighting skills repertoire isn't complete without aid skills. Here we have Vhemin, tending for humans, after—"

"After they murdered us!" Heser the Cheg blurted. He swung to Morgan. "My queen, we must get you to safety."

"We're quite safe," the queen replied. "We set this up."

"Evil sorcery has taken her mind again." Heser the Cheg spoke like this was a revelation given from on high. "We must find the villain and kill them."

"For the first time in months we think clearly." Morgan raised her voice. "Barret!"

A familiar crooked-backed Vhemin walked forward. The Vhemin looked at Heser the Cheg with suspicion, but didn't leap on him. "What is it?"

"What is it *my queen*," Heser the Cheg said.

"Have you been told to get fucked today?" Barret crossed her arms.

"Uh. No." Heser the Cheg looked lost.

"Allow me to be the first. Get fucked." She turned to Morgan. "What is it? There are people dying. A lot of them. You're truly fucked. I'm trying to unfuck things. Talking isn't unfucking."

"Where is Epifan du Callisto? Ah, there you are." The queen beckoned the white-faced lordling forward. She waved a hand. "Do the thing."

"The ... thing?"

"Lands, titles. That thing." Morgan sighed, like it'd been a long day, and dim-witted fools weren't going to shorten it.

Epifan drew steel. Barret took it from him like candy from a baby. She leaned in, nice and close, blade at Lord du Callisto's throat. "Do you want to die?"

"Again?" he squealed, looking to Geneve.

"Barret," Geneve barked. "They want to give you a promotion. The blade is to knight you."

"Like a Tresward?" The Vhemin didn't budge.

"Not even a little bit," Meri explained. "What will happen is this. Epifan will touch the sword to your shoulders, after you kneel. Then—"

"I ain't kneeling."

"After you kneel, he'll ask you to rise. Once you're on your feet, you'll be Lord Marshal of Ravenswall. You'll be in charge of the army." Meri tried a smile on the monster.

She let Epifan go. "I already lead the army."

"Officially." Meri tried tucking a few more stars in his smile.

"Officially, I lead the army. The human army's fucked. Most are dead or injured. Vhemin are starting to get back on their feet, because no one told you clowns about cutting our heads off."

"I did," Armitage said. "I told 'em a bunch of times."

"Thank you," Barret sneered. "Everyone's looking to me to lead, because I didn't die when I wore the blue-runed armor. There are hundreds of hungry, tired Vhemin out there. They want freedom. They want to be *paid*."

Meri clapped Heser the Cheg on the shoulder. "This is who I wanted you to meet. What I'd suggest is taking a walk with Barret and working things out."

Heser the Cheg looked as lost as an orphan. "Work things out?"

"Yes. While you're doing that, I suggest you raise the matter of who's going to be in charge. Barret will lead the Vhemin, and she will need a leftenant to lead the human contingent." Meri gave a small cough. "That is, if her Majesty agrees."

"Her Majesty wants to sit down." Morgan looked at Meri like she was appreciating something anew. Geneve didn't like that look, a fist of jealously curling in her gut.

"Her Majesty did ask me to act as her reeve." Meri smiled. "It comes with the title, I believe."

"So, who are we hanging for treason?" Heser the Cheg seemed stuck on that tiny detail.

"It was going to be me, until just now." Meri brightened. "I think we're all pleased it didn't come to that, aren't we?"

Chapter Forty-Five

The day wore on like an old wound. Meriwether felt threadbare by the end of it, but one thing kept a spring in his step when everything else seemed lost. *Geneve*. The red-haired warrior walked the corridors with him, keeping her peace more often than not, but also holding a close distance.

The sun had set long ago when they walked outside. The Vhemin here had been pressed into service. Morning Song left with Sight of Day, as if the two alone could fashion a spy network out of fragments.

Ormeon waited for them in the dim light. The Three no longer watched from above, but for Cophine's absence the stars shone on. As near as Geneve knew, the moons hadn't been seen in the sky since the battle. The dragon stretched. *//IT HAS TAKEN YOU A LONG TIME TO DO NOTHING.//*

"We did a lot," Meriwether said. "There was a lot of talking."

The dragon grinned, a glow from within silhouetting her teeth. *//WE VIEW DOING QUITE DIFFERENTLY.//*

"You just want to eat people," Geneve said. "Vhemin aren't for eating."

Ormeon sobered. *//YOU DON'T UNDERSTAND HOW WE'RE MADE. DO YOU REMEMBER THE ... TEMPLE?//*

Geneve looked away. "Not a lot."

"I do," Meriwether said. "I remember cylinders of glass, and Vhemin reduced to the consistency of rotted porridge."

//DRAGONS ARE MADE FROM THE SKINS OF THEIR ENEMIES.//

"Hold up. *Their* enemies? You weren't ... *alive* to have enemies."

//VEHEMENT SYSTEMS ARCHITECTURES ARE THE SAME. WE ARE LOCKED IN AN ETERNAL WAR. OUR CREATORS WANTED THE RIGHT INCENTIVES.// The dragon sounded almost sad as her head swung to the sky. *//TO HEAL, I NEED TO EAT VHEMIN.//*

"They don't need to eat dragons to heal," Geneve said. "They heal just fine without you."

//THERE WERE COMPETING DESIGN PROFILES.// Ormeon gusted a sigh, hot and dry. *//THE MANIFEST IS CORRUPT. THERE ISN'T MUCH WITHIN IT THAT LOOKS LIKE THE WORLD OF TODAY. ONE THING IS CERTAIN.//*

"Don't leave us guessing," Meriwether said. "It's been a long—"

//DAY, I KNOW. YOU SAID. WOULD YOU LIKE TO SEE A SURPRISE?//

"No." Geneve touched Meriwether's arm. "We've had enough surprises. We need to—"

//IT'S A GOOD SURPRISE.//

She growled. "Enough, dragon!" Meriwether laughed, and Geneve glared at him. "What is it?"

"Only you, my love." He stepped closer, stealing a kiss. "Only you would face a dragon and command her silence."

"She was annoying me."

Ormeon drew back. *//I'M SORRY THE FATE OF THE WORLD IS SO TRIFLING TO YOU.//*

"Don't be huffy." Geneve crossed her arms.

//HUFFY?//

"Yes. Now be still." The Knight turned from the dragon's wide-eyed incredulity. Meriwether felt her full regard. It made him feel small, but also awesome, because she was his, and he hers. "How do you feel?"

He took a step back. "What?"

"You. Feelings." She looked down, red hair falling across her face. "I'm no good at this. I wish Tilly was here."

"Tilly is *terrible* at feelings," Meriwether offered. "She is the exact example of someone worse than you. Not," he hurried on at her expression, darkening like storm clouds, "that you're bad at it. If I knew what 'it' is. Was. Um." He felt himself run down like an old clock.

"This." She flung her arm to the west. He took her meaning to be *the battle where we almost died*. When she spoke, her voice was softer, smaller somehow. "Your father's dead."

Meriwether felt his stomach churn. "I've been trying not to think of it."

"I know."

"Because I don't want to think."

"I know that too." She touched his arm, her armored fingers delicate against his sleeve. "But it's okay."

"It's really not. He was a madman. A murderer." Meriwether's words, slow at first, came in a tumble. Geneve let him speak, her eyes gentle, her hand not leaving his arm. "He tried to break me with the lash. Starved me when my gifts didn't work to his satisfaction. Kept me locked up, or paraded me about at his fancy. Killed my mother, drove my friends away, drove me away..." His voice caught, a tiny sound that *couldn't* be a sob there.

A tiny puddle of quiet spread from her, broken up by Ormeon's steady, comforting breathing, a bellows at his back. "Have you said goodbye?"

"I don't want to."

"You need to. You must." Geneve tugged his arm. "Come. We'll be there before you know it."

⁂

THE TERROR OF FLYING BY DRAGON DIDN'T REACH MERIWETHER through the morass of his thoughts and feelings. Ormeon took them over the battlefield, swooping low over the abandoned enemy encampment. She landed, leaving Geneve to lead Meriwether to the tent where Leander lay.

It was as he remembered. Trinkets. Spoiled food. Divans that looked faded in the pale starlight without Cophine's gaze. And, of course, Leander du Reeves, laying on the ground like a commoner. No rites, no care, not a soul to mourn his passing. The body wasn't pretty after two weeks in a tent in all manner of weather. The smell was almost physical, like an extra person there with them.

Meriwether stalled at the pavilion's entrance, but Geneve dragged him inside to his father's side. He stood shoulder to shoulder with her, reaching for words that wouldn't come. "I should be better at this by now. You'd think after my ... *experience* I'd know better."

"Say what you feel." Geneve sighed. "I wish I could have with my father. No, don't interrupt. I know it's not the same thing. That my father was basically kind, but misguided. Yours had a perfect path, but was without character. As opposite as they could be, yet ... we both need to say goodbye."

Meriwether clenched his hands. "What would you say?"

Geneve crouched by Leander's corpse. "I'd say I was grateful."

"You ... what?"

She smoothed hair from his father's brow. Leander's skin was dark, mottled, the body giving in to decay. She didn't seem to mind, tugging his shirt straight, then smoothing it with an armored hand. "He brought all of us to war. The Vhemin, doing what they do, against the Feybrind, fighting for their lives. Us, caught in the middle, and demons, hungering from the sidelines. Lord du Reeves almost killed Armitage. If not for one ornery dragon," her lip quirked, "his army of blue-runed monsters would have swarmed the highest seat in Or'sen. For all that, I'm thankful." Geneve stood. "He gave me you."

Meriwether didn't realize he was moving until he'd made it outside, to the cool night air. Its caress cooled him, comforted him. *I want to be sick. I want to hide. I want to cry.* He felt Geneve at his side, her slow pace quiet as always. "I can't be thankful. I ... *can't.*"

"You asked what I would say. Not you."

He thought about that. "I would wish for time to do it again. Perhaps if I'd been smarter, or stronger—"

"Meri—"

"No, listen. If I'd not run, I might have been *part* of what he needed. Stopped all," Meriwether gestured at the rows of tents, the bodies, the ruin, "*this*. Or, made it less. Tempered his burning ambition. Something like that."

"Do you think you could have?"

"I don't know. I should have tried."

Geneve walked a few paces past him, eyes on the moonless sky above. "Then I never would have met you. Or our blades would have crossed. I'd have killed you, and all without knowing," her fingers touched her breastplate over her heart, "this."

"Was it worth the price?" His words tasted bitter on his lips.

"I don't know." She shrugged. "But we've paid it anyway. Life is too short to bargain once all's done." Geneve glanced at him over her shoulder. "I wouldn't trade *us* for anything."

"Because we'll save the world from demons?"

"Because I love you." She turned away, striding toward Ormeon's shadowed bulk.

Meriwether turned to the tent. *Go back inside? Sure.* He walked in, seeing the same things, but feeling better for Geneve's words. He crouched by his father's side. "I'm sorry, for so many things. Most of all, that we didn't love each other. Or, that you didn't love me. Because, save me, I loved you. I'll carry the weight of that for all my days. If I'd been a little more *her*, I could have done something about it." He sniffed. "Goodbye, Dad. I love you. I wish you could've seen it." Meriwether left the pavilion. Ormeon waited outside. He wondered how he'd missed the weight of the dragon's tread on the ground, but maybe his lack of attention wasn't so surprising. "Hello, dragon."

//HELLO, HOLOMANCER. YOU'RE WRONG, OF COURSE.//

"Sorry?"

//ALL FATHERS LOVE THEIR SONS.//

"Is that in the manifest?" Meriwether turned away. "I'm sorry. That was unfair."

//IT'S NOT IN THE MANIFEST. IT'S WRIT ON THE CANVAS OF THE HEAVENS. IT BEATS IN THE BURNING HEART OF ALL THE STARS IN THE SKY. THE DIRT UNDER YOUR FEET

REMEMBERS IT. SO SHOULD YOU.// She leaned down, nose a meter from his. *//ARE YOU READY?//*

"I guess so." Meriwether walked past the dragon, heading for Geneve. She was a hundred meters away. The Knight took his hand in hers as he turned to watch. The dragon breathed deep, fire blasting out. The heat washed over them as the dragon created a funeral pyre of such majesty even the Three would be able to see it, if they still rode the heavens. Ash and smoke rose on light steps to the vacant seats of the gods.

Leander du Reeves was gone.

Chapter Forty-Six

*I*T'S TIME FOR YOUR SURPRISE.// Ormeon took them toward the waterfront. Geneve clutched Meri's arms to her as they flew. He'd been quiet since they left his father's side, thoughts around him like an intricately woven cloak. She wished she could help him, as he had her, when Iz died.

I'm not good at those things. I was made to stand as the bright shield of the world. This is ... something else.

Ormeon banked low. Geneve heard something that might be accused of a *whoop!* from Meri. The dragon looked back at them, grinning her balefire teeth, before tucking her wings tight and dropping to the wharves.

The dock area wasn't as occupied as it might have been. Before the attack, it'd been frequented by sailors and those trying to profit from them. It still had a few tired whores and merchants selling meat of questionable origin, but there wasn't much joy to be had. *Many of the people who used to work here are gone. It didn't matter what they did ... they died anyway.* Most people ran at the sight of Ormeon. They might have heard she was a friend, but it was quite different to see a fire-breathing monster land beside you.

Geneve slid from Ormeon's back, then helped Meri down. The

sorcerer stood, hands on hips. "Ho, dragon. Here we are. Where's the surprise? All I see is people like us. Tired. Sad. Missing those they love."

//THE MANIFEST IS WRONG ON MANY THINGS, BUT A CONSTANT IS HOW VIOLENT YOU ARE.// Ormeon gazed to the Three above. *//DID YOU KNOW YOUR BODIES WERE FORGED IN STARS EONS PAST?//*

Geneve glanced at Meri. "I fail to see—"

//WHAT YOU SHOULD SEE IS YOU'RE ALL MADE OF THE SAME THINGS. THIS WORLD. THE AIR YOU BREATHE. THE CLOTHES ON YOUR BACK. IT'S ALL STARDUST.// She sighed, a huff only a dragon could make so epic. *//ALL EXCEPT THE DEMONS.//*

Geneve stiffened. "We fought and killed them."

//THEY AREN'T MADE IN THE HEARTS OF STARS, BUT DON'T MAKE THE MISTAKE OF THINKING THERE ARE ONLY A FEW OF THEM. THAT'S WHAT UNMADE THIS WORLD. THEY ARE AS NUMEROUS AS ANTS. THE STARLIGHT THAT FORGED YOUR BEAUTIFUL HEARTS LEFT ITS MEMORY ON THIS WORLD. THEY SMELL IT. THEY YEARN FOR IT. DEMONS WILL CONSUME EVERYTHING.// The dragon gazed over the water. *//THE ANCIENTS KNEW THIS MUCH AT LEAST, BEFORE THE END TOOK THEM.//* She sighed again. *//TOO FEW DRAGONS, AND FAR TOO FEW DRAGONRIDERS.//*

"And holomancers, hey?" Meri's tone was bright, but Geneve heard the tremor in it.

Ormeon regarded the illusionist. *//THERE WERE ONLY THREE.//*

"Three gods? We know that—"

//THREE HOLOMANCERS. THEIR NAMES WERE MISTRAL CLARK, JOSEPH KAUR, AND CHAR TAYLOR. I REMEMBER THEIR FACES, BUT THEY WERE RETURNED TO STARDUST BEFORE YOU CALLED MOST OF MY KIND FROM THE GRAVE. YOU CAN MAKE AS MANY DRAGONS AS YOU HAVE VHEMIN. LESS DRAGONRIDERS, BECAUSE THEY NEED TRAINING— MASTERY OF THE STORM IS REQUIRED. BUT THERE WERE

ONLY THREE HOLOMANCERS. THREE PEOPLE WHO COULD SEE THE HEARTS OF DEMONS AND GUIDE THEIR DESTRUCTION.//

Meri swallowed. "That makes no sense. I'm an illusionist. There are plenty—"

//THERE IS ONLY ONE LIKE YOU IN ALL CREATION, LORD MERIWETHER DU REEVES. IT'S WHY THE DEMONS TOOK YOUR FATHER. IT'S WHY THEY HUNTED YOU. YOU ARE THE ONLY PERSON WHO CAN SEE THEIR WEAKNESS. AT THIS POINT, HERE AND NOW, THE THREE GAVE THIS WORLD WHAT IT NEEDS MOST. ONE HOLOMANCER, ONE DRAG-ONRIDER, AND,// she touched her scaled chest with a claw, *//ONE MAGNIFICENT DRAGON.//*

"That's ... quite a surprise." Meri looked like he wanted to be sick.

Geneve touched his arm. "Meri ... it's more than just us. There's Tilly, Sight of Day, and Armitage. Queen Morgan, Picotee, and Heser the Cheg." She felt her lips quirk at his name. "Barret and Morning Song. We're all here."

//YOUR DAWNING UNDERSTANDING ISN'T THE SURPRISE I WANTED TO SHOW YOU.// Ormeon pointed to the ocean. *//EIGHT HUNDRED YEARS AGO THIS WAS A GRASSY PLAIN. IT WAS A MONUMENT AND WARNING, IN ONE. THERE'S A DEVICE UNDER THE SEA.//*

Geneve strode to the water's edge. "What kind of device? The ancient's tools have been ... fickle."

//IT WILL TAKE YOU ACROSS SPACE TO WHERE YOU NEED TO BE.//

"And where's that?"

//I DON'T KNOW. THE DEMONS HAVE A FOOTHOLD ON THIS WORLD. THE DEVICE SEES IT. WHEREVER THEY ARE STRONGEST, IT WILL TAKE YOU.//

"But it's underwater." Geneve frowned. "That seems—"

//DEMONS MAY HAVE CHANGED THE OCEANS, OR TIME DID THAT FOR THEM. BUT THIS IS WHY THEY COME TO RAVENSWALL. TO DESTROY THIS DEVICE, AND ALL IT REPRESENTS. IT'S ONLY A MATTER OF TIME BEFORE THEY

MANAGE IT. THEY WORK THROUGH HUMAN AGENTS HERE, AND THEIR SUPPLY OF THOSE IS LIMITLESS.// Ormeon bowed her head. *//IF ONLY YOU WEREN'T MADE OF STARDUST, THEY'D NEVER HAVE FOUND HOW BRIGHT YOU ARE.//*

Meri joined her, hand finding hers. "How do we get to it?"

//YOU ASK.//

The sorcerer's voice took on a vibrant tone. "Oh ocean, reveal!"

Ormeon gazed at him. *//HAVE YOU FINISHED?//*

"You said—"

//THE OCEAN DOESN'T CARE. YOU NEED TO ASK THE DRAGON.// She eyed Geneve. *//ONE DRAGONRIDER. ONE HOLO-MANCER. ONE DRAGON. THREE TOGETHER CAN DO WONDERS.//*

"What if it takes us under the ocean? Or into a pit in the earth?" Geneve shivered. "Do demons need air and light?"

//THEY DO NOT. THEY NEED THE SOULS OF THE DAMNED.// Ormeon looked away. *//IT'S KIND OF THEIR THING.//*

"Will you come with us?" Geneve looked up at Ormeon. Saw her damaged pride, and how much she'd been hurt in the battle. "You carry no Storm."

"What she means is..." Meri bit his lip. "We want you to come. We could use the help. But are you coming because you're made to, or because you want to?"

//THEY ARE THE SAME. VEHEMENT SYSTEMS FELL FIRST. WARMONGERS MAKING WEAPONS FOR THE PETTY. THE ANCIENTS WHO CRAFTED DRAGONS ALSO MADE THE FEY BRANDED. THE FEY BRANDED WERE NEVER MADE FOR WAR, SO THEY MADE DRAGONS. NO CAT WAS MEANT TO CARRY A BLADE.// She sounded sad, as if remembering something the world shouldn't have forgotten. *//BUT THEY WERE MADE OF STARDUST TOO, AND COULDN'T HELP BUT STAND AS COMMANDED. NOW THEY ARE FEW. VEHEMENT SYSTEMS SPRAWL ACROSS THE WORLD, WITHOUT THEIR MAKER'S LEASH.//*

"None of that matters," Meri said.

Ormeon blinked. *//HAVE YOU GONE SENILE?//*

"It doesn't matter because we're all in this together. The Vhemin, the Feybrind, and us. We're on this world, and always will be. The only ones who shouldn't be are the demons, and they're doing a bang-up job of putting us at each other's throats. It's got to stop. No more leashes, no more masters, and no more us versus them. That's how we work, dragon. No dragon slaves, no cats as servants, and no monsters with blue-runed armor of terrible compulsion. Just ... us."

//FRIENDS?// Ormeon seemed surprised.

"Family," Geneve said. "We've all been made from different shattered pasts. You were born of death. My father couldn't tell me who he was. Meri's was a villain. Armitage lost his tribe, and Sight of Day his son. Vertiline followed a man for her entire life who never loved her. All that remains is ... each other."

The dragon held her peace for a spell, the bellows of her breath calling to the waves. *//NO COMMANDS?//*

"No." Geneve crossed her arms.

//HOW DO I KNOW WHAT TO DO?//

"Let your heart decide," Meri suggested.

//SOUNDS LIKE FUN.// The dragon beamed, jaws lit by ruddy light from within. *//I'M ON THE TEAM. NOW, ASK.//*

Geneve nodded. "Dragon, please show us the gate."

Ormeon arched her head up. The runes on the side of her head blazed red, then turned a brilliant white. The darkness was tossed back like an old blanket as night turned to day. Geneve turned away, unable to look at Ormeon and her terrible beauty.

//THREE COME. YOU WILL ANSWER. GATE, OPEN!//

The ground shook as Ormeon's brilliance faded. Sea trembled, then gushed aside as something massive shouldered its way from the deep. Barnacle-crusted stone rose like a swimmer broaching for a desperate lungful of air. Geneve saw a podium two hundred meters across. It had a stone roof supported by pillars of the material the ancients used to build everything.

Water surged against the docks, then subsided. If anyone had been sticking around after Ormeon landed, they were well gone now. The dragon pointed. *//YOUR CHARIOT AWAITS.//*

"We ... go over there?" Geneve frowned. "I don't want to go anywhere now. I want to sleep, and spend time with Meri."

The sorcerer's lips quirked. "Perhaps in a different order."

//WE WON'T GO ANYWHERE. TURNING IT ON IS QUITE DIFFERENT TO MAKING IT APPEAR. NOW, CLAMBER ABOARD.//

"I don't clamber," Geneve said. But she and Meri mounted Ormeon, the dragon taking them the short hop across black waters to the podium. As they approached the roof irised aside, and the dragon settled to the stone within. Geneve and Meri got down. The ground smelled of the deep ocean. A hundred fronds, shellfish, and scuttling things remained aboard.

There was no obvious control mechanism like the temple that birthed Ormeon. Meri turned a circle. "How's it work?"

//MAGIC,// the dragon said. *//IT'S QUITE SAFE FOR NOW. THE ACTIVATION SEQUENCE IS COMPLEX.//*

Geneve felt a hum deep under her feet. It made her teeth itch, and she covered her ears. The very air seemed to glow, and then she fell. Not down, because that didn't make sense. She thought she heard Meri say *we're falling sideways, to the left*, but she couldn't see him. Geneve couldn't see anything but white light that tasted of citrus and sandalwood.

𐤟

THE PODIUM SANK BENEATH THE WAVES, WATER RUSHING TO RESCUE stranded sea creatures.

Silence returned, and after a time, people. Not a one knew where the Savior of Ravenswall, her dragon, or the Lord du Reeves went. No one but a slim Feybrind, her eyes wide in shock and wonder.

THE END.

𐤟

THE FINAL WAR BEGINS.

The gods have turned away. The demons have taken root. The world teeters on the edge of ruin.

Geneve has fought her battles. She's faced assassins in the dark, walked through the fires of rebellion, and stood against monsters both mortal and divine. But everything that came before was only the prelude.

Now, the last reckoning is at hand.

Her sword is ready. The storm within her rages. But is it enough to stop the end of everything?

Turn the page to begin *Requiem's Justice*.

Because the fight isn't over. **It's only just begun.**

REQUIEM'S JUSTICE
A DARK FANTASY ADVENTURE

Revelations

The lightning brought terror.

Omrar was on his way home from the town fountains. He'd collected water for tomorrow, the heavy pole holding jugs swaying across his shoulders. It didn't pay to linger or to look idle. Idleness was a sin. It wasn't healthy to appear sinful, so he carried his water with short, hurried steps. His eyes were down, measuring his tread on the smooth, worn stones paving the streets of Imshir.

Sinning was rife, if the Arm were to be believed. It was the cause of all wrongdoing in society, and the Arm made sure everyone knew it was sinners that stole the moons from the sky. The Three had watched Omrar for as long as he could remember, but now ... they were gone. The Arm's watches tripled. People were dragged from their homes, strung up in the town square in front of the temple, and flayed alive before the baleful gaze of the Precept. His neighbor Lily, who supplied Omar's store with fresh bread, had been missing for two days. He'd heard screams in the night, and her ovens were quiet and cold the next morning.

So: water, quick steps, and straight home. Omrar remembered when the fountain held the sound of laughter along with splashing water. *That happened a lifetime ago. Or to another, in a different life. This life is fear.*

A rumble made him pause. It sounded like what came after lightning, but the sky held no flash. He looked toward Heaven's Gate. The mighty mountain shouldered the sky to the north. It was a natural wall against invaders, its rugged slopes vigilant but friendly. The setting sun left the mountain half in shadow, half-baked by waning rays.

Rumbling came again, longer and louder, and *then* came the flash. Not a simple lightning strike, but a pillar of twisting, incandescent light. It hammered the side of Heaven's Gate, rock exploding into the sky. From this distance they looked like slow-tossed pebbles, but Omrar knew the stones to be big as houses. The lightning wasn't a simple strike, one and done. The cloudless sky unleashed fury in a twisting column for ten seconds before stopping.

The town answered with screams of panic and the metal clamor of an alarm. The Arm were mobilizing, and being on the street—even with water for his store—wasn't a good idea. Omrar didn't want to tangle with the Arm. He had no wish to know firsthand what happened to Lily.

She made such good bread.

People emerged from their houses, some at street level, others on the rooftop gardens Imshir was famous for. All eyes were turned toward Heaven's Gate. Most had missed the cascade of rocks, but none could mistake the gout of lava that spewed forth from the mountain's side, as if the earth was injured and magma its lifeblood.

The rumble sounded again. Somehow smaller, but no less ominous. A second twisting pillar of lightning reached down, striking north of Heaven's Gate. The destruction it wrought was hidden by the mountain. Omrar clenched his teeth and put his back into the task of hurrying home. *The streets aren't safe. They were* never *safe, but the Arm will be looking for sinners to blame. I'm no sinner, but I'm ... convenient.*

Omrar had a small business that sold food, but no powerful family, or patrons in the Precept's palace. He knew if someone needed to die to appease the people, or the gods, he'd do just fine.

His store was the ground level of his home. The whole affair was a simple three-story building surrounded by adobe walls as tall as a man. The garden out the back held the day's laundry. Omrar imagined what the clean white cotton would smell like, or the coarseness of linen sheets against his skin. *Move, old man, or you'll never enjoy simple pleasures like folding washing again.*

The pole across his shoulders rattled against the chains suspending jugs of water. He should just leave it, but he needed the water. A man could be judged for sinning by inaction as much as the wrong action. Wasting water was a crime against the gods. Imshir was a paradise in a wasteland of desert, and the gods' gift shouldn't be wasted. So, he kept his burden, and hurried as best his old, bent frame could manage.

He was four blocks from home when a third rumble broke the air. Omrar managed to ignore the sounds of screaming as citizens cried panic or were dragged away by the Arm, but there was no ignoring the thunderous tolling of heaven's bell. A third pillar of twisting fury lanced from the sky, this time hammering the ground no more than a block away.

Omrar was tossed from his feet, water urns breaking as they crashed against the ground. He landed on his hip, feeling a twinge of pain. The air tasted of burnt copper and rage, as if the gods were accusing all Imshir of crimes unimaginable. The lightning twisted and curled, stealing away Omrar's sight with night-blindness. A fourth rumble sounded, and despite not seeing it, he *felt* the lightning impact. His body bounced, and he cried out.

Then, it was done. His hearing was gone as was his vision in the wake of the gods' might. He pawed across the ground, dragging himself to the side of the street as near as memory could guide him. *Please let me see. Please, just a glimpse of color.* There was no place in Imshir for the broken, the frail, or the helpless. There was barely enough space for a tired old man. He felt sick, desperate, his heart laboring like the old workhorse he was.

In fits and starts his hearing came back. The bells of alarm, overlaid by the hammer of horse's hooves drawing closer. His vision came back as splotches first, then a blurred image of the street, like an artist's watercolor, but drawn from a memory of a long time ago.

A contingent of the Arm cantered past, the metal shoes of horse's hooves sparking the cobbles a meter from Omrar's face. He scuttled back, drew his knees close, and urged his old body upright. It obeyed, but not without complaint. The Arm continued on past toward the lightning strike's site.

I should go. Get more water, or just get gone. Omrar knew the wisdom of a hasty retreat, but couldn't turn away. Before the gods stole his vision for a moment, he could've sworn the lightning brought something with it.

I saw someone come down in that pillar of fire. A person, even a godly one, might need help.

It was old habit talking. Time spent in the Arm before they'd passed from law to disorder, after the Precept took the good things from Imshir and bottled them inside his palace. But habit wouldn't be ignored. *I couldn't help Lily. Perhaps I can help ... whomever this is. A castoff from heaven will find no help from the Arm.*

Omrar hurried down the block, journeyed west for another, and rounded the corner to see a crater torn from the bedrock of Imshir. No one stood by, because unlike Omrar no one was stupid enough to go where the Arm would follow. He scuttled toward the crater. It was perhaps twenty meters across. The heat was intense, the ground flickering with tiny flames as released gasses caught. There was nobody here.

The crater destroyed the whole width of the street. The lightning caved in the wall of a house to the east and destroyed a wall to the west. That way Omrar caught movement. A figure, hunched low, daring a backward glance. His eyes weren't working well enough to make out more than semi-imagined details.

Omrar tried to follow as fast as his old bones would allow. He hobbled around the smoldering crater, heading after the figure. He passed through the broken fence and through a smoking garden. Ahead a gate banged closed, beckoning him on. *Old man, you should run, and not after that figure. I should get away before the Arm arrives.*

His feet didn't obey. It was as if they said, *What if the storm brought terror, but for the Arm? What if the figure is sent to save Imshir?*

"Stupid feet." Hand on the gate, he paused, listening. Horses drew closer, and with them, the harsh sound of men's voices raised in anger, fear, or the heady mix of both that would drive one to unthinking madness. He looked at his sandals. "Feet, stop talking and start hurrying."

Omrar made it through the gate into a small garden typical of Imshir. Stone fruit trees vied with ground vegetation. He spied turnips, and what might have been silverbeet, but he hated the stuff. He helped himself to a date no one would miss and pushed through the gloom. The garden was fenced like the rest, encircling this little Eden. A two-story house waited to the north. A line holding linens swayed.

There is no wind.

He headed for the line. A gap in the laundry the width of a large shawl or small sheet showed the figure's intent. *Camouflage.* The back-door was locked. He wondered where the figure got to when a strong grip spun him about.

He was faced with a woman. Her skin was lighter than his. Not white like ghosts and the ridiculous savages from Or'sen, but not the earthy tone he'd carried all his span. Green eyes hard as emeralds watched him. Young. Barely twenty summers, if that, but those green eyes held cares and demons aplenty. Her hair was red, perhaps dyed, cut short, but not short enough for modesty in Imshir. She wore the missing sheet, wrapped like a toga about shoulders that were broad and strong. Her hand didn't leave his arm, but neither did she use her obvious strength to push him around.

Her voice was even, calm, like riding lightning was a thing she did each Tuesday, right before lunch. She spoke, voice rising at the end in a question. The language was beautiful, melodic, and unfamiliar.

"I don't know what that means." Omrar shifted, nervous, but curious. He'd never met a god before. "Did you come with the lightning?" He pointed above.

Another series of words, cut short as she spun at something crunching beyond the gate. It gave him time to think. He recognized a word.

"Trebani? Yes, this is the Empire." He shook his head. "It's seen better days." Then he realized what shaking his head meant and nodded. "This is Trebani."

Her eyes narrowed. Another question in that gentle, soft language.

The gate he'd come through crashed aside, and the Arm walked in. Three were burly men, the fourth a slender woman with officer's banding on her arm. They saw Omrar, then the woman in the sheet. The officer's eyes narrowed. "Sin."

"It's hardly a sin for someone to be lost and alone." Omrar snapped his mouth shut, unsure of where the words came from.

The officer's face twisted to a sneer. "Old man, we'll deal with you in a minute. Take her. The Precept wants a word."

Her three men marched forward, curved blades coming from their sheaths. The green-eyed woman pulled Omrar behind her, then strode to meet them. Omrar goggled. *She has no armor. By the will of the gods, she wears a sheet. No blade's in her hand. She's going to die. The savior from the heavens will bleed out in this nice yet small and insignificant garden.*

She took two more steps while his brain tried to keep up. *I should help. I should get in there and do something. I used to be good at this, but all I'm good for now is making other people lunch.*

The green-eyed woman didn't care what he used to be good at. She stepped for the first of her attackers, hands wide, stance lowering. The blade hungered for her neck, but somehow she wasn't there anymore. Omrar wondered if it were his eyes still not working right, because she didn't seem to step, but rather flow. A hint of a golden luminance dogged her heels as she stepped behind the man.

He spun to follow her, but she hadn't finished moving. The gods-warrior made the officer, taking the woman's sword before she'd drawn it half-way. Whoever this Three-given fighter was, she didn't waste time with the monkey, going straight for the organ grinder. Officer's saber in hand, she kicked the woman in the gut, then spun back to her original attacker.

Or not. The green-eyed woman didn't look where she was going. Her sword seemed to guide itself, swinging an arc that glittered gold. *Wait, what? The saber is steel. Not brass or bronze. I'm going to die here, but I'm going blind first!*

The blade took the arms off her assailant, the sword meeting no resistance. It didn't make sense. No Arm blade was sharp enough to shave with, and she worked it one-handed. The sword cut through steel-banded armor, flesh, and bone as fast and slick as his own pairing knives dealt with tomatoes.

Like tomatoes, red gushed, and she moved again. The blade swung about, taking the head from the second man, who'd only just begun to register what his comrade's screams meant. Startled eyes stared at Omrar from the ground where his head landed, before life's light left them.

The third Arm, perhaps unused to seeing two of the Precept's best killed in less than five seconds by a previously unarmed woman in a sheet, checked himself. The officer looked about to move, so the green-eyed woman kicked her in the stomach without turning, as a mule might. The officer dropped, the air going out of her like it had better places to be. The green-eyed woman held her stolen saber cross-guard, waiting.

The last Arm lunged, and lost his hand for his troubles. He grabbed the stump, trying to stop the fountain of blood coming from it. Shock or blood loss took their toll and he sank to his knees, to be run through with the saber.

The gods-sent woman turned to the officer. She asked a question, her tone hard.

"You will die, and it won't be a good death," the officer wheezed.

Green eyes flashed, lips pressed in a line. More words, but one repeated more than others: *Meri*. A weapon? A person? Perhaps a place? Omrar knew of nothing wearing that moniker.

The officer tried to regain her feet. The gods-warrior let her, blade never wavering. "I swear by the gods you will die."

The saber flashed, and the officer fell, but in two places, sheared from shoulder, through ribcage, and out the other side. Another sentence, this one final, but also forgiving.

Omrar looked at the bodies, and listened for horses. He stole another sheet, moving toward the gods-warrior. "Here." She spun, blade ready. Omrar held his distance. "Your clothing, uh, sheet. It's covered in blood. This one isn't." He offered the sheet again. She looked to it, then her own, and nodded. More words, Meri repeated again, and again. It was unlikely Meri was a clothier, so... "Meri's a friend of yours?"

She touched her chest, over her heart. Omrar understood. "We best get you off the streets. If Meri is precious to you, the Arm will find him, and they will use him to break you."

The green-eyed warrior looked to the sky, then tossed her saber aside. Omrar led them from the garden, and to home.

Chapter One

"What do you mean, they're gone?" A vein on the side of Heser the Cheg's temple throbbed, angry and insistent.

Vertiline almost rolled her eyes. It was only through years of Tresward training that kept her face in check. If that kind of emotion ran rampant, she'd not be great at sword-fighting. *And if I roll my eyes, they'll spin so much I'll tumble across this fine throne room floor.*

The throne room was like it'd been the day before, except there was no Geneve, and no Meriwether either. The sinner had grown on her, but Tilly worried for her sister in battle. Not because a single day had passed without her. *I'm concerned she's dead. I'm worried she's done something stupid, because she's young, and when I was her age I signed up for a life of service to the Tresward, which was a terrible idea.*

In the throne room was the usual suspects. Morgan was on her throne, leaning head against hand, eyes closed in a way that suggested a migraine. Vertiline knew *exactly* how she felt. Picotee lounged in a chair toward the back of the room, eyes locked on the ceiling, the very picture of *this is a boring conversation.* Eyeballing Heser the Cheg was Armitage. The monster—

He's not a monster.

The Vhemin hadn't been himself since the battle. The injury he'd sustained left him moving with great care, as an ancient man might. Tilly had seen men hurt before, and what happened to Armitage wasn't a thing you walked off. Yet he walked, a challenge to common wisdom, and was spoiling for a fight, despite looking like his spine was a single piece of wood that didn't flex.

Sight of Day stood with hands clasped, golden eyes bright and patient. Morning Song was by his side, her emerald eyes brilliant. A scattering of Queensguard held attention by the queen, most of their focus on Barret, who looked like she had zero fucks to give.

Heser the Cheg was making a great show of being distressed, but Vertiline didn't understand why. Vertiline cleared her throat. *Better jump in before this takes up more time in my life I'll never get back.* "I don't see why you're upset."

Heser the Cheg, about to burst into another tirade, checked himself. "Because the Savior of Ravenswall is missing."

"Don't forget the runt," Armitage said. "He's important."

That vein on Heser the Cheg's temple pulsed again. "He's not—"

"He's not *here*." Vertiline's hand found the hilt of her sword, not because she wanted to skewer Heser the Cheg, but because swords were useful in conflicts, and this felt like one of those. "He is also the person who suggested she," Tilly pointed at Barret, "take your job, and the cat," her finger wandered toward Morning Song, "corrupt your intelligence network from within."

Heser the Cheg's mouth opened and closed a couple times before he found his mental footing. "What?"

"At least, that's what you're thinking." Vertiline's fingers tapped a casual medley on her pommel. "Without Lord du Reeves you might stand a chance of getting your job back, protecting your queen, and getting all the non-human interfering scum out of the throne room. It won't work."

Queen Morgan looked up at this. Face framed by raven locks, eyes like glass, voice like the hush before an earthquake. "It won't?"

"No." Vertiline sighed. "The sinner's worthless with a sword. He can barely run a block before his breath gives out. His magic is border-line useless. But what he's good at is *thinking*. He's already worked out there's a bunch of assholes," her arm pointed to a window, through which a shaft of sunlight bravely tried to face her, "out there, trying to get us killing each other, rather than killing them. So, if we get rid of the Vhemin and the Feybrind, we're on our own. Worse, we'll spend time murdering each other instead of the people who *deserve* murder. I've no time for that kind of lunacy."

The queen looked slightly put out, as if she'd been thinking along the lines of getting her kingdom back under lock and key and didn't like being called a lunatic. "There are other ways we can do this without positions of power being in the hands of, of..."

"Say it," Vertiline encouraged. "You know you want to."

"The enemy?" Heser the Cheg's voice held a questioning tone, like his eyes saw a trap but his brain hadn't interfered fast enough, lips already on their way to saying something stupid.

"The enemy who saved us all." Vertiline nodded. "The cats held the waterfront. They died in hundreds they couldn't afford there, on the battlefield proper, and all through the streets. The Vhemin fell in far greater numbers, some under the command of an evil man, others trying to get a little payback. All of us," she touched her chest above her heart, "practiced *dying* while others cackled in glee. If you're," she swung toward Morgan, who looked agitated enough to interrupt, "thinking of reverting to tradecraft with people who never responded when the need was dire, what do you think will be different this time? The lords will return with hugs and flowers?"

"Keep a civil tongue in your head," Heser the Cheg warned. "You address the Queen of Or'sen."

Vertiline snorted. "I've got no quarrel with her majesty, but she and I both know the Tresward don't bend the knee. This isn't about me versus the kingdom. Don't you see? That's the whole point. You've a Tresward Chevalier here, getting involved in *politics*," she spat the word, "because this is bigger than any faction. It's all of us."

"All of us, or none of us." Morgan nodded. "We agree."

Heser the Cheg frowned, stroking his chin. "Your Majesty—"

"Not today, Heser the Cheg." Morgan stood. "Picotee du Parneer, your queen needs you."

Picotee jerked upright. "You what?"

Morgan clapped her hands. "Find them. All available ships. I need to know where the Savior of Ravenswall is."

"To ... bring her back?" Picotee guessed.

The queen offered the eye-roll Vertiline had been dying to make. "No. So we can help them." Morgan turned to Morning Song. "Isn't that right?"

{Don't bring me into this.} Morning Song tried to slink back, but Sight of Day put a gentle, anchoring hand on her shoulder. It didn't look welcome.

"Tell us what you heard."

"I thought there were no witnesses," Heser the Cheg said.

"The reason I called you here was my spymaster woke me at an hour that is frankly impolite." Morgan smoothed her gown. "She witnessed everything."

{I wouldn't be a good spymaster otherwise.} Morning Song's emerald eyes found the floor, as if realizing she'd just formally accepted her new job. *{The dragon said they were going to where the demons were strongest.}*

"Then we need to get there too," Armitage said. "I don't like the idea of Geneve getting all those kills without us."

Sight of Day blinked. *{That was your outside voice.}*

"What's your point, cat?"

Vertiline cleared her throat. "We've got work to do, then."

Picotee tried to feign disinterest, but it didn't stick. "Doing what?"

"Barret, for recruits." Tilly swung her gaze to the Lady du Parneer. "Picotee for ships. Maybe the Tresward, to see if they can spare glass or steel. Lords and ladies. Barkeeps and weavers. We will go everywhere, and we'll do it fast."

Armitage winced. "There doesn't sound like there's a lot of room for food and booze on this trip. What makes you think the Tresward will help? Or Barret? Or the sea-bitch?"

"Watch it." Picotee's tone turned ominous. "It's easy to fall overboard, and the embrace of sea is mighty cold."

"Sounds just like your—"

"Anyway," Vertiline clapped her hands. "Let's get on."

Sight of Day stroked his chin. *{What makes you think anyone will help us?}*

"They're a part of this world too. We all face the same demons. And ... they owe us." Tilly looked at her feet. "Or Geneve. No one in this world is where they are without her. Not the queen." Morgan nodded. "Not the Tresward. And definitely not the sea-bi—"

"I get it," Picotee growled.

Vertiline touched her temple in salute, then strode for the door. She allowed herself the guilty pleasure of a small smile, feeling a spring in her step. *I forgot what my old family was like, but my new one is ... better?* "Heser the Cheg's not going to have *all* the fun."

Chapter Two

When Meriwether woke, he wished he hadn't.

If he were Armitage, he'd have said his mouth tasted of ash and ass. Geneve might have winced and stood up, but otherwise walked it off. He could imagine Vertiline holding up her metal hand, the gift given at agony's knifepoint, asking him, *Do you think it hurt more than this?*

Sight of Day might have given him a hug, then said, *{Get a grip.}*

He was alone, which made everything worse. *We were supposed to check out a platform, then fly back for a quiet night's rest.* Meriwether found himself on the ground, coarse and unyielding. Tiny pebbles scratched his skin, some sharp as knives but of a size fairies might use. The ground wasn't the type he was used to, with grass, or even sand beneath him. There was no convenient boulder to use as shelter from the sun.

Meriwether lay in a curved hollow set in the ground. It sloped evenly from all sides to meet him at the center, or bottom, depending on your point of view. The surface of the ground was worn smooth like the inside of a shield. The tiny pieces stabbing him mercilessly were chips of a glass-like material. It looked like he'd landed in a crater caused by great heat, every surface sloughed to a smoother, less definite form.

Also, he was naked.

Meriwether eased himself to his feet. A mountain lay to the south. It looked high enough to dissuade the casual climber, but didn't seem studded with cliffs or other unforgiving bastions. He scratched his back. "If I had to guess, where I need to go is on the other side of that huge hill."

A bird chirped from its vantage point of a low tree, but no one else seemed to be about to voice an opinion on the matter. Meriwether climbed out of the scorched depression in the earth, stretched, and looked around.

Grass, the odd tree, and no one for miles. The grass wasn't healthy, most of it dry and withered. Between the clumps of mostly-dead foliage lay rock and sand, which explained why he'd found himself stabbed by glass. *Take sand and enough heat, and glass is the eventual product.* He sighed, eying the mountain. *Maybe I should get it over with. Just climb it. I know I'll need to be on the other side, because it's the hardest place to get to.*

The smart regals said he'd be better off finding clothes first, and maybe a horse. But even before that, he needed to find a huge dragon and what was no doubt a very angry, red-headed Tresward Knight. If everyone arrived in a pit of fire without clothes, the people who first met her better be polite.

His mouth quirked into a grin as he thought of Geneve. Meriwether wasn't worried about her. Of the three people the ancient device transported to whatever-this-place-is-called, she was the best equipped to deal with demons, sword-wielding maniacs, or ancient terrors of the world. The dragon would probably be fine. *Truth, but I should be worried about myself.*

He squared off against the bird, which returned his regard with head cocked. "But I'm not. Worried, I mean. I'm in a place I've never seen with no clothes. I don't even have the book of High Magic. I should be terrified, but..." The bird hopped to the left on its branch, watching him. *But I'm not scared. I'm ... free.*

He didn't recognize this land at all. Not the mountain, the plains, or what looked like the shimmer of sea to the west. Which meant the land didn't recognize him either. No one knew the du Reeves name. Unlikely they'd heard of Leander, and the merciless crimes he'd perpetrated on the Kingdom of Or'sen. *Maybe they don't have Vhemin, Feybrind, or the endless war between us all. Could be a nice place to settle down. Now, if only I could find the dragon.*

A dragon seemed the best thing to aim for. "Giant flying lizard. Can't miss it." He turned another slow circle but saw no dragon. *Maybe Ormeon's on the wing.* He looked up, but didn't see a dragon there either. Something that looked like a vulture circled, but he didn't look near dead enough for it to come closer. "Ormeon!"

Nothing.

Clothes, then. He closed his eyes for a moment, concentrating. When he opened them, he was attired in his usual garments. A cloak about his shoulders, a shirt—complete with sword rent—above pants and boots. None of it was real, but it meant if he came across anyone other than a bird they probably wouldn't murder him for perversion. Foreign customs were tricky to navigate.

Meriwether walked in widening circles from his crater, trying to find any sign of ... anything, really. Aside from his feet getting sore, because walking on gravel, hot sand, and rock without shoes wasn't the easiest thing in the world, nothing changed. No Geneve, and no Ormeon either. No craters showing where they might have landed. Just the damn bird, which didn't seem concerned about him anymore. It followed him as he walked, moving from its original branch to another tree as he paced.

Time to get to the mountain. Meriwether faced the tree-studded edifice and set out. He took it slow, his desire to hurry, thus avoiding sunburn, governed by the beating his feet got. The bird kept pace well enough. It was small, about the size of his clenched fist, with bright-blue feathers covering everything except its chest, which was white, and around its eyes, which were a bright green. He had no idea what kind of bird it was, but it didn't have a poisonous barbed tail or breathe fire, so pretty much he was good with it following him.

The mountain drew closer by degrees. He smelled woodsmoke, and oriented himself slightly west, the breeze from that direction guiding him in. He walked until he found a small decline, too modest to call itself a hill to anyone but its friends. At the hill's bottom was a hut about ten meters a side, well built from long planks that might have been cedar. A fire pit lay beside it. The flames barbecued what looked like human bodies. Two Vhemin stood next to the fire, eating from skewers and warming themselves.

So much for no Vhemin. Meriwether backed up, nice and slow, right to the point where he hit something. He glanced over his shoulder at another Vhemin. The monster was about a head taller than him, and twice as broad in the shoulders. It wore half armor like a gladiator might, or someone who liked to show off their massive chest and ripped abdomen, which the creature had in spades.

"Hello," Meriwether said.

The monster slugged him in the side of the head, then tossed him over its shoulder. It walked to its fellows at the bottom of the not-quite-a-hill, tossing him to the ground beside the fire pit. It pulled out a wicked-looking knife about the length of Meriwether's forearm, curved in a way that promised it would hurt more than the regulation amount if it entered your gut. The Vhemin's friends grinned their shark-toothed smiles, snake eyes bright and feral.

"I see you're not up with the play. Allow me to explain." Meriwether curled over with a gasp as the monster kicked him in the gut. "Please. Let me explain," he wheezed.

The monster growled words in an unfamiliar tongue, brows furrowed in confusion.

"Right," Meriwether said. "The thing is, we're not at war with the Vhemin anymore. Big battle, lots of arrows and swords, and yes, there was a dragon, and demons too. After that, we decided murdering each other wasn't as useful as murdering the demons. Did no one tell you?"

The Vhemin pursed his lips, thinking hard. More incomprehensible babble. It sounded like Tebrani, if you sieved out the meaning and left nothing but swearing and death threats.

"No idea," Meriwether admitted. "But I think we should come to an accord before you die." The monster gave a guttural sigh, almost a snarl, then readied its knife, perhaps to plunge it into Meriwether's heart. "Don't say I didn't warn you."

Ormeon the Redeemer landed with a jarring *whump* that toppled the three Vhemin from their feet. She snatched the one with the knife in a clawed hand, raising the struggling figure to her jaw. She *crunched*, juices squirting, then chewed twice before swallowing. *//HOW DID YOU GET YOURSELF IN TROUBLE SO QUICKLY?//*

The other two Vhemin bolted. She whipped her tail around, swatting one into a smear, then snatched the other and gobbled it in three bites.

"Well. To be fair, it's been some hours since I woke." He blanched. "Do you have to chew so loudly?"

//THESE VHEMIN ARE FOR EATING.//

"Sure, help yourself." Meriwether stood, dusting himself off before remembering he wore no actual clothes. "Why am I naked?"

//BECAUSE NOTHING WORKS ANYMORE.// Ormeon sighed like a windstorm. *//WE'VE MORE IMPORTANT THINGS TO WORRY ABOUT. I CAN'T SEE THE DRAGONRIDER.//*

Meriwether felt his heart stumble. "What do you mean?"

//I MEAN, SHE'S GONE FROM MY SIGHT. ALWAYS I CAN SEE HER, BUT NOT NOW.// Ormeon crouched low. *//COME. THERE'S AN OLD TEMPLE ABOVE. WE CAN GET YOU SOME PANTS.//*

FLYING THE DRAGON WITHOUT GENEVE WASN'T EASY. NOT THAT Ormeon did anything *wrong*, per se, just that ... well, Geneve was something to hold onto. Without her, his hands tried to grip Ormeon's scaled hide, with varying levels of success ranging from *By the Three, I'm going to die* through to *I might just be getting the hang of this.*

"Tell me why you don't have a saddle!" Meriwether hollered over the wind.

//TELL ME WHY YOU'RE NAKED.// The dragon gave him an over-the-shoulder emberfire smile. *//I THINK I GET THE WORSE PART OF THE DEAL.//*

"How so?"

//I'M NOT RUBBING MY JUNK ON YOUR NECK.//

"Fair point." Meriwether might look like he was clothed, but there was nothing really there except a few stray moonbeams and a little imagination.

The dragon banked around the mountain's crown, her wings dipping to afford Meriwether a stomach-clenching view of trees and rocks below. A massive crater sat like an old wound in the mountain's side. Scattered about, looking like charred pebbles at this distance, were huge rocks. A massive, burned stretch lay like a river of ash down the mountain's flank.

I wonder what happened there?

//I HAPPENED,// Ormeon said.

"Are you reading my mind?"

//DID GENEVE NOT EXPLAIN THIS TO YOU? IT'S NOT MIND READING. IT'S ... NEVER MIND. YES, I'M READING YOUR MIND.// She descended toward a vertical basalt slab of rock, leaving Meriwether's stomach in the clouds above. Ormeon extended her feet, landing with a crunch Meriwether would feel in his spine for months.

"Nice landing."

She snaked her head around. *//WOULD YOU LIKE TO WALK HOME NEXT TIME?//*

"I said it was a nice landing!" Meriwether slid from her back, trying not to cause undue injury to himself.

//I'M READING YOUR MIND.// The dragon pointed a clawed hand at the basalt surface before them. *//BEHOLD.//*

Meriwether walked toward it, shoring up with his hands on hips about ten meters back. "It's a nice piece of rock. A little weathered, I'll allow, but with a certain," he waved his hand, "striation that lends character."

//I DON'T KNOW WHY SHE KEEPS YOU AROUND.// Ormeon dipped her head to be next to his. *//THIS IS THE DOORWAY TO AN ANCIENT TEMPLE.//*

"It's not a temple. The ancients didn't really have temples." Meriwether scratched his beard which, unlike his clothes, was real.

//COPHINE GRANT ME GRACE.// Ormeon closed her eyes, sighing a great dragony sigh. *//I KNOW THAT. BUT YOUR PRIMITIVE FORM OF REFERENCE THINKS ABOUT TEMPLES, SO IT'S A TEMPLE.//*

"What is it? Really, I mean." Meriwether put his hand on the stone surface. It felt old, as old as time itself. "Like, what did they call it?"

Ormeon gave him a little side-eye. //THEY CALLED THIS PLACE SAFE. HOME. HAVEN FROM PERSECUTION.//

"And they died?"

//AND THEY ALL DIED,// she confirmed. //TO YOU, IT'S A TEMPLE. FULL OF WONDERS AND HORRORS. I'M ALSO CONFIDENT THERE WILL BE PANTS OF MANY SIZES INSIDE.//

"Cool," Meriwether said. "How do we get it open?"

//IT SHOULD HAVE OPENED ALREADY.// Ormeon's voice held doubt. //I AM A DRAGON.//

"You say that like dragons can go anywhere."

She turned ruby-red eyes on him. //DRAGONS CAN GO PRETTY MUCH ANYWHERE.//

"Another fair point." Meriwether's hand strayed to his belt, where the tome of High Magic used to sit. The clutch was a nervous tic, nothing more. He'd memorized it. Remembering every symbol was different to understanding them, though. "The ancients would have a code word."

//THIS IS NOT A FORT CHILDREN PLAY IN.//

"Work with me here."

//THEY WOULDN'T HAVE HAD A CODE WORD. THE TEMPLE KNEW THEM FROM THE SMALLEST PARTS THEY WERE MADE FROM. CODE WORDS CAN BE STOLEN, BUT WHAT MAKES YOU REAL CAN'T BE FORGED ANYWHERE EXCEPT THE HEART OF A STAR.// Ormeon nudged the basalt with her nose. Aside from a grating noise, nothing happened.

"You mean, demons can't get inside?" Meriwether nodded. "Makes sense. They couldn't get into the place you were... made, either." He sniffed, remembering Tristan, and Geneve's love for the horse.

//HE WAS A GOOD MOUNT. I DIDN'T WANT HIM TO DIE.//

"I know, beastie. Anyway. The last temple opened to Red and me without any trouble. Like it knew us."

//IT KNEW THE RECIPE-MAKERS. ONE DRAGONRIDER, ONE HOLOMANCER.// She sat on her haunches. //IT WAS MADE FOR YOU, SO YOU COULD MAKE ME.//

"What was this one made for?"

//KILLING DEMONS.//

"Good talk." Meriwether crouched beside the cliff face, examining it. His inner eye could make out no magic. Nothing barred their path except good, honest rock. Movement caught his eye as the bright-blue bird landed to his right. It cocked its head at him. "Hello, bird."

The dragon looked at the bird. *//THAT'S NOT A BIRD.//*

"It looks like a bird." Meriwether held up his hand. "I know, I know. It's probably a death-dealing horror. Capable of killing ten men with a single chirp."

//IT'S NOT A DEATH-DEALING HORROR. I'VE CORNERED THAT MARKET.// Ormeon slunk behind Meriwether, nosing toward the bird. For its part, the bird didn't fly away in terror as Meriwether expected. *//HELLO, BUILDER.//*

Meriwether scoffed. "It's a *bird.*"

//IT CAN OPEN THE TEMPLE.// Ormeon stared at the bird, the blue-feathered creature staring right back. *//YOU DIDN'T ALWAYS WANT TO LOOK LIKE THIS, DID YOU?//*

The bird shook its head. Meriwether took a step back. "It understood you?"

//I CAN BE VERY PERSUASIVE.//

"I mean … your words." Meriwether crouched down, hand out to the bird. It eyed his fingers with more suspicion than it had Ormeon's maw. "Come on, friend."

Meriwether could've sworn it rolled its eyes, but it bounced closer, then flitted to his hand. Two small claws gripped his finger. He held it up to his eye line. "Where'd you come from, then?" It looked at the rock face, then back to him. "In there? But this has been sealed for…" *Hundreds of years*, he thought. *This bird doesn't look a day over thirty.*

//EIGHT HUNDRED YEARS OR'SEN HAS BEEN WITHOUT THE THREE'S GRACE.// Ormeon chuffed. *//THE NOT-BIRD IS VERY WELL PRESERVED.//*

"I'll admit, an eight-hundred-year-old bird is cool and all, but how does it open the temple?" Meriwether winced. "Sorry. I don't mean to imply you're a tool … oh, Ikmae's sometime balls. I'm talking to a *bird.*"

//PERHAPS YOU SHOULD ASK THE NOT-A-BIRD TO HELP.//

"Okay. Bird, can you open the door?" The bird cocked its head, turning a beady black eye in his direction before alighting and flitting to the door. It touched it with a bright blue wing, then returned to Meriwether's finger.

All three looked at the rock face expectantly. *//I ADMIT, I EXPECTED SOMETHING IMPRESSIVE.//*

"Maybe eight hundred years as a bird has taken some of the magic out?" The bird chirped, a tiny angry sound, then it flitted to touch the basalt again. With a groan like the sound of an earthquake, the basalt cracked down the center. Dust rained, causing Meriwether to cough and squint. The doorway opened wider, showing ... darkness. Meriwether cleared his throat. "I bet there are a lot of spiders in there."

Ormeon chuckled like a thunderstorm. *//THERE ARE WORSE THINGS THAN SPIDERS.//* She shuffled into the entrance.

Meriwether watched her hindquarters for a moment. "You think that's supposed to make me feel better?"

//IF IT HELPS, I THINK IT MORE LIKELY THAN EVER PANTS ARE TO BE FOUND WITHIN.//

The bird flitted from Meriwether's finger to his shoulder. He barely felt its weight, but the sharpness of its claws pricked his skin through his illusory shirt. "Pants would be good," he allowed. "Come on, bird. Stop holding me back."

With a glance at the sun, as if hoping to memorize it in case he never saw it again, Meriwether stepped into the dark maw of another temple of the ancients.

The Final War Has Begun.

THE END IS IN HER HANDS.

The gods have abandoned the world. Demons walk freely. The kingdom stands on the edge of annihilation.

Geneve has fought through darkness, betrayal, and fire. But the battle ahead isn't just for survival—it's for **justice, vengeance, and the fate of everything she holds dear**.

Her blade is drawn. Her enemies are waiting. The last reckoning is here.

Grab *Requiem's Justice* now!

https://www.books2read.com/RequiemsJustice

Because some wars don't end until the last sword falls.

About the Author

Richard Parry worked as a senior marketing manager in one of the world's top tech companies. It sounds cool, but it wasn't all cocaine parties. He lives in Wellington with the love of his life, Rae. They have two cats, Harry and Friday, who chase birds. The birds, who have the power of flight, don't seem to mind.

WAIT. DON'T GO!

Thanks for reading my book. If you enjoyed it, let's keep the party going:

📖 Join *Roll for Narrative* for reviews, storytelling breakdowns, and writing misadventures:

https://rollfornarrative.parrydox.com

✒ Lurk, judge, or say hi:

https://www.parrydox.com

P.S. An angel still gets its wings for every five-star review, but I'm told they're on backorder.

Also by Richard Parry

DAWN'S WARDEN

The Three Faces of Fate

The Undefeated Throne

The Fury of the Betrayed

THE SPLINTERED LAND

Tomb of the Six

Blade of Glass

The Storm Within

Requiem's Justice

The Copper Bard

Heartsong

The Hymn of All

THE EZEROC WARS

The Ezeroc Wars universe is big (and growing!). Get the reading guide here: https://www.parrydox.com/ezeroc-wars-reading-guide/

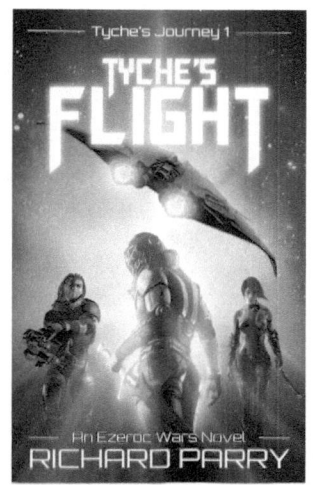

The Empire's Rogues: Volume 1

FUTURE FORFEIT

Not sure where to start? Get the reading guide here: https://www.parrydox.com/future-forfeit-reading-guide/

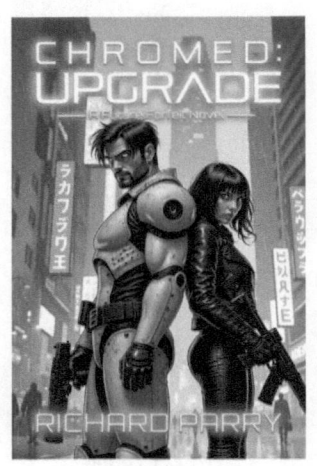

Chromed: Upgrade

Chromed: Rogue

Chromed: Restore

City Stories

Chromed: Consensus

Chromed: Delilah

Chromed: Meltdown

NIGHT'S CHAMPION

Night's Favor

Night's Fall

Night's End